Also by Scott Turow

THE BURDEN OF PROOF (1990)

PRESUMED INNOCENT (1987)

ONE L (1977)

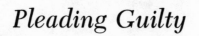

Pleading Guilty

PLEADING

GUILTY

———

SCOTT

TUROW

Farrar, Straus and Giroux

New York

*For seven years now, my colleagues at Son-
nenschein Nath & Rosenthal—lawyers and
non-lawyers alike, but especially my partners—have provided me with unflagging support in a variety of circumstances which have
occasionally surprised us all. Only I know better than they how little the law firm described
in the following pages either resembles our
firm or shares its atmosphere of sustained
decency. In gratitude for their comradeship,
their kindness—and their tolerance—this
novel is affectionately dedicated to the many
persons at Sonnenschein to whom my deepest
thanks are due.*

Where was my heart to flee for refuge from my heart? Whither was I to fly, where I would not follow? In what place should I not be prey to myself?

The Confessions of St. Augustine
BOOK FOUR, CHAPTER VII

•

The secret self—
ever more secret,
unhappy,
misled.

T A P E 1

Dictated January 24, 4:00 a.m.

TO: Management Oversight Committee
FROM: McCormack A. Malloy
RE: Our Missing Partner

Attached, pursuant to your assignment, please find my report.

(Dictated but not read)

I. MY ASSIGNMENT

The Management Oversight Committee of our firm, known among the partnership simply as "the Committee," meets each Monday at 3:00 p.m. Over coffee and chocolate brioche, these three hotshots, the heads of the firm's litigation, transactional, and regulatory departments, decide what's what at Gage & Griswell for another week. Not bad guys really, able lawyers, heady business types looking out for the greatest good for the greatest number at G&G, but since I came here eighteen years ago the Committee and their austere powers, freely delegated under the partnership agreement, have tended to scare me silly. I'm forty-nine, a former copper on the street, a big man with a brave front and a good Irish routine, but in the last few years I've heard many discouraging words from these three. My points have been cut, my office moved to something smaller, my hours and billing described as far too low. Arriving this afternoon, I steadied myself, as ever, for the worst.

"Mack," said Martin Gold, our managing partner, "Mack, we need your help. Something serious." He's a sizable man, Martin, a wrestler at the U. three decades ago, a middleweight with a chest broad as the map of America. He has a dark, shrewd face, a little like those Mongol warriors of Genghis Khan's, and the venerable look of somebody who's mixed it up with life. He is, no question, the best lawyer I know.

The other two, Carl Pagnucci and Wash Thale, were eating at the walnut conference table, an antique of Continental origin with the big heavy look of a cuckoo clock. Martin invited me to share the brioche, but I took only coffee. With these guys, I needed to be quick.

"This isn't about you," said Carl, making a stark appraisal of my apprehensions.

"Who?" I asked.

"Bert," said Martin.

For going on two weeks, my partner Bert Kamin has not appeared at the office. No mail from him, no calls. In the case of your average baseline human being who has worked at Gage & Griswell during my time, say anyone from Leotis Griswell to the Polish gal who cleans the cans, this would be cause for concern. Not so clearly Bert. Bert is a kind of temperamental adolescent, big and brooding, who enjoys the combat of the courtroom. You need a lawyer who will cross-examine opposing party's CEO and claw out his intestines in the fashion of certain large cats, Bert's your guy. On the other hand, if you want someone who will come to work, fill out his time sheets, or treat his secretary as if he recollected that slavery is dead, then you might think about somebody else. After a month or two on trial, Bert is liable to take an absolute powder. Once he turned up at the fantasy camp run by the Trappers, our major league baseball team. Another time he was gambling in Monte Carlo. With his dark moods, scowls, and hallway tantrums, his macho stunts and episodic schedule, Bert has survived at Gage & Griswell largely through the sufferance of Martin, who is a champion of tolerance and seems to enjoy the odd ducks like Bert. Or, for that matter, me.

"Why don't you talk to those thugs down at the steam bath where he likes to hang out? Maybe they know where he is." I meant the Russian Bath. Unmarried, Bert is apt to follow the

Kindle County sporting teams around the country on weekends, laying heavy bets and passing time in sports bars or places like the Bath where people talk about the players with an intimacy they don't presume with their relations. "He'll show up," I added, "he always does."

Pagnucci said simply, "Not this time."

"This is very sensitive," Wash Thale told me. "Very sensitive." Wash tends to state the obvious in a grave, portentous manner, the self-commissioned voice of wisdom.

"Take a look." Martin shot a brown expandable folder across the glimmer of the table. A test, I feared at once, and felt a bolt of anxiety quicken my thorax, but inside all I found were eighteen checks. They were drawn on what we call the 397 Settlement Account, an escrow administered by G&G which contains $288 million scheduled to be paid out shortly to various plaintiffs in settlement of a massive air crash case brought against Trans-National Air. TN, the world's biggest airline and travel concern, is G&G's largest client. We stand up for TN in court; we help TN buy and deal and borrow. With its worldwide hotels and resorts, its national catering business, its golf courses, airport parking lots, and rent-a-car subsidiaries, TN lays claim to some part of the time of almost every lawyer around here. We live with the company like family in the same home, tenanted on four floors of the TN Needle, just below the world corporate headquarters.

The checks inside the folder had all been signed by Bert, in his flourishing maniac hand, each one cut to something called Litiplex Ltd., in an amount of several hundred thousand dollars. On the memo lines of the drafts Bert had written "Litigation Support." Document analyses, computer models, expert witnesses—the engineers run amok in air crash cases.

"What's Litiplex?" I asked.

Martin, to my amazement, rifled a finger as if I'd said something adroit.

"Not incorporated or authorized to do business in any of the fifty states," he said. "Not in any state's Assumed Names registry. Carl checked."

Nodding, Carl added like an omen, "Myself."

Carl Pagnucci—born Carlo—is forty-two, the youngest of three, and stingy with words, a lawyer's lawyer who holds his own speech in the same kind of suspicion with which Woody Hayes viewed the forward pass. He is a pale little guy with a mustache like one of those round brushes that comes with your electric shaver. In his perfect suits, somber and tasteful, with a flash of gold from his cuff links, he reveals nothing.

Assessing the news that Bert, my screwball colleague, had written millions of dollars of checks to a company that didn't exist, I felt some peculiar impulse to defend him, my own long-time alliance with the wayward.

"Maybe somebody asked him to do it," I said.

"That's where *we* started," Wash replied. He'd taken his stout figure back to the brioche. This had come up initially, Wash said, when Glyndora Gaines, our staff supervisor in Accounting, noticed these large disbursements with no backup.

"Glyndora's searched three times for any paper trail," Wash told me. "Invoices. Sign-off memo from Jake." Under our pro-cedures, Bert was allowed to write checks on the 397 account only after receiving written approval from Jake Eiger, a former partner in this firm, who is now the General Counsel at TN.

"And?"

"There is none. We've even had Glyndora make inquiries upstairs with her counterparts at TN, the folks who handle the accounting on 397. Nothing to alarm them. You understand. 'We had some stray correspondence for this Litiplex. Blah, blah, blah.' Martin tried the same approach with one or two of the plaintiffs' lawyers in the hope they knew something we didn't. There's nothing," he said, "not a scrap. Nobody's ever heard the name." Wash is more shifty than smart, but looking at him—his liver spots and wattles, his discreet twitches and the little bit of mouse gray hair he insists on pasting across his scalp—I detected the feckless expression he has when he is sincere. "Not to mention," he added, "the endorsement."

I'd missed that. Now I took note on the back of each check of the bilingual green block stamp of the International Bank of Finance in Pico Luan. Pico, a tiny Central American nation, a hangnail on the toe of the Yucatán, is a pristine haven of fugitive dollars and absolute bank secrecy. There were no signatures on the checks' backs, but what I took for the account number was inscribed on each beneath the stamp. A straight deposit.

"We tried calling the bank," said Martin. "I explained to the General Manager that we were merely trying to confirm that Robert Kamin had rights of deposit and withdrawal on account 476642. I received a very genial lecture on the bank secrecy laws in Pico in reply. Quite a clever fellow, this one. With that beautiful accent. Just the piece of work you'd expect in that business. Like trying to grab hold of smoke. I asked if he was familiar with Mr. Kamin's name. Not a word I could quote, but I thought he was saying yes. God knows, he didn't say no."

"And what's the total?" I thumbed the checks.

"Over five and a half million," said Carl, who was always quickest with figures. "Five point six and some change actually."

With that, we were all briefly silent, awed by the gravity of the number and the daring of the feat. My partners writhed in further anguish, but on closer inspection of myself I found I was vibrating like a bell that had been struck. What a notion! Grabbing all that dough and hieing out for parts unknown. The wealth, the freedom, the chance to start anew! I wasn't sure if I was more shocked or thrilled.

"Has anybody talked to Jake?" That seemed like the next logical step to me, tell the client they'd been had.

"God, no," said Wash. "There's going to be hell to pay with TN. A partner in the firm lies to them, embezzles, steals. That's just the kind of thing that Krzysinski has been waiting for to leverage Jake. We will be dead. Dead," he said.

There was a lot that was beyond me going on among the three

of them—the Big Three, as they are called behind their backs
—but I now thought I could see why I was here. Through most
of my career at G & G I have been viewed as Jake Eiger's proxy.
We grew up in the same neighborhood and Jake was also a third
or fourth cousin of my former wife. Jake was the person responsible for bringing me to the firm when he left to become
Senior Division Counsel of TransNational Air. That is a long
tradition at Gage & Griswell. For over four decades now, our
former partners have dominated the law department at TN,
becoming rich on stock options and remembering their old colleagues with the opportunity for lavish billing. Jake, however,
has been under pressure from Tad Krzysinski, TN's new CEO,
to spread TN's legal business around, and Jake, unsure of his
own ground with Krzysinski, has given troubling signs that he
will respond. In fact, in my case he seems to have responded
some time ago, although I can't tell you if that's because I divorced his cousin, used to drink my lunch, or remain afflicted
by something you might politely call "malaise."

"We wanted your advice, Mack, on what we should do," said
Martin. "Before we went any further." He eyed me levelly beneath his furry brows. Behind him, out the broad windows of
the thirty-seventh story of the TN Needle, Kindle County
stretched—the shoebox shapes of Center City and, beyond that,
upraised brick smokestack arms. On the west bank of the river,
suburban wealth spread beneath the canopy of older trees. All
of it was forlornly sullied by the dingy light of winter.

"Call the FBI," I offered. "I'll give you a name." You'd expect
a former city cop to recommend his own department, but I left
some enemies on the Force. Reading my partners' looks, you
could see that I'd missed their mood anyway. Law enforcement
was not on the agenda.

Wash finally said it: "Premature."

I admitted that I didn't see the alternatives.

"This is a business," said Carl, a credo from which all further
premises devolved. Carl worships what he calls the market with

an ardor which in former centuries was reserved for religion. He has a robust securities practice, making the markets work, and a jet-lagged life, zooming back here to Kindle County at least twice a week from D.C., where he heads our Washington office.

"What we were thinking," said Wash, who laid his elderly hands daintily on the dark table, "some of us, anyway, is what if we could find Bert. Reason with him." Wash swallowed. "Get him to give the money back."

I stared.

"Perhaps he's had second thoughts," Wash insisted. "Something like this—he's impulsive. He's been running now, hiding. He might like another chance."

"Wash," I said, "he has five and a half million reasons to say no. And a little problem about going to jail."

"Not if we don't tell," said Wash. He swallowed again. His sallow face was wan with hope above his bow tie.

"You wouldn't tell TN?"

"If they didn't ask, no. And why should they? Really, if this works out, what is there to tell them? There was *almost* a problem? No, no," said Wash, "I don't believe that's required."

"And what would you do with Bert? Just kiss and make up?"

Pagnucci answered. "It's a negotiation," he said simply, a deal maker who believes that willing parties always find a way.

I pondered, slowly recognizing how artfully this could be engineered. The usual false faces of the workplace, only more so. They'd let Bert come back here and say it was all a bad dream. Or withdraw from the practice for a while and pay him—severance, purchase of equity, call it what you'd like. A person feeling either frightened or remorseful might find these offers attractive. But I wasn't sure Bert would see this as much of a deal. In fact, for three smart guys they seemed to have little idea of what had happened. They'd been flipped the bird and were still acting as if it was sign language for the deaf.

Wash had gotten out his pipe, one of his many props, and was waving it around.

"Either we find some way to solve this problem—privately —or the doors here will be shut in a year. Six months. That's my firm prediction." Wash's sense of peril no doubt was greatest for himself, since he had been the billing partner for TN for nearly three decades, his only client worth mentioning and the linchpin of what would otherwise have been a career as mediocre as mine. He has been an *ex officio* member of TN's board for twenty-two years now and is so closely attuned to the vibrations of the company that he can tell you when someone on TN's "Executive Level," seven floors above, has broken wind.

"I still don't understand how you think you'll find Bert."

Pagnucci touched the checks. I didn't understand at first. He was tapping the endorsement.

"Pico?"

"Have you ever been down there?"

I'd first been to Pico when I was assigned to Financial Crimes more than twenty years ago—sky of blue, round and perfect as a cereal bowl above the Mayan Mountains; vast beaches long and lovely as a suntanned flank. Most of the folks around here are down there often. TN was one of the first to despoil the coast, erecting three spectacular resorts. But I hadn't taken the trip in years. I told Carl that.

"You think that's where Bert is?"

"That's where his money is," Pagnucci said.

"No, sir. That's where it went. Where it is now is anybody's guess. The beauty of bank secrecy is that it ends the trail. You can send the money anywhere from Pico. It could be back here, frankly. If it was in the right municipal bonds, he wouldn't even have to pay taxes."

"Right," Pagnucci quickly said. He took this setback, like most things, in silence, but his precise, mannerly good looks clouded with vexation.

"And who's going to do the looking?" I asked. "I don't know many private investigators I'd trust with this one."

"No, no," said Wash. "No one outside the family. We weren't thinking of a private investigator." He was looking somewhat hopefully at me. I actually laughed when I finally got it.

"Wash, I know more about writing traffic tickets than how to find Bert. Call Missing Persons."

"He trusts you, Mack," Wash told me. "You're his friend."

"Bert has no friends."

"He'd respect your opinion. Especially about his prospects of escaping without prosecution. Bert's childish. We all know that. And peculiar. With a familiar face, he'd consider this in a new light."

Anybody who's survived for more than two decades in a law firm or a police department knows better than to say no to the boss. Around here it's team play—yes, sir, and salute smartly. No way I could refuse. But there was a reason I was going to law school at night while I was on the street. I was never one of these lamebrains who thought cop work was glamorous. Kicking doors in, running down dark alleys—that stuff tended to terrify me, especially afterwards when I got to thinking about what I'd done.

"I have a hearing Wednesday," I said. This took them all back for a moment. No one, apparently, had considered the prospect that I might be working. "Bar Admissions and Discipline still wants to punch Toots Nuccio's ticket."

There was a moment's byplay as Wash proposed alternatives—a continuance, perhaps, or allowing another G&G lawyer to handle the case; there were, after all, 130 attorneys here. Martin, the head of litigation, eventually suggested I find another partner to join me at the hearing, someone who could take over down the road if need be. Even with that settled, I was still resisting.

"Guys, this doesn't make sense. I'm never going to find Bert.

And you'll only make them angrier at TN once they realize we waited to tell them."

"Not so," said Wash. "Not so. We needed time to gather facts so that we could advise them. You'll prepare a report, Mack," he said, "something we can hand them. Dictate it as you go along. After all, this is a significant matter. Something that can badly embarrass them, as well as us. They'll understand. We'll say you'll take no more than two weeks." He looked to Martin and Carl for verification.

I repeated that there was no place to look.

"Why don't you ask those thugs down at the steam bath where he likes to hang out?" Pagnucci asked. Talking to Carl is often even less satisfying than his silence. He is stubbornly, subtly, but inalterably contrary. Pagnucci regards agreement as a failure of his solemn obligation to exercise critical intelligence. There is always a probing question, a sly jest, a suggested alternative, always a way for him to put an ax to your tree. The guy is more than half a foot shorter than me and makes me feel no bigger than a flea.

"Mack, you would be the savior of this firm," said Wash. "Imagine if it did work out. Our gratitude would be"—Wash waved—"unspeakable."

It all looked perfect from their side. I'm a burnt-out case. No big clients. Gun-shy about trials since I stopped drinking. A fucked-up wreck with the chance to secure my position. And all of this coming up at the most opportune time. The firm was in its annual hysteria with the approaching conclusion of our fiscal year on January 31. All the partners were busy choking over-due fees out of our clients and positioning themselves for February 2, a week and a half from now, when the profits would be divided.

I considered Wash, wondering how I ever ended up working for anybody in a bow tie.

"I say the same thing to you I've said to Martin and Carl," Wash told me. "It's ours, this place, our lives as lawyers are here. What do we lose if we take a couple of weeks trying to save it?"

With that, the three were silent. If nothing else, I had their attention. In high school I used to play baseball. I'm big—six three—and never a lightweight. I have good eye-hand, I could hit the ball a long way, but I'm slow, what people call lumbering when they're trying to be polite, and the coaches had to find someplace to play me, which turned out to be the outfield. I've never been the guy you'd want on your team. If I wasn't batting, I wasn't really in the game. Three hundred feet away from home plate you can forget. The wind comes up; you smell the grass, the perfume from some girl in the stands. A wrapper kicks across the field, followed by a ghost of dust. You check the sun, falling, even with all the yelling to keep you awake, into a kind of trance state, a piece of meditation or dreams. And then, somehow, you feel the eyes of everybody in the park suddenly shifted toward you—the pitcher looking back, the batter, the people in the stands, somebody someplace has yelled your name. It's all coming to you, this dark circle hoving through the sky, changing size, just the way you've seen it at night when you're asleep. I had that feeling now, of having been betrayed by my dreams.

Fear, as usual, was my only real excuse.

"Listen, guys. This was carefully planned. By Mr. Litiplex or Kamin or whoever. Bert's three sheets to the wind with his sails nowhere in sight. And even if I do find him, by some miracle, what do you think happens when he opens the door and sees that he's been tracked down by one of his partners, who undoubtedly is going to speak to him about going to prison? What do you think he'll do?"

"He'll talk to you, Mack."

"He'll shoot me, Wash. If he's got any sense."

Bereft of a response, Wash looked on with limpid blue eyes and a guttering soul—an aging white man. Martin, a step ahead as ever, smiled in his subtle way because he knew I'd agreed.

Pagnucci as usual said nothing.

II. MY REACTION

Privately, my partners would tell you I'm a troubled individual. Wash and Martin are polite enough to murmur some faint-hearted denial as they read this, but, guys, we all know the truth. I am, I admit, kind of a wreck from all directions—overweight even by the standards of big men who seem to get some latitude, gimpy on rainy days because I ruined my knee while I was a copper, jumping off a fence to chase some bum who never was worth catching. My skin, from two decades of drinking hard, has got that reddened look, as if someone took a Brillo pad to my forehead and my cheeks. Worse is what goes on inside. I have a sad heart, stomped on, fevered and corrupted, and a brain that boils at night in a ferment of awful dreams. I hear like far-off music the harsh voices of my mother and my former wife, both of them tough Irishwomen who knew that the tongue, for the right occasion, can be made an instrument of pain.

But now I was excited. After the Committee broke, I lit out from the Needle for the Russian Bath, eager and actually somewhat jealous of Bert. Imagine! I thought as I bounced along in the taxi taking me west. Just imagine. A guy who worked down the hall. A foul ball. Now he was off roistering with a stolen fortune while I was still landlocked in my squalid little life.

Reading this, my partners probably are squinting. What kind of jealous? they say. What envy? Fellas, let's not kid ourselves, especially at 4:00 a.m. It is the hour of the wolf, quiet as doom, and I, the usual insomniac mess, am murmuring into my Dictaphone, whispering in fact, in case my nosy teenaged son actually returns from his night of reprobate activity. When I finish, I'll hide the tape in the strongbox beneath my bed. That way, in the event of second thoughts, I can drop the cassette into the trash.

Before I began dictating the cover memo, I actually figured I would do it just as Wash requested. A report. Something anesthetized and lawyerly, prose in a straitjacket, and many footnotes. But you know me—as the song goes, I've done it my way. Say what you like, this is quite a role. I talk, you listen. I know. You don't. I tell you what I want—when I want. I discuss you like the furniture, or address you now and then by name. Martin, you are smiling in spite of yourself. Wash, you are wondering how Martin will react. Carl, you'd like it all in no more than three sentences and are bristling already.

The bottom line, then: I didn't find Bert this afternoon. I tried. The cab got me to the right place and I stood outside the Bath, looking over the run-down commercial street, one of DuSable's many played-out neighborhoods, with the gritty restaurants and taverns, storefronts and tenements, windows dulled by dust. The brick buildings are permanently darkened from the years when this city burned coal. The masonry seemed to gather weight against the sky, which had been galvanized by winter, heavy-bellied clouds, gray and lusterless as zinc.

I actually grew up not far from here on the West End of the city, near the Callison Street Bridge, a phenomenal structure of enormous brownish stones and concrete filigree, designed, I believe, by H. H. Richardson himself. A mighty thing, it cast a shadow for blocks over our gloomy little Irish village, a neighborhood really, but a place as closed off as if there were a drawbridge and walls. The dads were all firemen, like my father, or

policemen or public-payroll hacks or guys who worked in fac-
tories. A tavern on every corner and two lovely large churches,
St. Joe's and St. Viator's, where the parish, to my ma's constant
regret, was half Italian. Lace curtains. Rosary beads. Until I was
twelve, I did not know a kid who went to public school. My
mother named me for John McCormack, the famous Irish tenor,
whose sad ballads and perfect diction left her trembling over
the sadness of life and the forlorn hope of love.

"Seedy" is not the word for the Russian Bath; better "prehis-
toric." Inside, the place was vintage Joe McCarthy—exposed
pipes overhead, with the greenish lacquered walls darkened by
oil and soot, and split by an old mahogany chair rail. The motif
here was Land That Time Forgot, where was and would-be were
the same, an Ur region of male voices, intense heat, and swinging
dicks. Time would wear it down but ne'er destroy it: the sort of
atmosphere that the Irish perpetuate in every bar. I paid fourteen dollars to an immigrant Russian behind a cage, who gave
me a towel, a sheet, a locker key, and a pair of rubber shoes I
purchased as an afterthought to shield my tootsies. The narrow
corridor back was lined with photos in cheap black frames, all
the great ones—sports stars, opera singers, politicians, and
gangsters, a few of whom fit in more than one of these categories.
In the locker room where I undressed, the carpet was the gray
of dead fish and smelled of chlorine and mildew.

This Russian Bath is a notorious spot in Kindle County. I'd
never set foot inside before, but when I was working Financial
Crimes, the FBI always had somebody sitting on a surveillance
here. Pols, union types, various heavy-browed heavyweights like
to take a meet in this place to talk their dirty business, because
even the Feebies can't hide a transmitter under a wet sheet.
Bert is down here, relishing the unsavory atmosphere, whenever
he can break free—lunchtime, after work, even for an hour after
court when he's in trial.

Inside his head, Bert seems to live in his own Boys Town.
Most of my partners are men and women with fancy degrees—

Harvard, Yale, and Easton—intellectuals for a few minutes in their lives, the types who keep *The New York Review of Books* in business, reading all those carping articles to put themselves to sleep. But Bert is sort of the way people figure me, smart but basic. He'd been law review at the U., and before that an Air Force Academy grad and a combat pilot in Nam in the last desperate year of war, but the events of his later life don't seem to penetrate. He's caught up in the fantasies that preoccupied him at age eleven. Bert thinks it's nifty to hang out with guys who hint about hits and scores, who can give you the line on tomorrow's game before they've seen the papers. What these fellas are actually doing, I suspect, is the same thing as Bert— talking trash and feeling dangerous. After their steam bath, they sit around card tables in the locker room in their sheets, eating pickled herring served at a little stand-up bar and telling each other stories about scores they've settled, jerks that they've set straight. For a grown-up, this sort of macho make-believe is silly. For a guy whose daytime life is devoted to making the world safe for airlines, banks, and insurance companies, it is, frankly, delusional.

The bath was down the stairs and I held tight to the rail, full of the usual doubts about exactly what I was up to, including going someplace I didn't know without my clothes on, but it proved to be a spot of well-worn grace, full of steam and smoke, a breath of heat that rushed to meet you. The men sat about, young guys shamelessly naked, with their dongs hanging out, and older fellas, fat and withered, who'd slopped a sheet across their middles or slung it toga-like over their shoulders.

The bath was a wood construction, not your light color like a sauna that reminds you of Scandinavian furniture, but dark planks, blackened by moisture. A large room rising fifteen feet or more, its scent was like a wet forest floor. Tiers of planked benches stepped up in ranks on all sides and in the center was the old iron oven, jacketed in cement, indomitable and somehow insolent, like a 300-pound mother-in-law. At night the fires burned there, scalding the rocks that sit within the oven's belly, a brood of dinosaur eggs, granite boulders scraped from the bottoms of the Great Lakes, now scarred white from the heat.

Every now and then some brave veteran struggled to his feet with a heavy, indigenous grunt and shoved a pitcher of hot water in there. The oven sizzled and spit back in fury; the steam rose at once. The higher up you sat, the more you felt, so that even after a few minutes at the third level you could feel your noggin cooking. Sitting, steaming, the men spoke episodically, talking gruff half-sentences to one another, then stood and poured a bucket of icy water, drained from flowing spigots in the boards, over their heads. Watching this routine, I wondered how many guys the paramedics have carried out. Occasionally someone lay down on the benches and another fella, in a bizarre ceremony, soaped him from head to toe, front and back, with callus sponges and sheaves of oak leaves frothing heavy soap.

These days, of course, a bunch of naked men rubbing each other leads to a thought or two, and frankly, exactly what gives with Bert is not a matter I'd put money on. But these guys looked pretty convincing—big-bellied old-world types, fellas like Bert who've been coming here since they were kids, ethnics with a capital E. Slavs. Jews. Russians. Mexicans. People steeped in peasant pleasures, their allegiance to the past in their sweat.

From time to time I could catch the sideward glances. Many gay blades, I suspected, had to be stomped into recognizing that Kindle County isn't San Francisco. This crowd looked like they made fast judgments about newcomers.

"Friend of Bert Kamin's," I muttered, trying to explain myself to a solid old lump who sat in his sheet across from me. His graying hair was soapy and deviled up, going off in three or four different directions so he looked mostly like a hood ornament. "He's always talked about it. Had to give it a try."

The fella made a sound. "Who's that?" he asked.

"Bert," I said.

"Oh, Bert," he said. "What's with him? Big trial or somethin? Where all's he gone to?"

I took a beat with that. I had figured that would be my line. I could feel the heat now, agitating my blood and drying my nostrils, and I moved down a level. Where does a fellow go with five and a half million dollars? I wondered. What are the logical alternatives? Plastic surgery? The jungles of Brazil? Or just a small town where nobody you'd know would ever appear? You'd think it's easy, but try the question on yourself. Personally, I figured I'd favor a simple agenda. Swim a lot. Read good books. Play some golf. Find one of those women looking for a fellow who's honest and true.

"Maybe he's got someplace with Archie and them," said the old lump. "I ain't seen him too much neither."

"Archie?"

"Don't you know Archie? He's a character for you. Got a big position. Whosiewhasit. Whadda they call it. Hey. Lucien. Whatta you call what Archie does with that insurance company?" He addressed a guy sitting near the oven, a man who looked more or less like him, with a sloping belly and fleshy breasts pink from the heat.

"Actuary," answered Lucien.

"There you go," said the guy, sending suds flying as he gestured. He went on talking about Archie. He was here every day, the guy said. Clockwork. Five o'clock. Him and Bert always together, two professional fellas.

"I bet that's where-all he's gone, Bert. Hey, Lucien. Bert and Archie, they together or what?"

This time Lucien moved. "Who's asking?"

"This guy."

I made some demurrer that they both ignored.

"Name of?" asked Lucien, and squinted in the steam. He'd come in without his glasses and he stepped down to get a better look at me, clearly sizing me up, one of these guys too old to apologize anymore for anything. I gave my name and offered a hand, which Lucien limply grabbed backhanded, his right paw holding fast to the bedsheet around his middle. He took a breath or two through his open mouth, red as a pomegranate.

"You lookin for Kam Roberts, too?" he asked finally.

Kam Roberts. Robert Kamin. I was sure it was a joke.

"Yeah," I said, and brought out some blarney smile. "Yeah, Kam Roberts," I repeated. Don't ask me why I do these things—I'm always pretending to know more than I do. Since I was a naughty kid, I've been like that, faking one thing or another; there are so many selves rollicking around in here and it is a harmful indulgence for a man often out of control. I had the thought that "Kam Roberts" was like the secret password, I could ask a few more questions once I'd said it, but something, the peculiarity of the name or my odd tone of enthusiasm, seemed to deaden the air in the room.

In response, Lumpy and Lucien more or less withdrew. Lucien said he wanted to play cards and nudged his pal along, both of them shoving off with only a bare goodbye and a quick look back in my direction.

I stayed put in the steam, blanching like some vegetable and considering my prospects. Heat has its odd effects. In time, the limbs grow heavy and the mind is slower, as if gravity's increased, as if you'd taken a seat on Jupiter. This thing of men being men amid the intense heat revived some lost thought of my old man and the firehouse where all those guys spent so much of their lives together, bunking down in that single large room in which they dreamt uneasily, awaiting the hoarse call of the alarm, the summons to danger. We always knew when there'd been fires. You could hear the engines tearing out of the little firehouse four blocks away, the clanging of the bells, 'the sireens,' as my father said, the enormous roaring motors that sounded big enough to power rocket ships. My dad came home sometimes still carrying the fire with him, a penetrating scent that hung around him like a cloud. 'Smellin like the sinners down in hell' was how he put it, weary and beaten in by physical exertion and fear, waiting for The Black Rose to open so he could have a snoot before he slept. My dreams since are full of fire, though I can't say for sure if that's from my pa or the way my ma, when she was scolding, would pinch my ear and tell me I was in league with Satan and would need to be buried in britches of asbestos.

Cooked out, I stumbled back up to the seedy locker room. I was trying to squint up the number from my key when I heard a voice behind me.

"Hey, yo, mister, you. Jorge wants to see you." It was a kid with a bucket and a mop. I wasn't sure he was talking to me, but he tossed his head of sleek jet hair and waved for me to follow, which I did, clip-clopping after him in my thongs and wet sheet, leaving the locker area for something a hand-drawn sign called "The Club Room." Maybe somebody wanted me to buy a membership, I figured. Or to tell me about Bert.

Here again the furnishings were the latest, if the year happened to be 1949. Cheap mahogany paneling. Brown, speckled asbestos floor tiles such as would give any OSHA inspector an instant coronary. Red vinyl furniture with the stuffing oozing out the corners and, in one case, a black spring so long exposed it was beginning to rust. At a gray Formica table, with one of those old designs of vague forms like the sight through an unfocused microscope, four men were seated, playing pinochle. The youngest of them, a smooth-looking Mexican, nodded, and behind me the kid with the bucket scooted a chair.

"You lookin for Kam Roberts?" the Mexican asked. His eyes were on his cards. Lucien and Lumpy were nowhere in sight.

"I'm a friend of Bert Kamin."

"I asked you 'Kam Roberts.'" He considered me now. This fella, Jorge, was a thin guy, one of those unshaved stringy-looking Mexicans who make such amazing lightweights, always whipping the fannies of these sleek black guys with bulging muscles. Unforeseen strength like that always impresses me. "You got some i.d.?"

I looked at my sheet, heavy and almost translucent from the steam.

"Give me two minutes."

"How far you think you get in two minutes?" he asked and threw down a card. I took a while on that.

"My name is Mack Malloy. Bert's my partner. I'm a lawyer." I offered my hand.

"No, you ain," said Jorge. Story of my life. Lie and I make you smile. The truth, you only wonder.

"Who are you?" I asked.

"Who am I? I'm a guy sittin here talkin to you, okay? You're lookin for Kam Roberts, that's who I am. Okay?" Jorge studied me with what you might call Third World anger—this thing that really goes beyond skin color and echoes back across the epochs, some gene-encoded memory of the syphilis that Cortez's men spread, of the tribal chieftains that the helmeted European troops tossed into the steaming volcanic crevices. "Mr. Roberts here, that's Mr. Shit. You know what I mean?"

"I hear you."

He turned to a guy beside him, a thick old brute who was still holding his cards.

"He hears me." They exchanged a laugh.

Overall, this was not a good situation, being naked with four angry men. Jorge put both hands down on the table.

"I say you're a cop." He wet his lips. "I *know* you're a cop." Those dark Hispanic eyes had irises like caves and emitted no light, and I was lost in there; it was a second before I heartened with the thought that a copper was unlikely to end up beaten in the alley. "I'd make you nine days a week. You got a star tattooed on your tushy."

The three guys watching thought this was a terrific line.

I smiled faintly, that primate fear-flight thing, still trying to figure what it was this guy thought he knew about me. It had been more than twenty years, but I would bet I could remember every guy I cracked. Sort of like the kids from grade school. Some faces you don't forget.

"Whatever you lookin for, *hombre*, you don' find here. You check with Hans over in Six, you'll find out."

"I'm looking for Bert."

Jorge closed his eyes, heavy-lidded like a lizard's.

"Wouldn't know him. Don' know him and don' know nobody he knows. I tole the first copper what come around askin Kam Roberts, I tole him straight up, I don' want none of this shit. I tole him, see Hans, and now we got some fucker here playin What's My Line. Don' fuck with me." He worked his head around completely as if it were on a string, so that I knew I'd had it right to start: a former boxer.

I got it now, why he thought I was a cop, because the cops had already been here looking for Kam Roberts. I wanted to ask more, of course—which coppers, which unit, what they thought Bert had done—but I knew better than to press my luck.

Jorge had leaned in his confidential way across the table once again.

"I'm not supposed to have any this shit." That's what he paid Hans for, that's what he was telling me. I knew Hans too, a watch commander in the Sixth District, two, three years from retirement, Hans Gudrich, real fat these days, with very clear blue eyes, quite beautiful actually, if you could say that about the eyes on a fat old cop.

"I was on my way out," I said.

"See, that's what I thought."

"You were right." I stood up, my sheet wetting the floor beneath me. "We all have a job to do." My impression of an honest policeman didn't sell. Jorge pointed.

"Nobody got no jobs to do here. You want to sweat, that's fine. You come here runnin any scams, Mr. Roberts or whatever, we'll take a piece of your candy-ass, I don' care what kind of star you carry. To me, Mr. Roberts, man, I better not hear no Mr. Roberts again, you know?"

"Got it."

I was gone fast. Bert may have been a fake tough guy; these fellas knew a thing or two about making hard choices, and I was dressed and on the street in a jiffy, bombing down the walk, my insides still melted down in fear. Nice crowd, I told Bert, and, once I'd started this conversation, asked a few more questions like why he was calling himself Kam Roberts.

I was now up to the intersection of Duhaney and Shields, one of these grand city neighborhoods, the league of nations, four blocks with eleven languages, all of them displayed on the garish signs flogging bargains that are pasted in the store windows. Taxis here are at best occasional, and I stomped around near the bus stop, where a little bit of the last snow remained in a dirty crusted hump, my cheeks stinging in the cold and my soul still seething from the trip into that inferno of tough men and intense heat. Near my native ground, I found myself in the thick grip of time and the stalled feelings that forty years ago seemed to bind my spirit like glue. I was hopelessly at odds with everyone—my ma, the Church, the nuns at school, the entire claustrophobic community with its million rules. I took no part in the joy that everybody here seemed to feel in belonging. Instead, I felt I was a spy, a clandestine agent from somewhere else, an outsider who took them all as objects, surfaces, things to see.

Now this last couple of years, since Nora scooted, I seem to be back here more and more, my dreams set in the dim houses beneath the Callison Street Bridge, where I am searching. Four decades later, it turns out it was me who was secretly infiltrated. Sometimes in these dreams I think I'm looking for my sister, sweet Elaine, dead three years now, but I cannot find her. Outside, the wash flags in the sunshine which is bright enough to purify, but I am inside, the wind shifting in the curtains and the papers down the hall as I prowl the grim interior corridors to find some lost connection. What did I care about back then? Desperately, in the nights now, I sit up, concentrating, trying to recall the source of all of these errors, knowing that somewhere in this dark house, in one room or another, I will sweep aside a door and feel the rush of light and heat, the flames.

III. MY LAWYER

It was about seven-thirty when I got back to the office, and Brushy, as usual, was still there. Near as I can tell, none of my partners believes that money is the most important thing in the world—they just work as if they did. They are decent folks, my partners, men and women of refined instinct, other-thinking, many of them lively company and committed to a lot of do-good stuff, but we are joined together, like the nucleus of an atom, by the dark magnetic forces of nature—a shared weakness for our own worst desires. Get ahead. Make money. Wield power. It all takes time. In this life you're often so hard-pressed that scratching your head sometimes seems to absorb an instant you're sure will be precious later in the day.

Brush, like many others, felt best here, burning like some torch in the dark hours. No phone, no opposing counsel or associates, no fucking management meetings. Her fierce intelligence could be concentrated on the tasks at hand, writing letters, reviewing memos, seven little things in sixty minutes, each one billable as a quarter of an hour. My own time in the office was a chain of aimless spells.

I stuck my head in, feeling the need for someone sensible.

"Got a minute?"

Brushy has the corner office, the glamour spot. I'm ten years older, with smaller digs next door. She was at her desk, a plane of glass engulfed at either end by green standing plants whose fronds languished on her papers.

"Business?" she asked. "Who's the client?" She had reached for her time sheet already.

"Old one," I said. "Me." Brushy was my attorney in my wars with Nora. An absolutely ruthless trial lawyer, Emilia Bruccia is one of G & G's great stars. On deposition, I've seen her reform the recollections of witnesses more dramatically than if they had ingested psychoactive drugs, and she's also gifted with that wonderful, devious, clever cast of mind by which she can always explain away the opposition's most damaging documents as something not worth using to wrap fish. She's become a mainstay of our relationship with TN, while developing a dozen great clients of her own, including a big insurance company in California.

Not only does she bill a million bucks a year, but this is a terrific person. I mean it. I would no sooner try to get a jump on Brushy than I would a hungry panther. But she is not dim to feelings. She has plenty of her own, which she exhausts in work and sexual plunder, having a terminal case of hot pants that makes her personal life, behind her back, the object of local sport. She is loyal; she is smart; she has a long memory for kindnesses done. And she is a great partner. If I had to find someone on an hour's notice to go take a dep for me a hundred miles from Tulsa in the middle of the night, I'd call Brushy first. It was her dependability, in fact, which inspired my visit. When I told her I needed a favor, she didn't even flinch.

"I'd love it if you could grab the wheel on Toots's disciplinary hearing at BAD," I said. "I'll be there for the first session on Wednesday, but after that I may be on the loose." BAD—the Bar Admissions and Disciplinary Commission—is a sagging bureaucracy ministering over entrances, exits, and timeouts from the practice of law. I spent my first four years as a lawyer there,

struggling to remain afloat in the tidal crest of complaints regarding lawyerly feasance, mis, mal, and non.

Brushy objected that she'd never handled a hearing at BAD
and it took a second to persuade her she was up to it. Like many
great successes, Brushy has her moments of doubt. She flashes
the world a winning smile, then wrings her hands when she is
alone, not sure she sees what everybody else does. I promised
to have Lucinda, the secretary whose services we shared, copy
the file, to let Brushy look it over.

"Where will you be?" she asked.

"Looking for Bert."

"Yeah, where in the world is he?"

"That's what the Committee wants to know."

"The Committee?"

Brushy warmed to my account. The Big Three tend to be
tight-vested and most of my partners relish any chance to peek
behind the curtains. Brushy savored each detail until she suddenly grasped the problem.

"Just like that? Five million, six?" Her small mouth hanging
open, Brushy looked dimly toward the future—the lawsuits, the
recriminations. Her investment in the law firm was in jeopardy.
"How could he do that to us?"

"There are no victims," I told her. She didn't get it. "Cop
talk," I said, "it's a thing we'd say. Guy walks down a dark street
alone in the wrong neighborhood and gets mugged. Some shmo
cries a river cause he lost a hundred-thousand-bucks hoping
some con artist could make a car run on potato chips. People
get what they're asking for. There are no victims."

She looked at me with concern. Brushy sat here tonight in a
trim suit and a blouse with a big orange bow. Her short hair
was cut close, a little butch, and showed off two or three prominent acne scars that pitted her left cheek, like the dimples of
the moon. Her teenaged years had to have been tough.

"It's a saying," I said.

"Meaning what? Here?"

Shrugging, I went to the pencil drawer in the gunmetal cre-
denza behind her to find a cigarette. We both sneak butts. Gage
& Griswell is now a smoke-free environment, but we sit in
Brushy's office or mine with the door closed. From the drawer
I also removed a little makeup mirror, which I asked to borrow.
Brushy couldn't have cared less. She was chewing on her thumb,
still wrought up with the prospect of disaster.

"Should you be telling me this?" Brushy asked. She always
had a better sense than me for the value of a confidence.

"Probably not," I admitted. "Call it attorney-client." Privileged, I meant. Forever secret. Another of those witless jokes
lawyers make about the law. Brushy wasn't really my lawyer
here; I wasn't really her client. "Besides, I need to ask you
something about Bert."

She was still pondering the situation. She said again she
couldn't believe it.

"It's a nice idea, *n'est-ce pas*? Fill your pocket with some new
i.d.'s and several million dollars and jet off to be someone else
for the rest of your life." I made a sound. "It gives me the shivers
just to think of it."

"What kind of new i.d.'s?" she asked.

"Oh, he seems to be using some screwy alias. You ever hear
him call himself Kam Roberts for any reason—even just kidding
around?"

Never. I told her a little about my visit to the Russian Bath,
watching these guys built like refrigerators flail each other with
oak branches and soap.

"Weird," she said.

"That's how it struck me. Here's the thing, Brush. These birds
around there seem to think Bert has gone off with some man.
He ever mention anyone named Archie?"

"Nope." She eyed me through the smoke. She already knew
I was up to something.

"It made me think, you know. It's been years since I saw Bert
with a woman." When Bert got here more than a decade ago,

he was still squiring Doreen, his high-school honey, to firm functions. He'd made vague promises to marry this woman, a sweet schoolteacher, and in the years she waited she turned into a kind of sports-bar bimbo, with a drinking problem like mine and skirts the size of handkerchiefs and blond hair so ravaged by chemicals that it stuck out from her head like raffia. One day at lunch Bert announced she was marrying her principal. No further comment. Ever. And no replacement.

Always live to nuance, Brushy had perked up. "Are you asking what I think?"

"You mean something dirty and indiscreet? Right. I'm not asking you to speculate. I just thought you might be able to contribute pertinent information." I sort of scratched my ear lamely but it wasn't fooling her a bit. Pugnacious, you would call her look. She's not big—short, broad, and but for tireless health-club hours tending to the stout—but her jaw was set meanly.

"Who are you now? The Public Health Service?"

"Spare me the details. Yes or no will do to start."

"No."

I wasn't sure she was answering. Brushy is touchy about personal lives, since hers is always the subject of sniggering. Every office deserves a Brushy, a stalwartly single, sexually predatory female. She subscribes to a feminism of her own vision, which seems to be inspired by piracy on the high seas, regarding it as an achievement to board every passing male ship. She does not recognize any common boundary: marital status, age, social class. When she decides on a man, either for the position he occupies, the promise he radiates, or the good looks that stimulate other females to mere fancy, she is unambiguous in making her desires known. Over the years she has been seen in the company of judges and politicians, journalists, opponents, guys from the file room, a couple of former jurors—and many of her partners, including, should you be wondering, for one fitful afternoon, me. Big and good-looking, Bert had undoubtedly fallen within the circled sights of Brushy's up-periscope.

"It's not prurient interest, Brush. It's professional. Just give me a wink. I need your opinion: Is it he's or she's when Bert dances the hokey-pokey?"

"I don't *believe* you," she said and looked off with a sour scowl. In her pursuits, Brushy, in her own way, is discreet. She generally wouldn't talk under torture, and her advances, while relentless, always recognize the proprieties of the workplace. But for her sexual follies, Brushy still pays a heavy price. Her commitment to appetites that most of us are busy trying to suppress leads folks to regard her as odd, even dangerous; other females are often downright hostile. And among her peers, the younger partners, the men and women who started together as associates and survived those years together—the giddy all-nighters in the library, the one thousand carry-in meals—Brushy is on the outs anyway. They envy her advancement in the firm, and when they gather privately for gossip, it's often about her.

She is, in her own way, alone here, a fact which I suppose has drawn us together. Our one misfiring encounter is never a topic. After Nora, my volcano seems more or less extinct, and we both know that afternoon belongs to my wackiest period— right after my sister, Elaine, had died and I had stopped drinking, just when the recognition that my wife was busy with other sexual pursuits was beginning to assume the form of what we might call an idea, sort of the way all that swirling gas and dust in the remote regions of the cosmos starts to zero in on being a planet. For Brush and me our interlude served its purpose, nonetheless. In the aftermath, we became good pals, schmoozing, smoking, and playing racquetball once a week. On court, she is as vicious as a mink.

"How's the Loathsome Child?" Brushy asked. She eyed me in strict warning. We both knew she'd changed the subject.

"Living up to his name," I assured her. Lyle was Nora's and

my only kid, and his insular ways as a little boy had led me to refer to him with what I thought was tenderness as the Lonesome Child. When adolescence set in, however, the consonants migrated.

"What's the latest?"

"Oh, please. Let me count the ways. I find muddy footprints on the sofa. Dried soda pop on the kitchen floor. He comes home at 4:00 a.m. and rings the doorbell because he forgot the keys. The PDR doesn't list half the drugs he takes. Nineteen years old. And he doesn't flush the toilet."

At that last item, Brushy made a face. "Isn't it time for him to grow up? Doesn't that happen with children?"

"Not so as you'd notice with Lyle. I'll tell you, whatever you saved me on alimony, Brushy, she got even with that shrink. All that crap about how an adolescent male was too vulnerable to be without his father in these circumstances."

Brushy said what she always said: the first custody fight she'd seen where the dispute was over who had to take the child.

"Well, she got even," I repeated.

"What did she have to get even for?"

"Jesus Christ," I said, "you really haven't been married, have you? The world went to hell and I went with it. I don't know."

"You stopped drinking."

I shrugged. I am seldom as impressed by this feat as other people, who like to think it shows I have something, some element which if not unique is still special to the human condition. Courage. I don't know. But I was aware of the secret and it never left me. I'm still hooked. Now I depend on the pain of not drinking, on the craving, on the denial. Especially the denial. I get up in the morning and it strikes me that I'm not going to drink and I actually wonder why I have to do this to myself, same as I used to think waking from a bender. And inside there's the same little harpy telling me that I deserve it.

I had taken another cigarette and wandered to the big windows. The trail of headlamps and brake lights stippled the strip of highway, and an occasional building window was lit up by the isolated sparks of somebody else's life being squandered in evening toil. Stepping back, I caught a glimpse of my own reflection decaled over the night: the weary warrior, hair gone gray and so much ruddy flesh beneath my chin that I can never button my collar.

"You know," I said, "you get divorced, it's like being hit by a truck. You walk around in a fucking fog. You're not even sure you're alive. Maybe the last year, I've realized when I stopped drinking was probably what pushed her out the door."

Brushy had removed her pumps and crossed her feet on the desktop. With my remark she stopped wiggling her short toes against the orange mesh of her pantyhose and asked what I was talking about.

"Nora liked me better when I drank. She didn't like me much, but she liked me better. I left her alone. She could conduct her international experiment in living. The last thing she wanted was my attention. They have a word for this now. What is it?"

" 'Co-dependent.' "

"There you go." I smiled, but we were both rendered silent. It hadn't taken Brushy many guesses. As usual, the mess in my life was its own dead end.

I sat down on her sofa, black leather trimmed with metal rails. It was twenty-first-century decorating in here, "high-tech," so that the place had the warmth of a hospital operating room. Every partner furnishes as he or she likes, inasmuch as our offices are otherwise the same, three walls of union Sheetrock and a glamour view, all plate glass framed by piers of stressed concrete. We have been here in the TN Needle, a forty-four-story stiletto looming prominently against Center City and the prairie landscape, since it opened six years ago, keeping cozy with our biggest client. Our phones and electronic mail intersect with TN's; half our lawyers have stationery of the General Counsel,

Jake Eiger, so they can dash off letters in his name. Visitors to the building often say they cannot tell where TN ends and Gage & Griswell starts, which is just how we like it.

"So you're really going to do this, look for Bert?"

"The Big Three didn't think I had a choice. We all know my story. I'm too old to learn to do something else, too greedy to give up the money I make, and too burnt out to deserve it. So I take on Mission Impossible and buy myself a job."

"That sounds like the kind of deal somebody could forget about. Have you thought of that?"

I had, but it was humiliating as hell to think it was so obvious. I just shrugged.

"Besides," I said, "the cops'll probably find Bert before me."

She became rigid at the mention of the police. I took some time to tell her the rest of the story, about Jorge, the lightweight, and his three mean friends.

"Are you telling me the cops know about this? The money?"

"No chance. It's gone out of our escrow account and we haven't heard word one from them. It's not that."

"Then what?"

I shook my head sadly. I didn't have a clue.

"Actually," I said, "from the drift I got, I think they've been asking about Kam Roberts."

"I'm lost," she said.

"Me too."

"Well, I don't understand why you're willing to do this," Brushy told me. "Didn't you say he'd shoot you?"

"I was negotiating. I'll fend him off. I'll tell him I didn't believe it, I took it on to defend his honor."

"*Do* you believe it?"

I raised my hands: who knows? Who ever knows? I spent a moment with the wonder of it all. What is it really, this life? You're shoulder to shoulder with a guy eight hours a day, try cases with him, go to lunch, sit in the back row and make wisecracks at partners' meetings, stand beside him in the men's room and watch him shake his thing, and what the hell do you know? Zippity-do. You haven't got a clue about the inner regions. You don't know what he regards as dirty thoughts or the place he dreams of as a haven. You don't know if he constantly feels close to the Great Spirit or if anxiety is always nibbling inside him like some famished rat. Really—what *is* this? You never know with people, I thought, another phrase I picked up on the street and have been repeating to myself for twenty years. I repeated it to Brushy now.

"I can't accept it," she said. "This is so calculating. And Bert's impulsive. If you told me he'd signed up to be an astronaut last week and was already halfway to the moon, that would sound more like him."

"We'll see. I figure if I actually track him down, I'll always have a great alternative to turning him in or bringing him back."

She stared, green eyes hopped up with all her wily curiosity.

"And what alternative is that?"

"Bert and I can split the money right down the middle." I put out the cigarette and winked. I said to her again, "Attorney-client."

IV. BERT AT HOME

A. His Apartment

My partner Bert Kamin is not an everyday-type guy. Angular
and swarthy, with a substantial athletic build and long dark hair,
he looks good enough, but there is something wild in his eye.
Until she passed away, five or six years ago, Bert—former combat ace, trial shark, hotshot gambler and hoodlum hanger-on—
lived with his mother, a demanding old witch by the name of
Mabel. He didn't have a shortcoming she failed to mention.
Slothful. Irresponsible. Ungrateful. Mean. She'd let him have
it, and Bert, with his macho jaw set, tough talk, and chewing
gum, just sat there.

The man left after this thirty-five-year mortar assault is a sort
of heaping dark mystery, one of those vague paranoiacs who
defends his odd habits in the name of individuality. Food's one
of his specialties. He is sure America is out to poison him. He
subscribes to a dozen obscure health newsletters—"Vitamin B
Update" and "The Soluble Fiber Wellness Letter"—and he is
regularly reading books by goofballs just like him which convince
him that something new should not be ingested. I have unwill-
ingly absorbed his opinions over many meals. He lives in mortal

fear of tap water, which he figures has everything deadly in it
—fluoride, chlorine, and lead—and will drink nothing from the
city pipes; over the protests of the Committee, he's even had
one of those big green bottled water coolers installed in his office.
He won't eat cheese ("junk food"), sausage ("nitrites"), chicken
("DES"), or milk (he still worries about strontium 90). On the
other hand, he believes that cholesterol is an AMA-sponsored
fiction and has no brief against red meat. And he never ate green
vegetables. He will tell you they are overrated, but in fact, he
just never got to like them as a kid.

I was feeling Bert's presence pretty strongly now, all his screwball intensity, as I stood outside his place. It was about eleven
and I'd decided to check out his digs on my way home. Last
time I looked, break and enter was still a crime and I figured
I'd just keep this visit to myself.

Bert lives—or lived—in a little freestanding two-flat in a re-
habbed area near Center City. As I recalled the story, he'd
wanted to stay in his ma's house in the South End, but he got
into one of those coffin-side spats with his sister and had to sell
to make her happy. Here, he was pretty much at loose ends. I
arrived with my briefcase, which had nothing in it but two coat
hangers, a screwdriver which I'd borrowed from the mainte-
nance closet on my way out of the office, and the Dictaphone,
which I took on the bet that my dreams would wake me, as they
have, and leave me grateful for something to do in these awful,
still hours.

Twenty-some years ago, before they shipped me off to Financial Crimes to give me time to finish law school, I worked
in the tactical unit with a good street cop name of Gino Dimonte,
who everybody called Pigeyes. Tac guys are plainclothes, the
sort of roving linebackers of the Force who'll do further investigation on what the beat cop reports—stake out an arrest, round
up a suspect. I learned a lot from Pigeyes, which is one of the
things that ticked him off when I testified about him before a
federal grand jury; these days he's backwatered in Financial

Crimes and, as the legend goes, always looking for me, the same way Captain Hook had an eye out for the crocodile and Ahab for the whale. Anyway, Pigeyes taught me a million tricks. How to sneak the cruiser down an alley, headlights out, using the emergency brake to stop so that your suspect doesn't even see the red glow of the rear lamps. I watched him get into apartments without a warrant by making calls, saying he was UPS and had left a package downstairs, or that he lived across the street and thought there was a fire on the roof, so that our man would come rushing out and leave his door wide open. I even heard him phone and say there were suspicious guys around, and have a high old time when the dip stuck his mug out with an unregistered pistol in his hand and got his ass arrested and his front room tossed incident to arrest.

This was another of Gino's little bits, just a makeup mirror that a lady would carry in her purse or keep in the drawer in her office, as Brushy had. In most old buildings, the front door on an apartment has been trimmed at the foot to fit the carpeting, and with the mirror, if you get used to looking upside down, you can see a lot. I knelt there in the vestibule, putting my ear to the door to the upstairs apartment now and then to make sure the neighbor wasn't shaking around. As I remembered it, she was a flight attendant. I figured on trying her sometime, after I'd seen what was what in Bert's apartment.

It sure looked like Bert was gone. In the mirror I could see the mail piled up on the floor in heaps—*Sports Illustrated* and health and muscle magazines and flyers, and of course a bunch of bills. I rumbled around a little bit against the door, enough noise so that if there was anyone inside I'd get them moving, then after a while I used the coat hangers. I straightened them out, all but the hook, and joined them at the crimps. Using the mirror, I could see the chain lock hanging open. I must have spent five minutes trying to get a decent purchase on the knob of the dead bolt, and then it turned out the damn thing wasn't set. The old skeleton-keyed door lock and knob came off with the screwdriver in twenty seconds. I always told Nora: If they want to get in, they're coming in.

Maybe it was that thought of Nora, but as soon as the door swung open, I was attacked by the loneliness of it all, Bert's life. I felt like I'd gone hollow, unfilled space aching with the absence. It scares me to see the way single guys live. When Nora bolted for the great outdoors, she left most everything behind. A lot of the furniture is broken and torn, what with the Loathsome Child, but it's there, it's still a house. Bert's living room didn't even have a rug on the floor. He had a sofa, a 30-inch TV, and a huge green plant that I bet somebody sent him as a gift. In one corner, housed on its packing box, was an entire computer setup—box, keyboard, monitor, printer—with a folding chair in front of it. I had a sudden vision of goofy old Bert lost inside the machine, spending the dead hours of the night with his mind tracing the circuits of a chip, whizzing from one bulletin board to the next or playing complex computer war games, wiping out little green people with a death ray from space. Crazy guy.

I walked right through the mail as I came in, then thought better of it and plunked myself down on the hardwood floor among the gathered dustballs. The oldest items were postmarked about ten days ago, which seemed to fit Bert's suspected date of departure. One envelope had a footprint on it, maybe mine, or someone else's, or Bert's when he took off. The last thought seemed to make the most sense, since I found another envelope which had been opened. Inside was a bank card—one only— tucked into the little two-sided cardboard holder used to send out new cards annually. Maybe Bert had taken the other card to travel? The one that was there was embossed with the name Kam Roberts.

In the scattered mail I found another envelope addressed to Kam Roberts. I held it up to the light, then just ripped it open. A monthly statement for the bank card. It was pretty much what you'd expect with Bert during basketball season, charges run up in every town in the Mid-Ten. Bert thought nothing of flashing to the airport at five and getting in one of those flying buckets so he could arrive in some Midwestern college town in time to witness the walloping of the U.'s team, the Bargehands, known for generations as the Hands. There were a number of local charges, too, but I stashed all of it, the card and the bill, in my inside suit pocket, figuring I'd study the details later.

The only other item in Bert's mail that struck me was *The Advisor*, Kindle County's gay newspaper, with its sizzling personals section and some pretty embarrassing ads for underwear. Was he or wasn't he? Bert might tell me that he subscribed for the classifieds or film criticism, but to me it figured that Bert was in the closet. He's of my place in history, when sex was dirty and desire a hidden misery that each of us kept steeled within our own Pandora's Box and released only in clandestine darkness where we were promptly enslaved. Bert's inclinations are a deep-dark secret. He isn't telling anybody, maybe even himself. That's where Kam Roberts comes in; it's his drag. If he's meeting boys in the men's room of the Kindle County Public Library or visiting leather bars in another city where he's supposedly gone to watch the Hands, Kam is his name. All of this is surely what the TN engineers refer to as a WAG—a wild-assed guess. Yet standing in the apartment, I thought it made sense. No, he never put his hand on my knee or cast lascivious glances at the Loathsome Child either. But I'd bet the farm anyway that all Bert's twitches and costumes and lonely moods came out of which way his pecker was pointing. Which is his business, not mine. I really mean it. Frankly, I've always admired people with secrets worth keeping, having, of course, one or two of my own.

Which is not to pretend on the other hand that scoping all this out did not give me a combo of the creeps and some little thrill of kinky curiosity. So talk to me about my tendencies. But don't you wonder sometimes, really, what these guys are up to? I mean, who does what to whom. You know, tab A, slot B. They've got this weird secret thing, like the Masons or the Mormons.

I wondered if it was problems in his life as Kam that had the coppers looking for Bert. When I was on the street, there were always the sorriest scams with these fellows—a prisoner in the Rudyard penitentiary who somehow got a bunch of guys he'd found through the personals to pay him fifty bucks apiece with a letter promising he was "going to put a liplock on your love-muscle" as soon as he was released. There was one restaurant owner who installed a hidden camera behind one of the urinals and had a private photo gallery of Kindle County's most prominent penises. And you'd hear of plenty of outright extortion, boy-toys who threatened to tell the wife or the employer. There were a billion ways Bert could have gotten himself in trouble, and tossing all this around, big bluff old Mack felt pretty sorry for Bert, who wasn't trying to hurt a soul.

I made a tour of the apartment. Bert's bedroom wasn't much better than the living room—a cheap dresser set, his bed unmade. There wasn't a picture in the entire place. His suits hung neatly in his closet but his other stuff was thrown around the room in the familiar fashion of Lyle.

I went to the kitchen to check out the fridge, still trying to see how long our hero had been gone, another old cop move, smell the milk, check the pull date. When I opened the fridge, there was a dead guy staring back.

B. His Refrigerator

The dead, like the rich, are different from you and me. I was racing with that crazy bursting feeling as if I was going to pop out of my own skin. Not that I couldn't acknowledge a macabre interest. I actually pulled one of the kitchen chairs around and was sitting, say, three feet away, staring at him. In my time on the street I'd seen my share of corpses, suicides hanging from the basement pipes or in a bathtub full of blood, a couple of murder victims, and lots of folks who just plain expired, and I'm at the age now where every couple of weeks it seems like I'm going to a wake. However it is, I'm always impressed by the way a human being looks stripped of that fundamental vitality, like a tree without its leaves. Death always takes something away, nothing you could really name, but life somehow is a visible thing.

It wasn't Bert. This guy was about Bert's size, but he was older, maybe sixty. He had been folded into the refrigerator like a garment bag. His feet went one way, his legs were squashed down under him, his head was forced to about ninety degrees to make him fit. His eyes were bugged out unbelievably; they were that very light green you might as well call gray. He was wearing a suit and a tie, and around the collar of his shirt, the blood had soaked in and dried like a kind of batik. Eventually I noticed the black line dug into his neck and tied to a shelf hook to hold him up. Fishing tackle. Deep-sea stuff. One-hundred-pound test. The refrigerator light glowed like a bald head and threw a little orange into his gray face. Alive, he must have been a respectable-looking fellow.

I sat there trying to figure out what to do. I had to be good and careful, I knew that much. Still, I kept wondering what had happened. Bert's motives for disappearing seemed clearer. The most obvious reason to chill the remains would be to get some time to run. But there was no blood anywhere in the apartment. Unless there'd been a rug or a little more furniture before. Did wonky old Bert have murder in him? The Jesuits in high school told me nobody did, then the police force gave me a gun and told me to shoot and I was in enough basements looking for some slug who'd vanished down a gangway, ready to piss my trousers every time I heard the furnace creak, so that I knew I would have. Bert, in his own way, was pretty tightly wound. So maybe.

Option 2 was that this was somebody else's handiwork. Before Bert left or after? Before appeared unlikely. Not too many people are going to break into your apartment with a stiff and leave him in your refrigerator without your permission. After was possible. If somebody knew Bert was gone.

I really didn't want to call the cops. If I did, everything was going to come out. Missing Bert. Missing money. So long, client. So long, Mack and G&G. Worse yet, the way things work, murder suspect number one for a while would be me. That could be a real pain, given the number of coppers, pals of Pigeyes, who are laying for me, one of whom in time would realize he could charge me for the break-in. Sooner or later the police would have to hear about this. This poor bastard, after all, probably had a family. But the best way to tip them was anonymously, after I'd had some time to think things through.

I went about putting the place back together as best I could, wiped the refrigerator handle down, swept the kitchen floor to clear my footprints. I couldn't get the lock in the front door without opening it, since the outer plate screwed in from the other side. So I stood there on the threshold, upright, in plain view, fumbling for five minutes, fixing up the apartment I'd just broken into. I tried to imagine what the hell I'd say if the stew came home or if I raised the curiosity of somebody passing on the street, how I'd get myself out of trouble. Still, as I fooled around with the last screw, I liked it, my minute dangling over the cliff. Sometimes in life, things just happen. No planning. Out of control. That's one of those things guys like about being cops. I'd liked it too, just not the way I woke up in the night, with my heart galloping and my mouth like glue and the fears, the fears, licking me all over like some cat getting ready to do it to a mouse. It drove me to drink, was one of the things, and off the Force, though it has never stopped.

But nothing happened, not now. The stew never showed,

nobody on the street even looked my way. I went through the outer door with my scarf pulled up to my nose, and down the city walk, safe and happy, just like I am with daybreak coming now, knowing I can stop talking into this thing, having slipped away for one more night.

TAPE 2

Dictated January 24, 11 p.m.

V. A WORKING LIFE

A. The Mind of the Machine

Now and then everybody wants to be somebody else, Elaine. There are all these secret people rolling around inside—ma and pa, killers and cops and various prime-time heroes, and all of them at times reaching for the throttle. There's no way to stop it, and who's to say we should. What seemed sweeter yesterday than the thought of nabbing Bert and running with the money? It's just your brother, the old copper, explaining how it is that folks go wrong. Every guy I cracked said it: I didn't mean to, I didn't want to. As if it were somebody else who'd scored the smack or kicked the coins out of the vending machine. And it is in a way. That's what I'm saying.

I sat in my office this morning, venturing this two-bit commentary for the benefit of my dead sister, as I do a couple of times each day, and noodling over the statement that I'd pocketed from the Kam Roberts credit card. The thought of Bert being someone else impromptu still drilled me with that little secret jolt, but the particulars of his hidden life remained elusive. Besides the charges for air tickets and restaurants and motels in little Mid-Ten towns, there were items, five to fifteen dollars each, posted almost daily for some something called "Infomode," and there was also a series of cash advances totaling about three grand. Bert made more dough than me, maybe 275K, and I'd have figured he'd write a check to cash in Accounting if he needed folding money, rather than pay interest. Then we got really strange: a single credit item, over nine thousand bucks for something called Arch Enterprises. Maybe this was pal Archie, the wayward actuary, but what-for nine thousand dollars credit? I was writing comedy making up the explanations. *E.g.*, Bert returned a big insurance policy? And then we had the small-time peculiar, two nights' charges last month at U Inn, a kind of run-down hotel/motel right across from the university's main quadrangle, an odd spot for Bert to be checking in since his apartment was only a mile away.

I was pushing around these puzzle pieces when my phone rang.

"We have a serious problem." It was Wash.

"We do?"

"Very serious." He sounded undone, but Wash is not the fellow we turn to in crisis. There are people, like Martin, who talk about Wash as a legend, but I suspect he was one of those young men who was admired for his bright future and now is forgiven his lapses due to the supposed achievements of his past. Aged sixty-seven, Wash by my reckoning lost interest in the practice of law at least a decade ago. You could say the same of me, but I'm not an icon. This life can make you soft. There are always younger lawyers, agile-minded and bristling with ambition, to think for you, to write the opinion letters and draft the contracts. Wash has capitulated to that. He is, for the most part, a ceremonial lawyer, a soothing presence to old clients to whom he is connected by club affiliations and schooling.

"I just spoke with Martin," Wash said. "He ran into Jake Eiger in the elevator."

"So?"

"Jake was asking about Bert."

"Uh-oh." Ticklish inquiries from the client. I felt the usual moment of private gratitude that I wasn't in charge.

"We have to figure out what to tell Jake. Martin had to jump onto a conference call—we only spoke for a second. But he should be through soon. He suggested we all get together."

I told Wash I'd stand by.

In the interval I resumed my routine endeavor these days at G&G—trying to find something to do. When I came here eighteen years ago, it was with the promise that Jake Eiger would have lots of work for me, and for a number of years his word held true. I rewrote TN's Employees' Code of Conduct, I conducted a number of internal investigations—flight attendants selling drinks out of their own bottles, a hotel manager whose hiring standard for chambermaids was whether they swallowed after fellating him. Eventually that stuff tapered off, and in the last two years has stopped cold. I'm left doing odds and ends for Bert and Brushy and some of my other partners who remain on Jake's main menu, trying cases they are too busy for, doing firm committee work, still hoping, after eighteen years in private practice, that somehow, somewhere there's some million-dollar client who wants an ex-drunk former copper for its principal outside counsel. Between slouching work habits and a lack of clientele, my economic value to this enterprise is dwindling toward zero. True, I cash a hefty draw check every quarter, notwithstanding three straight years of reductions; and there are folks, like Martin, who seem inclined to support me as an act of enduring sentiment. But I have to worry about when someone like Pagnucci will call time's up—and then there's the matter of my pride, assuming I have any left.

Not happy thoughts as I looked over the Blue Sheet, our daily bulletin, and the remainder of the lost forest of memos and mail that are generated within G&G each day. I had some desultory work to do on 397, the air crash disaster that has provided nearly full-time employment for Bert and more than occasional toil for

me in the last three years. There were letters to sign and a draft
of payout documents which were due over with Peter Neucriss,
the lead plaintiff's lawyer, an exacting prick who'd force me to
rewrite them four times. Today's letters purported to be from
TN, written on TN stationery—various proclamations regarding
the settlement fund that we were supposed to safeguard and
which TN controlled—and I applied my flawless imitation of
Jake Eiger's signature, then went back to the Blue Sheet, shifting
for interesting news. Only the usual. A corporate department
luncheon to discuss interest rate swaps; time sheets due by 5:00
or we'd get fined; and, my favorite, mystery mail, a photocopy
of a check payable to the firm for $275 with a note from Glyndora
in Accounting asking if anybody knew who sent it and why.
There was once a check for about 750 grand that ran for three
days straight which I very nearly claimed. Carl and various sub-
alterns had also sent four separate memos to the partners,
hard copy and E-mail, telling us to giddy up and get our clients
to pay their fees before the fiscal year ended next week on
January 31.

This thought of bills coming due reminded me of the Kam
Roberts credit card. I told Lucinda where I'd be when Wash
called and rambled through the halls to the law library, a floor
above on 38. Three associates, all in their initial year of practice,
were yakking around a table. At the rare sight of a partner in
these surroundings, they embarked on a silent, quailed departure from each other's company to resume making profit of their
time.

"Not so fast," I said. I had recruited each of them. A large
law firm is basically organized on the same principles as a Ponzi
scheme. The only sure ingredients of growth are new clients,
bigger bills, and—especially—more people at the bottom, each
a little profit center, toiling into the wee hours and earning more
for the partnership than they take home. Thus we have a lecher's
interest in new talent and are always wooing. In the summers
we give fifteen law students a tryout on terms that make over-

night camp look like hard labor. Twelve hundred a week to go to baseball games and concerts and fancy lunches, an experience that is a better introduction to life as royalty than the practice of law. And who's in charge of sucking up to these children this way? Yours truly.

When I was assigned to the recruiting subcommittee, Martin tried to explain it as a tribute to my raffish charm. Young people would relate to my offhand ways, he suggested, my casual eccentricities. I knew that with his native bureaucratic dexterity he'd struck on some last-hope way to demonstrate my usefulness to our partners. The fact is I do not particularly care for younger people. Ask my son. I resent their youth—their opportunities, the zillion ways they are inherently better off than I am. Nor, frankly, are they particularly taken with me. But nineteen times each fall I sit in some desolate hotel room near a premier law school and watch them, in their lawyer costumes, strut their stuff, twenty-five-year-olds, a few so self-impressed you want to stick a pin in and watch them blow around the room. Jesus.

"I got this guy's bank card statement in discovery," I said, "and I'm trying to figure what he was spending money on. What's Infomode?" Amid the library's lavish surroundings, the three listened to me with the studied solemnity reserved to the young and ambitious. This was a comfortable, old-fashioned place with club chairs and oak bookcases and tables, and a second-floor balcony rimmed with gold-trimmed volumes that ran the circumference of the room. Leotis Griswell, the firm's late founder, had spent generously here, sort of on the same theory by which Catholics like to glorify their churches.

It was Lena Holtz who knew about Infomode.

"It's a modem information service. You know. You dial up and can go shopping or get stock-market quotes, the wire services. Anything."

"You dial up what?"

"Here." She walked me over to a laptop computer in one of the carrels. Lena was my touchdown for the year, law review at the U., from a rich family out in the West Bank suburbs. She'd had some rough times prior to law school and they left her with an appealing determination to use herself well. Five feet tall, with those teensy thin limbs so there always seems to be extra room in her clothes, she's not much to look at, not when you looked closely, but the pieces fit well. Hair, cosmetics, clothes—Lena has what is generally called style.

I had given her Kam Roberts's bill and she was already punching at the computer. A phone was ringing inside.

"See?" she said as the screen brightened with color proclaiming INFOMODE!

"And what kind of information can you get?" I asked.

"You name it—flight schedules, the prices of antiques, weather reports. They have two thousand different libraries."

"So how do I figure out what he was doing?"

"You could look at his billing information. It would come right up on the screen."

"Great!"

"But you'd need his password," she told me.

Naturally I was blank.

"See, this isn't free," she said. "They charge your credit card every time you enter a library. Like now, I logged on into his account."

"How?"

"The account number's right here on the bank card statement. But to make sure that I'm really authorized to use it, we need his password."

"What's the password? 'Rosebud'?"

"A kid's name. Birthday. Anniversary."

"Great," I said again. I sat hunched, watching little iridescent squiggles radiate on the screen, as if the letters were burning, fascinated as ever by the thought of fire. This might be why Bert had the card, so he could rack up Infomode charges in another name. I grabbed her arm.

"Try Kam Roberts." I spelled it.

The screen lit up again: WELCOME TO INFOMODE!

"Whoa," I said. Once an art student, always an art student. How I love color.

"Do Billing," she typed. The listing that scrolled up looked like the bank card statement, a log of charges incurred every day or two, which included the length of use and the cost. It was just what you'd expect of Bert. It was all for something called "Sportsline," or for another service they referred to as "Mailbox." I figured Sportsline reported the scores of games. I asked about Mailbox.

"It's what it sounds like. Get messages from people who are on-line. Like electronic mail."

Or, it turned out, you could leave messages behind, little memos to yourself or to someone who logged into your account with your permission. That was what Bert had done. The note we found was dated three weeks ago and seemed to make no sense.

It read:

```
Hey Arch——


              SPRINGFIELD
Kam's Special 1.12——U. five, five Cleveland.
1.3——Seton five, three Franklin.
1.5——SJ five, three Grant.


              NEW BRUNSWICK
1.2——S.F. eleven, five Grant.
```

Lena grabbed a yellow pad out of another carrel and wrote it down.

"Does this mean anything to you?" she asked.

Not a thing. Baseball scores in January? Map readings? The combination for a safe? We both stared desolately at the screen.

I heard my name from the P.A.s in the ceiling: "Mr. Malloy,

please go to Mr. Thale's office." The announcement was repeated twice, somehow more ominous with each rendition. I felt trouble darken my heart. What were we going to tell Jake? I rose, thanking Lena. She clicked off the machine so that Bert's message, whatever it was, vanished in a little star of light that lingered on the dull screen.

B. Washing

Relieved to have found me, Wash welcomed me to his office with a warmth you'd expect if you were entering his home. George Washington Thale III has the sort of charm meant to reflect breeding, a steady geniality he radiates even with the secretaries. When he turns all his attention and smooth manners on you, you feel like you've met somebody out of Fitzgerald, scion of an old rich world to which all Americans once aspired. Still, I never can forget the term "stuffed shirt." He has this big bag belly that seems to push up to his chest when he is seated. With his bow ties and his horn-rimmed glasses, his liver-spotted face and his pipe, he is a type, one of those used-up emblems of prosperity whose very sight makes you think that somewhere there's a kid waiting for his inheritance.

Wash asked after my well-being, but he was still fretting about Jake, and he promptly dialed Martin's extension on his speakerphone. In Wash's grand corner office, decorated in dark woods, with colonial objects brightened by dabs of gold or red, the practice of law generally has an easy, elegant air, a world where men of importance make decisions and minions at a distance carry them out. He has filled this space with memorabilia of George Washington—portraiture and busts, little mementos, things that G.W. was alleged to have touched. Wash is some ninth- or twelfth-hand relation, and his hapless attachment to this stuff always seems secretly pitiful to me, as if his own life will never measure up.

"I'm with Mack," Wash said when Martin came on.

"Good," he replied. "Just the men I'm looking for." I could tell from Martin's tone, a quart over on oil, that he too was in the company of someone else. "Mack, I just bumped into Jake and we began to talk about the progress on some of the 397 cases Bert's been handling. I invited him to stop in. I thought we all might want to talk about this together."

"Jake's *with* you?" Wash asked. He only now grasped what Martin had meant when he said we all should get together.

"Right here," Martin answered. Upbeat. Strong tone. Martin is like Brushy—like Pagnucci—like Leotis Griswell in his day, like many others who do it well, a lawyer every waking hour. He manages the firm; he plans the renewal of the river and the buildings on the shore. He counsels clients and gets fourteen younger attorneys in a room and plays war games on all his big-time cases. He flies here and there and engages in endless conference calls with parties strung out across most of the world's time zones, during which he listens, opines, edits briefs, and reads his mail. Something in the law is always at hand and on his mind. And he adores it—he is like a gourmet gorging down an endless meal, eating every goody on his plate. With Jake there, with crisis looming, he sounded chipper and self-confident, raring to go. But when Wash looked back, his aging, pale face was stricken and he looked more scared than me.

C. Introducing the Victim of the Crime

If you've ever seen *The Birth of Venus* with the goddess on the half-shell and all the seraphim bent back with the vapors because she is so great, then you've seen big-firm lawyers when the General Counsel of their major client arrives. During our first few minutes with Jake Eiger in Martin's vast corner office, getting coffee and waiting as Martin quelled the usual urgent calls, about half a dozen partners stuck their heads in to tell Jake how fit he looked, or that his latest letter on the Suchandsuch matter reflected the same pith and sensibility as the Gettysburg Address; they threw out offhand invitations to dinner, theater, and basketball games. Jake, as ever, accepted this attention with grace. His father was a politician and he knows the way, waving, laughing, parrying with various skillful jests.

I have known Jake Eiger most of my life. We went to high school together at Loyola, Jake two years ahead. You and I, Elaine, we were the kind of Catholics who grew up thinking we were a minority group, the mackerel snappers who ate fish on Friday and wore ash on our foreheads and made way for the ladies in black sheets; we knew we were regarded by Protestants as a clandestine organization with foreign loyalties, like the Freemasons or the KGB. Jack Kennedy of course was our hero, and in his aftermath America for Catholics, I think, truly was different. But you are ever the child, and I'll never really be sure there is a place at the table for me.

But Jake was a Catholic boy, German-Irish, who thought he'd joined the white man's country club. I envied him that and many other things, that his father was rich and that Jake was easy with people. Very good-looking, a movie-star type, he has smooth coppery blond hair that never leaves its place and is only now, with Jake a year or two past fifty, beginning to show less of the radiance that always made you think he was under a spotlight. He has prepossessing eyes—the kind of abundant lashes that you seldom see on a man and which gave Jake, since an otherwise unimpressive childhood, the misleading look of a worldly adult depth. There were always lots of girls after him, and I suspected him of treating them cruelly, wooing them in his soft way and rebuffing them once he'd gotten between their legs.

Still, when I was on my fourteenth version of who I would be, having decided against Vincent Van Gogh, Jack Kerouac, and Dick Tracy, and figured I'd give my dad's idea, law school, a try, Jake, of all people, became a kind of ideal. Our paths had split after high school but my role as Nora's intended brought us back in contact at little family dos, and Jake took it on himself to give me pointers and advice about law school and practice. Then when I got started at BAD he called upon me for a rather auspicious favor which he felt obliged to repay years later by bringing me here.

A rational person would be grateful to Jake Eiger for that. I made $228,168 last year, and that was after they cut my points for the third time in a row. Without Jake, I'd probably be in some interior office space with cheap paneling, practicing on my own, scrambling around to the police courts and otherwise looking hungrily at the silent telephone. But Jake flies and I float. He's still soaring for the stars and on his way has cut me loose to go to cinders as I plummet back through the atmosphere. A lesser type might be bitter, because without me Jake Eiger would be a handsome middle-aged guy looking for ways to explain why he gave up the practice of law many years ago.

"Wash, Mack—" Martin had clapped down the phone, dispensing with the last interruption, and his secretary had finally closed the door. "About Brother Kamin."

"Ah yes." I smiled brightly and waited to watch Martin dance this tightrope.

"Jake's aware, of course, that Bert is on another of his self-declared sabbaticals."

"Right." Smiles. Wash laughed out loud. Martin's such a card.

"And I thought, frankly, that it would make more sense just to share with Jake everything that we've been concerned about. Everything. I don't want any misunderstandings down the line."

Martin went on in a mood of impressive gravity. The room was quiet as he spoke, windowed on three sides, full of abstract paintings and the kind of kooky objets d'art that Martin adores —funny clocks, a side table whose glass top overlay an entire city carved of exotic woods, a shaman's crook that makes the sound of a waterfall when you turn it upside down. Rather than the standard photo of the family, a small soft-sculpture that rendered Martin and his wife and three kids in the mode of

Cabbage Patch Kids was perched on his credenza. Martin was behind the desk toward which all the room's furnishings subtly angle, a broad barely finished burl from the trunk of some thousand-year-old oak.

I saw where Martin was going long before Wash, who was in one of the Barcelona chairs that form a proscenium about Martin's desk. When Wash finally realized that Martin was detailing our suspicions about Bert, he made a vague move to object. But Wash clearly had no time to think it through and instead contained himself.

Martin removed his credenza key—he had it hidden in the rubber belly of a clock set in a hula dancer—and displayed the folder of documents I'd seen yesterday. He explained to Jake that we had found no paper trail authorizing these checks. As Jake began to sense that something had gone wrong, he started to fidget. But Martin, the man of principles and solid commitments, showed no wavering. It couldn't have been easy for him. G&G has been life to Martin since his days at Leotis Griswell's right hand, and he adores the hurly-burly, the business of bringing everyone together. That's his faith, that the team is greater than the sum of the parts. He's my Chinaman here, the man I admire, and he was being admirable now. Only yesterday the Committee had made its decision to wait before the client was informed. Yet Martin was manifesting his allegiance to something more significant than law firm Hoyle: Values. Duty. The lawyer's code. The client, unexpectedly, had asked a question which clearly invited the truth and Martin would not be party to withholding it.

By now Martin was explaining the Committee's plan, how I was searching for Bert in the hope he could be persuaded to relent. From Jake, Martin asked brief forbearance, a couple of weeks, with the promise that at the end I'd provide a full report. To sum up, he came and sat on the forward edge of his desk.

"If we can tell Bert that you, that TN, is looking at this in an understanding way," he said to Jake, "I think there's a chance, a real chance, to get the money back. If we do, we can, perhaps, avoid the scandal. That truly strikes me as best for everyone."

He stopped. Martin had made his appeal, all his formidable charm and powers turned on Jake. Now we waited. It was, on the whole, a moment of high daring. Gage & Griswell was probably about to join the lost city of Atlantis as a civilization that fell into the sea. I thought Wash might black out, and even my skin was crawling, anticipating Jake's reaction. Jake, for his part, looked worse than I'd ever seen him, the fatal gray of a man in shock.

"Unbelievable." That was the first thing Jake said. He got to his feet and walked a circle one way and then the other around his chair. "How am I ever going to handle this upstairs?" He asked this question mostly of himself, fingertips at his lips, and it was clear he did not know the answer. He stood there, visibly pained, not quite willing to discuss the repercussions, as if they were lexically beyond him, like a man who could not bear to utter dirty words.

"We're here to help you," Wash said.

"Oh, you've helped a lot," said Jake and winced at the thought.

TN lately had been on hard times, if a company with gross earnings of four billion every year can be described that way. Almost everything they own—the hotels, the rent-a-car companies, the airlines—is sensitive to fluctuations in travel, of which there had been damn little since our warlette against So-damn Insane. No surprise either, since anybody with a college business course could have told you that covey of enterprises would move cyclically. To diversify, TN a decade ago bought a traveler's check business and from that made an entry into the world of Sunbelt banking, just in time to watch their loan portfolio go to hell. After the suicidal fare wars of last summer, the company lost about 600 million bucks, the third bad year in a row. To stem the bleeding, the outside directors brought in Tadeusz Krzysinski as CEO, the first person ever to advance above the level of vice-president who was not homegrown.

Among many reforms, Tad has cracked the whip on expenses and by all accounts has been prodding Jake about his relationship with G&G, on the theory that there should be more competition for TN's legal work. Krzysinski has been heard to speak warmly of a 200-lawyer firm in Columbus he grew to like when he was in his last incarnation, as president of Red Carpet Rental Car.

This, to say the least, is a subject of concern at Gage & Griswell, since TN has never been less than 18 percent of our revenues. Martin and Wash have been trying to convert Krzysinski, lunching with him, inviting him to meetings, reminding him repeatedly how expensive it would be to replace our knowledge of TN's structure and past legal affairs. In response, Krzysinski has emphasized that the decision is Jake's—his General Counsel, like most, must have free rein to choose the outside lawyers he works with—a deft move since both Jake and G&G have their supporters on TN's board. But Jake has a seasoned corporate bureaucrat's lust for terrain. He covets a seat on the board, the title of Vice-Chairman, which only Krzysinski can award him, and evinces a toadying willingness to please his new Chairman, with whom in truth he seems frequently ill at ease. As often happens in corporation land, there's been more talk than action. Jake has sent only a few morsels to Columbus, as he does with many other firms. But in business, like baseball, senior management is often behind you right up to the day you get the ax.

Jake by now had turned to me. "This is very sensitive. Mack, I want to know about everything you're doing. And for God's sake," he added, "be discreet."

Jake is accustomed to being an executive. He stood a moment, medium height and lean, a hand placed over his eyes. He was wearing a smart double-breasted suit, a subtle glen plaid, and his initials—J.A.K.E.: John Andrew Kenneth Eiger—a favored decorative element, had showed on his shirtsleeve when he pointed at me. "Jesus Christ," Jake said in final reflection and with nothing further left.

Wash rose in his wake. In extremis his aging face had taken on the texture of a gourd, and he hung there, a mystery to himself, torn between remonstrating with Martin and comforting Jake, and finally chose the latter. A grade-schooler knew what he was going to say: Give us time. Don't be rash. Once we find Kamin, this can be worked out.

Behind the thousand-year oak, Martin watched them vanish and asked me, "So what do you think?" He had his hands across his tummy, his face tucked down shrewdly between the matching braces, so that his chin rested on his fancy handmade shirt of jazzy vertical stripes.

"I'll let you know as soon as I get feeling again in my limbs." My heart was still flapping. "I thought we weren't going to say anything."

Martin is one of those men who abound in the legal profession whose brains seem to make them a quarter larger than life. His mind is always zipping along at the speed of an electron. You sit down with him and feel surrounded on all sides. Jesus Christ, you wonder, what is this fellow thinking? I know he's turned over every word I've said three times before I get another one out of my mouth. Accompanying this kind of intellectual hand-speed is a canny grasp of human nature. To what uses all of this is put is not necessarily clear. Martin would not be mistaken for Mother Teresa. Like anybody else who has whizzed along the fast track in the practice of law, he can cut your heart out if need be. And talking to him, as I say, is a kind of contest, in which his clever, warm remarks, his conveyed sense that he knows just what you mean, is somehow never mutual. I know you; you don't know me. His true residence is out-of-bounds, somewhere in the neighborhood of Mount Olympus. But Martin was rarely as mystifying as he was now. He seemed unshaken by anything that had occurred here. He met my inquiry with an inscrutable little tip of the hand, as if he could not alter bygones.

"What do you think Krzysinski's going to say when Jake tells him about this?" I asked.

Martin closed his eyes to weigh the inquiry, as if it had not occurred to him yet, and when he looked back a little wrinkle of something close to humor, an embracing irony, briefly crossed his worn face. He stood to regard me, as another of his funny clocks began to chatter like a chipmunk somewhere in the room.

"I think you'd better find Bert," he told me.

VI. THE SECRET LIFE OF

KAM ROBERTS

A. Good News

Most of the time as I am recording this, talking it through, I do
not see the faces of Carl and Wash and Martin. I can't really
imagine them with the pages in their hands. So there must be
someone else I mean to talk to, sitting here in my rummage-
sale bedroom late at night. In the stillness the voice seems to
be the spirit, the way a candle is best represented by a flame.
Maybe the Dictaphone's a medium, then, a way to enhance
communication with the dear departed. Maybe this is really an
extended message to sweet Elaine, with whom I used to speak
three times a day. Today I've felt her absence starkly, the willing
ear to whom I've muttered stray remarks, even as I sat in my
office, shiftless and sour, feeling perplexed by the hunt for Bert.

I stared again at the statement from the Kam Roberts bank
card. My feet were on my desk, a large period piece with the
formidable tiered look of a steamship, its rosy surface lost in a
patchwork of discarded telephone messages, throwaway memos,
and various briefs and transcripts that I was yet to file. When I
came in at G&G with Jake Eiger's backing and made partner
during those initial years when Jake drowned me in work, I had

the option to redecorate this room but never got around to it, too drunk to care I guess. I've lived all this time with what is in reality secondhand stuff, the big walnut desk, the glass-paned bookcases, two leather gooseneck chairs with brass studs, a nice, if worn, Oriental rug, a personal computer, and my own clutter. The only object I care much about is on the wall, a terrific Beckmann print—the usual dissipated people in a café. By daylight I have a fine view of the river and the west edge of Center City, girded by the Interstate, U.S. 843.

I thought sullenly about how I was going to make Martin happy and find Bert. I still wanted to talk to the flight attendant in the apartment above his, but I didn't have her name—she hadn't left it on the mailbox—and the notion of putting myself in the vicinity of that stiff again gave me the willies. I phoned long-distance information for Scottsdale and after two calls found Bert's sister, Mrs. Cheryl Moeller, whom I'd met when the ma was buried. She didn't know where her brother was and had not heard from him in months, which was par for the course. She couldn't remember any pal of Bert's named Archie either. She didn't sound as if she liked her brother any better than she ever had and ended up reassuring me that Bert was going to turn up, as usual.

Fellas, Elaine—whoever I'm talking to—I have to tell you, your investigator was stumped. I went over the statement one more time. Why was Bert booking hotel rooms on game nights when he had an empty apartment a mile away? Purely on a flyer, I called U Inn. I got the hotel operator and did what we used to refer to in Financial as a pretext call. I said I was trying to get information on a guy I'd had a business meeting with at U Inn on December 18. I'd lost my entire file in a taxi and was hoping maybe they had a forwarding address or phone for him.

"What's this gentleman's name?" the hotel operator asked.

"Kam Roberts." I was looking for any clue to Bert's present whereabouts. I heard a few computer keys click, then spent most of eternity on hold, but finally got a fellow named Trilby who said he was the Associate Manager. He asked first thing for my name and number, which I gave him.

"I'll check our records, Mr. Malloy, and ask Mr. Roberts to call you."

Wrong idea. Bert didn't figure to stick around for an encounter with any of his partners.

"I'm on vacation after today. I really need to reach him. Any chance of that?"

"Just a moment." It was a good deal longer than that, but Trilby sounded quite pleased with himself when he returned. "Mr. Malloy, you must have ESP. He's a guest in the hotel."

My heart stopped.

"Kam Roberts is? You're sure?"

He laughed. "Well, I wouldn't say that anybody here knows him, but there's a gentleman by that name checked in to Room 622. Should I have him call you? Or can we tell him when you'll be coming by?"

I thought. "Can I talk to him?"

He returned after I'd heard an extended symphonic version of "Raindrops Keep Falling On My Head."

"There's no answer there, Mr. Malloy. Why don't you stop by at the end of the day and we'll get him a message you'll be here."

"Sure," I said. "Or I'll call."

"Call or come by," said Trilby. He was writing a note.

After I put down the phone, I sat a long time looking at the river. There was one building across the way, still wearing Yuletide festoonery, lights and a skirt of holly across the roof. It didn't make much sense. Bert had reason to be laying low—his partners, the police, and maybe even whoever had stuffed that bug-eyed businessman in his refrigerator were all after him. But why hide in Kindle, where sooner or later he'd run into somebody he knew? Whatever, I had to get down there fast, before

Bert got this lamebrained message in which I'd used my actual factual name, the sight of which undoubtedly would lead him to scoot once more.

I took the elevator down and crossed the street to the health club where I play racquetball with Brushy. I jumped into my sweats and shoved my wallet in a pocket, then started jogging. It was 28 degrees so I hauled my broad Irish backside down the avenues with some dispatch, but I ran out of wind after about four blocks and went back and forth, running till my smoked-up lungs felt like I'd breathed in bleach, then stopping and letting sweat freeze up on my nose.

I cruised out of Center City into the neighborhoods where the two-family houses roosted like hens behind the frozen lawns and the leafless trees, stark and black, loomed above the parkways. Lured by my mood, I jogged a few blocks out of my way into the edges of the ghetto, so I could pass St. Bridget's School. It is a stucco building split by long cracks the shape of lightning. There, for more than thirty-one years, Elaine was the school librarian—"feeding the starving," as she put it. This was a person of iron convictions. With our ma, I turned myself into a sort of human tetherball, always close enough to be pounded back in another direction when she'd go off her nut and rage about one thing or another, but Elaine was smarter and held her distance. She developed, through this exercise, I suppose, a strongly contrary temperament. When everyone was sitting, Elaine was standing; she wandered around the kitchen when the family dined. She preferred her solitary self to any company, and that never seemed to change.

She ended up one of those Catholic spinsters, a spiritual type who never quite joined the secular world, at 5:00 a.m. Mass every morning, always palling around with the nuns and identifying people, and even store locations, throughout the tri-cities by their parish. She had her worldly moments, some gentlemen friends with whom she sinned, and she was a terrific card too, one of these clever old Irish gals with a bracing wit. All Ma's

sharpness was still resident in her, but where Bess took to the
cudgel of spiteful words and judgments, Elaine's humor was
aimed principally at herself. These little muttered cracks as you
left your seat, turned your back, and always an arrow to the
heart. Her only failing she came by naturally—she drank a bit.
The night she left our house, goofy from plum brandies, and
turned up the off ramp and headed onto U.S. 843 was the final
drunken evening of my life.

In AA, where I've lapsed just like I have in the Church,
impressed by the faith but unwilling to engage in the required
daily rituals—in AA they told me to submit myself to a power
outside myself. Don't count on beating the demon on your own.
The help I ask for, Elaine, is yours. And sometimes as I do it,
as I ran down the bleak streets toward the U Inn or sit here in
the night whispering into the Dictaphone, I puzzle on what
strikes me as a piece of nasty truth.

I miss you ten times more than Nora.

B. Bad News

Eventually I reached the outskirts of the U., with its handsome
progressive neighborhood, integrated since early in the century,
its bookstores and vague bohemian air. U Inn was at the corner
of Calvert and University, and I did a long tour of the parking
lot, then jogged right through the front door, waving to the
doorman, playing today's role as another hotel guest, a traveling
business type living on snacks from the mini-bar and morning
aerobics. I ran all the way to the elevator, hopped in with a fat
woman who was whistling to herself, and rode up to 6.

Room 622 was quiet. I stuck my ear to the door and rattled
the knob. As I figured, there were not going to be any of Pigeyes's
tricks in a mid-city hotel. The doors were reinforced and the
locks had been replaced with those solid-state electronic gizmos,
little brass boxes with lights that required sliding in some plastic

card they give you these days instead of a key. I knocked hard. Nothing doing. A suspect fellow in a lizard-skin jacket came by and I kept my eye on him until he got some ice and disappeared under the exit sign at the other end of the dim hall. The hotel corridor was quiet, except for the whine of a vacuum inside one of the rooms.

I'd planned the next move. The guy on the phone had told me nobody here knew Kam on sight. I had some second thoughts, but I had to count on sliding by. That was the point of leading a perilous life. I needed to find what in the hell Bert'd been up to. And I'd be a lot better off sneaking up on him than announcing myself. I took the Kam Roberts credit card out of my wallet.

At the reception desk in the lobby, I talked to a cute blonde, a student, I imagined, like many of the employees.

"I'm Mr. Roberts in 622. I went out for a little trot and like a fool I grabbed my credit card when I left instead of my room pass." I showed her the credit card casually, tapping an edge on the counter. "If you could just get me another."

She disappeared in back. This was frankly a pretty rummy place, especially after the big-bucks life where you get used to going first class. The shabbiness of course was excused by a convenient location—there wasn't another hotel within a mile of the university—and an atmosphere of self-conscious boost-erism. The U Inn, as you would expect, is pretty rah-rah. Every-thing was roped in U. colors, vermilion and white, and near the desk there were pennants and pom-poms and U. sweatshirts tacked to the walls. The Hands basketball schedule, a cardboard poster featuring a color photo of Bobby Adair, this year's wanna-be star, was pinned up on either side of the desk, and as I studied it I realized that a Hands basketball game probably would have brought Bert back to town no matter what.

But there was none today. Not even last night. Or tomorrow. In fact, a lot of things didn't fit. The home games were set on the schedule in vermilion, the away games in black. I didn't have Kam's bank card bill with me, but I'd been staring holes in it for eighteen hours and I was pretty sure that I had committed most of the entries to memory. What bothered me was that the days didn't match. December 18, the last time Kam was here, the Hands were at home. But according to the schedule, they'd been in Bloomington and Lafayette and Kalamazoo since then, and on different dates than the ones when Kam had rung up charges in the same towns.

"Mr. Roberts?" The blonde had returned. "Can I see your credit card again for a moment?" I'd kept it out and she removed it from my hand. I had some instinct to start running, but the girl looked like she'd rolled in off a haywagon, with those sweet eyes the color of cornflowers. One of America's twenty million blondes with looks too standard to conceal any scam. She disappeared again into the office, but was gone just a second.

"Mr. Roberts," she said when she returned, "Mr. Trilby would like to see you for one minute in back." She opened a door for me and pointed to the small rear office, but I hung on the threshold, heart fluttering like a moth.

"Is there a problem?"

"I think he said he had a message."

Ah yes. Me old bud Mack Malloy had called. A perceptive fellow, Trilby probably wanted to tell me that Mack sounded like a phony. There were three men in back, a black man behind a desk who I took to be Trilby and the wormy-looking guy I'd seen upstairs in the hall. The third one turned to face me last.

Pigeyes.

I was in deep.

C. Would You Care If Your Partner Did This to You?

This is not an especially pretty story, Elaine. Pigeyes and I worked tac nearly two years, life and death and plenty of whiskey, lots of laughs, I'm the former college-boy art student, wet behind the ears, he's the guy who's been street-smart since he was seven. I'm talking out loud about Edward Hopper and Edvard Munch when we drive down city streets at night and he's feeling up every hooker. Some team.

Working with this guy was always an adventure. Pigeyes was one of those cops in the old style, who think parents take care of kids, you go to church and pray to God to save your soul, and everything after that sort of depends on where you stand, how you look at it, right and wrong, you know, sometimes you have to squint. I'd been riding with him about eighteen months when we hit a dope house, just a small packaging factory in a dismal apartment building. We had followed some little shitbum off the street, pretty sure we'd seen him swapping packages, and then, afraid we'd got made, decided to go through the door in the name of hot pursuit before any backup arrived. Pigeyes was always that kind of cowboy—he thought he was in the movies, strung out on the rush of danger as bad as if he were sticking a spike in his arm.

Anyway, you've seen the next scene at the Odeon: We come through with guns drawn, a lot of yelling and carrying on in two or three different languages, people jumping out the windows and onto the fire escapes, and some poor bastard running first one way, then the other with a seal-a-meal under one arm and a scale under the other. I kick in the door of the john and there's a gal sitting on the can with her print skirt around her belly, holding a baby in one hand, using the other to push a baggy full of powder up herself.

We got four people facedown on the floor. Pigeyes did his usual raging, sticking his service revolver in their ears and saying various terrible things until somebody whimpered or literally shit their trousers, then he turned his attention to a little card table in the corner of the living room which was covered with money, I mean a lot, lying there in heaps like it was just paper. Pigeyes had radioed for the narcs to come help us with the arrest, but without skipping a beat he counted out two piles of bills, three or four grand each, and handed me one. I took it but handed the money back in the car, after Narcotics had shown up.

'What's this?' he asked.

'I'm goin to law school.' I'd been accepted by then.

'So?'

'So I shouldn't be doin this shit.'

'Hey, get real.' He read me out then. He beat me up with the truth. Did I think the narc guys wouldn't take a nibble out of this? What were we supposed to do, leave it in a nice pile so that the shitface beaners could have it all back when Judge Nowinski decided we weren't in hot pursuit? Were we gonna wait around and hope that the mopes in the Forfeiture Unit actually took some time off from the golf course to try to get a writ, in which case the cash'd get lost in the clerk's office or maybe in some judge's chambers? Did I think the beaners were gonna say something? Every one of them didn't know nothin, man. They were wet and waitin for a trip across the river. 'Or do you just want to be able to go tell Momma?' he asked.

'Hey, give me a break.' We'd sort of been down this pass before. What he did, he did, I figured, he wasn't the only one and he made some effort not to involve me. Now he wanted me aboard. 'You do what you wanna, I'll do what I wanna. I got a rest-of-my-life to think about. That's all.'

He sat there watching me, a nasty-looking fellow normally, with a sullen face going to jowls and those little whiteless eyes, his expression now slackened and mistrustful. This was what they call a delicate situation. Like being with the Yakuza. You got to cut off a finger to prove you're in. What was he up to? I think, in retrospect, he had a point to make, that before I departed for the world I ought to know that there's no judging, that everybody has their moments. So I brought the money home and showed it to my wife and, after leaving it in my sock drawer for three weeks, gave it to my sister for St. Bridget's. Yeah,

Elaine, that's where it came from, it wasn't, like I said, a stationhouse collection. I got a note back from the eighth-grade class president which I've kept for all these years, a pointless thing to do, since I wasn't going to tell anyone the real story, inasmuch as I was a policeman who was supposed to arrest Pigeyes's unlawful ass right on the spot, not sing "Que Sera, Sera," or make a charitable donation of what was, in law, money I'd stolen.

Two months later I started law school and a few weeks after that I was Form 60'd to Financial. Pigeyes threw a nice bash when I left. Everything for the best.

The police, any city you go to, are kind of a sneak fraternity. The Force. Close-knit. Trust each other first and most and nobody very much. There are lots of reasons, maybe the most important being that no one really likes the police. Who should? All these types looking sidewise and waiting for you to slip. I was a cop myself, but when I see a black-and-white just sitting on the corner, the first thing I think is, Why's this bastard got his eye on me?

Also, cops are really by themselves. This retinue of lawyers, prosecutors, judges, wardens, that whole world of rules, they're as far away as Pago Pago when you're in that basement looking for the robbery suspect Mrs. Washington saw running. You go through the basement door and wait there on the threshold, come out five minutes later shaking your head in disappointment, just can't find him, that whole crew, lawyers, wardens, so on and so forth, they have nobody to chew on. It's only you—not just your life on the line, but you're the only reason this guy is going to get caught. There's no system. That's why it's so easy to whack the mouthy bastard when he's cuffed in the back of the black-and-white and is still talking about your mother or the violation of his constitutional fucking rights, never mind the seventy-seven-year-old guy he just hit in the head with a paving stone the better to steal his T-check. Because it was only you. And he's yours. And only other cops really understand that.

Which is how come, even forgetting everything else—that you're a sneak fraternity, that nobody likes you—even forgetting all that, coppers don't do it to coppers. When you're there, when it's only you, you do your best. And if some days you're not up to your best, then you're no worse than anybody else, are you? Tomorrow you can try again. Who's to judge? You start that game, I saw you be bad, shit, it's the whole Force tellin tales.

Shift scene: Two years later I'm coming out of Constitutional Law II, here's two Feebies, real types, drawls and polyester suits and white shoes, who want to talk to me—did I work with Gino Dimonte, la-di-da, a few warm-up pitches, then the hard stuff—was I on a dope bust three years ago April? I do the arithmetic real fast. One of the dopers has finally gotten cracked federally rather than stateside and has found some Ivy League AUSA happy to cut him a few months in summer camp if he'll talk about Kindle coppers with their hands on dirty money, and the doper naturally doesn't give him everybody he has on the pad who he might need again, he gives him Pigeyes, who used self-help. I know all this at once, I see just where they're going, and I'm like 'Yeah, okay, yeah, I think I remember that one, oh yeah, that one, there was money on the table.' A bubble in the brain. What am I thinking? It was the weirdest goddamned thing. Five seconds in the law school hallway and I've changed my freaking life. There was not a cop who heard about this— and believe me, they all heard about it before the ink was dry on the 302s, the FBI agents' reports—who didn't think I'd done it because I felt with law school I was now a cut above. Coppers are very sensitive about class and have always got it on the brain, they just can't get over the fact that they make forty grand to keep the world safe for millionaires, eat a bullet for Daddy Warbucks, who'll use your corpse to wipe his shoes. But it wasn't that, I wasn't trying to make new friends, and in point of fact, I never much liked snitches. And it wasn't my sterling character for the truth. Who am I kidding? I've fibbed for worse reasons than to help a pal. It's just that, at that moment, I was standing there in the law school, with its wainscotted walls, and something came over me, that thing going back to when I was a kid when I'd realize I didn't belong, that feeling that the world was objects. That's where I was, I guess, the smartass fourth-grader looking at his life as Something in This Picture Does Not Fit and always thinking the Something was me.

Anyway, I got about three-quarters through the story when it hit me like a bolt that this would not work out. The agents had come on with the usual street immunity, just be straight and you're okay, you won't even get lint on your new suit, but I realized suddenly that the feds were not my only problem. I would have to explain this to Bar Admissions and Discipline, to BAD, and they were pretty tough on the new recruits. Immunity. Felonies. Breach of trust. I was not going to make a good impression with this story of stolen dope money in my sock drawer. So the tale ended with me and Pigeyes in the car and me telling him to inventory my end and his end too, handing the money back so he could turn it all in to the evidence room.

Things sort of went in natural sequence after that. I testified in the grand jury, just what I'd said in my statement to the agents, nothing more. The last six months I was a policeman, I was assigned behind a file cabinet, I didn't get near the street, and even the khaki crew, the unsworn personnel, would spit in my coffee when I turned my back. Then Pigeyes got indicted and I went to court and testified against him. He had paid about thirty grand to Sandy Stern, who a few years ago I would have described as a Jew defense lawyer, and Sandy made it look like the government did not have much of a case. They had a couple of the shitbum dopers who had to admit they'd had their faces planted on the floor; a narcotics officer's inventory of two grand in cash on the table when the beaners said there had been forty; and they had me. Of course, I was up there only sort of telling the truth, with my old pal Pigeyes giving me the death look, and something uneasy came to the surface, like bones bubbling up in tar. Stern asked if I was jealous of Pigeyes, felt he was a better cop than me, and I said yes to that, and I agreed that I never checked with Evidence to see what Pigeyes had inventoried. I allowed as how there were beaners who didn't know one Anglo cop from another, and I even said yes when Stern asked if Yours Truly was in fact the only police officer who admitted having received money removed from that table. The AUSA got this look like he needed Preparation H and the jury came back not guilty in two hours. When I walked out of the courtroom I had really lit the scoreboard: I don't think there was a soul there, not the judge, not even the toothless buffs out in the peanut gallery, who didn't think I was lower than pond slime. Nora, never one to miss a point of vulnerability, put it nicely: 'So, Mack, now do you think you got what you want?'

Did I? There were a few strange turns, I admit. One of the strangest was that BAD publicly embraced me. They thought ratting out your friend was a mark of character and gave me a job, since I'd demonstrated such fidelity to the rules of upstanding conduct in another calling. As for Pigeyes, he was ruined. For the jury it's always opening night, but the cops had all seen Stern's act before and they didn't need a trial to know that Pigeyes was dirty. All his buddies in the department, and there are a million, they'll do him favors day to day, get him twice as much for uniform allowance, but as far as going higher, he smelled bad, to the brass he was wearing lead boots. He's been on his unhappy trail down the hill ever since, getting the kind of discipline they practice out of Rome, sending the pederast priest to dwell at a convent. Pigeyes's punishment is Financial Crimes. Personally, I'd always liked the intricacy of Financial, the fact that there was more to investigating a case than finding the perp's girlfriend and sitting on her house until he came by for a cha-cha, but for Pigeyes, a proof mark will never take the place of drawing his gun.

From what I hear he has a sad life now. These days the rare dope bust he horns in on, he's picking powder off the table, not money. Behind his back, guys call him G-Nose or Snowman, and it's not cause he likes winter weather. He was always a copper's copper, full of twitches and complexes, sort of hated everyone, so there never was a Mrs. Pig, just the usual copper-bar girls and chickies on the edge of trouble who thought it was a good idea to give a cop a screw. He did not have much. Until now. Now he had me.

D. Pigeyes and I Renew Acquaintances

"Didn't I *tell* you this guy was gonna turn up? Didn't I *fucking* tell you?" Pigeyes was so happy, gloating like some cock who'd gotten every hen in the coop, that I thought he was going to fall over and give himself a hug. I had, I admit, some glum thoughts about my partners who had set me off blind on a path that led straight to my life's greatest enemy—even counting my former wife—a man who, judging by his comments, was clearly expecting me.

"Refresh me," he said, "memory serves, this ain't you." He was holding the credit card.

"I'm sorry, Officer?"

"Detective, shitface."

"Detective Shitface, I'm sorry." Personally, I didn't believe I'd done it. But there you have it. Chasing Bert and teasing myself with the notion of another life, I was becoming a new man. By the door, the younger cop in lizard, in his longhair do with shiny sidewalls, grimaced and turned a full pirouette. I was looking for it. But he didn't know the history. If Pigeyes kicked the bejesus out of me, he could never fit a story good enough. He stared at me with those little black eyes without any visible whites, while this reality crowded in on both of us. Then he extended one finger, thick as a stake, and gave me his own unique look, a laser right to the heart.

"Not again," he said.

Trilby spoke up at that point, a pudgy black man of middle years, sitting behind his desk. He and his sidekick out front had done a nice job of setting me up. The coppers obviously had been here long ago looking for Kam and had left instructions to get in touch if anybody connected with him ever reappeared. While I was on hold, Trilby was probably on the line with Pig-eyes, who gleefully thanked whatever idol he worshipped as soon as he heard my name. To this point, Trilby had watched our exchange out of one eye, face sort of averted, so he could claim he hadn't seen it, if anything bad happened. Now he stuck up his courage to ask who I was.

"A drunk," said Pigeyes.

It's always strange how that shot can reach me.

"I'm a lawyer, Mr. Trilby."

"Quiet," said Pigeyes. He wasn't that tall, probably lying when he said he was five ten, but he was built like your freezer, no neck, no waist, a lot of slack flesh on a real solid structure. His anger gave him a kind of aura, an impression of heat. You knew he was there. He was dressed in a sport jacket and a knit shirt, beneath which his undershirt showed. He was wearing cowboy boots.

His partner could see he was hot and edged past him; Gino sunk back toward the door. With the second cop, we started again.

"Dewey Phelan." He pulled his badge from his pocket and we actually shook hands. Good cop, bad cop. Mutt and Jeff. Fuck, I invented this game, but still I was relieved to be talking to skinny young Dewey here, maybe he's twenty-three, with pale skin, a lumped-up complexion like custard, and that greasy black hair falling into his eyes.

"Now the question, Mr. Malloy, you understand what it is, is we kind of think you were trying to go into a hotel room that isn't yours. See? So maybe you could explain that." Dewey wasn't really great at this yet. He shifted between feet like a five-year-old who had to go tinkle. Pigeyes was back near the door, arm on a filing cabinet, just taking this in with a sour expression.

"I'm looking for a partner of mine, Officer." Better the truth. There was only so much I could bluff, and right now everything was concentrated on looking chipper.

"Uh-huh," said Dewey. He nodded and tried to think of what to ask next. "Your partner, what's his name? What kind of partner is he?"

I spelled Kamin. Dewey wrote in his little pocket spiral, which he rested on his thigh.

"False personation," said Pigeyes. Back at the filing cabinets he gestured at the credit card which Dewey was now holding. Pigeyes was going to charge me with the crime of pretending to be someone else. I had forgotten up to now that the state claimed any interest in who I was or wanted to be.

I looked to Dewey almost as if he were a friend. "You know, Gino and me," I said, "there's some history. But you can explain this to him. It's not false personation when you use somebody's name with their permission. That credit card belongs to Kamin. See?"

Dewey didn't. "You got this card from him, is that what you're saying? From Kamin?" He looked back to Pigeyes for a second, maybe to check how he was doing. I had the sense, though, I had told them something. There was a little of that light-bulb look in both faces. Bert was Kam, or vice versa. They hadn't known that. "It's Kamin's card?" Dewey asked.

"Right."

"And he gave it to you?"

"It's Kamin's card, I came here to look for him, as far as I know it's Kamin's hotel room. I'm sure he'll tell you I had his permission."

"Well, we'll have to ask him."

"Natch," I said.

"So what's his address?"

I'd raised him one too many. I saw that, but not quick enough. Sooner or later, when Bert didn't answer their phone calls, they'd turn up at his place. And the shit would fly when they opened the refrigerator. I tried momentarily to figure how many days it would be until we got to that point and what would happen then.

Dewey, in the meantime, had written down Bert's address and stepped away to chew things over with Pigeyes. Dewey, no doubt, was telling Gino they didn't have any real good reason to hold me and Pigeyes was saying, Like hell, he had me in sweatpants using someone else's name. But even Pigeyes would realize that, given our colorful past, if he pinched me and it didn't hold up, the civil suit I'd file for retaliatory arrest would lead to his immediate retirement.

All in all, I was beginning to figure I'd come out okay, when I heard Gino say, "I'm gonna get her." He was back in a blink with the sweet-looking student who'd been at the front desk. I imagined he wanted to review my antics out there with the card, see if maybe she'd give him some handhold on me he had missed. I was wrong.

"This isn't the guy, right?" he asked her.

This office was small and getting crowded, five of us now and most of the space to begin with occupied by Trilby's desk, which was clean but for pictures of his children, all grown, and his wife. There was a U. pennant on the paneled walls and a clock. The girl looked around.

"No, of course not," she said.

"Describe him."

"Well, for one thing he was black."

"Who's that?" I asked.

Dewey gave me a warning look, a minute shake of the head: Don't interrupt. Pigeyes told the girl to go on.

"Late twenties, I'd say. Twenty-seven. Kind of receding hair. Athletic build. Nice-looking," she added, and shrugged, maybe by way of apology for the frank observations of a white girl.

"And how many times have you seen him?"

"Six times. Seven. He's been here a lot."

I spoke up again. "What is this, a show up? What'd I do supposedly, steal this guy's wallet?" I was guessing now, earnest if confused.

"Hey, dude," said Dewey. "I think it's time for you to be quiet."

"You're questioning me, you're talking about someone in my presence. Come on, I want to know who."

"Oh my God, can you believe this guy?" Pigeyes turned away and bit his knuckle.

"Hey, so tell him," said Dewey. He hitched a slight shoulder. What was it to them? Gino eventually caught the drift. A glimmer struck home.

"Here, fine," said Pigeyes, "knock yourself out." He moved his hammy paw toward the girl. "Tell Mr. Malloy here who we been talking about."

The girl did not get any of this. She shrugged, farm-plain, a little thick in her white blouse.

"Mr. Roberts," she said. "Kam Roberts."

"Your pal." Across the room, Pigeyes's hard little eyes glowed like agates. "So now tell us something smart."

VII. WHERE I LIVE

The house in which Nora Goggins and I made our married life was a little square thing, brick with vinyl siding and black shutters, three bedrooms, in a sort of middle-of-the-middle suburb called Nearing. Nora always said we could afford more, but I didn't want it; we had a summer place out on Lake Fowler and that was plunge enough for me. There were so many extraneous expenses—the Beemer, my suits and hers, the frigging clubs. I suppose, in retrospect, it means something that our home wasn't much. Ivy clings to the bricks, plantings that went in when we bought and now have vines thick as tree branches which are beginning to develop bark and sinister tendrils that have found the cracks in the mortar and are gradually pulling the entire place down. When I got the kid, I got the house. Nora cashed out. Nearing will never be glamorous and Nora knows a thing or two about value anyway.

Nora is a Real Estate Lady, you've seen them before, suburban gals dressed to kill at lunch. She could not stand it at home. She limped to the finish line with Lyle, got him into high school, but I could tell that she had done a calculation on some scratch paper somewhere and figured what percentage of her brain cells were dying every day. Even drunk, I sensed a wild, unhappy thing in her that was not going to be tamed. I remember seeing her once; she was in the garden. She had a different homebound passion each year and that summer it was vegetables. All the green things abounded: the cornstalks with their broad leaves like graceful hands, the jungle density of the peas, the ferny tops of asparagus spread like lace. She stood in our tiny suburban back yard with Lyle at her knee and looked toward the distance, a mind full of lonely visions like Columbus, who saw round when everybody else saw flat.

Eventually she tore off into the land of open houses, showings, new on the market, with a ruthless glee, lit up like a rocket— she loved it, being back in the grown-up world. She was like twenty-one again—regrettably in all ways. When I figured out something was doing, a year or two along, I was more or less immobilized. I was no longer drinking, so I'd sit at home with painful fantasies, thinking about the guys relocating from Kansas City who got something special off Nora's own Welcome Wagon. She was pointing out the features of her inner sanctum and I, the former sot who'd done more wandering than a minstrel, was at home conducting a perverse and private romance with Mary Fivefingers. Isn't that the worst part of sex, that we *think* about it? Guys especially. You know how that goes, we don't have babies so we only have one way to prove the point. "You gettin any?" It's like asking a fat person if they've had a chance to eat. I swear, I was depressed for days after my last physical, when the doctor asked, in the modern way, if I was sexually active and I had to answer no. But then, I digress.

In her roaming, Nora was joined by her manager, a gal named Jill Horwich with whom she was always having a drink or sneaking off to a convention. Jill was like a good number of the Real Estate Ladies, divorced, the main support of a passel of kids, and I figured she liked screwing around because it was low-stress, some tomcat in a bar better than a fellow making himself a fixture in the kitchen, one more mouth to feed. Nora somehow seemed impressed by Jill's way of life.

But it was hardly news that Nora was adventurous. Soon after I met her, on date number two, it was Nora Goggins who gave me my first blow job. I still count the moment when she peeled back my zipper and greeted John Peter eye to eye, taking hold with the confidence of some nightclub vocalist grabbing the mike, as among the most exciting instants of my life. It was not a boy's thrill I'm talking about either. I knew I'd found a rare one, somebody braver than I was, a trait that I found irresistible, especially in a Catholic girl. I figured this was someone to follow through the jungle, who'd show no fear of the wild creatures and had the inner strength to clear a path of her own. Instead, it meant that she was a person of strong opinions who would feel thwarted by our life. She picked on me, told me regularly how I failed her emotionally, and apparently conceived of secret yearnings that I could never satisfy.

The noise I made coming in tonight brought the Loathsome Child in person bouncing off the staircase, rubbing his eyes, shirtless but wearing his jeans, looking as if he had been foraged on by some roaming beast. He is a scrofulous creature, frankly, my size but still not well developed, with a few errant hairs that crop up along his breastbone amid the acne. His peculiar haircut, which looks like a golf green cut onto an overgrown hillside, was disheveled. We ended up together at the kitchen table, both of us making a meal on Cheerios.

"Tough night?"

He made a vaguely affirmative sound. His hand was across his face and he rested his arm on the cereal box as if it was the only thing keeping him from collapse. He had put a shirt on by now, some chic rayon chemise I'm sure I paid for. The red stripe on it, I decided, was not design but ketchup.

"What time did you get home?"

"One."

He meant afternoon, not morning. I checked the clock: 7:48 p.m. Lyle was just rising. He pretty much lives backward. He and his pals consider it uncool to get started anytime this side of midnight. Nora, of course, attributes Lyle's libertine existence to the poor example his drunken father set when he was growing up.

"You should try reading St. Augustine. He has much cautionary advice about a life of excess."

"Oh, shut up, Dad."

Maybe if there were just a trace of humor in this I wouldn't have been so hot to smack him. As it was, I had to contain myself with the thought that if I hit him he would tell his mother, who'd tell her lawyer, who'd tell the judge. If I believed they'd take the kid away I'd have knocked him cold, but it would only end in more restraining orders and restrictions on me.

According to that splendid education I received out at the U., it was Rousseau who began in Western culture the worship of the child, innocent and perfect in nature. Anyone who has raised a human from scratch knows this is a lie. Children are savages —egocentric little brutes who by the age of three master every form of human misconduct, including violence, fraud, and bribery, in order to get what they want. The one who lived in my house never improved. Last fall it turned out that the community college, for which I'd dutifully given him a tuition check at the beginning of each quarter, did not have the bastard registered. A month ago I took him out to dinner and caught him trying to pocket the waitress's tip.

About three times a week I threaten to throw him out, but his mother has told him the divorce decree provides that I will support him until he's twenty-one—Brushy and I had assumed that meant paying for college—and Nora, who thinks the boy needs understanding, especially since she doesn't have to provide much, would doubtless find this an occasion for yet another principled disagreement and probably seek an order requiring Lyle and me to get some counseling—another five hundred bucks a month. Thus, the thought often stabs me with the ugly starkness of a rusty knife: I am afraid of him now too.

Believe me, I am not as cheerful as I sound.

Rising for another bowl of cereal, my son asked where I had been.

"I was dealing with uncomfortable aspects of my past," I told him.

"Like Mom, you mean?" He thought he was funny.

"I ran into a cop I used to know. Over at U Inn."

"Really?" Lyle thinks it's neat that I was a policeman, but he couldn't pass up the opportunity for role reversal. "You aren't in trouble are you, Dad?"

"If I ever need to be bailed out, chum, I know where I can find an expert." I gave him a meaningful look, which sent Lyle at once across the kitchen.

It had killed Pigeyes to let me go. He and Dewey had talked it over for about fifteen minutes and apparently decided that they had better check out my story about Bert. Gino gave me back the credit card and told me to hold on to it because I'd hear from him soon. It didn't sound like he'd be bringing a bouquet.

Slurping up my dinner now, I wished I hadn't been so hasty with Bert's name. The problem, slowly dawning on me, was that when Pigeyes and Dewey open Bert's refrigerator, the next stop would be G&G. They'd want to know everything about Kamin. At that point—probably within the next week—it would be hard to keep the missing money out of our answers. And once this was a police matter, everybody would be posturing. Even if Krzysinski kept his cool now when Jake gave him the lowdown, there'd be no hush-hush after the cops arrived, no diplomatic solutions. It'd be sayonara, G&G. I needed to get going.

Still, the news that there is a living breathing human named Kam Roberts has left me feeling like an astronomer who just discovered that there's a second planet in our orbit, also called Earth. If he wasn't Bert—and Bert wasn't twenty-seven, black, or losing his hair when I last saw him twelve days ago—then why is Kam Roberts using Bert's name upside down and getting his mail at Bert's house?

I'd been carrying the note that Lena had copied off Infomode in my shirt pocket. I studied it for a second and in total desperation even showed it to Lyle. I told him it seemed like Bert had written it.

"That dude? One who took us to a couple Trappers games? Got to be sports with him, man."

"Thank you, Sherlock. What sport in particular? Safe-cracking?"

Lyle was blank. I might as well have asked him about Buddhism. The kid had left a pack of cigarettes on the table and I took one as a garnish.

"Hey." He pointed. "Buy your own."

"I'm saving you," I said. "I'm conserving your health and future."

The kid didn't think I was funny. He never did. If I start counting the endeavors in this life at which I have failed, I'll burn out the batteries on this thing. But somehow Lyle and I stand on our own plateau. When I was an active drunkard, there were moments while I was crocked that my love for this child would come over me with breathtaking intensity. It was always the same image, this chubby two-year-old running to beat all hell, his laughter free as a waterfall and sweeter than music, and I loved him so dearly, with such heartsore tenderness, that I'd sit over my highball glass shameless at my tears. These were the most intimate moments I had with my kid, this kind of imaginary contact while he was fast asleep and I was in some barroom half a dozen miles from home. Practically speaking, I did him little good. Near as I can figure, that makes me the same as three-quarters of the dads I know who just sort of phone it in as fathers. But somewhere along the line Lyle recognized my vulnerability, that when it comes to him I am wholly paralyzed by regret. Call it what you like, getting even or being nuts together, we both know that him pushing my buttons and me refusing to jump has the same screwed-up emotional dynamic as, say, ritual torture or some family form of S and M. Lyle by his behavior berates me, while I cry out by suffering this punishment that I love, if not him, then something he alone represents.

With the cigarette I retreated and knocked around the living room. I had gone back to the health club to dress and to the office to pick up the file for Toots Nuccio's hearing tomorrow and I read at it a bit. Eventually I wandered upstairs, doing my nightly usual, trying to sneak up sidelong on sleep. Should I describe my bedroom, site of my nighttime dictation? Hiroshima after the bomb. Books and newspapers and cigarette butts. Scattered highbrow journals and law reviews read in my brainier moods. A brass colonial lamp with a broken shade. Beside my cherry highboy, there is a rectangle of carpeting less faded than the rest, dimpled at each corner by the casters from Nora's dresser, one of the few pieces of furniture she took. With Lyle around, there is not much point in cleaning anywhere, and my little corner of the world now seems crushed and flattened on all sides.

Next to my bed is a dropcloth and a half-finished canvas on an easel, upon whose ledge sit many tubes of paint, thumb-dented and fingerprinted with the bright pigments. Artist at work. When I was eighteen, I was going to be Monet. As a child in my mother's house, as a victim of her shrill tirades, I took a certain comfort in concentrating on what did not change, on the permanence of a line and the silence of the page. I don't know how many times, in how many schoolrooms, I drew the people from the funnies, Batman, Superman, Dagwood. I was good too. Teachers praised my work, and nights when I was sitting around The Black Rose with my old man I'd amuse his cronies by faultlessly rendering a photo from the paper. 'Boy's great, Tim.' He took the usual bar-time pleasure from this, man among men, letting others boast about his son, but at home he would not cross my ma, who took a dim view of this vocation. 'Drawin flippin pictures,' she'd mutter whenever the subject was raised. It was not until I got a D in a drawing class in my first year at the U. that I began to see she had a point.

Here's the problem: I see well only in two dimensions. I don't know if it's depth perception or something in the brain. I envision the picture but not the figure it is drawn from. If counterfeiting were a legitimate profession, I would be its Pablo Fucking Picasso. I can reproduce anything on paper as if it were traced. But real life somehow defeats me. Foreshortened, distorted— it never comes out right. My career as an artist, I had realized shortly before I joined the Force, would be a sort of secondhand hell in which I'd never do anything original. So I became a lawyer. Another of those jokes, though when I make it, my partners flinch.

At home, in private, I like to pretend. Normally, when I jolt awake at 3:00 a.m., it's not Wash's report or the Dictaphone that occupies me. Instead, I repaint Vermeer and imagine the thrill of being the man who so saucily transfigured reality. I am here often in the middle of the night, the light intense, the glare from the shiny art book page and the wet acrylics somehow dazzling, as I try to avoid thinking too much about the image that leapt up from the flames to wake me.

And what image is that? you ask. It's a man, actually. I see him stepping out of the blaze, and when I start awake, heart banging and mouth dry, I am looking for him, this guy who's got my number. He's around the corner, always behind me. Wearing a hat. Carrying a blade. In dreams sometimes I catch the gleam winking as he treads through the path of blue light from a streetlamp. This is an always thing, all my life, me and this guy, Mr. Stranger Danger, as the coppers put it, the guy who's out there and gonna do you bad. He's the one that mothers warn their daughters to watch out for on a deserted street. He's the mugger in the park, the home invader who strikes at 3:00 a.m. I became a copper, maybe, because I thought I'd catch him, but it turns out he still gets the drop on me at night.

Jesus, what is it I have to be so scared of? Five years on the streets and still with all my fingers and toes, a job that I'm busy trying to make secure, and skills of one kind or another. But I am looking at the big 5–0, and the numbers still stir something in me, as if they were the caliber of a gun that is pointed at my head. It gets a body down. I lie here in the bed in which I screwed several thousand times a woman who I figure now never really cared much about what I was doing; I listen to the phlegmy report from the rotted muffler of what I used to call my car and desolately hold to the departing sounds of that roaming creature who was once a tender child. What is there to be so scared of, Elaine, except this, my one and only life?

Tonight I woke only once. It was not as bad as sometimes. No dreams. No knives or flames. Just a single thought, and the horror of it for a change was not too large to name.

Bert Kamin is probably dead.

T A P E 3

Dictated January 26, 9:00 p.m.

VIII. MEN OF THE CITY

A. Archie Was a Cool Operator

When I got to the office on Wednesday morning, Lena was waiting for me.

"Is this guy a gambler?" You could see she already knew the answer was yes.

"Show me." I followed her toward the library.

When I interviewed Lena on campus at the U. last year, I noticed there was a hole in her résumé—seven years to finish college. I asked if she'd been working.

'Not really.' She had grasped her briefcase, a little redhead with a worldly eye. 'I went through a rough spell.'

'How rough?'

'Rough.' We scrutinized one another in the interview room, a soundproofed spot no bigger than a closet; it would have done well for torture. 'I thought I was in love with a guy,' she said. 'But I was in love with the dope. I'm NarcAnon. That whole thing. Once a week.' She awaited my reaction. There were a half dozen other good firms in the city and we were interviewing early. If candor didn't work, she could lie to the next bunch, or hope she'd make it through someplace before anybody asked.

She'd had A's. Somebody would take a chance. You could read all these calculations in her strong features.

'AA,' I said and shook her hand. She'd done well here. Brilliantly. She had taken control of her life with an athlete's determination, which, whenever I witnessed it, colored me from the same palette of murky feelings—envy, admiration, the ever-present conviction that I am a phony and she the real thing.

In the library she stationed me by a p.c. and went through the codes to bring Bert's message up on the screen. I stared at it again:

```
Hey Arch--


            SPRINGFIELD
Kam's Special 1.12--U. five, five Cleveland.
1.3--Seton five, three Franklin.
1.5--SJ five, three Grant.


            NEW BRUNSWICK
1.2--S.F. eleven, five Grant.
```

"See," she said, "I looked in Sportsline. It's not only scores. They also have a sports book. From Las Vegas? It shows the odds and spreads. Here." The list went on for pages: basketball, college and pro, and hockey, with a point spread for every game, each one listed on a separate line. "Then I asked myself," she said, "do any of these sports have anything to do with Springfield or New Brunswick?"

There was some kind of basketball shrine in Springfield, Massachusetts, but I drew a blank on New Jersey.

"Football," she said, "that's where they played the first college football game. In New Brunswick. And the first basketball game was in Springfield."

I made her flip the screen back so I could look again at Bert's message. Three weeks ago, the NFL playoffs had laid waste to my weekend.

"These are games," she said. "I think he's betting one side of the spread or the other." She looked at me to see how she was doing, which was fine. "It makes sense," she told me. "Franklin and Grant—they're on money, right? I mean bills. I don't quite get Cleveland."

"Grover Cleveland's on the thousand."

"He *is* betting," she said. "Heavy too. How's he covering his losses?" An addict, Lena had an ingrained view: For sin you pay sometime.

I considered her question. Betting between five and ten grand a day, Bert had the look of a man likely to steal.

"I can't figure what this means," she said, "Kam's Special?"

I had no idea.

"And who's Arch?" she asked.

That one was more obvious to me.

"A bookie." Actuaries, of course, are oddsmakers in white shirts. Archie, I guess, couldn't resist plotting probabilities on something more amusing than mortality tables. It was a funny thought, some buttoned-down type making book in one of these steel towers.

"Look," I said to Lena, "if this character Archie had my guy's account number and the name Kam Roberts, he could call in and take bets out of the mailbox. Right? And he could do that with dozens of other people too, if he had the same kind of arrangement with them."

"Why would he want to?"

"Because bookmaking is illegal and it's a better business if he doesn't get caught." Even when I was on the street, before wiretapping got so big, guys kept a book on the run. Somebody with no nose would knock on a door in a poor neighborhood and offer to rent an apartment for a month, three grand, no questions asked. They'd use the place for four weeks, then go somewhere else, hoping to stay ahead of the feds. But these days, no matter how they do it, when they're taking bets over the phone there's the chance the G is listening. Archie took calls from no one. You could scout out the Sportsline and leave your bets for Archie in your Infomode mailbox. Archie was an electronic tout, man of his times.

Which also explained the reference to Arch Enterprises on the Kam Roberts bank card statement. Archie had solved the bookie's age-old dilemma—how do I collect without giving the legbreakers a call to knock 6 for 5 out of you by Friday? This was clean, professional. It was all charged to the credit card. Wins and losses. Probably once a month a debit or credit memo went through. For a winner, it was as good as cash—you could wash your airline tickets, dinners out, a suit, a tie, everything you charged. If you lost, Arch got paid by the bank. No doubt everybody employed intermediate devices. In all likelihood Arch Enterprises was the subsidiary of some holding company owned in turn by a trust. Maybe created in Pico Luan?

"What's this case about?" Lena asked. "Can I work on it?" Better than bond indentures and coverage claims.

I thanked her at length, then took the bill back to my office, somewhat saddened by myself. As usual, I had let my lurid imagination get the better of me. Archie was not Bert's lover. He was a bookie. Even so, there was a lot of this that didn't fit. I still didn't know what Bert had to do with Kam, and I couldn't figure why Pigeyes and his pals were chasing him. It wasn't for gambling, which would be a vice investigation. Pigeyes and Dewey were working this out of Financial Crimes. But this information did do one thing. It made my wee-hours theory look even better, and I said it to myself again out loud, if quietly: "Bert's dead."

Icicles of steely light drifted out on the river. You had to consider Bert's situation with what I call cop logic. Look for the simple explanation. The gentleman in the Amana had not tied a fishing line around his neck by himself. Bad People had a point to make. And given the location of the body, it seemed that

point had something to do with Bert. And now Bert had disappeared, and I find out, to boot, that he was in the middle of
some off-the-wall gambling scheme, just the kind of scene where
people end up sore over money and who shorted who, subterranean disputes that get settled with bloodshed, since you can't
file a lawsuit. I wondered if Bert had another fridge in his basement.

One thing for sure, I wasn't going back to check, especially
now that I'd sent Pigeyes in that direction. It would have been
enlightening to take a peek at what was on the computer I'd
seen in Bert's living room, to see if there were more references
to Kam, his specials and his life. Settling for second best, I visited
Bert's office down the hall. The door was locked—that was Bert,
manic and jealous of his clients' secrets, not to mention his own.
They'd moved his secretary to another station while her boss
was AWOL, but I knew where she kept the key and I let myself in.

Bert's home had that fly-about look, but fitting his compul-
sions, the office was crazy clean. Every object dusted and in its
place. Lawyers' furnishings are pretty standard: diplomas on the
walls, pictures of the family, and a few discreet mementos that
nod toward the high points of their legal career and are likely to
impress clients. Wash, for example, keeps the reminders of certain big deals in one bookcase—announcements from the *Journal*
preserved in little Lucite blocks; deal "bibles" in which the
thousands of closing documents, all on foolscap, are bound in
leather with the name and date of the transaction etched in gold
on the binding. Even I have a framed sketch, done by one of
the local TV station's artists, of me arguing a big jury case for
TN concerning their firing of a pilot who'd been hired as John
and later took on the name and genitalia of Juanita.

Looking around Bert's office, all you'd know is this guy's
sports-crazy—game memorabilia were wall-to-wall: autographed
baseballs, a Hands jersey, signed in indelible marker by every
member of the '84 championship team, which was framed and

hung from one of the concrete pilasters. Nothing else was visible he cared about, except the huge goofy water cooler in the corner.

Working on 397, I learned all Bert's passwords on the network, and I popped on the computer and cruised through the directories, pressing the buttons to glimpse different documents in the hope that there'd be more signs here of what was doing with Kam Roberts and Archie. But there was nothing. Instead, I started looking over Bert's endless correspondence, sort of idly poking for clues but also, I admit, enjoying some of the twisted thrill of the snoop, surveying old Bert's life as a lawyer.

His odd ways have held Bert back with clients and he's brought in few of his own. He is what they call a "service lawyer," like me, somebody who does the work that one of our hotshot partners has been hired for. But with that limit, the Committee loves him. Bert clocks a good twenty-five hundred hours every year, and with his own fierce methods gets great results in court. Every case is a full-bore commitment. Got a client with a small problem, say, falsely representing that night is day, Bert will defend him without blinking. He is one of those lawyers who agrees with the other side about nothing. Everything leads to correspondence. Move the dep from two to one, Bert will send you a letter. Which bears no resemblance, by the way, to the conversation it claims to record. I say my client's having open-heart and Bert's letter says the guy can't appear because he scheduled a doctor's appointment. With stunts like that, Bert's made enemies of half the trial lawyers in town. In fact, that's why I started working on 397 in the first place, because Jake can't be bothered with 150 plaintiff's attorneys, and most of those guys want to turn on a tape recorder before they're willing to say so much as good morning to Bert.

Out in the hallway I heard my name being repeated on the paging system, asked to dial Lucinda's extension. That meant it was time to go to Toots's hearing. I was about to turn off the p.c. when I saw a name in Bert's letter directory that struck sparks off my heart: Litiplex.

I fiddled with the buttons to call up the file. I was nervous, sure that I'd hit the wrong key and obliterate the whole thing, but I didn't, although there was not much to see, just a short little cover memo.

GAGE & GRISWELL
Office Memorandum
ATTORNEY WORK-PRODUCT
PRIVILEGED AND CONFIDENTIAL

20 November

TO: Glyndora Gaines, Supervisor
     Accounting Section
FROM: Robert A. Kamin
RE: 397 Check Requisition—Litiplex, Ltd.

Per the attached, re agreement with Peter Neucriss, please draw for my signature separate
checks to Litiplex, Ltd. in invoice amounts as
indicated.

I read this over four or five times. Finally, when I'd made as much sense of it as I could, I printed it.

"Hey."

I started. I hadn't heard the door open over the printer's whine. It was Brushy. She was standing with my coat and hers and the file on Toots's case all bundled in her arms.

"It's ten to. We're just going to make it." I guess I had some telltale look, because she came straight up to Bert's desk chair where I sat. I had a thought of fending her off so she couldn't read Bert's little memo over my shoulder, but on the whole I was too pleased with myself and my skills of detection to make much of an effort at that.

"Holy smokes," she said. "What's 'the attached'?"

"Hell if I know. I searched—there's no other mention of Lit-

iplex. I suppose I'll have to go ask Glyndora. I've been meaning
to talk to her anyway."

"You said the Committee told you there wasn't any paperwork
to cover the checks."

"They did."

"Maybe this memo is phony," she said. "You know, so Bert
had something to show if anybody asked why he signed the
checks."

That was possible. It even made sense. The odds against Bert
reaching any kind of "agreement" with Peter Neucriss approached the level of mathematical certainty. Neucriss is Kindle's number-one personal-injury lawyer, a portly little demon
whose commanding ways and courtroom successes have led him
to be called "The Prince" to his face, with "of Darkness" added
when he turns his back. He and Bert haven't exchanged a civil
word since the *Marsden* case some years back, when Neucriss
in closing referred to Bert as "the attorney from the fourth dimension" and got a laugh out of the jury. It would make sense,
I supposed, to talk to Neucriss too, although that was never a
welcome prospect.

"Will you tell me what happens," she asked, "when you talk
to them?"

"Sure," I answered, "but no blabbing. You know: attorney-
client. I don't want this getting around before I figure it out."

"Come on, Malloy," she said. "You know me. I always keep
your secrets." She gave me her own special smile, whimsical,
flirtatious, tickled with herself and her hidden adventures, before she rushed me out the door.

B. The Colonel

"State your name please and spell your last name for the record."

"My name is Angelo Nuccio, N, u, c, c, i, o, but since I'm a
kid folks like to call me Toots." The Colonel, as he is generally

known, displayed a grand showman's smile for the members of Bar Discipline Inquiry Panel D arrayed beside him at a long table. We were trying our case, such as it was, before them, a three-member jury of other attorneys, volunteers with a part-time yen to sit in judgment of others. In response to Toots, the chair, Mona Dalles, yielded something, but the two men at either side of her maintained expressions of utter self-imposed neutrality. Mona is at the Zahn firm, G&G's biggest competitor, and is known as amiable, level, bright—qualities that were not helpful on Toots's case if you looked at it from the perspective of the defense. What we needed was somebody certifiable. A large reel-to-reel tape recorder spun in front of Mona, preserving, for those who might care to listen in the future, the final stage of one of the county's most vivid public lives.

Colonel Toots is eighty-three years old and a physical wreck. His bowed little legs, one of which had been shot up at Anzio, are brittle with arthritis; his lungs are smoked out, curled up, as I imagine them, like dead leaves, so that he has developed a wheezy little breath that punctuates every word. He has diabetes which is imperiling his sight, and various circulatory ailments. But you have to give it to him, the guy is still full of it—Colonel Toots has been running on premium all his life. He is a man of the city who has been a bit of everything—a soldier in three wars, and a ludicrous chest-thumping patriot; a pol; an accomplished clarinetist who on two occasions has rented the entire Kindle County Symphony to back him when he did a not-bad run-through of a Mozart number for clarinet; a mobster; a lawyer; a friend of whores and gunmen and virtually anyone else in the tri-cities who common sense taught him might count. When I was a copper twenty years ago, he was still in his heyday, an elected city councilman from the South End who, when not politicking, was fixing judges, selling jobs, or, so it was claimed, killing a fellow or two. You could never tell for sure with Toots. He was an absolute stranger to the truth. But a storyteller such as might have beguiled Odysseus, charming even when he recounted matters that better sense told you were absolutely revolting—how he bought votes from "shines" for turkeys ("November is a good month for elections") or once shot the knees out of some dunce who refused to pay a poolroom debt.

At eighty-three, Colonel Toots has survived just about everything but BAD, which has fired at him an even half dozen times over his career and is still reloading. During a recent federal investigation, it developed that Colonel Toots for fourteen years running had paid the country club dues of Daniel Shea, the chief judge of the county Tax Division, a court where Toots' firm was especially prominent. Judge Shea had wisely died before the U.S. Attorney's Office could indict him on various income tax charges. The government couldn't prove that any matters in Shea's courtroom had been influenced, so there wasn't much of a case on Toots. But the payments violated a number of ethical provisions and the Justice Department had referred the matter to BAD, where my former colleagues, beetle-browed do-gooders, knew at once they had Toots's number, eighty-three years old or not.

So at 10:00 a.m. this Wednesday morning, Brushy and I and our client had arrived at the old school building where BAD is housed. Our presence in itself was a sign of defeat. At my client's urging, I'd employed various gambits to put this off for over two and a half years. Now the ax was certain to fall.

I stipulated to the Administrator's case, a collection of grand jury transcripts offered by Tom Woodhull, the Deputy Administrator, who years ago had been my boss. Standing up to rest his case, Woodhull appeared himself—unruffled, tall, handsome, and completely inflexible. I called Toots to the stand at once, hoping to appear eager to begin the defense.

"When did you become an attorney?" I asked my client, after he had given a gaudy review of his war record.

"Was admitted to the practice of law sixty-two years ago, nineteen days. But who's counting?" He supplied the same corny smile he used every time we went through this.

"Did you attend law school?"

"At Easton University where I was taught contracts by the late Mr. Leotis Griswell of your firm, who was my conscience throughout my professional life."

I turned away from the panel for fear I might smile. I had told Toots to drop the Jiminy Cricket routine, but he did not take easily to correction. He sat in his chair with his walking stick against his knee, a little trail of spittle on his lips from all the heavy mouth-breathing, a bulbous tuber of a man, all belly and cigar, with woolly eyebrows that meandered halfway up his forehead. He wore what he always wore—a shocking-green sport jacket, somewhere in color between your lighter watermelons and a lime. I would wager a considerable sum that neither of the men on the panel owned a tie that bright.

"What has been the nature of your law practice?" I asked next, a tricky question.

"I would say I had a very general practice. I would say," said Toots, "that I was a helper. People came to me who needed help and I helped."

This was about as good as we could do, since Toots in sixty-two years as a lawyer could not name a case he had tried, a will he'd drafted, a contract he'd written. Instead, folks came to him with certain problems and their problems were solved. It was a very Catholic concept, Toots's practice. Who, after all, can explain a miracle? Toots helped many public officials too. There was someone in almost every significant public agency with whom Toots maintained a special friendship. There was a debonair Assistant Attorney General for whom Toots bought suits; a particularly important State Senator who'd had three additions to his home built by a contractor friend of Toots for the remarkably low cost of fourteen grand. This generosity had made the Colonel quite an influential fellow, especially since his methods were always understood. He relied first on his rogue charm. After that, he had other friends, guys from the neighborhood who'd smash your windows, torch your store, or, as happened once to a club singer who got crosswise of Toots, perform a tonsillectomy without benefit of an anesthetic.

"Did you practice in the Tax Division courts?"

"Not at all. Never. If I was goin there today I'd need to ask directions."

I glanced down at Brushy to see how this was going. She was seated beside me, wearing a dark suit, trying to record every word on a yellow pad. She gave me a wee smile, but that was just being friends. She was too tough to hold out any more hope than I did.

"Now, did you know Judge Daniel Shea?" I asked.

"Oh yes, I known Judge Shea since we was both young attorneys. We was terrific friends. Like this."

"And did you, as the Administrator here alleges, pay the country club dues of Judge Shea?"

"Absolutely." Toots had not been quite as sure when the IRS asked him the same question a number of years ago, but he had cut the interview short; it would not prove too damaging when Woodhull began his cross-examination, which was guaranteed to be wooden in any event.

"Can you please explain how that occurred?"

"That would be no trouble at all." Toots grabbed hold of his walking stick and shifted, as it were, into forward gear. "In about 1978 I run across Dan Shea at a dinner for the Knights of Columbus and we started talking, as fellas do, about golf. He told me that he had always wanted to get into the Bavarian Mound Country Club, which was right in his neighborhood, but unfortunately for him, he did not know a soul who could sponsor him. I volunteered for that job with pleasure. Shortly thereafter that, the president of the club, Mr. Shawcross, called to my attention the fact that Dan Shea was having some trouble making his dues. Since I was his sponsor, I felt it was up to me to pay them, and that's what happened ever since."

"Now did you mention these payments to Judge Shea?"

"Never," he said. "I did not want him to feel embarrassed or uncomfortable. His wife, Bridget, was in very bad health then and the expense and trouble was weighing quite heavy on him. Knowing Dan Shea, I'm sure that he had meant to get to this and it slipped his mind."

"And did you ever discuss with him any of the business in his court that your firm had there?"

"Never," he said again. "How could I? The younger fellas in my office do any number of things. It never crossed my mind that they was in that court. There's so many courts these days, you know." Toots spread his arms wide and smiled, revealing the worn yellow stubs of what were left of his teeth.

Brushy handed me a note. "The cash," it said.

"Oh yes." I touched my tie to revert to role. "We've stipulated that when Mr. Shawcross was in the grand jury, he testified you made these payments in cash and asked him not to discuss them with anyone. Could you explain that, please?"

"That would be no trouble at all," said Toots. "I did not want it to become known among the members of the club that Judge Shea was having a problem with his dues. I felt that would embarrass him. So I paid in cash, hoping that the bookkeeper and all of them would not see my name on a check, and I asked Mr. Shawcross to very kindly keep this to himself." With effort, he cranked himself about to face the panel. "I was just trying to be a friend," he told them. I didn't notice anybody up there reaching for a hanky.

Woodhull spent about fifteen minutes stumbling around on cross-examination. Toots, who hadn't missed a word on direct, was suddenly virtually deaf. Woodhull repeated every question three or four times and Toots often responded simply with a vague, addled stare. About noon Mona called a recess. That was enough for today. Seven lawyers, we all got out our diaries to see when we could resume. We went through the mornings and afternoons clear from today to next Tuesday before everybody was free.

"How'd I do?" Toots asked on the way out.

"Great," I said.

He lit up childishly and laughed. He thought so too.

"Why does a guy who's eighty-three want to be disbarred?" asked Brushy after we'd put him in a taxi. "Why doesn't he just resign from practice?"

Toots's forty-year career as councilman for the South End had come to a conclusion in the early 1980s, when it turned out that the city's Parks and Playgrounds Commission, which Toots controlled by appointments, had voted for a decade straight to award its refuse-hauling contract to Eastern Salvage, a company owned through various intermediaries by one of Toots's sons. Since then, Toots's life had been confined to his role as the man for desperate occasions. He needed his law license to lend his activities some air of legitimacy. I explained all this to Brushy as we walked back toward the Needle through the noontime crowds. There had been a light snowfall last night which had been ground to gray mush and crept over the toes of our shoes.

"There's no listing in the Yellow Pages for Fixers. Besides, it would stain his honor. This is a man who wanted to wear his medals to the hearing. He can't accept the public disgrace."

"His honor?" she asked. "He's had people killed. Those guys in the South End? He eats lunch with them. Dinner."

"That's an honor too."

Brushy shook her head. We entered the Needle and rose by elevator to G&G's reception area, where oaken bookcases had been erected and filled with dozens of antique books, bought by the gross, to lend the proper air. Our offices had been redecorated at Martin's direction a couple of years ago in the manner of an English hunting lodge. This main reception area was refurbished with planked pine and tufted leather chairs of royal maroon and little landscapes and hunting scenes on the walls, pictures in brass frames with broad green mats, second-rate decorative crap, but who was asking me? That kind of stage setting, though, made it easier to fall into some kind of fugue state—new faces every day, young people striding about with urgent anguished looks, all this important stuff going on that didn't have a damn thing to do with me. Bonds issuing. Deals closing. You could see it all from a considerable distance: Men with phallic symbols around their necks. Women with half their legs exposed. What on God's green planet were they up to? Why was it that they cared and I didn't?

"I've told him we can't win," I said of Toots. "He kept asking me to get continuances."

"I see that." She thumped the file. "Two years four months. For what?" She was backing down the corridor. She had a meeting with Martin but reminded me about racquetball at six.

"Time."

"What's he going to do with time?" asked Brushy.

"Die," I said, before turning away.

IX. TOUGH CUSTOMERS

A. Slave Queen of Accounting

Like the engine room of an oceangoing vessel, where soot-spotted hands shovel coal into great fires, the firm's Accounting Department burns on belowdecks. On 32, between an investment banking operation and a travel service, the location has a sub-basement feel, because it is cut off from the three other floors we occupy. Yet in many ways this is the heart of G&G: to Accounting our billable hours are reported on a daily basis; from Accounting our statements for services go out every month. Here the great profitmaking motor of the law firm whines away at high r.p.m.'s.

One of the most peculiar things about going from BAD to G&G was getting used to a world where money—which as a cop and then a public lawyer I regarded as inherently evil—is, instead, the point of axis of an entire universe. Money's why the clients hire us—to help them make more or keep what they have. God knows, it's what we want from them. It is what we all have in common. At this point in the calendar, when our fiscal year concludes, the firm takes on the air of a campus before the Big Game. We have partnership meetings about collecting that can't be easily distinguished from pep rallies, where Martin, and especially Carl, make speeches designed to give us the stomach to demand our clients actually pay our bills. It was one of Carl's many clever innovations to move the close of our fiscal year back a month to January 31, in order to give clients the chance to book our fees in either calendar year. On February 2, Groundhog Day, after the receipts are totaled, the partnership meets in tuxedos, while the Committee announces each partner's "points"—our percentile share of firm income.

Accounting is housed in a couple of rooms, garish with fluorescence, nine women in an environment of white Formica. Their figures are reported daily to the Committee and various CPAs. The staff supervisor, the resident person in charge, is Glyndora Gaines. When I came in she was on her feet, studying a clipping torn from the newspaper. The paper itself was spread on her desk, the only thing there besides a framed photo of her son. As soon as she saw me, she walked away.

I was in my overcoat, on my way out to see Peter Neucriss. I'd called Glyndora three or four times now without response, and I asked if she'd gotten my messages.

"Busy," she said, the gal who'd just been reading the *Tribune*. I followed her around Accounting while she slammed through cabinets.

"This is important," I added.

I got a look that could have smelted lead.

"So's what I'm doing, man. We're 10 percent below budget and looking for ways to reallocate every expense we got. Don't you want to make *money*?"

Boy, this is a lady with an attitude—capital A—one of those powerhouse African-American women whose chief regret seems to be that she has but one life to fume over the indignities of the last few centuries. No one gets along with her. Not the attorneys, the paralegals, the staff. During her years as a secretary Glyndora worked with half the lawyers in the firm. She couldn't cut it with another woman and lasted only a week with

Brushy. She'd been far too intimidating for Wash—and many others. In all the ensuing scrapes Glyndora's been protected by—guess who?—Martin Gold, patron saint of the local eccentrics. He seems to find her amusing and, as I knew well, is inclined to forgive every sin except sloth for the sake of ability. Able Glyndora is. That's the problem. She resents the way she's been enslaved by circumstance. She had a kid at fifteen, whom she raised on her own, with no chance after that really to make her way.

Recognizing that Glyndora could not resist the chance to prove how capable she is, Martin had ultimately teamed her with Bert, the lawyer for whom she'd worked longest. Glyndora filed his motions, kept his schedule, wrote the routine correspondence, filled in the blanks on the standard interrogatories, made excuses when he took a powder, even went to court for him in a couple of emergencies. (And had an income about 10 percent of his, if you'll excuse the son of a union man.) The only problem was that about a year ago they began to fight. Here I am not being euphemistic. I do not mean occasional cross looks or even one or two sharp words. I mean standing in the hallway bellowing. I mean papers flying, clients in the doorways of the conference rooms staring down the halls. I mean Scenes. Finally, someone who must have been in the army or on a police force got the right idea: promote her. Glyndora was less a tyrant as a boss than she had been as an employee and she clearly enjoyed having a universe of her own. Bert, naturally, carried on like a baby when they took her away. And Glyndora undoubtedly enjoyed that too.

"Glyndora, it's this Litiplex thing. The money." That stopped her. We were in front of a row of bone-colored cabinets. Her face was narrowed by her customary suspicion. "When you searched for the paperwork, I think you could have missed a memo. From Bert. Maybe attaching some kind of agreement with Peter Neucriss?"

She shook her head immediately, a copse of long hair, dulled by straighteners. I nodded firmly in response.

"Hey, man." She swept her hand wide. "I got 80,000 files here and I had my nose in each one. You think you can do a better job, Mack, help yourself. We lock up at five."

The phone rang then and she picked it up, long sinister sculpted nails painted bright red. Glyndora is past forty and showing little wear. This is one good-looking woman and she knows it—built like the brick shithouse you've always heard about, five foot ten in her stocking feet and female every inch of it, a phenomenal set of headlights, a big black fanny, and a proud imperial face, with a majestic look and an aquiline schnozzola that reports on Semitic adventures in West Africa centuries ago. Like every fine-looking human I have ever met, she can be charming when there's something she wants, and with me, in certain moods, she's even something of a tease, picking up, I guess, on a certain susceptibility. I've lived most of my life with women like this, who were suffering from the peculiarly female frustration of feeling there had never been any way out to start—and besides, a body can't ignore how she looks. I've heard men speak of Glyndora with admiration for years—but only from a distance. As Al Lagodis, an old pal from the Force, told me one day when he came by for lunch, you'd need a dick like a crowbar.

She had no use for me now. "I told you, Mack," she said when she was done on the phone, "I don't have time for this."

"I'll see you at five. You can show me what you went through."

She laughed. Glyndora and non-essential overtime were mutually exclusive.

"When?" I asked.

She picked up her purse, dropping something into it, and gave me a little tight smile that said, Go jump. She was on her way down the hall, where I couldn't follow. I said her name to no avail. She left me by her desk. The newspaper from which she'd ripped that item was still open. It looked like it had been an article, an eighth of a page. A little portion of the headline remained. WES, maybe part of a T. West? I looked up. Sharon, one of Glyndora's underlings, was watching me, a little brown woman in a pink outfit that was half a size too tight. Twenty feet away, she eyed me from her desk with suspicion—worker against boss, woman versus man, all of the workplace's silent little competitions. Whatever I was looking for, she figured, I shouldn't know.

I tried a silly smile and stepped away from the forbidden zone of what was Glyndora's.

"Tell her to call me," I said.

Sharon just looked. We both knew I had no chance.

B. Prince of Darkness

TransNational Air Flight 397 went down in a horrible fireball at the Kindle County Municipal Airfield in July 1985. A TV crew was coincidentally at the airport to cover the arrival of the Peking Circus at a nearby gate and so the footage played again and again across the country, you've probably seen it, 397 bouncing on its front wheel and taking air again, looking a bit like a kiddie's book where the hippopotamuses dance ballet, all quite slo-mo and graceful until the thing canted forward, hit square on its nose, and fire ignited, flashing through the cockpit first and then rolling back through the plane, lighting the windows as it went, until the engines and underbelly blew off in a memorable eruption of orange and yellow flame. No survivors—247 fried.

At this point, the plaintiffs' lawyers took the field, the guys and gals who prate to juries about the misery of the widows and orphans and then take a full third of what is forked over in sympathy. As someone who works the other side of the street, I'll spare the high and mighty—let me just note that Peter Neucriss, Barracuda-in-Chief of the local plaintiffs' bar, had filed three lawsuits in behalf of the families of crash victims not only before the remains were buried but in one instance before, quite literally, they had cooled. Within six months, there were more than 137 cases on file, including four class actions in which some enterprising lawyer claimed to represent everyone. All of these cases were consolidated before Judge Ethan Bromwich of the Kindle County Superior Court, a former law professor at Easton whose brilliance is exceeded only by his regard for his own abilities. And in every single suit, TransNational Air, our client, was the lead defendant.

Being the airline in an air crash case is sort of like driving a bumper car at the carnival. There are more drivers than you can count; no one knows or cares about rules of the road; everyone's headed in his or her own direction; and every single one of them seems to get his jollies out of ramming you in the behind. It's not just that there are 247 individual victims, each one with relatives and lawyers looking for money to assuage their misery, but you also have ten or twelve co-defendants, ruthlessly pissed off to be involved. Everybody gets sued, not just the airline and the pilot's estate, but any poor son of a bitch who left so much as a fingerprint on the plane: the folks who made the body, the engine manufacturers, the flight controllers, even the company that distilled the gas—anybody with deep pockets who might conceivably be blamed or forced by the prospect of a decade of expensive litigation to throw a few million bucks in the pot. And every one of those folks has a stop-loss insurer who steps to the plate looking for a way to deny coverage to the company that pays their premiums, or, if that won't work, to blame somebody else and get them to pay. There are weathervanes that do not point in as many directions. We blame the people in the flight tower; they in turn say the ailerons weren't working; the manufacturer speaks of pilot error. The plaintiffs all stand on the side and gloat.

About a year after 397 went down, Martin Gold began an effort that seemed to me as romantic and ill-considered as the Crusades: settling 397. Martin has a mind like a cloud chamber, that device where nuclear physicists trace the course of complex atomic reactions; he is probably the only lawyer I know who could even have embarked, let alone succeeded, on a negotiating process which, at one point, had him taking calls from 163 different attorneys.

Under what Martin is always careful to refer to, even sometimes in the office, as "The Bromwich Plan" the defendants, meaning for the most part their insurance companies, put together a fund of $288.3 million. In return the plaintiffs, led by Neucriss, agreed that the damages in all the cases together could not exceed that sum. Over the last five years, every individual case has been either tried before a Special Master, or more often settled, with Captain Bert heading the TN litigation team and supervising administration of the settlement fund which G&G has held in an interest-bearing escrow.

Recently, as the last of the damage trials have been resolved, we've had an unforeseen development: there's going to be millions left over which, accordingly, will remain the property of little ol' TransNational Air. Indeed, the only problem for TN has been keeping this news to ourselves, since it would be a public-relations nightmare to explain how, when everything is added and subtracted—legal fees, interest, the surplus, and TN's initial contribution to the fund—the company netted close to $20 million by killing 247 people. More pertinently, the plaintiffs' lawyers, who have never seen a dollar they didn't think was rightfully theirs, would use that vulnerability to weasel themselves a bigger share, and the co-defendants of course would wail piteously. We have been on a self-conscious campaign to make sure that every plaintiff has been paid out and signed a release before we submit our final accounting on the settlement fund to Judge Bromwich. Nonetheless, if you put liquor into Tad Krzysinski, TN's CEO, in an intimate setting, you can get him to laugh pretty hard at the inevitable jokes about crashing more planes.

When I was finally allowed to see Neucriss about 4:30, he had a tuna steak on a plate before him. Just out of court, he was enjoying a light supper, preparing for an evening's toil. He had a full kitchen and a chef in the office. The immediate air was savored with ginger, but there was still the frantic feel of trial. Peter's $100 foulard was dragged down; the sleeves were rolled on his white-on-white silk shirt; he stood as he ate, rumbling out every free-associated thought as a command. Four or five associates came charging in and out with questions about exhibits that they would need tomorrow. It was a bad-baby case, worth in Peter's hands at least $10 million. The mother was going on in the morning.

Meanwhile, I sat there in the mendicant pose in which Peter prefers to see everyone around him. I was hoping to get a quick answer and go. I had brought over drafts of the payout documents on 397, and had casually mentioned Litiplex, using the routine Wash said had been employed with others—correspondence we couldn't place, maybe Peter had an idea?

"Litiplex." Peter touched his forehead. He stared, unseeing, toward the middle distance. "I did talk to somebody about that."

"You did? Was it Bert?"

"*Bert?*"

"He's been out of town, I haven't been able to ask him."

"Right. Visiting his family on Mars." Neucriss rolled his eyes. "No. Who?" He drummed his fingers, he yelled for one of the secretaries, then stopped her with an explosive clap of his hands. "I know who asked me about Litiplex. Jesus Christ, what a squirrelly bunch you are. Don't you guys even talk to each other? Gold. Gold brought it up. Is he out of town too, or just out to lunch?"

My heart went flat, I wasn't even sure why, except I knew something was wrong. There were plaintiff's guys Martin could talk to with confidence, whereas even hello on the street with

Peter required full body armor for Martin and an Alka-Seltzer afterwards.

"Martin?" I asked.

"No, good as. Yeah, Gold called three or four weeks ago. Doing the same soft-shoe as you, talking to me about something else, then trying to slide this Litiplex name in so I wouldn't notice. What the hell are you guys up to now?"

Nothing, I said. Lying to Peter is not even a venial sin: speaking to a Frenchman in French. Wash had said Martin phoned a couple of plaintiffs' lawyers with discreet inquiries about Litiplex, but it had never crossed my mind they might include Neucriss. In the meantime, I tried to smooth over the concerns all this Q and A about Litiplex seemed to have raised. Just getting ready for distribution, trying to cover all details, who more likely to know all than Peter?

With Neucriss, flattery is always the best way. Perhaps because it is the social world's realm of ultimate restraint, the law seems to attract more of these types, the utterly self-impressed who regard the bar as the pathway to a frontier where will and ego can go virtually unbounded. The sole partner in a seventeen-lawyer firm, Neucriss is the only lawyer I know who earns more every year than a good left-handed pitcher makes in the National League. Between $4 and $6 million are the printed estimates, and this year, with some $30 million worth of settlements in the 397 litigation about to pay out, his income will, as he puts it in his own unctuous way, "reach the eight figures."

This success has not been achieved by adherence to scruple. Peter's political contributions are vast—he hits every limit and gives in the name of his sixteen associates, his wife, and his children. Even so, he leaves nothing to chance. His witnesses are skillfully tutored; documents disappear; and in the bad old days, perhaps not entirely gone, when cash on the barrelhead bought judicial favor, Neucriss was figured to do this as well. Worst of all, his very prominence is a sort of revolting advertisement of the fallibility of the jury system. Ten minutes with this guy and you know the story: ego run wild, some form of character disorder. But somehow, from juries, Peter's schmaltzy performance, his self-congratulatory baritone and silvery mane, have drawn nothing but rave reviews for forty years. He goes on, with all of us knowing that no matter what his triumphs, his wealth, the national accolades, all the purchased adoration, the only motive force in nature surer than gravity is Peter's desire for more.

He continued talking about Martin, always a raw nerve with him.

"Oh yeah. What was Gold's line? Something like yours. A letter to be forwarded. I asked him, 'What game is this? Post Office? I thought that was adolescent foreplay.' " Neucriss roared at himself, his mouth still full. Being profane, he kept Martin on edge.

"But what about it, Peter? Litiplex? What is it?"

"Listen to this. How the hell do I know? For crying out loud. Call information. Ask them about Litiplex. Jesus Christ," he went on, "how do you stand stuff like this, Malloy? One hundred forty lawyers running around bumping into each other. Two senior partners sorting the mail. And now you'll bill Jake Eiger five hundred bucks for looking at an envelope and tell him it's the plaintiffs' lawyers who make legal expenses so high."

Jake and Neucriss were sort of on speaking terms, since Jake's dad was one of those pols to whom Neucriss had barnacled himself decades ago. Peter, in the meantime, was off and running, going on about big law firms, the Gog and Magog of his universe. In his own oleaginous way, he was even attempting to appeal for my support. He knew where I stood at G&G— the entire legal world, local and national, was mapped in his head. Hanging on there by my fingernails, I might be brought to side with him against my partners. Instead, I fended him off lamely with wit.

"If I didn't know better, Peter, I'd think you were offering me a job." As soon as I said it, I heard that the tone was all wrong. Neucriss's quick eyes registered something, the possibility of corruption, which around here is always in the air, like carbon dioxide. He held on just a second before rejecting that thought.

"Not you, Malloy. You're an old plowhorse." That's all he said. Dead or dying went unspecified, but either way, my bones in his view would soon be tromped upon, ground down by some other dray treading my row. He went back to work and I went on my way, fighting him off, trying not to be diminished by his estimate, but of course feeling absolutely flattened. I wasn't even worth buying off.

I was on the street, my overcoat open for the short walk to the Needle, buffeted by the thick pedestrian traffic on all sides, workers departing in the sullen dwindling light of winter. Overhead, the sky was dimming to the color of a burnt pot. The morning snow was now nothing but a dampness on the walks, freezing over amid the little hummocks of salt that rimed the concrete and would stain my shoes.

In the interval, I tried to figure what was doing. I wouldn't say I believed Peter. It was safer to bet on the Easter Bunny. But I couldn't figure why he had anything to hide. I was feeling surly, in a formerly familiar cop-mood in which everyone was a suspect. Bert. Maybe Glyndora. Even, possibly, God's emissary on earth, Martin Gold. The vague unpredictability of Martin's behavior bothered me especially: the way he'd been with Jake; the fact that Martin had called Neucriss, which he ordinarily did only when somebody was paying premium rates. I stopped on a corner where a little boy in a hooded sweatshirt was hawking papers, while a sudden wind snapped my muffler in my face. Here I stood in the city where I've lived my entire misbegotten life, the canyons I've been prowling for decades, feeling depressed and undermined, full of the convincing if momentary illusion that I didn't know where in the hell I was.

C. Somebody Else's Girl

For unexplained reasons, I always found it a shock seeing Brushy's pale meaty thighs in her athletic shorts. Her adolescent acne still flared on the parts of her body that were ordinarily concealed, high up on her arms and in the V-neck of her tennis shirt, but I found her appealingly girlish. She did not spend much time letting me look her over, though, and began to bat the ball around the racquetball court. We went through more or less the same routine each week. I moved well left and right, and had superior reach and better strokes. Brushy swung with an awkward roundhouse, elbow locked, but she scrambled all over the white-walled court like a squirrel and got to every shot; she'd run me over rather than call hinders. Each week we'd play the first two games even. I careered around, yelling oaths and curse words whenever I mishit the ball. Then Brushy, who had not hit drop shots out of deference to my knee, would dink one ball after another, until I was limping and so short of breath I could faint.

We were at the usual fateful pass between the second and third game in the little low corridor outside the court, toweling off. She wanted to know what had come of my visits with Glyndora and Neucriss.

"Zero," I said. "Nobody knows nothin. Maybe you were right. Bert was just trying to phony up something to cover his tracks." She started asking me questions and I told her a little about Archie and his betting scheme, and my misadventures yesterday, in which, in my version, I had stood up heroically to my old nemesis from the Force.

Brushy took in as much as I said and with her usual cool deliberation got fast to the bottom line.

"So whose credit card is it," she asked, "Bert's or Kam's?"

I had no idea.

"Where'd you find this card anyway?" she asked.

I was still keeping that part to myself. I didn't want anybody to put me near Bert's refrigerator. I invoked the magic words "Attorney-Client" and pushed Brushy back onto the court, where she shortly whipped my butt once more, 21–7, dropping shots to the corners and banging the ball off the ceiling like a storm of large blue hail.

"Would it kill you if I won just once?" I complained as we were leaving.

"I know you, Mack. You have a weak character. You'd want to win every week."

I denied it, but she didn't believe me. She was heading off to the ladies' locker room, and I asked about dinner, which we did now and then when we were both in the office late.

"I can't. Maybe later this week."

"Who's the lucky fella?"

Brushy frowned. "Tad, if you must. I'm meeting him for a drink." Brushy's occasional rendezvous for lunch or cocktails or dinner with Krzysinski had been going on for some time, and nobody at G&G knew what to make of them. Tad had been on the job at TN no more than a month when he was personally named in a securities fraud case which Brushy had handled and won, filing a successful motion to dismiss. Purportedly, Krzysinski was just staying in touch, but everybody at the firm alternately suspected or hoped that he was getting the usual from Brushy, since any direct line to the top was valued, given the precariousness of our relationship with TN. The part that didn't fit was that Krzysinski had the rep of a serious family man, nine kids, and had been known to fly back from Fiji so he could be around for family Mass late afternoon on Saturday. On the other hand, as my mother would say, the devil finds a way into the safest home.

I greeted Brushy's news with a lascivious wag of my brow.

"Ooo la la," I said. Between us, Brushy generally took this kind of joshing pretty well, but today she called the foul.

"I resent that," she answered, and her eyes heated up. Brushy wanted to be thought of as a counselor to titans, a hotshot who'd be a logical drinking partner for a Fortune 500 King. Instead, here was her ace partner and pal assuming that she'd have one hand on her martini and the other on Tad's privates. I stood there in the hallway, a foot taller, sweating, and felt myself vulnerable for the lack of any smart remark.

"You happen to be wrong," she went on, "and you're getting to be worse than anybody else. Why do you suddenly think *my* sex life is *your* business?"

"Because I don't have one of my own?"

She remained in a huff.

"Maybe you should work on that," she told me, and marched off down the narrow white hall that led to the locker rooms. The door was too heavy to slam but she gave it a try.

It was rare, but there were instants like this when between Brushy and me there was the throb of something, maybe lost opportunity. Especially in her early days, Brushy let a guy know she was available not long after you said how do you do, and for ten years or so we'd had this running thing about the great fun I was missing. I smiled but kept my distance. Not, by the way, that I was a man of perfect virtue. But it was bad enough being known around the office as a lush, and something about Brushy seemed to make her a daunting proposition, maybe just the well-worn story of a college student who worked in the mailroom and let it be known after one magic summer night that Brushy had so inspired him that they'd had, count them, nine separate encounters between 7:30 p.m. and the following dawn, an achievement that led the young man to be known thereafter solely as *Nueve* and cast such a pall over every man in the place that there was a palpable atmosphere of celebration the day the kid finally left to go back to school.

Anyway, during that period when my life seemed to be demonstrating some law of thermodynamics or entropy, all to the effect that if things could fuck up they would, with my sister dying and Nora wandering and Lyle in his teenaged funk and me sworn off the bottle, I finally spent an afternoon with her at the Dulcimer House, a class place around the corner. Sex with Brushy was, well, brief. I did not completely fail, but various thoughts of home and spouse, a staid life, and even social disease had suddenly crowded within me, leaving me weak as water and quick as mercury.

'So what?' Brushy had said, and I welcomed her kindness. For Brushy it was all conquest anyway. No doubt she felt better finding that she hadn't missed much.

As for me, I probably expected it. The only good sex I've had was when I was drunk, which must tell you something about me, I wish I knew what. Still, something was easier when I could blame each mishap on the bottle. I was so gassed, et cetera— that's why I spent two sawbucks on the hooker who sucked me off in the back of that taxi; that's why I plugged that girl, even after she puked. A lot of guys lose the capacity that far along, but now and then after half a bottle of Seagram's 7, I lit up like a firecracker.

Without it, there is not a lot left to be said. Every now and then some fancy still strikes me, the oddest things—some gal in a cosmetics ad or some ordinary-looking female whose skirt hikes up in a provocative way as she is crossing the street—and I find myself engaged in Man's Oldest Amusement. I know this is revolting to imagine, a grown man, a big one, with a hand on his own throttle, but we're not really talking about much. Afterwards I am full of Catholic shame, but also curiosity. What's wrong with me? I wonder. Am I just half-dead in that region, or is it that no woman can be as good as what I dream up myself? And what is it I dream? you ask. People. Couples, frankly. I admit it, I like to look. X-rated movies, but in my own theater. The man is never me.

So that's what I was thinking as I came out of the locker room into the reception area of Dr. Goodbody's Health Club. There were a couple of chairs with a little table between them where most of the papers for the week were piled up, as well as the

usual health and fitness magazines, and feeling somewhat morose
anyway, I plopped myself down there, having half a mind to
look for something in the newspaper, although at the moment
I could not quite recollect what. The sports page was full of hype
about the Super Bowl on Sunday and the high point of local
interest, Friday night's Hands game with UW–Milwaukee. The
season records of the Hands and the Meisters were in a box on
the inside pages, and I noted, in passing, that Bert or Kam,
whoever, had won the $5,000 wager he'd called Kam's Special
on Infomode, the U. over Cleveland State. I diddled around
with that thought. The card statement had a $9,000 credit for
December. He'd been winning, Kam or Bert, which meant nobody had a reason to steal to pay Archie.

I remembered then, suddenly, why I'd wanted to see the
paper—to check what Glyndora'd torn out. I went through the
day's *Tribune* twice with no luck, and was ready to quit when
I found it at last in the late edition, an item from the City section:
WEST BANK EXEC MISSING. The wife of prominent insur-
ance industry executive Vernon "Archie" Koechell confirmed
that her husband had not appeared at home or work for the last
two weeks. Koechell's disappearance had been reported to the
Kindle Unified Police, who were investigating a possible connection to an undisclosed financial crime. On the jump page,
there was a picture of Archie, a noble-looking business type with
a round mug and a widow's peak. The photo was old, twenty
years, but I recognized him, no doubt of that. We'd met face to
face, so to speak, and I'd be a long time anyway forgetting the
man I'd seen in Bert's refrigerator.

X. YOUR INVESTIGATOR

RESUMES SOME OLD BAD HABITS

A. Your Investigator Is Misled

Glyndora lives in a triplex in one of these resurrected areas in the shadow of the projects. I swear to God, when I come back from the dead I want to be a real estate developer. Sell people a three-room apartment for two hundred grand and when they go out in the morning their car has no hubcaps. Two blocks away you could see the kids, in tattered coats in this season, playing basketball and looking through the chain-link with their devastated dead expressions. But here the construction was reminiscent of a Hollywood set, perfection in every visible detail, and the feel that you could put your hand right through it. The effect was Williamsburg. Little wooden doodads at the roofline and wrought-iron rails; starving saplings, bare sticks in January, were planted in little squares removed from the pavement. One could not help thinking of a theme park.

"Glyndora, it's Mack." I had found her address in the firm personnel directory, and I wasn't expected. I made my apologies for bothering her at home through the buzzer intercom. "I need to talk to you and I don't have a lot of time."

"Okay." Silence. "Talk, man."

"Come on, Glyndora. You don't need to be so entertaining. Let me in."

Nothing.

"Glyndora, cut the crap."

"Call you tomorrow."

"Like you did today? Listen, I'm gonna stand down here freezing my chestnuts and pressing on this buzzer and shouting your name. I'm gonna make a big goddamn scene, so that your neighbors wonder about the company you keep. And in the morning, I'm going straight to the Committee to tell them how you've been horsing me around." Something here might pass for a credible threat. Especially the Committee. I stomped around on the stoop another minute in the dark, breathing smoke beneath the brass colonial lamp, with my chin nuzzled into my muffler. Finally I heard the buzz.

She waited for me at the top of the stairs, backlit by her own home and barring the way to her door. She was wearing a simple housedress and no makeup, and her stiff hair had been released from barrettes and looked somewhat shapeless. I more or less moved her across her own threshold, waving my hands to show I wouldn't take no for an answer. Inside, I seated myself at once on her sofa and opened my overcoat. I did my best to look heavyset and immobile.

"Aren't you going to offer me coffee? It's cold out there."

Standing near the door, she showed no sign of moving.

"Look, Glyndora, there are a couple of things. One, maybe you can think again about whether you ever saw a little memo from Bert about the Litiplex checks. Two, the name Archie Koechell mean anything to you?"

She was going to stare me down, the way sideshow performers overcome certain fearsome creatures, cobras or bears. She put her hands to her waist and slowly shook her head.

"Glyndora, you answered Bert's phone for years and this guy

Archie is a big pal of his. Think again. He's an actuary. And he's missing. Just like Bert. There was an article in the paper today. Maybe you saw it?"

Nothing. The same fiercely baleful expression. I blew on my fingertips to warm them and again asked for coffee.

She went this time, but not before she cussed me, tossing her head about in disbelief. I wandered around the apartment. Very nice. The sort of discreet middle-class taste I would have preferred in my own home. Light carpeting of a Berber weave and patterned fabrics with big flowers on the cushions of the rattan-sided furnishings. There was a kind of decorator painting, a lot of innocuous wave motion, over the sofa. Otherwise the walls were bare. Glyndora was not a person attached to images.

She was gone awhile. I looked into the kitchen, a little galley affair hinged to the cramped space the architect had probably called the "eating area," but she was not in there. No coffee brewing either. I could hear her movements through another door or two and thought I detected her voice. Maybe in the john, or putting on her battle regalia. It would not be unlike Glyndora to be holding an animated conversation with herself, but I also had some thought of picking up the phone to see if she had reached out for somebody else. I held my breath, but I could not make out a word.

Across from me, in a corner of the dining room, was a little round étagère, a multilevel thing of chrome and glass. There were various glass animals—Steuben, if you asked Nora Goggins's ex-husband—and pictures of Glyndora's kid, a high-school graduation photo, complete with mortarboard, and a smaller snapshot, more recent, in a frame. An okay-looking guy, lean and muscular, the mother's strong build and good looks gender-translated, but with an impish unfocused expression that had never emanated from Glyndora since the day of her birth.

"You still here?" Over my shoulder, she looked remotely amused, probably with herself.

"Still warming up."

She had combed her hair a little and reddened her lips, but her manner remained unyielding.

"Look, Glyndora," I said, "you're a smart guy and so am I, so let's skip the horseplay."

"Mack, you ain been no po-lice for twenty years, and I ain never been no mope. So just take it somewhere else, man. I'm tired." Glyndora is often at her blackest around white people, especially when she's on the offensive. In the office today, she'd spoken the same English as me.

"Come on, Glyndora. I already told you how it is. I'm the Question Man and you're the Answer Lady. Otherwise we can all sit down and discuss this tomorrow—you and me and the Committee." I hoped the renewed threat, which had been enough to get me through the doorway, would make her relent. But the notion seemed to perk her up with a kind of tough amusement.

"I gotta do what you say, huh?"

"Sort of."

"That figures, man. You like that, right?"

I shrugged.

"Yeah, you like that. Just you and me and I ain't got no choice."

"Come on, Glyndora."

"Yeah, that's why you got to come round after dark to my house. Cause I ain't got no choice."

Glyndora has what you might call issues. For her it always comes down to this, master and slave. She was moving in my direction now, sashaying slightly, a hip-rolling walk that was both deliberately provocative and defiant; I got back to my feet to greet her, but she still came a little bit closer than she was supposed to. She knew what she was up to and so did I, we'd both been to the movies. She was just going to back me down with her boldness. She'd cinched the waist on her dress and projected herself and her formidable anatomy at me, rocking a little on her toes, hands on her hips. She might as well have said, I dare you.

"So tell me, Mr. Mack. What-all is it I *gotta* do for you?" Up close, her dark skin was a complex of colors, pointillistic. She was giving me a taunting smile, revealing a gap in her teeth which I'd never noticed over the fifteen years I've known her.

I said again, quietly, "Come on."

She stayed right there, head high, eye mighty. As a grownup I have believed that priests, schoolteachers, and criminal investigators should have no carnal knowledge of the people over whom they exert authority. Temptations, naturally, abound. What it is with some gals there's no telling, but it sometimes seems they'd stand in line to screw a copper. You can take a guy built like a Franklin stove, half bald and dirty looking, a fella who'd sit at the end of the bar all night and attract no company, and once you put a uniform on him and a pistol on his hip, the guy's a freakin ladykiller. It's just a thing. Some fellas on the Force, it was a dream come true, they'd work for free, and others, so what.

For me, this was one of the few areas in my life where I had actually exhibited self-control. Naturally I was not perfect. There was a party girl from Minnesota one time who made me dizzy, witness in a white-slavery case in which we were making our usual effort to catch some of The Boys by hiding behind a tree. Twenty or twenty-one years old, beautiful blond thing who looked so innocent you'd have thought she'd sailed in off some fjord. Terrible life. Ran from home because her old man was cornholing her each night, fell in with the wrong crowd in the city, and Jesus, forgive me for sounding as if I had a Catholic education, but then did everything in the world to degrade herself. There was some big TV star, a comedian whose name you'd know, who paid her two g's each time he was in town for her to come to his hotel and let him take a dump on her and then—prepare yourself—watch her eat it. This I am not making up. Anyway, Big Bad Mack thinks she's pretty neat. And Christ, this is her life, she catches on like that, the way a plant will turn to face the sunbeams. And so one day it comes to pass, I'm supposed to take her from the stationhouse to her apartment, pick up some address book where she has the name or two of some big-time gumbas, and we both know what's cooking, nature is about to take its course, and she opens the door to this rummy place—I remember the door was like a pockmarked face; somebody had taken an ax or crowbar to it—and inside is this little Chihuahua, this pygmy animal, spotted with black sores from the mange or some similar doggy disease, charging our feet. She tells it once to scoot and then chases this poor mutt around, . kicking and cursing it with a look of such fixed and intense hatred that it sort of let the air out of my heart. It woke me up, I admit it, seeing the ugly mark all that cruelty had made on her, beaten up, assailed, like her door.

And I was awake now with Glyndora. Chugging right up to fifty and potbellied, I was not, I knew, the image rousing Glyndora in a parched erotic heat at night. But something wild and screwy was turned on in me, especially to see how far this was going to go, and feeling the daring that is always leaping up in me, else I die of fear, I took each index finger and with a thrilling directness settled them one at a time on the point of each breast, then, gently as somebody reading Braille, let my fingertips come to rest on the thin fabric of her dress. I could feel underneath the lace pattern of her brassiere.

The moment that then passed between us was what we used to call on the street p.f.s.—pretty fucking strange. Nobody was supposed to mean it. I wasn't supposed to squeeze her tits and Glyndora wasn't supposed to like it. We were playing chicken or the Dozens. It was as if we were both on camera. I could see it in my mind's eye—the bodies here and the spirits hovering fifteen feet above, wrestling like angels over someone's soul. In theory, we were merely disputing power and terrain. But with all these faces, the secret self was set free and was frisking about. Those rich brown eyes of hers remained dead set on mine, thoroughly amused, determinedly defiant: I see you. So what? I see *you*. But, folks, we were both pretty goddamned excited.

This contact, encounter, call it what you like, lasted only seconds. Glyndora pushed her arms up and slowly parted my hands. Her eyes never left mine. She spoke distinctly.

"You couldn't handle it, man," she said and turned for the kitchen.

"Are we taking bets?"

She didn't answer. I heard her say instead that she needed a drink.

I was ringing—the body after 4,000 volts. It was the whole idea of it, me playing with her playing with me. Mr. Stiffy downstairs was definitely awake too. I heard her banging around in a cabinet and swearing.

"What?" I asked. She had no whiskey, and I offered to go out to get her a pint. I wanted her to relax. This could be a long conversation, a longer evening. "You make coffee." I pointed at her but didn't linger as I leaned into the little kitchen; I was afraid to see what showed. Something in me was already clinging to the weird intimacy of that instant between us. With any invitation, I might have kissed her goodbye.

So I went charging out toward the Brown Wall's, a local chain I'd seen on the way in, a grown man running down the street in the dead of winter, with his flag half unfurled. The store was in the neutral zone, between the projects and the upscale, its bricks spray-painted with gang signs, its windows holding gay displays but guarded by fold-back grates. I grabbed a bottle of Seagram's off the shelf, feeling I'd seen something pornographic when I looked at all those glass soldiers arrayed side by side. As an afterthought, I detoured to pharmaceuticals for a three-pack of Trojans, just in case, I told myself, because a Scout is always prepared. Then I barreled back down the block oblivious to the three gangbangers who stood on the corner in their colors checking me out. I took all the front steps in one bound and hit the buzzer, waiting to be restored to paradise.

I rang intermittently for I'd say maybe a minute and a half

before I began to wonder why she was not answering. My first
thought? That I'm a big dumbbell? That I'd let the little head
think for the big one? No, I actually worried about her. Had
she fallen ill? Had one of the neighborhood muggers come
through the window and done her while I was gone? Then I
recalled the little fatal click behind me that I'd made nothing of
as I flew down the staircase. Suddenly, as I stood on the stoop,
shriveled by the cold, I realized that was the sound of the dead
bolt being set, of a lady locking up for the night.

I will say this for myself—I did not go gently. I punched that
buzzer like it was her fucking nose. After about five minutes,
her voice came up clearly, just once, and not long enough to
allow any reply.

"Go way," she said, alive and well and not waiting for me.

Let me be honest: it was not a good moment. I had beaten
Lyle to the car tonight, my shitbox Chevy; Nora got the good
car, a jade-green Beemer which I always drove with a pleasure
that made me feel as if I had taken a pill. I retired to this worn-
out wreck, where I was always ill at ease with the stains Lyle
and his friends left on the seats, and tried to assess the situation.
Okay, I told myself, some gal won't let you in, then puts the
make on you, then locks the door. The point is . . . ? Fill in the
blank. Pictures? Maybe some dope was in the closet with a
camera.

I had to give her credit, though. Glyndora knew where the
belly was on this porcupine. Let him strike out with the ladies
once again, then put liquor in his hand. In my palm, the bottle
had a strange magical heft. I always had drunk rye, same as my
old man. God, I loved it. I felt a little thrill when my thumb
passed across the tax labels on the bottle's neck. I was a civil
drunk who did not get started until nightfall, but by two in the
afternoon I could feel a certain dry pucker back in the salivary
glands and the first shot was always enough to make me swoon.
I used to think all the time about Dom Perignon, the monk

who'd first distilled Champagne. He fell down a flight of stairs and announced to the brethren who rushed to his rescue, 'I am drinking stars.'

It all seems so goddamned sad, I thought suddenly, looking out in the bleak night toward Glyndora's apartment. My breath was fogging the windows and I turned the engine over for heat. The whole appeal of this venture had been to take some sudden startling control over my existence. But I felt again some faraway master puppeteer whose strings were sewn into my sleeves. The fundamental facts were plain again: I was just a lowdown bum.

I wondered what I always do—how'd I end up this way? Was it just nature? In my neighborhood, if your old man was a copper or a fireman, you took it for granted he was a hero, these mystical men of courage donning their helmets and heavy coats to brave one of nature's most inscrutable events, how substance turns to heat and color, how the brilliant protean flames dance as they destroy. When I was three or four, I'd heard so much of this stuff, sliding down the pole and whatnot, that I was sure that when he wore his boots and fire slicker my old man could fly. He couldn't. I learned that over time. My father was no hero. He was a thief. "T'eef," as he used to pronounce the word, never in application to himself. But like Jason or Marco Polo, he brought back treasure from each adventure.

I often heard my father explain his logic when he engaged my mother in bouts of drunken self-defense. If a house is burning to the ground, woman, why not take the jewelry before it melts, for heaven's sake, you're there risking life and limb—you think you went outside and asked the residents, as they stood there with the flames shooting through their lives, that they'd say no? When I studied economics in college, I had no trouble understanding what they meant by a user's fee.

But I was not inclined to forgive him. I used to wonder as a kid if everybody knew the fireman stole. Everyone in my neighborhood seemed to understand—they'd come nosing around, looking to buy cheap the little items that were nicked and fit well in the rubber coats. 'Why'd you think they made them pockets in the coats so big?' my father used to say, never to me but to whoever had sidled by to examine the table silver, the clocks, the jewels, the tools, the thousand little things that entered our household. He'd laugh as he made these subverted displays. 'Where'd it come from?' the visitor would ask, and my father would chuckle and say that bit about the coat. Kind of dumb, of course, but he wanted people to think that he was bold—all frightened people do, they want to be just like the people who scare them. I had a cousin, Marie Clare, who came by once and asked my father to keep an eye out for a christening dress for her baby and he got her a beauty—why'd you think they made them pockets in the coats so big?

For me, as a kid, the shame of it sometimes seemed to blister my heart. When I started confession, I confessed for him. 'My father steals.' The priests were never uninterested. 'Oh yes?' I wanted to leave my name and address in the hope they'd make him stop. A boy's father is his fate. But this kind of stealing was a matter of society, forgivable and common. They told me to respect my father and pray for his soul, and better mind my own conduct.

'So much of life is will.' I had spun the golden cap off the pint before I knew what I'd done, and repeated that old phrase to myself. I had heard it from Leotis Griswell, not long before he died. I looked into the open bottle as if it were a blind eye, and was reminded for whatever reason of looking down at something else, another seat of pleasure. The sharp perfume of the alcohol filled me with a pang, as acute and painful as the distant sighting of a lovely woman whose name I'll never know.

So much of life is will. Leotis was speaking to me about Toots, his old student. Leotis had the skill I'd noted in many of the best lawyers, ardent advocates who at the same time held their clients at a distance. When he talked about them he could often be cold-blooded and he did not want me to be beguiled by Toots. 'He'll make excuses to you about his harsh life, but I've never cared much for sociology. It's so negative. I don't need to know what holds down the masses. Any fellow with an eye in his head can see that: it's life. But where does that rare one come from, what is the difference? I still spend hours wondering. Where the strength comes from *not* to surrender. The will. So much of life is will.' A certain subtle incandescence refracted through the old man as he said this, the feeble body still enfolding his large spirit, and the memory of it and the standard he set as a person punished me now.

Still, Leotis had it right, about life and will. It's an appropriate belief for a man born in the last years of the nineteenth century, yet it's out of phase for anybody else. Now we believe that a nation is entitled to self-determination but a soul is a slave to material fate: I steal because I'm poor; I feel up my daughter cause my ma did that to me; I drink because my ma was sometimes cruel and called me names and because my father left that trait, like some unhappy lodestar, in my genes. On the whole, I still prefer Leotis's outlook, the same one they taught me in church. I'd rather believe in will than fate. I drink or don't drink. I'll try to find Bert or I won't. I'll take the money and run or else return it. Better to find options than that bondage of cause and effect. It all goes back to Augustine. We choose the Good. Or the Evil. And pay the price.

And this, this may be the serpent's sweetest apple. I did not even seem to swallow.

I am drinking stars.

Thursday, January 26

B. Your Investigator Loses Something Besides His Self-respect

I have awakened so many mornings vowing never to do this again that there was almost pleasure in the pain. I felt like something fished out of the trash. I held absolutely still. The

sunlight was going to be like a bullet to the brain. Along the
internal line from head to gut there was a bilious feeling, some
regurgitive impulse already stirring. "Slow," I told myself, and
when I did I sensed for the first time that I wasn't alone.

When I opened my eyes, a kid was looking square at me,
Latin he seemed to be, crouched about an arm's length away
on the driver's side beneath the dash. He had one hand on the
car's tape player, which he'd lifted half out, revealing the bleak
innards of the auto, colored cables and dark spaces. Cutting the
wires would be the next step. The door was cracked behind him
and the dome light was on. There was a little sniffle of cold air
riffling across my nose.

"Just cool," he told me.

I didn't see a gun, a knife. A kid, too. Thirteen, fourteen. Still
with pimples all over the side of his face. One of your sweet
little urban vampires, out in the early-morning hours rolling
drunks. Fifty coming, I could still pound this little fuck. Hurt
him anyway. We both knew it. I checked his eyes again. It would
have been such a frigging triumph if there was just a dash, a
comma, an apostrophe of fear, some minute sign of hesitation.

"Get out," I said. I hadn't moved. I was sort of folded up like
a discarded shopping bag, piled sideways onto the passenger's
seat. With the adrenaline I was waking fast and turning dizzy,
whirly city. My tummy was on the move.

"Don't fuck around, men." He turned the screwdriver to face
me.

"I'll fuck with you, shorty-pants. I'll fuck with you plenty. And
after I do, you won't be fuckin anybody." I gave my head a sort
of decisive nod. Which was a bad mistake. It was like tipping
back in a chair too far. I rolled my eyes a bit. I picked myself
up on my elbow. With that, it happened.

I puked all over him.

I mean everywhere. It was dripping from his eyelashes. His
nappy head had got little bits of awful stuff all over. His clothes
were soaked. He was drowning in it, spluttering and shaking,

cursing me, an incoherent rap. "Oh men," he said. "Oh men." His hands danced around and I knew he was afraid to touch himself. And he was out of there fast. I was so busy waiting for him to kill me I actually didn't see him go until he was running down the street.

Well, Malloy, I thought, you are going to like this one. I patted my back all over a few times, before I straightened myself up, then realized that this story, like the tale of what really happened between Pigeyes and me, was going to go untold. After all, I had been bad. Weak. I'd had a drink. A bottle. I had fucked around with fate.

My guy at AA, my angel, guardian, hand in the dark, was a fella named Giandomenico, LNU, as we said on the Force, last name unknown, none used. Even though I haven't shown at a meeting in sixteen months, I knew he would talk to me and tell me that I still had what it took to do it. Today was no different than the day before yesterday. It was a day I wasn't gonna drink. I was going to get through today and work on tomorrow then. I knew the rap. I'd memorized all twelve steps. Somehow over the long haul I found AA sadder than being a drunk, listening to these folks, 'My name is Sheila and I'm an alcoholic.' Then would come the story, how she stole and whored and beat her kids. Jesus, sometimes I wondered if people were making things up just so the rest of us wouldn't feel so bad about our own lives. It was a little too much of a cult for me, the Church of Self-denunciation, I used to call it, this business of saying I'm a shit and I turn myself over to a higher power, LNU, who'll keep me safe from John Barleycorn, the divil. I welcomed the support and got all warm and runny about a number of the people who showed up each week and held my hand, and I hope that they're still going and still safe. But I'm too goddamned eccentric, and reluctant to contemplate the mystery of why, with my sister's death, I no longer felt the uncontrollable need to drink. Had I finally filled even my own bottomless cup of pain? Or was this,

as I often feared in my grimmest moments, some form of celebration?

Glyndora's little complex was across the street, gray on gray,
the colors almost indecipherable in the subdued elements of
winter, still looking like a stage set except for the sign in front,
announcing that units were available, from 179 grand. What was
her point last night? Was that whole thing, that interlude, just
for laughs? I didn't think Glyndora enjoyed that kind of subtlety.
She told you off face-to-face. But for some reason she had wanted
me out of there. Was she afraid I would catch on to something?
A boyfriend, maybe? Somebody's clothes were in the closet,
shoes by the door. Archie's? Or Bert's?

I straightened myself up. I had a pretty good yuk thinking
about Lyle getting in here with his buddies south of midnight
and taking a whiff. I'd bet a lot of money he wouldn't know who
to blame. He'd sit here trying to recall who'd hurled night before
last. The little bastard had left worse for me. Still, I opened all
the windows and threw the floor mat on the street. I shoved the
radio back into the fragile plastic membrane of the dashboard.
I thought about that little thief running all over the North End
in the cold, searching for a hose. He'd smell like something
when he got to school. Yep, I was feeling mean and humorous.
I gathered myself together and slid across the seat behind the
wheel, and only then noticed the absence against my hip. I began
to swear.

The goddamn kid had got my wallet.

XI. EVERYTHING IS JAKE

A. Your Investigator Gets Interrupted

If Bert Kamin was dead, then who had the money?

This question struck me suddenly as I stood before a mirror at Dr. Goodbody's, where I'd come to clean up before heading on to the office. A shower and shave had not done much for my condition. I still had the shadowy look of some creep on a wanted poster and my headache made me recollect those cavemen who used to open vents in their skulls. I phoned Lucinda to say where I was, asking her to make the calls to cancel and replace my credit cards. Then I found a lonesome corner in the locker room to figure things out. Who had the money? Martin had said that the banker he talked to in Pico had hinted that the account where the checks went was Bert's. But that was hardly authoritative.

A refuge, even a phony one, is where you find it, and I was irritated when the attendant told me I had a call. One of the things I hate worst about the world of business at the end of the century is this instant-access crap: faxes and mobile phones and all those eager-beaver, happy delivery people from fucking Fed-

eral Excess. Competition in the big-bucks world has made privacy a thing of the past. I expected Martin, Mr. Impatience,
who likes to call you with his latest brilliant idea on a case from
some airplane at eleven o'clock at night as he's bounding off to
Bangladesh. But it wasn't him.

"Mack?" Jake Eiger spoke. "I'd like to see you ASAP."

"Sure. Let me get hold of Martin or Wash."

"Better the two of us," said Jake. "Why don't you come up
here? I want to give you heads-up on something. About our
situation." He cleared his throat in a vaguely meaningful way,
so I suspected at once what was coming. The powers-that-be at
TN had reviewed this fiasco—Bert and the money—and con-
cluded there was a certain large law firm they could do without.
Cancel the search party and pack your bags. I was going to get
to give my partners the news as a "leak."

It had been some time since Jake and I had sat down man-
to-man. They became uncomfortable meetings after my divorce
from his cousin—and Jake's decision to stop directing TN cases
to me. We never speak about either subject. The unmention-
able, in fact, is more or less the bedrock of our relationship.

As usual, a long story. Jake was not an especially good student;
I've always suspected he got into law school on his father's pull.
He's bright enough—downright wily at times—but he has trouble putting thoughts on paper. A whiz at multiple choice but
gridlock when he was writing essays. His own term was "cryp-
tophobic," but I think in today's lingo we'd say learning-disabled.

I had been at BAD about a year when Jake invited me to
lunch. I thought it was some kind of family obligation—one of
Nora's aunts hopping his keester about buy Mack a meal and
give him some advice, maybe he'll amount to something. But I
could tell he was uneasy. We were at some snazzy rooftop place
and Jake squinted in the sun. The wind flapped the fringe of
the umbrella overhead.

'Nice view,' he said.

We both were drinking. He was unhappy too. Jake's hand-someness has always had room only for boyish easiness. The worry was like a painted sign.

'So,' I asked, 'what?' There had to be something. We did not have a real social relationship.

'Bar exam,' he said.

I didn't understand at first. I thought it was one of those clever, stylish remarks he made that was beyond me, rich-kid talk. He was just starting his third year at G&G, Wash's favorite flunky, three years out of law school, with one year spent clerking for a judge, and the bar ordinarily would have been long behind him. I ordered lunch. You could see Trappers Park from there and we talked awhile about the team.

'I should get out there,' Jake said. 'Haven't had much chance.'

'Busy? Lots of deals.'

'Bar exam,' he said again. 'I just took it for the third time.' And he looked from the distance to me, the level sincere ago-nized way he probably took in the ladies he wanted to lay. I did not need a guidebook to know I was being compromised.

'Three strikes and you're out,' he said. Three failures and you had to wait five years to take the test again. I knew the rules. I was one of the guys who made them. 'The firm has to fire me,' he said. 'My old man'll die. Die.' His career as a lawyer would, practically speaking, be over, but no doubt for Jake his father would be the worst part.

While I was growing up, Jake's dad was a colleague of Toots's in the City Council and a considerable figure. Invested with the medieval powers typically exerted by a councilman in DuSable, Eiger *père* lived in our close-knit Catholic village like a prince among the folk. June 18, 1964, the day I turned twenty-one, my father took me to Councilman Eiger to ask him to find me a place on the police force. I'd had a couple of years of college by then and was sort of supporting myself selling vacuum clean-ers door-to-door; I had bombed out around the art department and was a kind of bookstore beatnik, your average troubled youth, an Irish lad still at home with his ma, absolutely mystified about which way to go in life. The Force at least would get me off ground zero and keep me out of the service too, not something I said out loud to anybody, and no left-wing politics involved either, just a pit stop on the life track I didn't want to make, never one to enjoy taking orders from anybody. Three years later I wrecked my knee and had a free shot at law school, no draft, no Nam to trouble me, and went, mostly to be in school again, another of those funny accidental ways things just happen in a life.

Sitting there in the ward office, which looked like a basement rec room decorated with maps and political posters from past campaigns and four of those clunky old-style telephones, big and black and heavy enough to be murder weapons, absorbing most of the space on his desk, Councilman Eiger assured me that my police application would get every consideration. You had to love him, a man so richly endowed with power and so generous about its use. He was the kind of pol you could understand, whose lines of loyalty were long inscribed and well known: first himself, then his family, then his friends. He was not against law or principle. They were just not operative elements. I was a cadet in a previously selected entering class at the Academy within three weeks. Now his son was sitting in front of me, and even though Jake denied his father was aware of anything, the message was the same. I owed. I owed the family. You knew his old man would see it just that way.

I made my one and only stab at rectitude.

'Jake, I think we ought to talk about something else.'

'Sure.' He looked into his drink. 'I took the test last week. There was a question—I fouled up so badly—a civil-procedure question, you know, revising a divorce decree, and I wrote this ream about matrimonial law.' He shook his head. Poor old handsome Jake was about to cry. And then he did. A grown man almost, sobbing like a kid into his gin and tonic. 'Hey, you know, I'm sorry.' He straightened himself up. We ate in absolute silence for about ten minutes, then he said he was sorry again and walked away from the table.

One of the peculiar things you learn in life is that what makes Great Institutions great is the stuff people attach to them, not their actual operation, which is often purely prosaic. The scoring of the bar exam was like that. We sent the bluebooks out to ten graders around the state, one for each question. The booklets came back UPS, thousands of stacks, piled up no more ceremoniously than rubbish. The secretaries sorted them for days, then added each individual's totals, and the staff attorneys checked the arithmetic. Those were the results. Seventy passed, 69 failed. Jake was at 66 when I found his stack on another assistant administrator's desk the night I decided to go hunting for it. The guy who graded Jake's civil-procedure answer had given Jake three out of a possible ten. A 3 and an 8 of course can look a lot alike, even if you don't have a gift for forgery. I wasn't taking any risk; no one would ever know. Not counting me, of course.

Still, you wonder, why'd I do it? Not because of Jake, God knows, not even because my old man and my ma'd have been ashamed to think I wouldn't look after a friend. No, I suppose I was thinking of Woodhull and his minion, who confused ethics with ego, those judgmental prigs, my colleagues, one more team I didn't want to play on, one more group I would not allow to claim my soul. Same reason I did it to Pigeyes, then lied, unwilling to play for either side.

Jake took me out to lunch the week after the results were mailed. He was pleased as a puppy. He slobbered all over me and I wouldn't say a thing. I congratulated him when he told me that he passed. I shook his hand.

'You think I'm going to forget this, but I won't,' he said.

'*No comprendo.* Thank yourself. You took the test.'

'Don't give me that bull.'

'Hey, Jake. Practice makes perfect. You passed. Okay? Give us both a break.'

'You're all right. You know, after my performance last time —I got sick. I thought to myself, A cop, for Chrissake. You talk like that to a guy who was a *cop*.'

His look said everything. Us pals. Us guys. That smug fraternity thing Jake over the years has never lost. His life now is country-club golf courses and screwing around behind the back of his third wife, but there, twenty-one years before, I could see I'd restored the central faith of his life: we were special people who could outwit harm if we stuck with each other. I wanted to spit in his eye.

'Forget it, Jake,' I said. 'Everything.'

'Never,' he answered.

And I knew it was a curse.

B. Your Investigator Visits Herbert Hoover's America

Waiting for Jake, I sat in reception on 44, TN's Executive Level, feeling inferior. There is a jazzed-up air of self-importance here that routinely deflates me. Someday someone will explain to me why this system of ours that is supposed to glorify diversity and individual choice becomes instead the vehicle by which everybody ends up choosing the same thing. With its airlines, banks, and hotels, TN did business last year with two out of every three Americans who make more than 50 g's. Many of those folks think of TN as nothing better than a kind of flying bus, but in a mass society it turns out that even a trivial connection to twenty-five million lives, especially prominent ones, imbues an institution with an extraordinary aura of grandiosity and power.

Jake's secretary steered me back and His Handsomeness rose to make me welcome. The office is so vast that when I walked in he actually waved. Once we were alone, Jake sat on the corner of his desk, one foot on the rich carpet. You could not help thinking it was a pose he'd seen in some ad in a magazine. He had his jacket on. His hair was perfectly combed. To fill air time, Jake usually likes to talk to me about the old neighborhood, guys from high school, our place among the generations. But today he came to the point directly. As I'd feared, he had Bert on his mind.

"Look, old chum, I have to admit I'm playing catch-up. What in God's name is going on down there?"

"I wish I could tell you, Jake."

"And you," he went on. "You're not helping much. I understand you went to see Neucriss."

Word travels fast.

"He was on the phone to me before your elevator had reached the ground floor," said Jake, "wanting to know what was wrong. Can I ask what in the world you were doing?"

"Hey," I said amiably. I never offend Jake. I had all those years watching my old man kiss the fire captain's ring. "You know, I'm playing hunches. We can't figure what the hell Litiplex is. Maybe the plaintiffs know. I didn't realize that Martin had already tried the same thing with Peter."

Jake took that in levelly. He was assessing me.

"Yes, but he had. And when you showed up, you really began ringing bells. We can't have this kind of fumbling." Neucriss, on the phone, had obviously had a great time: These klutzes you employ at three hundred an hour. Get a load of this. Two of them busy forwarding the mail. Ho, ho, ho. Jake had felt the needle and I was paying the price.

"Look, Mack, my friend, let's review the bidding." Jake is a master of these phrases, the corporate idiom, one more style he is on top of. It softens the edges, but he's still as ham-fisted as his father and I knew him well enough to see that no matter how fashionably, he was about to be coarse. "He"—Jake pointed to the door of the chairman's adjoining suite; he had lowered his voice—"the Polish gentleman next door. He likes me, he doesn't like me. Who knows day to day? Let's assume he's not president of the fan club. All right? Let's say he thinks I use the wrong lawyers and I pay too much to the ones I choose. All assumed. But he's going to put up with me. Do you know why?"

"The board?"

"The board, that's right, the board. Because there is a faction there, a number of members who believe I fly without wings. And do you know why that is?"

"Why?"

"Because I—and the lawyers I chose—handled a $300 million disaster for this company, a litigation mess where we'd reserved $100 million to pay for our share and we—I, your firm, Martin—we handled that and actually *made money* for this company. Almost $20 million. Every dollar left in that trust account is a badge of pride. For all of us. And a point on the scoreboard. All right?"

I nodded. "Sure," I said. I had to sit still for this, tutored like a child, simpering and pretending he was inventing cold fusion.

"Now let's look at this supposed business with Bert. Very disturbing. Frankly, personally, I don't even believe it. If I did, I'd be more alarmed. But in the end, if we're patient about getting to the bottom of it, perhaps review the accounting, I think it may develop that something else is going on. But it appears as it appears— Fine, investigate. Look into it. That's the responsible thing to do. But, old man, let's keep our eye on the ball. If you go out and rile up the plaintiffs' lawyers so that they want a bean counting before we distribute next month—if you do that and fellows like Neucriss catch wind of the fact that we're running a surplus, they're going to do their utmost to lay hands on every dime. Not to mention our co-defendants. So no matter what you think has happened with Bert, all that would be far, far worse for us all. Okay? So let's move ahead carefully. I told you the other day. *Be discreet.*"

More or less on cue, Tad Krzysinski, Board Chairman and CEO, poked his head through the side door. In a perfect world, this guy would be somebody you could comfortably hate, a prig like Pagnucci, a wild fucking success drunk on ego. He is nothing like that. No more than five foot four, he is a sunny little fellow, and in every room he enters it feels as if somebody has suddenly installed a compact nuclear reactor, a force so vital you half expect to be blown back through the walls.

"Hack," he greeted me, and advanced to pump my hand. He is a musclebound former gymnast with an engaging eye. I took a moment to wonder, as usual, about what gave between Brushy and him, but he always seems so goddamn cheerful there is no way to tell.

"Tad," I said. The guy holds no brief for proprieties, never anything but who he's first to tell you he is, the son of a plumber, one of eight kids, now with nine of his own, a three-hours-of-sleep guy who by his own admission cares only about his family, his God, and increasing the wealth of the people who've put their faith in him by plunking down their dough to buy TN's common shares. You could see that just nodding and shaking hands he scared Jake to death. They were the two sides of ethnicity, the Americans, once excluded, who since the sixties have found their way in corporation land—Jake, a deracinated wimp who aspired to everything vain the upwardly mobile envisioned, and Krzysinski, who accepted like Holy Writ all that stuff the immigrants believed about hard work, fortitude, and the capacity to alter the face of the world. I stood there uneasily between them, with a sudden recognition that this was an impossible match. Jake had powerful boosters on TN's board, but Krzysinski had to hate him. Which was what Jake meant about the 397 surplus being his lifeline.

"Well, I see you here, Hack, we must be in trouble again." Tad pounded my shoulder good-naturedly and laughed at his own joke and then talked to Jake about a problem they had in Fiji. TN of course owns hotels everywhere. Tokyo. Paris. But they got to the Far East ahead of everybody else, which in these lean times means those operations have become particularly important. Many days Tad is far more concerned about Prime Minister Miyazawa than Bill Clinton. Somebody ought to sit down and think about this, because your corporate types are soon going to be a stateless superclass, people who live for deals and golf dates and care a lot more about where you got your MBA than the country you were raised in. It's the Middle Ages all over again, these little unaffiliated duchies and fiefdoms, flying their own flags and ready to take in any vassal who will pledge his life to the manor. Everybody busy patting himself on the back because the Reds went in the dumper is going to be wondering who won when Coca-Cola applies for a seat in the UN.

As Tad at last disappeared, Jake darted a nettled look at his back.

"Let's take a walk." Jake headed down the hallway and I followed, acknowledging the people I knew. For me, a visit up here called for a lot of glad-handing, trying to remind folks on the counsel's staff I was neither drunk nor dead. When we reached the elevator, a messenger, one of the members of that minimum-wage cavalry that slams through the Center City traffic on bikes, came charging out, wearing an optic-orange vest over his worn parka. Jake and I stepped in, now alone.

"I want to be sure we're singing from the same hymnal," said Jake. He jammed the button labeled "Doors Close" and turned to face me when they had.

"Bert?" I asked.

"That matter," he replied.

The elevator began to move and Jake pumped the button for the floor below.

"You know what I want—make this tidy," Jake said. "And if Kamin really doesn't turn up?"

"Yes?"

He took a step so that he was no more than a foot from me,

his finger still anchored on the door-close button as the car slowed.

"No one up here has to hear any more." He looked at me solemnly before the doors peeled back slowly and he stepped again into the brighter light.

XII. TELLING SECRETS

A. Boys and Girls Together

"SOS," I said as I poked my head into Martin's office. His secretary was gone and I'd given a quick knock and leaned in from the hall. Glyndora was standing there with him.

"Oh shit," I said. It just sort of popped out and they both stared. It was an odd little moment. Glyndora shot me a look that might have contemplated my death, and my first thought was that she was here complaining about my investigative technique. That was one of Martin's many roles, Mr. Fix-It, in charge of the disgruntled, the waylaid, the weak. Our first year can't cut in practice, a partner flips out or has a problem with substance abuse, Martin takes care of you. You'd say compassion, but there's no there-but-for-the-grace; it's more his Olympian thing. I'm here, the mountain.

But Martin seemed unconcerned when he saw me. He actually smiled and casually waved me into his office with all its funny overstated objects. He said something about Glyndora showing him yesterday's numbers on cash received, the Managing Partner and the head of Accounting measuring our progress at year end. Somehow, though, I remained struck by the pose in which

I'd initially found them. Nothing untoward: she was at a distance from him, a few feet from his chair. But she was on his side of the desk, and Martin was facing her and the milky light coming from the broad windows behind her, sitting with his legs outstretched, hands on his tummy, relaxed, open to her in an uncharacteristic way, less our Martin, ever on alert. Maybe, though, it was just the shock of seeing Glyndora, who was still charged up for me like a magnet.

Martin, at any rate, said they were about done, and with that hint she arranged herself and strode past me in the door without so much as turning my way. I admit I was disappointed.

"I just had a conversation with Jake," I told Martin when she was gone.

"Troubling?"

He could see it in my face, I imagined. My heart was still skittering around like a squirrel. Jake in his own way had given off quite a sinister air. I began to describe my encounter with Jake, and Martin listened, absorbed. When you actually study him, Martin has distinct ethnic looks; he's one of those hairy darklings you'd expect to see loading a truck, with a dense beard that lends his face a bluish cast. His father was a tailor who cut the clothes of various gangsters and Martin refers now and then to his upbringing when it is availing to charm a client of humble roots or to worry an opponent; he has a number of racy stories about delivering tuxedos to the famous Dover Street brothel in the South End. But unlike me, Martin takes no refuge in the past and allows it to make no claim upon him. He evinces the airy noblesse of a fellow who grew up summering in Newport. He is married to a graceful, tall British woman by the name of Nila, whom you sort of picture in a garden with a Pimm's Cup the minute you see her. Large hats and shirtwaist dresses, with petticoats. He is thoroughly the man he decided on being, and that fellow showed little reaction to what I related, except that something abruptly caused him to interrupt.

"Better save this," he said. "My colleagues and I should probably hear it together." He meant the Committee. "Carl is in
town again today."

Martin proposed a meeting at four and left me to arrange it.
I went back to Lucinda to ask her to make the calls, though I
tried to reach Pagnucci, since I wanted a word with him myself.
Then I stood over my secretary's desk for a moment, examining
the list of my credit card issuers she'd reached. It struck me for
the first time that the Kam Roberts card had been in my wallet
too. I had no idea what to do about that.

Brushy came ambling by in her sturdy fashion and did a
double-take when she saw me.

"Jesus, Mack, you look horrible." No doubt that was true.
Jake had stirred my adrenaline but it still felt like my heart was
pumping motor sludge. "You sick?" she asked.

"Maybe a touch of the flu." I turned away, but she followed
me into my office out of concern. "Could be I'm depressed."

"Depressed?"

"From our conversation yesterday."

"Hey," she said, "you know me, spirited Mediterranean type.
I say things."

"No," I said, "I thought you had a point."

She looked herself, little chopped-down hairdo, big pearl ear-
rings, honest face, solid and peppy like she could step out of
her heels and give you a good block.

"Maybe I did." She sort of smiled.

"Yeah," I said, "I even went out and had a minute last night
where I thought I might practice my hokey-pokey."

I could have filled in her dental chart.

"And?" she demanded.

" 'And' what?"

"And?" she said once more, Ms. Mind Your Own Personal
Business.

"And I ended up getting rolled."

She actually laughed out loud. She asked if I was okay, then sang, far off-key, a few bars of "Looking for Love in All the Wrong Places."

"You don't have to gloat."

"Why should I gloat?" she asked and laughed again.

I turned my back on her to look through the mail. More memos from the Committee about the lagging pace of collections; the Blue Sheet. I heard her close the door, and the click of the bolt gave me a weird little amorous thrill, some vagrant inspiration from our conversation and the last twenty-four hours, an idling recall of what happened when men and women were alone. Brushy, however, did not have anything like that on her mind.

"Did you see the paper?" she asked. Apparently there'd been another small piece this morning about Archie, basically just saying he still hadn't been found. She described it and asked, "Do you think that's the guy? The one they talked about at the steam bath?" She never missed a detail.

"I think," I said, and then, not quite understanding myself, added, as I thumbed through the mail, "he's dead, by the way."

"Who's dead?"

"Him. Archie. Vernon. Dead-dead."

"No," she said. "How do you know?"

So I told her. "Bert has a problem in his refrigerator that baking soda will not help." She took a seat on my worn-out sofa, threshing her fingers through her short hair as I described the corpse.

"How could you not tell me this?" she asked.

"Hey, get real. The better question is why I tell you anything at all. This one's attorney-client, no kidding. The coppers'll sweat me if they find out I was anywhere near that body."

"Did Bert kill him?"

"Maybe so."

"*Bert?*"

"Your idea," I said.

"Never."

"Probably not."

"So who?"

"Somebody else. Probably the heavy-cuff-link crowd."

"Those guys don't do that anymore, do they?"

"Don't ask me," I said, "you're Italian."

"Come on," she said. "I mean to regular people."

"This guy wasn't regular people, Brush. If you make book you've got to be connected."

"Why?" she asked.

" 'Why'? Because this is *their* business. Coast-to-coast. And these guys don't believe in competition. You keep a book, fine and dandy, but you give them a share—they call it paying the street tax. Otherwise you suffer physical harm or they snitch you out to their favorite law enforcement type. Besides, they provide many valuable services. You got a customer who's slow-pay, these guys can hurry em up, believe you me. You can't do business without them."

She stared. She still didn't see why.

"Here," I said, "it's like your insurance client. What's the name?"

She reminded me, a fair-sized outfit that sent her their coverage litigation in the Midwest. A significant piece of business, and even saying the name she had a hard time managing her pride.

"Let's say they have four billion in property and casualty coverage in California," I told her. "How do they make sure that they don't go under when the hills burn?"

"They reinsure."

"Exactly. They find a few large, reliable companies and literally insure their insurance. And bookies do the same thing. A good bookie isn't a gambler. Any more than your insurance client is. Bookie makes 10 percent vig on your bet, win or lose. You bet 100, you owe him 110. That's where his money is. On any given game, he wants you to bet the loser and me to bet the winner. He gets $110 from you, keeps $20 vig, and gives 90 to me."

Brushy interrupted.

"No chance, Malloy. He'd use *your* money to pay *me*."

"Very amusing." I faked a little pop to her biceps and went on. "Anytime his book puts him at risk, when he has a lot more win money than lose money or vice versa, he'll do like the insurance company. Lay off. Reinsure. Call it whatever. And in this business, you want to lay off, you better be part of the network. Otherwise no one's going near you. Besides, if you need Mr. Large and Reliable, the outfit who can always handle your action, it's them."

"So what did he do wrong? Archie?"

"Maybe he was screwing around with the street tax." Guys had gotten fixed for less than that. With his gimmick with the credit cards, Archie might have thought he didn't need them. But even an actuary using the Vegas line was going to have to lay off. What I could use was a little heart-to-heart with some-body connected. At that moment Toots crossed my mind.

Having run out of answers, I asked Brushy about lunch.

"I can't," she said. "Pagnucci's in town. I said I'd have lunch with him."

"Pagnucci?" This was not one of Brushy's known allies or liaisons, but remembering yesterday I bit my tongue. "What's doing?" I asked. "Groundhog Day?"

That was her guess. In our firm, a partner is guaranteed to make 75 percent of what he earned the twelve months before, drawing it out after each of the first three quarters of our fiscal year. Then on January 31 the Committee divvies up the re-mainder and announces the results on Groundhog Day. Every-body puts on a tuxedo and goes to the Club Belvedere for dinner. We are served in elegance and joke with each other. On the way out, we each receive an envelope listing our share of firm income. Nobody carpools to this event. Each partner returns home alone, full of the elevating light of success or in fitful depression. The carping begins the next day and often goes on most of the remaining year until the next Groundhog Day. Some people campaign with the Committee, listing all their good deeds and achievements, the many new clients, the great rate of collections. To minimize discord, Pagnucci, who does the first draft of the point distribution, makes the rounds of influential partners to be sure they can accept the Committee's view of their worth. At least, that's what I hear. Pagnucci has never made luncheon reservations with me. The only info I get generally is by gossip, before or after the event, since your share, like your private parts, is supposed to be known only to you. When I got my first cut three years ago, I was in enough of a snit that late one evening I took a peek in the drawer in Martin's credenza, where he stashes the point-distribution record. I just about opened a vein after seeing all the layabouts and losers making more money than me.

"How about if we do lunch tomorrow?" Brushy asked. "I'll get some place with tablecloths. I want to talk to you." She touched my knee. Her round face was warm with feeling. Emilia Bruccia is probably the only person I know who feels any concern for my spirit.

B. Police Secrets

After Brush left, I got on the phone and called McGrath Hall, headquarters of the Kindle County Unified Police Force. Twenty-two years, but I knew the number by heart. I reached Al Lagodis, who was now up in Records, and told him I was gonna swing by. I didn't give him a chance to say no, and even so, I could hear he was about as enthusiastic as if I'd told him I was selling raffle tickets for some charity.

The Hall is a big graystone heap the size of a castle on the south rim of Center City, just where the big buildings stop and the neighborhood turns littered and bleak, full of taverns with garish signs sporting mention of dancing girls, places where lushes and perverts, released from the big buildings at lunchtime, drink beside the hustlers. I was at the Hall in ten minutes. I had to check in at the front desk and they called Al to fetch me.

"How are you?" Al gave me both eyes, a look of dead sincerity, as he was walking me back.

"You know."

"That good?" He laughed. Al and I go back to the time when I was in Financial Crimes and he thought I did the right thing on Pigeyes. Not that Al did anything himself, except, I always suspected, a little confidential muttering to the FBI—deep background stuff, a cup of coffee and some hard information that he'd refer to as "rumors." I always figured it was Al who put the Feebies onto me. He was one of the few folks here who would still talk to me afterwards—although he preferred to do it when nobody was around. Two decades and old Al was still going all shifty-eyed, hoping nobody saw him with Mack Malloy, legendary no-good guy. Around here not much changes. There were gals now, stepping through the dim old halls, wearing guns and ties and shirts that to my eye were not really designed for folks with tits, but even they have got that cop-roll, do-me-something stride.

"Nice digs," I said. He had a cubicle, steel partitions painted police blue, that rippled plastic stuff for windows, and a door. No ceiling. Life where you keep your voice down and can literally touch each wall when you stretch. Al worked Financial fourteen years. When Pigeyes was transferred in, he transferred out— discretion and valor, you know how that is—and went to the Records Division, which anyway is a better end to the road. He is now one of those coppers whose hard-charging days are behind them, who've found their cul-de-sac on the police life map and can hide here till it's retirement time, pretty soon now for Al, come age fifty-five. The Hall is full of these types, guts like saddlebags and smoked-out voices. He works 8:00 to 4:30. He supervises the clerks and fills out forms. Nobody shoots at him, nobody kicks him in the ass. He has his memories to keep him warm and a wife to set him straight whenever he's had a brewski too many and begins that lamebrained talk about how nice it would be to get back on the street. A good sod, with features blown out by alcohol.

"Need you to check me out on a couple things," I told him.

"Shoot." I was seated right beside his little desk and he could reach out from there to shut the door, which he did.

"You worked Financial a lot longer than me. I've gotta get information from Pico Luan—i.d. on who controls a bank account."

Al shook his head. "No," he said, "forget it," then asked, trying to be casual, "Whatta we got here?"

I was dodgy. "I'm not completely sure. I'm real confused. Here, let me try this one on you. Guy tells me he had a conversation with the General Manager of a bank in Pico Luan, long-distance telephone, and the G.M. sort of gives him between the lines whose account it is. How's that sound to you?"

"Not like any of them I ever talked to. Not on the telephone. Those guys got a patter. Go over to the Embassy. See your diplomat with the palm oil. Fill out a form. Wait an eon. Then another one. They'll send you a beautiful document back, honest to Christ, you never saw so many seals and ribbons, you'd think it was the fuckin VFW on parade, but it's spit, they won't tell you momma's first name when it comes to whose money's really in the bank. You been down there. You know how it is."

I knew, but I hadn't thought twice on day one, when Martin told us about calling the bank, because, after all, it was Martin. Now suddenly I was wondering how I sat still for that. 'Like trying to grab hold of smoke.' Jesus, I thought.

"Once or twice," said Lagodis, "we were desperate, we hired some sickening creep called himself a lawyer who claimed he had inside connections at the banks. What a snake charmer this character was. Ninety-nine and forty-four one-hundredths per-cent stinko, if you ask me. You could give him a try. Me, I believe more in the guys who get up and walk at the tent meet-ings." Al shook his head again, but I told him I'd take the name.

Scraping his chair across the floor, he walked out into the clamor of the central Records area, computer terminals and files, a number of empty desks at the lunch hour. From where I sat, I saw a sole uniformed type eating a burger out of the wrapper and glancing over the *Tribune*. The Hall, the h.q., units like Records especially, remain a sort of central backwater where it's like everyone took Valium, you'd swear every thirty seconds took a real-world minute, but I felt sort of cheerful to breathe again this gloomy bureaucratic air, this stolid, police thing of being utterly invulnerable.

The sad truth is that being a copper won't ever quite leave me. I never was in a flatter moral landscape. Or happier, as a result. Cops see it all—the Scout leader who scouts out the little boys, the business guy who makes 300K and gets caught stealing more, the mother who's beat her baby black and blue and wails in agony when you come with Child Welfare to take the kid away. You see her reach out, kneel and plead, tears a river, you see the utter knotted-up violence of her own agony, you see that you are taking her whole universe, cockeyed or not, that every-thing was in this child, not only her wild pain but some squalid hope, if maybe she could just get the suffering out of herself into some realm where it was more tangible, it might be easier to control. You see it and wonder how can you understand if some of that's not in you? It's just that today you're on the right side, you're wearing blue.

" 'Joaquin Pindling.' " I was reading the card Al handed me. "Jesus, what kind of name is that?"

"He'll cost you a buck or two, I promise that. Course, maybe a guy like you," offered Lagodis, "lots of personality, you could go down there yourself and make new friends, get information on your own."

"Kind of friends who'll leave me lighter in the pockets?"

"Anything's possible. Then of course could be somebody don't feel as friendly as you do. Then you become a sort of firsthand big-time expert on Due Process in Pico Luan."

"Now that's a subject, I'll bet."

"Oh yes indeedy. I talked with a couple visiting scholars once. Prison conditions in Pico Luan, friend, not like the Regency on the Beach. They let you crap in this big hole in the middle of the cell, deep, deep, goes down who-knows-where-the-fuck. Nighttime the guards like to play hide-and-seek with the white guys. Watch where you step, mon. You lose, you find out where who-knows-where-the-fuck is."

"Got it."

Al waited a bit, seeing how it was. He was still on his feet. He was wearing a tie and, here in the dead of winter, a short-sleeve shirt a little snug over the beer gut. I told him I'd run into Pigeyes, but he'd already heard. This was the Force. That was yesterday's news.

"He let me go too," I said.

"Better be no next time. He'll tear off your head and shit down your neck. From what I hear, he skins his knees he still mentions you. I think what it is is his feelings got hurt."

"That must be it." I had some idea to ask if Al knew what Gino was investigating, in hopes of getting a little more info on Kam, but all in all, I'd probably pressed my luck already.

"Yeah," said Al, just filling in, hitching up his trousers, which dropped six inches every time he rocked on the balls of his feet. "You got a lot to watch out for," he told me.

That part wasn't news.

XIII. WHO SAYS LAWYERS

AREN'T TOUGH?

A. Toots's Walls

I was received in Toots's law offices with the air of ceremonial grandeur undoubtedly lavished on every guest. Stumbling along on his cane, his cigar extinguished but comfortably couched inside his jaw, he introduced me to each secretary and half his partners, the greatly renowned Mack Malloy, who was helping out the Colonel on that ethics thing. Then he showed me into his office and propounded a lengthy commentary on each memento on the walls.

Toots's office should have been moved intact to a museum somewhere, if not as a monument to twentieth-century political life then to one individual's capacity for self-appreciation. It was a virtual Colonel Toots Nuccio shrine. There were of course signed photos of the Colonel with every Democratic President from FDR forward, and two with Eisenhower, Toots in uniform in both. There were plaques from B'nai B'rith (Man of the Year), Little Sisters of the Poor, and the Kindle County Art Museum. There was a special award from the symphony, a clarinet cast in bronze; religious relics received from grateful clerics; and a lengthy salutatory letter from the Urban League, perhaps the only compliment Toots had received from people of color in the last thirty years, but which nonetheless had been framed. There was a gavel he'd been given from the City Council upon his retirement, his years of service engraved on the brass hand that circled the mallet head, and scores of photos of Toots with sports stars and political luminaries, some so long gone that their names had vanished from memory. At the absolute focus of attention, mounted immediately above his ponderous old desk, were his medals, aligned in a glass-doored case with a separate little high-intensity lamp that trained on Toots's silver star, which was pinned to black velvet. I spent the required instant marveling at it, wondering as I always would if it had been awarded for real bravery or as part of one of Toots's inevitable deals. Within these walls, one tended to realize that self-congratulation, the collection of banners and ribbons, was far more real to Toots, far more important than the events they were intended to commemorate.

"So," he said, finally seated, "I didn't figure you made house calls."

"Occasionally. There's something I want to talk to you about."

"This here hearing?"

I told him it was something else and hiked my chair a little closer.

"Toots. Can a fella ask a question? Between friends?"

He gave me the usual fulsome stuff, for me anything. I replied in kind, saying he was the only person in the tri-counties I knew who might be able to answer this. He smiled, deeply pleased by any compliment, without regard to its sincerity.

"I wondered if you might have heard something around town. There's an insurance guy, an actuary, who the papers say is missing. Vernon Koechell. They call him Archie. What I have to find out is if you know any reason for somebody to pop him."

Toots laughed quite merrily, as if I had made a saucy remark just within the borders of good taste. The shrunken old face showed not a sign of even vague offense, but I noticed that he

had drawn back on his walking stick and within the milky elderly
eyes was perhaps lodged a trace of something lethal.

"Mack, my friend, can I make a little suggestion?"

"Sure."

"Ask another question."

I stopped on that.

"See, Mack, I got a rule for life. Always followed it since I
didn't even have hair on my chin. I known you a long time now.
You're a smart fella. But let me share my thinking with you:
Don't talk about other people's business. It's their business and
it's for them to worry about."

I received this advice solemnly. Looking at me, Toots winked.

"I hear you, Colonel, but I've got a real problem."

"Whatsa matter? He rate you on your policy or what?"

"Here's how it is, Colonel. I have a partner missing, a guy
named Kamin. Bert Kamin. Where he's gone, I haven't the
foggiest. But this guy Archie, he's got a white shirt on and a
nice tie, but he's keeping a book. And my guy Kamin's laying
bets with him. At least that's the way it looks." I peeked up at
Toots. I had his attention.

"Anyway, Archie, he's quite dead. That's a fact. Something I
know. And pretty soon, any minute now, the coppers are going
to show up to talk to me about that. And I'm frankly not inter-
ested in getting myself in Dutch with the wrong folks. So that's
why I ask. I gotta know what's doing here, because I may have
to do some fancy steppin'." I tried to look hangdog and sincere,
reverencing one of the many powers that dominated Toots's life.
He wasn't really buying it.

"You a straight shooter, Mack?"

"As much as the next guy."

Toots laughed. He liked that. He removed the cigar and in
the gloomy light of the room considered the mangled end. It
looked like a hunk of seaweed pulled up on a line.

"You understand with bookies," he said.

"Not everything."

"See this here— Guy makes a book, you know, he's got to lay off, right?"

"Like insurance companies. He doesn't absorb all the risk. I understand that much."

"This guy, he had some very good luck. Somehow he always had laid off his losing action."

I waited.

"How could he lay off only losing bets? Doesn't he lay off beforehand? I mean, before the event. The race, the game, whatever?"

"That he does," said Toots.

I was on very delicate ground. Toots worked lovingly on his cigar.

"You mean he knew how these events were going to come out? Is that what you're saying? He knew these games were fixed?"

"You see," said Toots, "you share risks, you share no-risks. *Capisc'*? A fella's gotta look out for his friends. Otherwise he don't got friends, he got enemies. Right? That's how life is, right?"

"That's how it seems to be, Toots. There are no victims."

Toots liked that one. No need to explain it to him.

"So you see," he said, "you asked a question, you asked another question, you told me some things, I told you some things, we had a talk. Okay? Somebody asks, some things you know, some things you don't know. Right?"

"Right."

"Sure," said Toots. He gave a quick, smug, frightening little laugh. "So. We gonna win this hearing?"

"I wish I could tell you yes, Colonel. The hill's pretty steep."

He shrugged, here in his element capable of seeming worldly-wise, ripened by life.

"Give it your best. I ain't gonna get the death penalty, right?"

We agreed on that.

"And who's there, you or the skirt?"

"The skirt's good," I told him.

"They say," said Toots. "So they say. Bit of a punchboard, I hear." I'd known he would check her out.

"Woman of the world," I answered.

"A big world," he said.

"I'll try to be there, Colonel. I have to worry about this too. Archie. Bert."

He understood. Sometimes a fella got himself into a spot. He walked me to the door.

"Remember my rule." He pointed with the cigar. Don't talk about other people's business. I had it firmly in mind.

B. Accounting Secrets

On the way back into the Needle, the elevator stopped at 32. No one got on, but I felt destiny beckoning and I jumped off and trod the hall to Accounting. When I came through the door, the unit manager, Ms. Glyndora Gaines, was sitting right there.

I took a seat beside her. Her desk was completely clean, windswept but for one file she was examining, a state of order which added to the usual impression of a dominant, unremitting soul. Glyndora continued to look over the file, determined not even to acknowledge me. Maybe there was a trace, a vapor, of a smile being willed to oblivion.

"Glyndora," I said quietly, "just as a matter of curiosity, not saying I'm gonna do it, but you know, what if. What if I go tell the Committee the way you've been screwing me around? What if I act like I'm one of your bosses, instead of a chump?"

I was trying to sound sort of reasonable, maybe not pleasant, but calm. In the big room out the door, a dozen people were whizzing around, overwhelmed by the year-end rush, adding machines chugging out tape and phones giving their little electronic chirp. Checks were at a number of desks in colorful stacks.

"You gone talk to the Committee? Then tell them this." She

rose up in her chair as she took a surveying glance toward the doorway. "Tell them you come to my apartment, you pounded on the buzzer causing all kind of commotion, talking all kinds of jive about Bert, and when I let you in, man, there wasn't barely one little word about Bert. The next thing, dude's got one hand on my titty and the other on my ass, and the only way I got rid of his rasty old self is cause this boy talkin all that AA shit went out to buy something to drink. Tell that to the Committee."

She smiled in her way, tight like she was fastening down a bolt or a screw, and sized up the effect all this had. With Glyndora everything is a contest and she knew she had me beat. My side of the story was going to sound weak. Worse than that, ridiculous. Nobody would believe I was just posing with my hand on her breast. And if they knew I had been drinking again, my time as Deadeye Dick, Private Detective, would probably be over, not to mention my employment.

"Glyndora, you know exactly what's going on here."

She leaned forward against her arms, making her frontal equipment prominent in a blouse of orange flourishes. A layer of purple shadow lay thickly on her lids like pollen.

"Here's what I know, Mack. You are weak, sucker." She was leering again, amused by the thought that she knew my secrets. But I'd been there too and learned some of hers. I pointed.

"And you like white guys." I let that out and nodded myself, maybe imitating her. Even so, I regretted it. She stiffened; she reared back. We were headed where we always headed—me beats you, hah hah. One more contest. The Dozens, some kind of phony signifying. It was nothing I wanted, and I did what seemed under the circumstances somewhat daring and reached out to grab one of her hands. The touch, my big pink hand on her brown one, was shocking to us both. And that was the point.

"Hey," I said, "you know, I'm like you, I work here. I'm not trying to be your lord and master. Have I ever done that? Call me callous, I'm crude, et cetera, et cetera. But have I ever gone out of my way to do some kind of job on you? These guys tell me 'Find Bert' and I wanna find him. I'll tell you the truth— it's something I *need* to do. So just give me a break, okay? Be a person." In the bleakness of the tone I'd assumed, I suddenly heard a confession to myself. All along, I'd talked about this whole escapade, tracking down Bert, as a boondoggling effort at life reform. But that was kidding around, teasing myself with fantasies of running away with the money or earning my partners' esteem. Yet somehow I'd staked a lot more on this venture than I had admitted. Maybe my life was on its last legs. Maybe my chances were few. But I saw now that I'd promised myself that I was not coming out of this funhouse the way I'd gone in. Somebody within me believed that and was connected to what even in this meager, glimmering form you'd have to call hope.

And in admitting that, I was doing to Glyndora the one thing she tried to warn everyone against—being vulnerable, hanging it out for her to tromp on. She stared, disbelieving, insulted, and not altogether happy with the physical approach. She withdrew her hand from mine and slid her chair back so she could view me from a more distant perspective as we continued sizing each other up. Glyndora has her routine, the Hey-I'm-a-tough-black-bitch number, and she does it on autopilot, a piece of racial rhetoric that's as much mask and cipher as Steppin Fetchit onstage. Oh, I know she means it. I know she's tough. Like Groucho, who would not want to be a member of any club he could join, Glyndora wants to be the first one to reject you. Mission accomplished. But swimming through her eyes on occasion is some misgiving, a recognition that she's someone else. I don't know if she gets caught up in crackpot fantasies about how she is being poisoned by aluminum pots or whether she is a secret reader of the Koran. But there is more to her than she lets on. And that's the final insult she hurls at most of us. That she'll never let us in. Yet Glyndora has her secret place. He says with confidence, a denizen of his own secret places. Somebody who'd been there briefly with her the evening before and was knocking on the door again now.

"I *need* to find Bert," I repeated.

Finally she leaned toward me and spoke in a softer tone, maybe an appeal of its own.

"No, you don't, Mack. You just gotta tell them you looked." That was a message. Glyndora was playing the role of medium, of oracle, but even so, I wasn't sure if I was being beseeched or warned.

"You have to give me more, Glyn. I'm clueless. Who are you fronting for? I mean, at least tell me about the memo."

Her posture became rigid again, her face hard. It was like watching a book slam closed.

"You're asking too much, man." It wasn't clear if the excess was on her end or mine, if I wanted information I wasn't entitled to or if it came at a cost she wasn't willing to pay. But the answer, whatever, was no. She stood up and walked past me. She was running for cover. I thought about what I ought to do. I could demand her keys and toss her office. I could hire a service and get thirty temps to tear through the files. But I'd just made a deal. Without turning, I spoke before Glyndora could get far.

"One thing," I said. Her heels stopped clacking, so I knew she was hanging there by the threshold. "I never put my hand, not once, on your behind."

When I looked back, she was smiling a little, something like that. I'd gotten that much. But she wouldn't give any actual ground.

"Says you," she told me.

C. The Devil Himself

"It's a pact with the devil." Thus spake Pagnucci as Carl, Wash, Martin, and I sat in the same paneled conference room where we had encountered each other at the start of the week. There was a moment of rare winter sun, a part of the circle escaped from the clouds like something hanging out of a pocket. The heavy drapes had been permanently sashed by the decorator and the long walnut table was bright with the glimmer of the late light, thick as caramel. I had found the three of them waiting for me and quickly reviewed my conversation with Jake Eiger that morning. I skipped Bert's memo and my trip to Neucriss. Glyndora had made me shy of both subjects, and I wasn't eager to take on Martin, whose motives remained perplexing to me. He and Carl gravely received the message I'd brought, but Wash was slower on the uptake.

"He's telling us that if we can't put this crime right, it will go unreported," Martin said to him. "Jake is concerned about Jake. He can't go to his Chairman, to Krzysinski, with this without endangering his own position. After all, who put Bert in charge of the 397 escrow in the first place? He wants us to keep our mouths shut."

"Ah," said Wash, who did a poor job of hiding the fact that he was quite pleased. "And where do we end up with Jake?"

"In bed, I would say," said Martin. "Holding dirty hands. He can't very well cut us off, can he? He's our hostage."

"And we're his," said Pagnucci, invoking by his remark a pointed silence.

"But," said Wash, continuing to muddle it through, "we've reported the matter to the client. We've done our duty. If he chooses not to do his—" The back of his elegant white hand traveled off to the land of moral oblivion. Wash was already sold. A tidy solution. Five million gone and a secret forever.

"Jake says he doesn't believe it, actually," I offered. "He says that he's hoping that an accounting will prove it's not true."

"That's horseshit," said Pagnucci. "He's posturing. We know the client isn't really informed. If we go along with this, it's the same thing as having said nothing at all."

With the only difference of course that there was a far lower

risk of detection. Auditing of the escrow account from which the
money had disappeared was under Jake's direction and control.
He'd cover us in order to cover himself. That was the meaning,
I realized now, of that remark he'd made to me this morning
about an accounting.

We were silent again, all four of us. Throughout this session,
my attention remained on Martin. Wash had already set
his course down the path of least resistance, and for Carl the
problem-solving method was equally apparent, a question of
benefits and costs. In his head, the pluses and minuses were
already totaling. But Martin's calculations, in line with his character, figured to be more complex. Like an Aristotelian figure,
his eyes were raised to heaven in the course of higher contemplation. Martin is your veritable Person of Values, a lawyer who
does not see the law as just business or sport. He's on one million
do-good committees. He's against the Bomb, the death penalty,
and damage to the environment, for abortion, literacy, and better housing for the poor. He's been the chairman for years of
the Riverside Commission, which is devoted to making the river
clean enough to drink or swim in, goals that frankly will not be
achieved until long after we have colonized Mars, but he'll still
take you for a walk along the tangled, littered banks, soft with
prairie grasses, and describe out loud the bike paths and boat
piers he sees in his head.

Like any Person of Values who is a lawyer, Martin is not in
it for goodness alone. These activities make him prominent, help
him attract clients. Most of all, they invest him with the same
thing that knowledge of the law imparts to us all: a sense of
power. Martin gets off with his hand on the throttle. When he
talks about the $400 million public offering we did for TN two
years ago, his eyes glow like a cat's in the dark. When he says,
'Public company,' he says it the way the priest passing out wafers
says, 'The body of Christ.' Martin has a grasp of the way business
runs America and he wants to help be in charge.

Yet it's not just the sense of being important by attachment that excites him. It's also what his clients want to know: right or wrong, allowable or no. He's the navigator, the person with the compass, the man who tells the high and mighty, if not about morals, then at least about principles and rules. His clients can go out in the vineyard and get their boots covered in muck. He's back in the office, charting their course by the stars. When Martin goes to sleep at night and asks God's blessing, he tells the Lord that he helped his clients move with grace and speed through the difficult and ambiguous world He has made for us. Though perhaps not even Martin can tease out the logic, he believes that he is engaged in an enterprise that is fundamentally good.

Listening to this, I'm sure you're humming "The Battle Hymn of the Republic" and marching in place. All right. I'm just trying to tell you how it is. But don't sneer. It's easy to be a poet sitting behind the gates of a university or a monk in a monastery and feel there is a life of the spirit to which you are dedicated. But come into the teeming city, with so many souls screaming, I want, I need, where most social planning amounts to figuring out how to keep them all at bay—come and try to imagine the ways that vast unruly community can be kept in touch with the deeper aspirations of humankind for the overall improvement of the species, the good of the many and the rights of the few. That I always figured was the task of the law, and it makes high-energy physics look like a game show.

Wash finally interrupted this extended silence by posing the question that no one had been willing to ask: "How would anybody ever find out?"

Martin actually smiled and without saying more looked to each of us, ducking his chin in a brief, suggestive way. The gesture by itself, his mere acknowledgment of what was held within the room, was vaguely shocking. The next step would be to dip a pen in blood.

"Where would you say Bert went?" I asked. "There are three hundred people here asking already."

"Say that, so far as we know, he's in Pico Luan," answered Pagnucci. "Retired from the practice. That'll pass the red-face test. Forward his mail to the bank there. None of that is what bothers me."

"Retired?" I asked. "Just like that? He's forty-one years old."

"There is not a soul who knows Bert Kamin well who wouldn't believe him capable of something so impulsive," said Wash, waving his pipe around. He had a point. Bert had done stranger things half a dozen times in the last five years. "This is doable," said Wash, "quite feasible. And as to your concerns, Carl, about Jake ignoring our report—" Wash filled the pipe bowl with fire from his lighter. "I personally do not believe Jake Eiger would lie." It was something of a non sequitur but we all saw what Wash was up to. If it ever proved that the secret had not held, we could say that we had placed our faith in Jake—to be honest, reverent, and true, to protect the best interests of TN, to tell what-all must be told. The silence upstairs we took to reflect TN's desire to save face and to protect the settlement fund from raiding by the plaintiffs' lawyers. We would express shock about Jake. In the face of calamity, Wash, who had placed Jake at TN like a spore years ago, would trot out his protégé for drowning.

But Martin saw through Wash instantly.

"If we go that route," said Martin, the man I love, a fellow who could make Keats think twice about whether beauty is truth and vice versa, "and the day comes that we have to explain, we'll all lie. You'll hear four different versions of what went on in this room." His look panned each of us and settled on me.

"Lest I repeat myself," he said now, "I hope you find Bert."

D. The Head of Finance

Pagnucci said, "That was troubling," as we headed toward my office after the meeting, strolling down the book-lined corridor. Martin and the decorators have decided that it is the right touch to fill the halls with the gold-spined federal and state reporters, though it's hell on the associates, who never know where to find the volumes they need.

Carl was in town from D.C. for the second time this week. Eager to please TN, and to minimize their dealings with other large firms, we had opened the Washington office fifteen years ago to handle matters before the FAA and CAB. When airline regulation went the way of white tennis balls, we had about thirty lawyers with nothing to do. Enter Pagnucci, a former Supreme Court law clerk to Justice Rehnquist, with six million dollars in annual billings, thanks to Ronald Reagan, who in 1982 made Carl the youngest member ever of the Securities Exchange Commission.

The saying about law firms is that there are finders, minders, and grinders, referring first to people like Carl and Martin and Brushy who find big-time, big-money clients to employ them, then the service partners, guys like me, who make sure that skilled work is carried out by supervising the third group, the young toilers laboring in the library amid the ghosts of dead trees. The sad fact is that there are far fewer finders than minders and the finders increasingly demand more of the pie. Carl left his former firm because they were not contemporary enough, meaning they did not pay him what he thought he was worth, and his very presence among us on those terms means we have to make sure the same thing does not happen here. There are only so many ways to do it. Maybe you can get the associates to stay another quarter hour past midnight, or pile on charges for ludicrous extras—fifty cents a page for running sensitive documents through our shredder—but in the end the best way for the top guys to stay ahead is if they have fewer people to share with, fire a few minders and give Carl their points. Lots of people around G&G claimed we'd never do it, but the pressure's there, and Carl, who heads the subcommittee on firm finances, has never expressed the same resolve. No doubt he thought that's what I wanted now—to lobby him about next year's pay—and as soon as my door was closed he raised another subject.

"So what's the latest from the Missing Persons Unit?"

"Gaining a little ground," I said. "Still no sight of our man."

"Hmm," said Pagnucci. He allowed himself a bit of a frown.

"I had a request to make to you as head of finance."

He nodded. No words. He was steeling himself. Unconsciously he raised a hand to his head. There's a bald spot the size of an orange at the back of his head and you can tell from the way he's always fussing that it drives him nuts—the imperfection, the lack of control, the fact that he is as subject as anyone else to the whims of fate.

"Suppose I told you I want to take a trip to Pico Luan?"

Carl deliberated. Even crossed up, he was disinclined to quickly agree.

"You didn't think that was such a clever idea earlier this week."

"It's the only lead I have left."

Carl nodded. He'd been right from the start; he could accept that. For my own part, I felt too much vestigial loyalty to tell him there was something squirrelly about Martin's account of his phone call to the International Bank of Finance.

"There's a lawyer down there I'd like to retain. Subject to your approval." I handed him the card I'd gotten from Lagodis. "The guy's supposed to do black magic getting stuff out of the banks."

Pagnucci made a sound but otherwise failed to react. Off-camera, Pagnucci has quite a life, this trim little guy with a stiff little mustache cuts some figure. He's on wife number four—each of them blondes, drop-dead gorgeous, who are getting progressively taller as his marriages wear on—and he runs himself to work in one modified Formula One car or another, Shelbys and Lotuses, all kinds of hot stuff. At some point, maybe all day, his fantasy life must be running wild, John Wayne movies probably, banal stuff like that. But in the office, none of it shows. Not a muscle twitches. He did not seem to have any more to say now. He touched the corner of his mustache with a lacquered fingernail.

"I was going to charge the trip to the recruiting budget, frankly," I said. "I'll probably take someone with me to witness any interviews. But I wanted you to know so there's no squawk when the bills come through."

"Have you talked to Martin or Wash about this?"

"I'd rather not." I was telling Carl a good deal now and he absorbed it like all else in silence. I was taking a chance. But Carl by his nature liked keeping things to himself. And I couldn't see him vetoing his own idea.

"You're turning out to be a much more complicated fellow than I imagined," said Pagnucci. I tipped my head slightly. I thought it might be a compliment. Before he opened my door, Carl said, "Keep me in the loop," then drifted off, smug and unruffled, leaving behind his usual aura: every soul for itself.

Rational self-interest is Carl's creed. He worships at the altar of the free market. The same way Freud thought everything was sex, Pagnucci believes all social interaction, no matter how complex, can be adjusted by finding a way to put a price on it. Urban housing. Education. We need competition and profit motive to make it all work. It is, I know, quite a theory. Let everybody struggle to get their bucket in the stream and then do what they like with the water they fish out. Some will make steam, some will take a drink, a few fellows or ladies will decide to take a bath. Entrepreneurship will flourish; people will be happy; we'll get all this nifty indispensable stuff like balsamic vinegar and menthol cigarettes. But what kind of ethical social system takes as its fundamental precepts the words "I" "me" and "mine"? Our two-year-olds start like that and we spend the next twenty years trying to teach them there's more than that to life.

I stayed down for the evening, cleaning up what I'd ignored while running all over town the last couple of days. Memos and letters. I returned all my calls. I hadn't eaten much. I was tired, my eyes and bones felt acid-etched from the hangover. Now and

then I closed my eyes and thought I could still catch far back in
my throat the fierce taste of rye, which I savored.

Eventually I picked up the Dictaphone. The city out the window at this hour has a sort of painted stillness, all black forms
and random lights: a woodcut pattern—gray on indigo and jet.
A lone car races up the ridges of the superhighway. I am one
more life in hiding amid the occasional heaving and cranking of
a big building in the darkness, talking to myself. A single coast
guard icebreaker's mast light bucks along the river.

It seems increasingly obvious, even to me, that I'll never show
a word of this to anyone on the Committee. Ignoring the insults,
which I could cross out, I've lied to or hidden things from each
of them half a dozen times. And for you, sweet Elaine, a Dictaphone or some typing won't really make our communication
improve. So we all wonder: who am I talking to?

In my mind's eye, there are faces. Don't ask me whose. But
I see some reasoning and sensate being who will get hold of this
thing, some someone of largely indecipherable characteristics
who I nonetheless find myself addressing now and then. You.
The universal You. U You, in my mind. Gender, age, and dis-
position unknown. Experience unimagined. A somebody floating
like dust in the outer reaches of the cosmos. But still—I think,
bud, this is for you.

Of course, I try to imagine reactions. You could be a copper,
or a Bureau agent, with a soul rough as sandpaper, who locks
this up at night to make sure your wife does not get ruffled by
the bad words, while you, when you're alone, rifle the pages
looking for another passage about my hand on my crank. Maybe
you're some fifty-year-old Irishman who thinks I don't sound a
bit like you do. Or a kid who says this is boring. Or a professor
who concludes it is generally vile.

Whoever, I want something from You. Not admiration, God
knows, I don't feel much for myself. What more can I call it but
connection? Comprehend. Let that mighty magic lightning flow
across the gaps of space and time. From me. To you. And back.

The way the bolts explode from sky to earth and then bounce again into the heavens and the universe beyond. Going on forever, to the regions where the physicists tell us matter equals time. While in one spot on this single humble planet, a tree is split, a rooftop smokes, a human being sits awake and startled by the miracle of energy and light.

T A P E 4

Dictated January 30, 1:00 a.m.

XIV. YOU GUYS

A. The Murder Suspect

Friday a.m. I was heading in through the revolving doors of the Needle when a young guy stopped me, pockmarked skin and a slick-backed do and a fancy jacket made from the skin of some creature with a two-chambered heart. Familiar from someplace, like an actor you've seen on TV.

"Mr. Malloy?" He flipped his tin at me, and naturally I recognized him then, Pigeyes's wormy companion, Dewey.

"You guys," I said.

"Gino'd like a word with you." I looked in all directions. I didn't believe I could get within one hundred yards of Pigeyes without picking up some sensation of him, like a missile detector homing on infrared. Dewey was indicating the curb where I saw only a rusted conversion van.

I asked what would happen if I said no.

"Hey, fella, you do what you wanna do. Me, I wouldn't fuck with him. You're in a lotta deep doo-doo." Pigeyes was in a mood, Dewey was saying. There was a vaguely plaintive quality to his address. Life forges all kinds of fraternities and Dewey and I were in one of its strangest: partners of Pigeyes. There were only so many people on earth who could understand his plight, and dogmeat or not, I was still one of them. We looked at each other a moment as the Center City crowd scurried past, and then I followed him to the curb and the van, which looked like a weary delivery truck bearing sclerotic rust marks on its rocker panels and six of those grayed-over bubble-type portholes, two in the back and two on each side.

When Dewey opened the rear doors, Pigeyes was inside, along with a black guy, another copper. It was a surveillance van. No way to be sure how long they'd been watching me; long enough to know I wasn't upstairs. They could have followed me from home or, more likely, called Lucinda and learned that I hadn't arrived. There were video cams mounted on swivels over each of the portholes and two rows of recording equipment in small wooden consoles behind the driver's seat. The entire interior had been carpeted in a mangy gray shag, which had matted and worn away on the floor and was marked here and there with cigarette burns. Guys spent long nights in here, begging each other not to fart, watching whoever they watched, dopers or Mafia dons or nuts who'd said they wanted to kill a senator. There were cup holders fixed to the walls and carpeted benches over the wheel wells. Pigeyes was sitting next to the electronics, wearing one of those short-billed county caps. I suppose this was his getup when he was undercover. I nodded rather than use his name and Dewey took my elbow to help me up. Inside, the van smelled of fried food.

I was impressed by Pigeyes's access to this equipment. Surveillance was a separate department unit. When I was on the Force, they would have shitcanned a request for assistance from Financial Crimes faster than junkmail. But Pigeyes sort of had his own police department, his own affiliations and rules. His cousins were coppers and so were two of his brothers, and he had one of "his guys" as he put it, in every nook and cranny of the Hall. He could fix up any little problem—leave or sick days, expense money to take care of a snitch. Naturally he'd return favors—outside the Force, too, for that matter. The guys he grew up with, fellas who these days were importing tunas stuffed with brown heroin or gambling for a living, were all the time giving him a holler when they got in a jam and Gino'd always help out. No questions asked. The Pigeyes National Bank of Favors Owing and Owed. The only thing I found disconcerting was that he was spending his markers to watch over me.

As soon as I took a seat on the wheel well, Pigeyes was on his feet. Make no mistake, he was unhappy.

"I know one fucking douche bag, Malloy, who isn't as fucking smart as you think you are." He waited for me to buy the straight line but I wouldn't bite. "You knew I was sitting on the goddamn credit card, didn't you?"

I looked at the black copper, tall, wearing a tweed jacket and a wool vest but no tie. He was lurking around near the equipment. The van, I would bet, was assigned to him.

"He's having those visions again," I said.

"Don't smart around." Pigeyes pointed. "That's some story he's tellin, this kid. How much did you pay him?"

"I don't know what you're talking about," but of course I did now. Pigeyes had been tracking Kam Roberts the same way I had—with the Kam Roberts credit card. Being a police officer, and one in Financial Crimes, he had clear advantages. The bank card people needed pals in Financial, guys who'd maybe visit some deadbeat who was twenty grand over his limit to suggest that a payment was due soon, otherwise this could go down as a criminal fraud. Now it was payback. Every time a transaction was posted to Kam Roberts's account, the computer center down in Alabama would call Pigeyes. He could track Kam all over the planet, and when Kam showed up in the tri-counties, Gino could skedaddle over to wherever, collar Kam if he was lucky, or at least ask where Kam had been and what he looked like and tell the store owner, the hotel manager, if this guy or anyone asking for him popped up again, to pronto give Pigeyes a jingle. That, I now realized, was how he'd set up on me at U Inn.

All well and good, but apparently Gino and Dewey had spent the last day chasing all over the North End, exploring a rash of purchases of CD players, high-top sneakers, Starter jackets and video games, receiving consistent descriptions of a thirteen-year-old Latino who was not a twenty-seven-year-old black man with receding hair.

Dewey was using a fingernail to pick at his teeth as the three of them watched me.

"I didn't pay him," I said.

"Sure you didn't," said Dewey. "He says he took your wallet off you while you're passed out in some Chevy near the projects."

"Sounds right to me."

"Not to me," piped in Pigeyes. "What I hear, you're on the Life Plan down there at AA. They take attendance?"

I looked pretty clever from Pigeyes's perspective. On the street, everyone knows you use a juvenile to do dirty business, because practically speaking, there's no such thing as jail for a kid that age. The gangbangers employ twelve-year-olds to make dope runs, even as triggermen. Pigeyes figured I gave the kid the Kam Roberts card and told him it was Shop-Till-You-Drop or the coppers come round, in which case here's your story.

"You're buying him time to run, Malloy." I wasn't sure if Gino meant Bert or Kam Roberts, or if they were actually one. "What's this guy to you?"

"Who?" I asked.

"Who am I looking for, fuckface?"

"Kam Roberts?" I really was guessing.

He mimicked me, a long face, a bit of Brando. " 'Kam Roberts?' " He repeated the name half a dozen times, his voice capering up the scale. Then he turned vicious. There was a rheumy turn to his eyes and something inflamed near the bridge of his nose; I could see why people were talking about Pigeyes and dope. On the other hand, he'd always been fast to anger.

"You fuckin tell me right now where he is. Now."

"You holding paper on him?" I still wanted to know what it

was for, what Kam, whoever he was, was supposed to have done.

"Uh-uh, no way, Malloy. You give, you get. No one-way streets."

"You have the wrong address, Pigeyes. I don't know a thing about this guy beyond what I told you last time." I raised two fingers. "Scout's honor."

"You know what I think, Malloy. I'm thinkin, you're dirty here." Pigeyes's instincts were highly reliable and his inclination to view me with suspicion did not need to be explained. "I think it's adding up. We been looking for your friend Mr. Kamin." Pigeyes placed his hands on his knees. He put his face right in mine. His breath was heavy; his flesh was laden with a dense, cruel light. "You wouldn't happen to have been in his apartment in the last couple days?"

I'd known for seventy-two hours this was coming, but the papers were already writing about Archie, and the homicide dicks have all got deals with the reporters—dinner and drinks and spell the name right before the sixth graph—and I thought for sure we'd be hearing an item on News Radio 98, with one of the secretaries scooting down the hall going, Oh my God, did you hear about Bert's place? So this one caught me by surprise.

You probably know it already, U You, but I really am crazy. Saying that, I mean what people usually do, not that I act without reason, but that my reasons, lined up with each other, don't make too much sense. Contradictory, you'd say. In conflict. I'm such a smart-guy who has all the answers, then I whistle in the dark with all these fears racing inside me and, worse yet, pull stunts like breaking into hotel rooms and apartments that would give the heebie-jeebies to the daring young man on the flying trapeze. But now and then even a knucklehead like me gets a wake-up call from reality and without warning I felt, in the radiance of Pigeyes's usual aura of menace, that I was in danger. Somehow with all my preoccupations, my good-time visions about what I'd do when I caught Bert, I hadn't recognized the opportunity I'd handed Gino. I'd known he'd vet me, give me a proctoscope, the third degree. But I had touched a lot of things in Bert's apartment. Doorknobs inside and out. The mail. Homicide was there now, taking lifts off every surface. My sworn enemy, Detective Gino Dimonte, finds a dead body, my prints, and evidence of a lot of peculiar behavior on my part. Guess what comes next? The panic arrived with the same sudden welling power as tears.

"I told you, the guy's my partner. I go to his place all the time." Gino knew just what I was up to. If I admitted I was in the apartment recently, I'd give him the break-and-enter cold, a forcible felony, and a leg up on the murder, since I put myself close to the body. If I denied it, I'd have no way to explain my prints.

"Bull," Pigeyes said. "You're such a pal of his, you know his friends? You know a bookie named Vernon Koechell?"

"No."

"Never heard of him?"

"Don't know him."

"That's not what I asked, Malloy."

I'd been down at the Russian Bath talking about Archie, and it would not take too much bullying to turn somebody's memory around about who'd brought up the name. Pigeyes could monkey with a lot of things, in fact, the evidence techs and the path reports. The people who owed him and played his way were all over the department, and I'd broken their code. A lift off the doorknob could be identified as coming from the refrigerator or the vegetable crisper. My hairs found in the kitchen might eventually appear on Mr. Koechell's lapel. I suddenly knew why there'd been no news flash about Archie's body. It would be easy to mum this in the papers, for a few hours anyway, if the coppers needed time to lay hands on the killer. In the folds beneath my chin, I could feel a slick of telltale dampness beginning to gather.

"This bird Koechell—I been looking for him. Did you know that?"

"No." I was relieved to give one honest answer.

"Some questions I need to ask him about his buddy Kam Roberts."

In the midst of all this sensation, mixed up and intense, I suddenly knew what Pigeyes was investigating—at least what it had been to start. It came into clear view like a birdie flapping through a cold sky as I recalled my conversation with Toots. Fixing games. Kam Roberts and Archie. That's why it was being looked at out of Financial Crimes instead of Vice. 'Kam's Special—U five.' Bert maybe had been in on this too.

"I got lucky, sort of. One of those good news, bad news things. Run into some rummy asshole I used to know, sort of sweat him a second, and bingo, this guy gives me the name of Robert Kamin, tells me go look for this dude, seems he knows Kam Roberts. And I do. I even take a look round Robert Kamin's place."

"With a warrant?" I asked. It was a question, an obstacle. The fear was still all over me now, like a brick on my heart.

Pigeyes sneered. "Listen, jagbag, a warrant for his apartment don't make any difference for you." We both knew he was right. "Here. Show him the warrant."

Dewey reached for a briefcase next to the passenger's seat. I closed my eyes briefly, in spite of myself.

"Now I'm asking you again, Malloy, you didn't happen to be in that apartment, did you?"

I was a copper during those years when it was starting that the police had to give somebody arrested Miranda. I never saw the point. It was a nice idea, I recognized that, put everybody on the same footing, rich guy and poor, they'd all know the same rules. But the problem was human nature, not social class. Because a man in a corner is never going to shut up. If he shuts up, if he says what I knew I should say, call my lawyer, then he's going to the station, he's going to get booked, he's going to court. For a guy in a jam, there's only one way out, to keep explaining, hoping that somehow bullshit buys liberty.

"Pigeyes, what do you think I did?"

"I asked if you were in that apartment." He pointed at Dewey to make a note. "That's twice he's not answering."

"Gino, I'm the guy who gave you Bert's name and told you to go shag him. Write *that* down," I said. Dewey, of course, didn't move. "What kind of sense does that make, if I'm hiding something?" He knew where I was going—if I killed Archie, why would I suggest they go looking for Bert? But I knew the cop answer: If everybody didn't do dumb things, nobody'd get caught.

"Malloy, nothing with you makes sense. You're not a sensible guy. You tell me why you send some punk with pimples on his ass to run all over the city with that fucking credit card? You tell me why the guy I'm looking for and the guy you're looking for got the same names inside out? You tell me why you're looking for this Robert Kamin in the first place? Or how come you don't know nothing about his asshole pal Vernon Koechell? You tell me why you're fronting for this fucking homo?"

Homo. I wasn't making the reference. I didn't know if he meant Archie or Kam or Bert.

"Now maybe," said Pigeyes, "third time's the charm. We'll try it again, and listen up. Yes or no. Last few days, were you in that apartment?"

I felt like he'd shoved his whole fist into my throat.

"Pigeyes, do I need a lawyer?"

"Hey, I thought you were a lawyer." All three of them laughed. The black guy covered his face with his hand. My, my, my. He was wearing a square diamond ring that was bright on his fingers. "See, here's why I ask. Cause I looked all over that place, Kamin's. Checked the dust on the window ledges, postmarks on the mail. I opened the fridge to see any food spoiled, pull date on the milk carton and orange juice. Know what I found?"

"No," I said. Without looking away from me he pointed at Dewey to make another note. I tried to be resolute but he was drilling holes in my peepers, reading every thought in my head. He knew he had me. He'd seen me frightened before. He knew the look and he savored it. And I knew him too. I'd watched him drag these poor kids into the station for questioning and go put on a stained butcher's apron he kept in his locker, knowing there was nothing these young bloods wouldn't believe about the Kindle police. He had the same expression. He was going to deliver the rabbit punch now, the body, and how the path report, the hair samples, the digestive track enzymes, somehow spelled Malloy. He bent close, he put his harsh face right back in mine. Mr. Stranger Danger in person.

"Not a fuckin thing," he said. "That's what I found: not a goddamn fuckin thing. This guy's gone two weeks at least. And if you ain't been in that apartment, you tell me how you come up with a credit card that the bank says they only mailed twelve days ago?" He took a real bite on the words and smiled a little bit as he did it.

And so did I.

B. He Looks Like Kam Roberts

I felt mostly cold in the wake of my panic. I might have belched or sung a song. I felt a little like I could fly. Gino had said, distinctly, that there was nothing in the refrigerator, and so far as I could see, he was having too much fun intimidating me to bother to lie. Who had moved the body and why were questions for later.

Satisfied he had nailed me, Pigeyes stumbled back through the divide between the front seats and sat to have a chuckle; he laughed so hard he held on to his hat. He'd had a great time. His buddies here, Dewey and the black guy, they were smiling right along. Nobody was feeling sorry for Malloy.

Pigeyes finally wiped his eyes. "Let's be straight guys, okay? I don't give a flying foreign fuck what you're up to, Malloy.

Robert Kamin? I don't care if he diddled the senior partner's wife—or the senior partner, for that matter. All I want is this guy Kam Roberts, whoever he is. You gimme that, he gimmes that— Go have your fucking little life. Sincerely." Gino touched his chest. I thought he was wearing the same shirt he had on the other day.

"You gonna tell me why you need him?"

"You gonna tell where I find him?"

"Gino, I don't know." He weighed that, the doubt hinged in his eyes. "I never met the guy in my life. The card gets billed at Kamin's place. Don't ask me why. That's all I know." That, and Infomode, one or two little things. But they were my business. Besides, who knew better than Pigeyes that sometimes I lie? "That's it. Okay? You did a great job breaking my balls."

Pigeyes motioned to Dewey. "Show him."

Dewey went for the briefcase. They had a sketch. It was on mat board, done with pencil and stored in a little plastic sleeve. Surveillance van. Police artist. Pigeyes had a lot of support. Dewey handed the drawing to me.

A black guy, late twenties, nice-looking, receding hair.

"Ever see him?" Dewey asked.

And this was the strangest goddamn part. I had.

"I'm not sure," I said.

"Maybe?"

Where? I would never remember. Not now anyway. If it was coming, it would hit me when I was half asleep, or scratching my fanny, or trying to recollect some clever gambit I had meant to include in a losing brief. Maybe he was the guy at the cleaner or a fella on my bus. But I had seen him.

I kept shaking my head. "This is him? Kam?"

Pigeyes rolled his tongue over his teeth. "Who is he?" he asked.

"Gino, I swear to God, it beats me. I see him on the street, I'll make a citizen's arrest. You're the first guys I call."

"Would Robert Kamin know?"

"I'll have to ask Robert Kamin next time I see him."

"When would that be?"

"No telling. He seems to be somewhat indisposed."

"Yeah, he seems to be." He shared looks, a smile, with the two other coppers. Finding Bert, I suspected, had recently occupied a lot of their time. "What about Koechell?"

"Honest to God, I never met him." I raised a hand. "Honest. And I have no idea where he is now." That was true too.

Pigeyes contemplated all of this.

"Which one's the homo, by the way?" I asked. "Koechell?"

Pigeyes put his hands on his knees again, so he could get up in my face.

"Why ain't I surprised that's of interest to you?"

"If you're trying to disparage me, Pigeyes, I'm going to have to call the Human Rights Commission." We were heading back to where we had been. Fun and games. Gino's bladder had run dry on the hot piss of vengeance for only a moment. The reservoir was filling and he was ready again to lower his fly. It came back to him as the lodestar of his universe: he really did not like me.

"Suppose I tell you," he said, "that you could fit a Saturn rocket up Archie Koechell's hind end, you gonna tell me how come you're so curious?"

"I'm just looking for clues to Bert's social life. That's all. Guy's out of pocket. You know that. My partners are worried and asked me to find him." I gave an innocent little shrug.

"You find him, I wanna know. He talks to me about Kam, he can go home. But you screw around, Malloy, it's the whole load: break and enter, credit card fraud, false personation. I'll fuck you up bad, big guy. And don't think I won't enjoy it."

I knew better than that. Dewey opened the van door from inside and I stepped down to the street, enjoying the daylight and the cold, the greatness of all outdoors. Twice now, I thought, two miracles. I spoke words of thanks to Elaine. Pigeyes had let me go.

XV. BRUSHY TELLS ME WHAT SHE WANTS AND I GET WHAT I DESERVE

A. Brushy Tells Me What's on the Menu

For our luncheon on Friday, Brushy had chosen The Matchbook, a quiet old-line place that tried to preserve some atmosphere of leisured sanctuary for the business class. You walked down from street level into a feeling of soft enclosure. The ceiling was low; the lack of windows had been obscured by little puddles of light projected onto the faux marble wallpaper from the top of the plaster columns dividing the room. The waiters in black waist-coats and bow ties did not tell you their first names or get so chummy that you started hoping the meal might be on them.

Following my adventure with Pigeyes, I'd had an uneventful morning, ruminating periodically about the body vanished from Bert's fridge. I wanted to believe that its disappearance had nothing to do with my visit to the apartment, but I was having a hard time convincing myself.

Eventually I tracked down Lena in the library. She had her feet up on her oak carrel and was absorbed in one of the heavy gold-bound federal reporters as if it were a novel, giving off the fetching aloof air of all brainy women. I asked if she had a passport and a free weekend and still wanted to work on that gambling case, the one where she'd cracked the bookmaking code on Infomode. She was enthusiastic. I did the usual law firm delegating, shit always rolling downhill, and told her to call TN's executive travel service, pull strings if need be to get us on a plane to Pico Luan Sunday and a decent hotel, the beach if they could. She took notes.

"So," I said, when Brush and I were seated side by side in a booth at the back. The maître d' had greeted Brushy by name and took us to a rear corner on a raised terrace of the room, with a column and a plant buying a little more privacy. The table was adorned with big linen napkins and a splendid anthurium, looking like a priapic valentine, and a huge cloth, stiff and white as a priest's collar, that ran to the floor. I looked about and marveled. For Center City, The Matchbook was a great place. A few years ago I would have pleasantly surrendered to temptation and had a drink at lunchtime, which would have been the end of my day. I asked Brushy when she was here last.

"Yesterday," she said. "With Pagnucci."

I'd forgotten. "How was that?"

"Strange," she said.

"What did he want? Groundhog stuff?"

"Just a little. Basically I think he was trying to figure out why I keep having lunch with Krzysinski."

"Jeez, I hope you slapped his face."

She squeezed my knee with a grip strong enough to cause pain.

"He wasn't being like that. It was business."

"Pagnucci? What a surprise. What did he want to know?"

"Well, he said it's a turbulent period for the firm. He wondered how I viewed things, my practice. He made it sound like a management review."

"Sort of checking you out for a mid-life crisis?"

"Sort of. I thought he was trying to set a context. You know, for Groundhog Day. Points. But the way he ended up putting it was, did I think that my personal relationship with Tad was strong enough that TN would remain a client of mine, come what may?"

" 'Come what may'?"

"His words."

I took a moment. Brushy and Pagnucci would make a great team, a litigator and a securities guy, two up-and-coming Italians.

"Did he actually say it? That he was thinking of leaving the firm and taking you with him?"

"Mack, we're talking Pagnucci here. He barely gets a word out. He made it sound, you know, like some remote curiosity."

"Like a dinner party game. Who Would You Be If You Weren't You?"

"Exactly. And I cut him off. I told him I was fond of my partners and proud of the work we do and that I didn't spend my time thinking about questions like that."

"Good for you. Leotis couldn't have done better. Was he abashed?"

"He completely agreed. He fumpfered around. 'Of course, of course.' He tried to act as if it was nothing to him."

"Carl obviously thinks I'm not finding Bert, the money's not coming back, TN's going bye-bye, and the firm is too. Right?"

"Maybe. He's probably just being cautious. Considering all the angles. You know Carl."

"Maybe he *knows* I'm not going to find Bert."

"How would he?"

I couldn't figure much that made sense. Especially after Carl had blessed my voyage to Pico.

The waiter came and we ordered iced teas, then Brushy on second thought asked for white wine. We looked over the menus, a foot and half if they were an inch, old-fashioned, with vellum pages and a tasseled binding. I remained puzzled by Pagnucci's game, but Brushy cut me short when I returned to the subject.

"Mack, do you really think I wanted to have lunch so we could talk about Pagnucci?"

I told her if I had, I probably wouldn't have come.

"I want you to try to be serious about something," she said. "You hurt my feelings yesterday."

Within, I recoiled. Some ancient retractile mechanism set in. Another lecture from another woman about how I'd disappointed her. We were going to have feminist reconstruction of my spicy remarks about her wandering loins.

"Hey, Brush, I thought we went past that. It's me, us, you and me. Pals forever."

"That's the point." She faced me in a casual way, so that we were more or less knee to knee. Her back was to the adjoining wall and she propped an arm on the top of the banquette and leaned her full face and her soft hairdo against a hand in an appealing fashion. She looked frank and friendly, like a teenager in her rec room. "I thought the next time you danced the hokey-pokey, Malloy, it was going to be with me."

That one took me a sec.

"You did?" This was apparently one of those male-female understandings that so often eluded me.

"Yes, I did." She pouted. Cutely.

"I guess, Brush, I thought I'd missed my chance. I figured we'd just sort of finished that."

"I guess I figured we'd just sort of started." Her little eyes were luminous and very much alive, full of the quest. Like a great institution, say a university or the President of the United States, Brushy was seldom formally rejected. According to the know-alls with whom I served on recruiting, nosy fishwives who somehow always heard this stuff, Brushy over the years had mastered a perfect line: 'I'm wondering if I should let you make love to me.' The nonplussed or the sincerely uninterested could back off, with little harm to either party. I was touched that she'd actually gamble, but I was confused in the presence of real emotion. While I went blank, she, as usual, took the lead.

"Unless," she said, "there's no spark." I felt, with that, her fingers laid daintily on the meat of my thigh, and then as she held my eye, her palm touched down and her hand skated home. She gave my little business a squeeze which in the scheme of things might best be called affectionate. I had no doubt anymore why she'd wanted a place with tablecloths.

How to respond? The adrenaline, the shock inspired an elevated mood, a kind of lunacy which in retrospect I attribute to the dizziness of the rare feeling that something significant was at stake. She was, as I have always known, a hell of a gal. And I was vaguely amused by how close this was to what I'd imagined with Krzysinski. But Brushy had the talent of all seductive females, to recognize a guy's fantasies and play along with them, without feeling debased.

"I would say there's a spark," I told her, still caught up in that fixed look, her green eyes with their clever gleam. "I would say you'd make a hell of a Boy Scout."

"*Boy* Scout?"

"Yes, ma'am, cause you keep rubbing that stick, you're gonna get a lot more than a spark."

"I'm hoping for that."

We were eye to eye, nose to nose, but in the dignified air of The Matchbook there would be no embrace. Instead, I turned a bit on the bench, diddled my fingers a little on her knee, then, leaning close like I was about to impart a little joke, slid my hand up her hosiery toward the female zero point, thinly guarded by the layer of panty hose. I looked her square in the eye, gathered the fabric, and gave it a sharp yank so that Brushy actually flinched. But she kept watching me, highly amused, as I found the gap I'd rent and tenderly as I could nuzzled two fingertips against her labia.

"Is this what we call equal opportunity?" she asked.

"Maybe. But you see, Brush, I got further than you. It's still a man's world."

"Oh," said Brushy, and lay back a bit, grabbing the tablecloth and tenting it in a casual way over my hand, which was already beneath her napkin. She opened the menu and rested it between her waist and the edge of table, making it more or less a roof, a privacy panel. Then her hips came forward and her knees parted. She lit a cigarette. And took hold of her wine. She faced me, taking her pleasure with a wild gimlet eye, a woman who loved life when it reduced itself to this basis.

She said, "I'm not sure I'd agree with that."

B. Would You Call This a Success?

In the room at Dulcimer House things were going pretty well until I took off my shorts. Then Brushy screamed. She covered her mouth with both hands.

"What's that?" She was pointing at me and it wasn't because she was so impressed.

"What's what?"

"That rash." She steered me to the mirror. There I was with half a boner and a livid band, shaped like a land mass, covering my hip. There was an island extension that broadened as it crossed my circumference and disappeared in the pubic over-growth. I stared, feeling direly conspired against. Then it hit me.

"The fucking Russian Bath."

"Ah hah," she said.

She reared back when I moved toward her again.

"It's dermatitis," I said, "it's nothing. I didn't even know I had it."

"That's what they all say."

"Brushy."

"You better see your doctor, Malloy."

"Brushy, have a heart here."

"It's the nineties, Mack." She stalked naked through the room. She pushed through her clothes and I was afraid she was dress-ing, but it was only a cigarette she was after. She sat across from me on an overstuffed brocaded chair, smoking, naked as a jaybird with her heel on the fancy fabric, leaking female fluids on the nice furniture. The stick figures do well for clothes racks, but naked, a woman with Brushy's Rubensesque proportions was still a lovely sight. I remained rosy and pointed for action, but I could tell from her posture that I had reached my sexual high point at lunch.

I lay down on the bed and, feeling I had every right to, began to moan.

"Mack," she said, "don't be like that. You're making me feel bad."

"Jeez, I hope so."

"It'll just be a few days," she said. She gave me a doctor's name and said he might even prescribe over the phone. She sounded authoritative, but I stowed all those questions she didn't like me to ask.

I quieted eventually. Soon I was back to being myself, primarily sad, staring at the classy ceiling here at the Dulcimer House, where the plaster decorations around the light fixture radiated off in various whitish doodles. We had been here once before, of course—with similar success. I had felt it was a mistake to start, checking into the same hotel—the same amiable stroll over here, a little frozen up with anticipation and propriety, trying, within hailing distance of the office, to look like anything but two people going to fuck; the same kind of sycophantic desk clerk; the same sort of room with heavy furnishings, a bit too dated to be tasteful. One more failure to connect. I felt rather imprisoned by the cycles in my life.

"I got drunk two nights ago, Brush," I said suddenly. "What do you think of that?"

"Not much," she said. I didn't think she meant she had no opinion. When I cranked my head around to see her in the chair, still naked, still smoking, I could tell from her level expression that this hadn't been a thunderbolt. "You looked pretty awful yesterday," she said. She asked if I had enjoyed it.

"Not particularly," I answered. "But I can't seem to get the taste out of my mouth."

"Do you think you're going to do it again?"

"Nope," I told her, and then, feeling almost as tough as she is, added, "I might."

I lay there feeling all the weight of my big fat body, this belly like a medicine ball, these saddlebags of fat that ride my back above the hipbones.

"Oh, don't you get sick of it?" I asked. "Another Irish lawyer. Another Irish drunk. I'm so tired of being myself—of fucking things up the way I do. It's a tiredness not lost in sleep and only worse on waking. I can't help thinking how great it would be to start new. A really clean slate. It's the only thing left that excites me."

"It makes me sad when you talk like that," she said. "It doesn't become you. You're just asking for someone to tell you that you're really okay."

"No, I'm not. I wouldn't believe it."

"You're a good man, Malloy. And a good lawyer too."

"No," I said, "no. Wrong on both fronts. To tell you the truth, Brush, I don't really think I'm cut out for the law anymore. Books and bills and briefs. It's a black-and-white life and I'm a guy who loves color."

"Come on, Mack. You're one of the best lawyers there. When you do it."

I made a sound.

"In the old days, you were there all the time. You had to enjoy some of it."

When I drank, I worked like a demon, billed twenty-two, twenty-four hundred hours a year. I was in the office until eight and in the bars until midnight—then back in the Needle at eight the next morning. Lucinda used to bring Bufferin with my coffee. When I set about changing my life at AA, that was another of the habits I broke. I went home at six—saw the wife, the kid.

And was divorced inside a year. It doesn't take Joyce Brothers to figure out what that proves.

"The truth?" I asked. "I don't even remember. I don't remember what it was like to be busy. I don't remember where I stood at the firm before Jake decided I was a useless piece of dung."

"What are you talking about? Are you grumping because he doesn't send you work right now? Believe me, Mack, you have a great future with that client. Krzysinski respects you. Give that time. It'll work out."

Krzysinski again. I mulled on that, then set her straight.

"Look, Brush, there is no future. Jake stopped sending me work because he knows it's his ass if anybody at G&G drops the ball and he figures I'm a guy who can't catch a pop fly."

"That's not so."

"Yes, it is," I said. "And he's probably right. I mean, I liked trying cases. Getting up in front of a jury. Waving my hands around. Seeing if I could make them love me. But nobody's sure I can handle the stress anymore and stay sober. Including me. Without that, I don't like it all. I'm just hooked on the money."

I felt bruised, lying there, pounding myself with the truth. But I knew I was on the mark. Money was worse than booze or cocaine. God, it could just go in the sweet rush of spending. You start visiting the tailor, buy the Beemer, maybe pick up a little country house, find a club or two not picky enough to keep you out. Next thing you know, two sixty-eight before taxes, and you're looking in the button drawer for coins to pay your bridge tolls. Not to mention being a drunk who used to arrive home routinely, pulling my pockets inside out under the light of my front porch, wondering, sort of abstractly, where it was all those twenties went. (As well as my house keys, which on one occasion I eventually realized I'd thrown into the tin cup of some beggar.) Now I had an ex with a nice German car and a house in the country and God to thank that I paid alimony and had something to show for the money I made.

"We all are," she said. "Hooked. To some extent. It's part of the life."

"No," I said. "You meant what you told Pagnucci. You love it. You love G&G. You'd work there for free."

She made a face, but I had her nailed and she knew it.

"What is it?" I asked. "Seriously. I never got it. To me, you know, all these lawsuits, it's my robber baron's better than your robber baron. What do you get off on? The law?"

"The law. Sure." She nodded, mostly to herself. "I mean, all this right and wrong. It's nifty."

" 'Nifty'?"

She came over and lay beside me, belly down. She had those bandy legs and her bad skin, but she looked awfully good to me, a perky little derriere. I patted her rear and she smiled. The flag was unfurling again, but I knew it was no use. Besides, she had her mind on the law now, and that, as I'd told her, was really the love of her life.

"It's the whole thing," she said, "all of it. Money. The work. The *world*. You know how it is when you're a child, you want to live in a fairy tale, you want to play house with Snow White, and I mean, here I am, hanging out with all of these people I read about in the *Journal* and the business pages of the *Tribune*." Brushy, Wash, Martin, all of them, they kept track of the movements of big-time corporate America—financings, acquisitions, promotions—avid as soap opera fans, gobbling up the *Journal* and the local business press every morning with a hunger I felt only for the sports page.

"Like Krzysinski."

She darted a warning look at me but answered straight.

"Like Krzysinski. And they *like* me, these people. And I like them. I mean, I think about what a mess I was when I got here. I was the only female lawyer in Litigation and I was scared to death. Remember?"

"Couldn't forget." She had been on fire in the self-consuming fashion of the sun. Brushy knew she was a woman in a man's world—just ahead of the female gold rush to law school—and she confronted her prospects with a combustive emotional mix of hell-bent determination and ravaging anxiety. She was the only girl in a family of five, born plug in the middle, and her situation here matched something that had faced her at home, some yes-and-no game she was always playing with herself. She'd do something brilliant, then come to one of her confidants—me or somebody else—and explain, with utmost sincerity, how it had all been accidental and would never be repeated, how she felt doomed by the expectations created by her own success. It was exhausting—and painful—just to listen to her, but even then I felt drawn to her, the way certain free molecules always react. I shared, I suppose, all these alternate moods, the brashness, the fear, the inclination to first blame myself.

"And now. All these people—they *need* me. I did this piece of takeover litigation for Nautical Paper a couple of years ago. My father worked there for a while, you know decades ago, but after we'd won the case I got this note from Dwayne Gandolph, the CEO, thanking me for the great work I'd done. It made me dizzy. Like inhaling Benzedrine. I brought it to my folks' home and we all passed it around the dinner table and looked at it. The entire family was impressed with me—*I* was impressed with me."

I understood what she was saying, perhaps more than she did, that her membership in this world was too hard-won not to be valued, too much a symbol to her to be understood as anything else. But she was smiling at herself for the moment. Gosh, she was great. We both thought so. I admired her enormously, the distances she'd dragged herself and her baggage. I gave her a smooch and we lay there necking for maybe ten minutes, two grown-ups, both of them naked in the daylight in a goddamn hotel room, just kissing and touching hands. I held her awhile, then she told me we had to go. There was G&G, the office, work to do.

We both laughed when she poked her fist through the hole in her panty hose. She put them on anyway and asked how I was doing finding Bert.

"I'm not going to find him," I said. She went quizzical and I told her what I hadn't yet said to anyone else—that I thought Bert was dead.

"How could Bert be dead?" she asked. "Who has the money?" It required only an instant, I noted, for her to reach the question that had come to me after a week.

"It's an interesting window of opportunity, isn't it?"

She had sat down in the chair again, half-dressed and posed against the fancy brocade. I loved looking at her.

"You mean," she said, "if somebody knew Bert was dead, they could blame it on him?"

"That's what I mean." I was off the bed, stepping into my trousers. "But they'd have to *know*," I said. "They couldn't be guessing. If Bert shows up again, they'd look pretty bad."

"Well, how would they be sure?"

I looked at her.

"You mean someone killed him? From the firm? You don't believe that."

I didn't, in fact. There was logic to it, but little sense. I told her that.

"These are just theories, right? Bert being dead? All of it?" She wanted more than my reassurance. She was being her true self, relentless, beating the idea to death like a snake.

"Those are theories," I told her, "but listen to this." I told her then about my meetings yesterday, first with Jake, then with the Committee. This time I caught her off guard. She sat far forward, her mouth formed in a small perfect *o*. She was too distressed to feign valiance.

"Never," she said finally. "They'll never agree to something like that. That kind of cover-up. They have too much character."

"Wash?" I asked. "Pagnucci?"

"Martin?" she responded. Brushy's reverence for Martin was even greater than mine. "You'll see," she said. "They'll do the right thing."

I shrugged. She could be right, and even if she wasn't, she was improved by thinking the best of her partners. But she could see she hadn't really persuaded me.

"And Jake," she said, "my God, how sleazy. What's wrong with him?"

"You just don't know Jake. If you'd grown up with him, you'd see another side."

"Meaning?"

"I could tell you stories." I fumbled in her purse for a cigarette. I was tempted to tell her about the bar exam, but realized on second thought that she'd think less of me than Jake.

"You don't trust him, right? That's what you're suggesting. He wasn't brought up to be trustworthy?"

"I know him. That's all."

In the green chair, she was stilled by disquiet.

"You don't like Jake, do you? I mean, all that palling around with him. That's bull, isn't it?"

"Who wouldn't like Jake? Rich, good-looking, charming. Everyone likes Jake."

"You've got a chip on your shoulder about Jake. It's obvious."

"All right. I have a chip on my shoulder about a lot of things."

"Don't wait for me to say you're wrong."

"I'm bitter and petty, right?" She could tell what I was thinking: I'd heard the tune before, someone else had sung the words, another chanteuse.

"I would never say petty. Look, Mack, he's lucky. In life, some people are lucky. You can't sit around despising good fortune."

"Jake is a coward. He's never had the balls to face what he should have. And I let him make me a coward with him. That's the part that frosts me."

"What are you talking about?"

"Jake." I looked at her hard. I could feel myself turning mean, Bess Malloy's son, and she saw it too. She stepped into her pumps and fixed the clasp on her purse. She'd been warned off.

"This is attorney-client, right?" she finally asked. "All of this. About Jake saying not to tell?" She wasn't being humorous. She meant that the communication was privileged. That she was forbidden to repeat it, to TN or anyone else, and thus that BAD could never criticize her for failing to come forward, as, ethically, each of us was obliged to do.

"That's right, Brushy, you're covered. There's no shit on your shoes."

"That's not what I meant."

"Yes, it is," I said, and she did not bother to answer back. A certain familiar melancholy attacked me midline, spreading from the heart. Ain't life grand? Every man for himself. I sank down on the bed, on the heavy embroidered spread which we'd never removed, and couldn't quite look at her.

Eventually she sat beside me.

"I don't want you to tell me any more about this. It makes me feel weird. And confused. It's too close to home. And I don't know what to do. How to react." She touched my hand. "I'm not perfect either, you know."

"I know."

She waited.

"I think this thing is frightening and out of control," she said at last. "All of it. I'm worried about you."

"Don't worry. I may bitch a lot, Brush, but in the end I can take care of myself." I looked at her. "I'm like you."

I wasn't sure how that sat and neither was she. She went to the chair and picked up her purse, then on second thought stopped off to kiss me. She had decided to forgive me, that things, everything, could be worked through. I held her hand for a second, then she left me there, sitting on the bed, alone in the hotel room.

XVI. INVESTIGATION APPROACHES CLIMAX, INVESTIGATOR GOES FURTHER

My afternoon with Brushy left me in a state. Longing—real longing—took me as a walloping surprise. I reeled around in an adolescent fit, captured in transported recollections of the impressive qualities of Brushy's person, her pleasant scent of light perfume and body cream, and the pure transmission of some as yet unnamed form of human-emitted electromagnetic sensation which continued to grip my thorax and my loins. From my house that night I called her at home, reaching only her machine. I told myself that she was in the office, a number I did not have the bravery to dial.

I had called her doctor, who'd prescribed a salve, and I went to the john to give myself another treatment. In my sensuous thrall, I soon found myself otherwise engaged. Unspeakable activities. I sweated in my bathroom, imagining wild amours with a woman who'd been naked in my arms a few hours before, and wondered about my life.

I had just reholstered when I noticed the catarrh of an engine idling outside. I was stabbed at once by the kind of probing guilt my mother would have cheered, chilled by the thought that Lyle and his pals might have seen my filmy shape through the wobbled glass blocks of the bathroom window. I would have made quite a sight, backlit, bending and swaying as I squeezed the sound from my own sax. I heard the front door bang and gave some thought to remaining locked up there. But that was not my approach with Lyle. In any circumstance, I felt committed to staring him down.

I encountered him as he galloped up the stairs. In his various rangy parts, he looked a little more organized than usual; I suspected he was with a girl. His spume of hair was combed and he had on a Kindle County Unified Police Force leather jacket, not mine but one he'd purchased from the cop supply house on Murphy Street and which he wore in unspoken comment on the time when I had what he judged a more authentic life. He stomped past me, muttering something I did not catch at first.

"Mom's downstairs," he repeated.

"Mom?"

"Remember her? Nora? It's boys' night out." I wondered if it meant anything positive that he was treating his parents' foibles with humor rather than undiluted contempt. We were in the dim interior hallway between the upstairs bedrooms, and after a few steps he turned back to me with a smirk. "Hey, man, what the hell were you doing just now? In the john? We were like taking bets."

"You and your mother?" I asked. I summoned all my courtroom dignity and told him I was blowing my nose. Frankly, he could not have cared less, but when he walked off down the dark corridor, I felt so hollowed by shame I thought I might stumble. Often humiliated and seldom saved. Is it just a Catholic thought that sex will always get you in trouble? God, I thought. God. What a moment that must have been. A boy and his mother laying odds on whether the old goat's actually up there having a wank. I headed down in an appropriate mood to see my former wife.

Nora was standing in the bright lights of the front entry,

framed by the white molding and the storm door, holding on to her purse and not venturing any farther inside. I kissed her cheek, a gesture she received stoically.

"How are you?" she asked.

"Jolly," I said. "You?"

"Jolly."

Serve and volley. Here we were, a total standoff after twenty-one years. After flips and swirls and curly dos, Nora had let her hair go straight, so that it hung lank and fine and almost black, looking as it does on those Japanese gals who seem to have surrounded their faces with a lacquer frame. She had given up makeup too. I saw Nora infrequently enough that she was starting to look different to me. The work of time was no longer undetectable for being observed day by day. Her chin was getting full and her eyes were sinking into shadow. She looked okay, though, except for her manifest agitation at being here.

Nora had a different life now, one that she thought of as better and truer than the decades she'd spent with me. New friends. New interests. A big-city life. Female circles principally, no doubt, with meetings, lectures, parties. I'm sure that days went by before she woke to any recollection of me—or Lyle. One foot inside this house and something fearsome gripped her, I suspected, not nostalgia, but the terror that she would be confined again, imprisoned, held hostage once more from her real self.

"You can sit." I swung a hand beyond the black slate of the foyer to the worn meal-colored carpet of the living room.

"It's just a minute. He wanted to stop for money. He's going to take me out."

"Money?" With that, I heard footsteps overhead. He was in my room, rooting for cash. Nora heard the same thing, and gave me the wrinkle of some happy, suburbanized expression she'd seen on TV.

"He's no better," I told her. "Not a bit."

The plainness of this observation seemed to catch us both; somehow a sense of tragedy reared up between us so large that

I thought we'd both go down like bowling pins. You could never get around the future with Lyle, the way he was now and the suspicion that it foretold something grim, that he was worse than an unhappy kid, but was one of those people—everybody knows several—who turns out to be lame, crippled, not even up to the dismal functions, like holding a job or hanging in with someone else, which allow us our meager share of daily satisfactions. In the moment of recognition nobody—not Nora, not me—could run from the unhappy evidence that our lives were once one thing, not merely a failure of spirit but an institution of cause and effect of which neither law nor will could annul the unfortunate consequences. Those would roll on through another generation or two.

"And whose fault is that, Mack?" she asked. The answer, if we were going to be honest—which we weren't—was probably elaborate. We could start with Grandma and Grandpa and go on from there. But I knew Nora. We were starting a game of Matrimonial Geography, in which Nora would point out how all roads on the map of blame led only to me.

"Desist," I said, "cease. Let's fight about something less predictable. A new subject. Just skip Lyle, money, or me."

"Look at your life, Mack. You're Mr. Entropy. What can you expect from him?" Her observations through the bathroom window seemed to have emboldened her, though ordinarily she did not need much excuse.

Mr. Entropy, I thought. There were entire universes saved from self-reproach by that remark. Jesus, this was one person who didn't take long to get under my skin.

"He's thirty years younger than me and doesn't have the same well-worn excuses." I smiled tightly and she made various faces, implying it was all right, she could take being stiff-armed. We confronted one another in simmering silence until Lyle returned and blew past me, taking his mother in tow.

In the aftermath, I settled by the TV in the living room. The Hands were playing UW–Milwaukee the usual tough first half

—both their bench and self-confidence would give out in the last twenty minutes, when they would resume their role as this decade's Mid-Ten doormat. Within, I continued prolonged fomenting. Nora fucking Goggins. Entropy! How long had she been storing up that one? There was always a hundred megaton warhead in her silo.

When I stopped drinking, Nora used to tell me I was really no fun anymore, a line that served the great principle of relationship transitivity by which she could both put me down and make excuses for herself. If I was no fun, she should have fun on her own. We reached a seven-week period where she went off for weekend conventions three times and then finally a midweek night when my bride of nineteen years simply did not come home.

When I marched through the door the next evening, the house was clean, I could smell a hot meal, a relative rarity, and I immediately made out the plan: life as normal. The idea was that I should ask nothing. Neither of us had enough fingers and toes to count the occasions when I'd pulled more or less the same stunt in those nineteen years, nights when I was so drunk that I sometimes felt I had to hang on to the grass to keep from falling off the earth, though usually the barkeep knew enough to give her a call. Nonetheless, about 9:30 I finally glued together my courage.

'I was with Jill,' she answered. Jill Horwich, her erstwhile manager and bartime buddy.

'I know you started out with Jill. I want to know who else you were with.'

'Nobody else.'

'Nora, don't bullshit me.'

'I'm not bullshitting.' When I fixed her with one of those looks she might have given me, she said, 'I don't believe this is happening.' She was on her feet, twisting the wedding ring around on her finger, posed in a corner of the living room where a lovely brass vase with gladioli was arranged. I was, I admitted, struck at that moment by the enduring phenomenon of beauty. 'Mack, leave it be. I know I don't have the right to ask that. But I am.'

'Motion denied,' I said. 'Let's go. The sticky truth.'

'You don't want to know.'

'You're right, I don't. But I'm asking anyway.'

'Why?' She looked at me bleakly.

'I suppose I sort of think it's important.'

Silence.

'So who's the guy?'

'There is no guy, Mack.'

'Nora, who were you with?'

'I told you, Mack, I was with Jill.'

Press your buzzer when you have the correct answer. It was the next afternoon before I got it, sitting in my office, being, as usual, no use to anyone, talking as I recall to Hans Ottobee, an interior decorator hired to do something about my furnishings. Nineteen years, you think you've seen everything from a person and then some guy mentions a modular wall unit and somehow you see something else. I always loved cubism. What a wonderful illusion that you can see all sides at once.

At home that night, I didn't wait long. She'd cooked again. I took my plate of pot roast from the oven and started right in.

'So how long have you been like this?'

'What do you mean "like this"?'

'Spare me. When did you start?' I finally got the heart to look at her straight on, which was more or less the end of the game.

'Always.' She blinked. 'As far as I know.'

' "Always"?'

'Do you remember Sue Ellen Tomkins?'

'From the sorority?'

She just nodded.

'I don't think women are like men,' she said. 'I don't expect you to understand.'

'Jesus,' I said.

'Mack, this is taking incredible courage for me.'

She apparently did not consider that it wasn't particularly easy for me. People who stay married, who hold on for the long pull, put up with a lot from each other: personal oddities, bad habits, ill health. For some it's tolerance, others commitment, many, like me, fear the unknown. For a while I tested myself with the notion that I should put up with this too. People stay married without sex. I'd known plenty. After all, I grew up a Catholic. And who even said it had to be like that? But it just sort of cut to the heart of things. I never saw this issue in normative terms. I wasn't worried that it was a perversion, or something that would have made my sainted ma faint, and I gave Nora no points just because it was the latest in style. It just seemed like an awful lot not to know. For her not to tell. For me not to recognize.

So what was it like for her, those many years with drunken old Mack, whose sails on rare occasion would blow full of lust and fall upon her, riding her waves, mast in her harbor? What did she think? How much was she faking? Inquiring minds want to know. I sat there tonight with the wretched dark broken by the flickering of the sporting event and the announcer's occasionally hysterical pitch, trying to fathom it all, and found myself, for me, admirably charitable. I doubt she knew what to think. She must have felt uncertain, not really herself. Not resentful. Not engaged. How could she not know? you ask. The law governs acts, not evil intent alone, and we seem to take that lesson to heart. In this life—Catholic theology notwithstanding—we are what we do. She must have thought about her college friend from time to time and been surprised to find herself stimulated by the memory. She must have put it off to voyaging youth, the same untamed daring that let her give fellas blow jobs on the second date, and dismissed her continuing reflections as part of the universe of unruly and unsavory things rattling around in the average human mind. At times she must have confronted herself starkly with the question—*Am I?*—and at other instants comforted herself with the facts: husband, boys in the past, her

roots in the present, her child. It must have taken her by surprise
to have been so pleased the first time Jill Horwich laid a hand
on her shoulder and then, feigning inadvertence, brushed
against her breasts. That's what I think. I didn't know, whatever
the disbelief with which that state of knowledge—or grace—is
greeted. We see a person, hear a voice, are drawn most inti-
mately to them, and yet so much remains unknown. No matter
how earnestly we search, the mysteries abide. As Nora would
tell you, we do not even know for certain when we look in the
mirror.

Practicing man's original sin, I have found my own unruly
mind passing over the image of the two of them, with Jill's face
buried up to the brows in Nora's female region and my wife
lolled back in an ecstasy she only aspired to with me. I see this,
I admit, with an unseemly exactness of detail, imagining it from
Nora's eyes, another of those figures I can't manage to paint.
Afterwards, I am morose, immobilized by grief. But often in the
instant of sensation and heat, in that image of Nora finally free,
relishing her own sensations like the finest music, I have a certain
flight myself, as if something similar were even possible for me.

So that's what I thought, staring frozenly at the TV, suddenly
recollecting how much I loved to drink and hating my surroundings. I swear, aren't the Irish the tackiest decorators in the world,
dark and cheap, with so many fucking little knickknacks collared
in dust that I never can find an inch of space on a tabletop to
put down a glass, and too much lace and all the required family
pictures? My ma's place looked just like this too, kind of a savage
irony, since Nora hated Bess, both her tightfisted, pursed-
lipped, judgmental ways and her flipside moods where she was
worshipfully reverent of her men. More's the marvel, since as
time passes and I close my eyes, it feels as if they both filled
the same space inside.

The TV screen was full of a big close-up of the referee. As I
watched the picture, some extraordinary sensation of discovery

took hold of me: I was at once suddenly focused, rescued, finally free.

"That guy!" I shouted in the empty house. I knew him, I'd seen his face.

In Pigeyes's drawing.

That was Kam Roberts.

XVII. I COULDN'T HAVE BEEN MORE SURPRISED IF THE HANDS HAD WON

A. Phantom of the Fieldhouse

Among the many noble institutions that, years ago, had first sought Leotis Griswell's counsel was the U. For his partners, this connection was priceless, inasmuch as it allowed us to obtain prime seats for football and basketball games and private tours of important university facilities like the bevatron or the fieldhouse, where the Hands played their games. I'd been down on the lacquered playing floor, with the huge-knuckled hands drawn at the center line amid a collar of vermilion, had capered down the tunnels and visited the locker rooms. Most important now, I'd also been to the ugly little changing room, where the refs dressed before games and sat out halftime and, after the final buzzer, immediately showered and put on their street clothes and dark glasses and escaped by mixing into the throng, rather than waiting for any lurking villain who wanted to engage in his own instant replay of various calls.

Flying out of the house, I grabbed only a tweed sport jacket and drove recklessly over the river back into the city, wary of black-and-whites as I spun the dial to find the game on the radio. I had to lower the windows to clear the odor from yesterday morning and the Chevy was frigid. I blew on my fingers when I stopped at each light. It turned to halftime, the Hands down by only a bucket. I was desperate to get there while the refs were off the floor so that I'd have some chance to get hold of this Kam.

Approaching this guy, whatever his name was, was going to be dicey. As far as I was concerned, the bookies and he could fix what they liked, but I didn't expect him to be carefree about that, and almost everything I might mention was likely to spook him. I was curious, naturally, although it didn't take much imagination to see how having a ref in your pocket could be, as they say in the law, outcome-determinative: a foul here and there, an out-of-bounds, a jump ball, a goal tend, a travel, all called or not. You could probably swing twenty to thirty points a game without being too obvious, given the usual grousing about officiating and the fact that in a sport like basketball, where everybody's always pushing and moving, a ref can only be expected to see so much. Archie had a great thing with this Kam, no question, but I had retired as a policeman. All I needed was to know about Bert—alive or dead, and if the former, how to make contact. For my sake, aside from my usual snoopy impulses, I didn't even need to know where Bert fit in their scam.

The fieldhouse, "The House of the Hands," as it was known, was the usual old university structure, a formidable mass of the same red-clay bricks from which most of the U.'s buildings were constructed. The House was relieved of utter grimness by roof-line adornments of turrets and battlements and gunsight notches blocked out of stone. Someone will have to explain to me someday why the architectural plans for so many of the land-grant universities seem to have been borrowed from Clausewitz. What was the idea, that if the South rose again these buildings could be converted to armories?

At the moment I could have used my own militia, since without it I could not find any place to park. The attendant at the lot across the street stoutly refused the two twenties I tried to force on him to get the Chevy inside, and I tore off around the block, sweating, swearing, itchy and bitchy, running out of time. Outside the fieldhouse the hawkers with the pennants and cups, buttons and banners, were milling with nothing to do, putting up with the little black kids in hooded sweatshirts and tatty coats who hung out just to get a scent of the game and the players. A dribble of early departees emerged through the gates two or three at a time. There were no more than five minutes left of halftime by now. The teams would be out there warming up, trying to look loose and jovial while they strutted their stuff without opposition, jamming and blocking, doing drills; the refs would soon follow them back out. I finally left the car on the street in a red zone. With luck, if I found this guy, I could be back out in ten minutes.

I did not have a ticket. This didn't occur to me until I saw the gate attendant. They guarded the entrances throughout the game due to the little kids outside, who employed considerable craft figuring out how to get in. I ran back to the ticket windows in front, which were closed when I got there. I had to get a glum kid to go fetch some old biddy, who raised the shade halfway, eyed me serenely, and said, "I'm sorry, we're totally sold out."

"I'll take standing room."

"Fire marshal doesn't allow that here in the House." The shade dropped. I heard her walking away while I pounded on the glass.

Back in front, I found some guy with three young kids, leaving to put them to sleep; he did not mind parting with his ticket stub for ten bucks, and I ran back to a different gate. The two student ushers, a boy and a girl in their red sport coats, were both overweight and obviously amorous, still overcome by that first thrill of love, the amazing news that in the flight of life, solo thus far, there might be a co-pilot. Watching them, I had an abrupt thought of Brushy, pleasing and then somehow muddled and pained. I bulled through the stiles between them, shaking my head and smiling and telling anyone who could hear how glad I was that I'd remembered the car lights. As I rushed on, I heard the boom of the horn and the crowd suddenly rousing itself: the second half was starting. I was in the dark rampway by then and I stood beneath the enormous welling crowd noise muttering, "Fuck." I could be one of those jerks who run out on the court, but the best that would come of that would be a trip to District 19, maybe even a clubbing.

Instead, I slowly paced through the warren of brick corridors, trying to remember where the refs' changing room was. The old interior bricks of the place were all painted in a heavy enamel, a garish Hands' vermilion that refracted the spectral light. The air had a sort of salty smell, not so much sweat as excitement, the way lightning leaves the pungency of ozone in its wake. Already there was a lull in the clamor, which meant that the Hands were fading. Passing by a ramp up, I caught a look at the big four-sided scoreboard suspended on taut cables between the rafters and the blue ribbons of smoke floated in from the hallways. Milwaukee had put up six points in the first forty seconds out of the locker room. Maybe the Hands weren't even on the court.

Finally I found what I was looking for, a simple wooden door painted the same red as the bricks and labeled "Authorized Personnel Only." I caught my only break of the night. The security guard in his ill-fitting red jacket was down the concrete corridor a good fifty yards, his radio clutched to his ear as he meandered, probably on his way for a leak now that halftime was over. I grabbed the knob and went through like I knew what I was doing. There were steel stairs, then a long low passage lit by bare incandescent bulbs, a janitor's gangway running downward beside the boiler pipes and plumbing into the field-house basement, where the refs changed.

To be under there while the game roared above was strange. Overhead there was glamour. The ash floor gleamed under the phenomenal brightness of the stadium lights. The cheerleaders, heartbreaking emblems of youth, simple in their grace, like flowers, flounced their skirts and jumped up and down. In the stands that timeless thing that goes back to when we ran in packs was strumming like the current in a high voltage wire in 18,000 sober citizens who were now nothing but one mass of screaming freaks. People with troubles, with a disabled kid or a mortgage they couldn't meet, were shouting so loud that tomorrow they wouldn't be able to speak at work, but now they were thinking of nothing but whether some long-bodied kid in shorts could throw a leather ball through a hole.

And the refs would be out there, dressed in black and white amid the colors and brightness, the very figures of reason, the law, the rules, the arbiters, the force that kept it a game, not a fistfight. Down here was where they got ready, where they steadied themselves and came to grips with reality, and believe me, it stank. Literally. I remembered from visiting before. The changing room would be gamy with sweat, a little closet with a seven-foot ceiling, an architectural afterthought carved out of the service channel that runs for the sewer pipes. The walls were wood, painted some miserable yellowish eggshell lacquer that glimmered cheaply under the unshaded bulbs. There were two little partitioned changing cubicles and a shower and a crapper, each behind a blue canvas drape, a setup that offered about the same level of privacy that inmates get in a holding cell.

At the bottom, the gangway joined a tunnel that ran up at an angle, leading to the court. Noise and light were funneled down, and as I got close to the door of the changing room, looking up the concrete channel to courtside, I could see the legs and red coat hems of two security guys stationed there to guard this area. The crowd above and the fury of the game, the pounding sounds of the court, the whistles, the yells, reached down here like exotic music.

The door to the changing room was like the one I'd come through above, an old wood thing painted red, with three raised panels. If the security guys up there were smart, they'd have locked it. If not, I'd hide inside, waiting. When I rattled the knob, it didn't give; I shook it twice and swore. I'd have no choice but to lurk about ten feet down the gangway, hoping for a chance as the refs came rushing down the tunnel right after the game. I was likely to get grabbed by security guys. They'd drag me away as I was screaming something dumb like "Kam! Kam Roberts!"

I was still holding the doorknob when I felt it move. The bolt shot back inside, and as my heart seized up, the door opened toward me.

Bert Kamin looked me up and down.

"Hey, Mack," he said. "Jesus, am I glad to see you." He waved me inside and threw the bolt at once when I was beside him. Then he told me something I already knew.

He said, "I'm in a lot of trouble."

B. Troubled Heart

Bert has never really mastered the gestures of amiability. In my unworthy suspicions about him, I imagined he was reluctant to put a hand on your shoulder for fear of what he might reveal. But the fact is that Bert is just strange. His usual manner is of some hey-man hipster. He chews his gum and gives forth with cynical carping from the side of his mouth. I'm never sure exactly who he thinks he is—he comes on like somebody who didn't quite get the sixties, who wanted to be in on what was happening but was too tough or unsentimental to take part. He reminds me at times of the first guy I ever busted, an engaging little rat named Stewie Spivak who was a student at the U. and seemed to enjoy peddling dope much more than taking it.

Bert stood there now bucking his head, telling me I looked good, man, I looked good, while I appraised him too. His dense black hair had grown to an unbarbered length and his hands kept moving to shove it in place; he was unshaved and that weird out-of-kilter light in his eye was brighter than ever. Otherwise, he was neatly turned out in a black leather jacket and a fashionable casual ensemble: Italian sweater with a snazzy pattern, pleated trousers, fancy shoes and socks. Was this the attire of a man on the run? He didn't look quite right, but then he never did.

"So who sent you?" he asked me.

"Who sent *me*?" I reeled around on that line. "Come on, Bert. Who the hell are you kidding? Where've you been? What are you doing here?"

He hung back, squinting a bit, trying to comprehend my agitation in the forgiving way of a child. He remained happy for familiar company.

"I'm waiting for Orleans," he finally said.

"Orleans? Who in God's name is Orleans?" At that Bert's eyes glazed—an aura of galactic mystery took hold. I might as well have asked the secret of the universe, of life. The level of misunderstanding between us was immense—different dimensions. In the silence I noticed that a radio was on. Locked away here in this dungeon, he was still listening to the game. The ceiling was low enough that he was hunched over a bit out of caution, which furthered the impression of something more yielding in his character. He hadn't replied yet when I figured out the answer to my own question.

"The referee," I said.

"Right." He nodded, quite pleased. "Yeah. I'm not supposed to be in here. You either."

Kam Roberts was Orleans. I was piecing it out in my head. Archie owned Orleans, and Orleans, the referee, was Bert's friend. Archie was dead and was once in Bert's refrigerator and Bert was alive and hiding from somebody, maybe just the conference officials of the Mid-Ten. It was not adding. I tried it again, hoping to settle him down and get better information.

"Bert, what's going on here? The cops are looking high and low for you and, especially, for Orleans."

He jumped then. There was an old teacher's desk, probably

requisitioned from a classroom, on which the radio sat. Bert had rested against it until I mentioned the police.

"Whoa, whoa, whoa," he said. "For Orleans? The police are looking for Orleans? Why? You know why?" I realized then what was different about him—his emotions were unmasked. Grim and adolescent before, he now seemed almost childish. He was jumpier than I recalled, but also pleasingly sincere. I felt like I was dealing with a younger brother.

"Bert, it's not like the traffic reports, they don't explain. I've been putting little bits together here and there. My guess is that they think your buddy Orleans there has been shading games. For bookies."

He took this badly. He brought his long fingers to his mouth to ponder. The refs' room, as I'd remembered it, was strictly low-rent. On the other side of the court, where the Hands changed, the boosters had provided carpet and whirlpools, weight rooms, a country-club air. But there was nothing similar here. In the center of the room, there was an old backless bench of varnished oak splintered at a corner, and against the wall facing the door three crummy-looking lockers listed. They were rusted in places and one of them was pretty much staved in from a foot or fist hurled by some ref who'd heard those remarks from the crowd about his mother, his eyesight, the size of his penis a little more clearly than he'd allowed out on the floor.

"Bert, there's a lot of screwy stuff going on. There's a body in the refrigerator in your apartment. At least, there was. I think it's another pal of yours. Did you know that?"

He glanced up barely, grimly preoccupied, and nodded a bit.

"That's jail, right?" he asked.

He couldn't have meant murder.

"Fixing basketball games? I'd say that one's pen time, yeah."

He swore. He took a step to the door and then stopped.

"I gotta get him out of here."

"Bert, wait a minute. Why was this guy in your refrigerator?"

"How'd they find out, you think? The cops? About Orleans?"

Talking to Bert is always the same thing, his subject is more important than yours. You have to follow him around like a puppy or a three-year-old child.

"I have no idea, Bert. Frankly, they seemed to have known about Orleans before they knew about you. Actually, they're looking for somebody named Kam Roberts. Is that him?"

He answered me this time. "It's complicated." Then he pounded a fist on his thigh. "Shit," he said. "I don't understand. How'd they find Archie? Nobody knew he was in there."

Nobody knew Archie was in there and Bert liked it that way. A brief qualm of something, a feathery spooky feeling like being touched by a moth, passed over me. I scrutinized Bert's vacant manner for signs as I explained to him how it was, that I, not the cops, had seen the body.

"By the time they got there, somebody'd adiosed the corpse. Maybe you know who."

He had the nerve to draw back and look at me as if I'd lost it, then he reverted to his calculations. If the cops hadn't seen Archie, he asked, what brought them to Orleans?

"Bert, how am I supposed to know? They were down at the Russian Bath asking questions. Would they have heard about Kam Roberts there?"

"Oh right," said Bert. "Right, right, right." He snapped his fingers a number of times and did a few paces. "God, me and my mouth, man. My fucking mouth." He held still, in considerable pain. When he opened his eyes, he looked right at me.

"If anything happens to me, Mack, can you make sure he gets a lawyer? Will you promise me, man?"

"I promise you, Bert, but give me a hint here. What's gonna happen to you? What are you afraid of?"

With that, there was the first sign of the old Bert, the sometime madman, always on the brink of falling into his own volcano. Red fury mobilized his expression.

"Come on, Mack! You said you saw what they did to Archie."

"Who we talking here? Outfit?"

I got that much from him, a nod.

"And they want what? Money?" That was my first thought, that they were demanding to be made whole for the losses Archie had palmed off on them.

He looked at me.

"Orleans," Bert said.

"Come again."

"They want Orleans. You know, man. How to find him. Who he is. I mean, that's what they wanted from Archie."

"Did he tell them?"

"How could he? He didn't have any idea where I was getting this stuff. I had a guy I called Kam. That's all he knew." Bert was bouncing around pretty good now, twitchy, scrambling all over the little refs' room like a hamster in a cage. But I thought I was following him. Bert was giving Archie advance word on game outcomes. "Kam's Special." Archie knew only that.

"Did Archie tell them about you?"

"He said he wouldn't. At first. And then the last time I talked to him, he told me— You know, he was pretty emotional. He said they'd kill him if he didn't let them know where it was coming from. They wanted Kam. They gave him like twenty-four hours to bring them Kam. You know, he was beggin'." Bert dared a little look my way, just to see how I handled that thought, some guy pleading with you for a secret to save his life. Which Bert didn't reveal. That's why he was only peeking at me.

"I knew he'd give me up. I already figured I'd have to run. I was edge-city, I kind of snuck home, and I like open the fridge, and I'm so fucking freaked out, I'm like out of my mind, for Godsake what they did to him—" His voice cracked, it broke, big bad Bert Kamin. He squeezed his hands to his eyes. The sight was so strangely out of keeping with what I knew and expected of Bert that a little inky blot of suspicion again darkened my heart. This might all be showtime. Bert after all was a trial lawyer, which meant he was part hambone. But Bert's long dark face appeared earnestly tortured and weak. "What they fucking did to him. And I'm next. I knew that. They're not kidding around, these guys."

My days as a copper sort of deprived me of any respect for the mob. Mind you, there are policemen who fall in with them, who gamble, particularly, and end up on the vig, with their asses owned in a city minute. And there is even an Italian son or two who I always was told had come on the Force because the uncle was some big something who wanted a toehold in the department. But as guys, who are they? Just a bunch of dark Mediterraneans who didn't finish high school really. If you've seen a guy selling fruit down at the market you've seen your basic mobster—some dese dems and dosers with a lot of jewelry who couldn't find something better to do. Accepting the fact that human beings are pretty mean, who but some guy who feels like a pygmy gets his jollies out of making everybody crap in their boots? And they are also the most overpublicized group in history. A city this size has maybe fifty, seventy-five guys max who are really inside, and a bunch of little rats running beside them hoping to gobble up crumbs. That's the mob. They live out in these bungalows on the South End because they don't want the IRS asking where they got the dollars for anything else; they drink coffee and Amaretto and tell each other that they're tough and worry over which of them's wearing electronic underwear, FBI issue. Bad dudes, no doubt about that, not folks you want to get crosswise of or even have to dinner, but their business these days is shrinking. The gangs control drugs. Hooking, that's mostly for oddball stuff now, golden showers, Greek, not straight sex; pornography's the same. The only place they can really still turn a buck is gambling.

"And what do they want to do with Orleans? Kill him?"

"Maybe. I mean, who knows. Do you know? They say not. That's what Archie said, they won't hurt him."

"So what do they want?" I asked, but I caught up at that moment. Orleans was a golden goose and golden geese are not slain. They would want him to give them what he'd given Archie.

Points. Fixes. Games. I said that to Bert. "They want him to perform, right?"

"He'll never do it. It's not him. Even if he wanted to, he'd mess it up somehow. They'll kill him. Sooner or later."

"And that's why *you're* running? Here's what I don't get, Bert. What's that to you? In the end."

He didn't answer, but it was there for a second, just a sudden stricken look, his dark face riven by feeling. And I'm slow, Elaine, lumbering, like the coach said in high school, but I get there eventually. Bert was in love with him. With Orleans. There's no real etiquette for this. It's still not the thing to do, to tell your gay friend that you knew all along. So we said nothing.

"Anyway," I said eventually. "You're protecting him."

"Right. I've got to."

"Sure," I said.

He was back by the desk, haunted, caught up in the vastness of all these troubles. He said it aloud a couple of times—"God, what am I going to do?"—and then without any real warning or connection he focused on me.

"And what's with you?" he asked. "I don't get why you're here, man. Who sent you?"

"Our partners, basically, Bert."

He drew back again. He closed one eye. "For what?"

"They want the money back, Bert. No questions asked."

I'd caught him, surprised him. He hung there, mouth vaguely parted as he sought the right words. Taking a step closer to him, I was startled by my own impulse. I was actually halfway to some sly remark, some ingenious quip about splitting the dough. It was as if I'd stuck a hand inside myself, trying to find out what was there. But it was just the same awful mess and I said nothing.

There was a tremendous commotion outside about then. Footsteps, pounding, lots of voices. My first thought was that the ball had rolled down the tunnel and they were playing the game right there. Someone began hammering on the door so that it seemed ready to jump out of the frame. But that happened only

after Bert had looked me square in the eye, blinked, and swallowed so his large Adam's apple wobbled in his long throat where
the hair grew coarse and unshaven. His face was utterly empty
of guile.

He asked me, "What money?"

XVIII. RUNNING MAN

"Okay, pissface, open up." I recognized Pigeyes's voice. "Come on, Malloy. Give it up. Come on," he kept saying. He'd had me again. The guy gets a surveillance van to watch me gambol down the avenues and I don't wonder. I was a dangerous fool. I had been followed.

Bert started to speak and I lifted a finger in warning. When I mouthed the word "Police," Bert circled his jaw and did a brief swoon.

Pigeyes was still pounding, while I waited. The tail could not have been that good because I'd have heard somebody behind me in the gangway. So they were guessing. It was a good guess, but there was always the chance they'd go away.

I found my datebook in my pocket and wrote Bert a note: "If I can get rid of these guys, grab your pal as soon as the game is over and scram." We both started hopping around, trying to figure out where he should hide, while Pigeyes went on walloping the door and calling me names. Finally we noticed the shower and I helped Bert chimney up so that his back was braced against one tile wall and his feet were parallel. I drew the blue curtain slowly; none of the rusty hooks gave even the slightest tinkle. It looked okay.

By now somebody was working on the door hinges. I heard the tapping of a hammer and a screwdriver.

"Who is it?" I called sweetly.

"It's Wilt Chamberlain. Open up so we can play one on one."

Pigeyes was dressed the same as yesterday. With him, he had his reptile-skin sidekick, Dewey, who was holding the screwdriver and hammer, and the two security guys I'd seen at the top of the runway up to the court, who were along for the ride.

"*Voi*-fucking-*là*," Gino said. He pointed a finger at me and said, "Back." He was awfully pleased. He'd got the drop on me twice now, counting U Inn. You'd never take this out of Pigeyes. He loved hunting some scumbag down, the whole pure adventure. Plenty of squirts come on the Force like that, adventure their watchword, it's all in their head, car chases, street scenes, kicking doors in, girls in the cop bars who can't wait to see them get hard. But the biggest adventure most of the time turns out to be department politics, seeing who gets back-stabbed in the latest downtown deal. Oh, plenty of excitement in the abstract. Every day you go to work and know in some fraction of your heart you might not come home. But usually, everyone does. Instead, there are hours of paperwork; there are nights of lame jokes and burning your tongue on bad coffee; the same old same-old on the street. Lots of folks, and I'm one, they get their fill and move on, knowing that life's life and can only be so much of an adventure. The guys who want adventure and stay—Pigeyes—they're the ones who seem to go wrong. Being a smartass, a wise guy, a rogue on your own—that's an adventure too. That's how they figure. That's one of the reasons he is like he is.

The two security types followed Pigeyes in, both of them looking around, deeply chagrined. As Bert said, no one was supposed to be in here. Dewey stayed at the door. I talked to the security men, one white guy, one black, with matching potbellies, and the same vermilion sport jackets with the university crest on the breast pocket, both with polyester trousers and cheap shoes. This was too good a gig, getting paid to watch basketball games, for me even to have to guess what these fellas did for a day job. Coppers off duty, or my ma wasn't named Bess.

"You didn't let him get away with that old thing that he was looking for someone, did you?" I asked. "I've seen him badge his way into Sinatra. He'll say anything to get in for free."

Pigeyes cast me a dirty look as he wandered around. He flipped the doors on the three banged-up lockers against the far wall, not really expecting to see anything inside.

"What gives, Malloy?"

"I'm hiding."

"Funny place."

I told him about representing the U., getting the tour, learning about all the out-of-the-way places in here. "Billy Birken from Alumni Relations took me around." The name, I could tell, bought me a little something with Security.

Sensing this, Pigeyes said, "He's full of shit" and, as if to prove it, pointed one of his thick fingers at me. "Who you hiding from?"

I went to the door and grabbed the doorknob, which was so old and so often handled that the brass had worn off. I leaned past Dewey, who laid a hand lightly on my chest as I scouted the hall. Both the gangway and the tunnel runway up to the court were clear. I looked back at Pigeyes.

"You," I said and with that gave Dewey a little shove so he wouldn't be hit as I slammed the door between me and them and took off. I turned back once to make sure they were all right behind me.

I got a hell of a lot farther than you would think. Four hardass cops shagging my fanny, but all of them heavier smokers than me, and they were lagging after the first twenty feet. Mack the Moose with one bum wheel made a hairpin when I got courtside and bolted up the aisle beside the first-tier seats, taking the stairs three at a time. As I came up from beneath, the smell and color of the enormous crowd in all its great clamoring power seemed startling, like falling into the hot breath of some beast. Pigeyes was shouting prosaic things like "Stop him!" but nobody seemed inclined. People watched us—those who didn't crane around so they could keep up with the game—with the same amused curiosity they'd take in a parade. It was nothing to them, part of the spectacle. Though it slowed me down, I could not keep myself from laughing, especially with the thought of Bert sneaking out of the room. One guy in a Milwaukee sweatshirt yelled, "Sit down, you clowns."

When I reached the mezzanine level, my knee hurt like a bastard from my gallivanting, but I was holding my lead. Huffing and puffing, I went down the exit passageway, ran past a big refreshment stand, with its Coca-Cola sign clock and long stainless-steel counter, and took a quick right up the old concrete stairs for the upper tiers. I could hear their voices ringing up the stairwell behind me. On the top level, I popped into the men's room and hustled into one of the stalls and waited. In about five minutes the game would be over and I'd have a chance to get out with the crowd. But that meant entertaining Pigeyes at my house. Besides, if they lost me completely, they might go back to the changing room, near which Bert would be lingering, waiting for Orleans. So I hid out another minute or two, then adjusted my sport jacket and found a seat in the second balcony.

There were about forty seconds left on the big game clock when Pigeyes sat down beside me. The Hands were losing now by eighteen and were taking bad shots for treys, with the Meisters picking up the long rebounds. Gino was winded. His forehead was bright with sweat.

"You're fucking," he said, "under arrest."

"For what? There a law against running in a public place?"

"Resisting."

"Resisting? I'm sitting here talking to you almost like we were friends." Dewey came up then. He put his hands on his knees for a minute to catch his breath, then he sat down in the seat on the other side of me. The place was emptying, but there were enough people left to keep me safe. "I wanted to see the end of the game."

Pigeyes told me to fuck myself.

"Did you tell me I was under arrest, Gino? Did you have a warrant?"

Pigeyes looked at me levelly. "Yes," he said.

"Fine," I said. "Show me the warrant. Hey, miss," I called to a fat college girl two seats down, and reached for her sleeve. "Would you please witness something?"

The girl just stared.

"Don't be a smartass, Malloy."

"Battery of a police officer," said Dewey.

"The way I remember, you put your hand on me first."

They exchanged a primitive look. I could remember how much I hated lawyers when I was a cop. The game horn went off then. Various people swirled out on the floor, the cheerleaders, photographers, TV crews, more security guys and kid ushers, the players from both benches. Bert Kamin was right at the edge of the court, among a hundred gawking fans. I saw him from three levels above, a distance of two hundred feet. He motioned to Orleans and went running down the tunnel behind him.

"I think they could play in this conference," I said, "if they had a big man inside."

"Listen, pencil-dick. You're way past being humorous."

"Have I forgotten something, Gino? Did I take a shower with you?"

"Keep it up, Malloy." He sighted me down the line of a finger. "We been on your ass since six tonight. You tear out of your house, you run around here like some fuckin mutt smelling heat, I say you're here for a meet. You got a call and you showed, lickety-split."

"And who would I be meeting?"

"Stop playin, Malloy. Who am I looking for?"

He still didn't have the remotest idea who Kam Roberts was. He was suspicious of course, because this was a basketball game and that was what Archie was fixing. But he didn't know how. Eventually, of course, the significance of my presence in the refs' room would come to him. But he'd been too busy running after me for that glimmer to strike home yet.

"I'm going to tell you this again, Pigeyes, and so help me, if I'm lying then put me in the paddy wagon. I've never met this Kam Roberts. Never said boo to him."

"Then it's the other guy. What's-it. Bert."

"I'm a basketball fan."

"I've had it a lot with you, Malloy. Not a fucking little. A lot. I want to know what gives."

"Forget it, Gino." I puckered my lips and made that little motion, the lock and the key.

He wasn't kidding about having had it. He was all gone. Looking into Gino's eyes, no one would be surprised to find that humans are carnivores.

"Stand up." I didn't at first, but when he repeated it, I figured I'd about run out the string. He tossed my pockets then. He pulled them out viciously so they were hanging from my trousers. He threw my keys and folding money down on the floor. He jammed his hands in my sport coat and found my datebook there, which he went through page by page until he got to the note I wrote Bert. He passed Dewey the book and was so overheated that his lips were sort of rumbling around on their own. Finally, for lack of anything else to do, he spat a big wad on the floor.

"Illegal search," I told him. "With only two, three hundred witnesses. And all of them holding season tickets. I don't even have to take names."

He snatched the datebook from Dewey and threw it as hard as he could toward the scoreboard over the court. It flipped around in the air over the seats, then opened along its main seam and looked like a swallow in flight, diving at last and disappearing between the lights. Pigeyes got up close and lowered his voice.

"I'm coming back with a subpoena."

"Do what you like. You start subpoenaing a lawyer, Pigeyes, with all those privileges and stuff, you'll have some poor assistant prosecuting attorney still dragging to court after you've got your thirty."

"Malloy, I cut you too much slack, twice now. I could have jacked you up good with that credit card, and I'm feeling what I always felt about you. That you're an ass-wipe. That you don't know dick about how to say thank you."

"Thank you, Pigeyes."

It was as close as I'd come yet to getting cracked. He was about ready to handle the beef. Public place. Lots of witnesses. He didn't care. He'd make up some outrageous insult I'd uttered, one that took in his manhood, his mother, the Force, in one breath. I didn't flinch either. A scaredy-cat like me, but I was ready to take what was coming. Go figure. Something with me and this guy. I couldn't back off or give him a break. We were an always thing, me and Pigeyes. With the death rattle I'd have one hand groping to yank on his chain.

And he, in the meanwhile, had to hold back. He didn't have the room he wanted. It was the past, I suppose. I had more liberty with him than just any stray dog on the street. An instant passed before Gino got his impulses under control. Then he did what he liked to do. He threatened me.

"I'm still making you as dirty on this thing. You were stinkin with sweat yesterday when I was puttin you in it. And I'll find out why. I'm going to be as close behind you as a fart. You better mind your fuckin manners. Cause when I tag you, Malloy"—he touched me on the lapel, just his fingertips—"you'll be It."

He and Dewey walked away. They were about half a row down when Gino turned back.

"And by the way. We got an amazing videotape of your bath-

room window. Strictly fucking amazing. I'm gonna show it in
the Squad Room tomorrow night in case you want to come by."
He had that slug smile, oily, evil, enjoying the contemplation
of pain.

I picked up my things eventually, after they were gone, figuring all in all it probably wasn't going the way I would have
liked. A guy from the cleaning crew appeared, filling a huge
trash bag and advancing me little dark looks in the hopes I would
beat it, but I stayed put. I was wondering about Bert. Did he
have the money or not, and if he didn't, who did? In the big
empty stadium, I felt the perpetual nature of doubt, the way it's
always with us. In life, we just never know.

It struck me eventually that I was going to have to find some
way to get home. I walked out, hope against hope, but I knew
it. My car had been towed.

XIX. SATURDAY

A. Possible Connections

On Saturday morning I went to the office. I had little to do but attend a lunch of the Recruiting Subcommittee and answer my junk mail, but I came in as a matter of habit on Saturdays. It kept me from fighting with Lyle and impressed those of my partners who saw the sign-in sheet. I liked the day, in fact, wandering down the uncrowded streets of Center City where other attorneys headed to work, moving at leisure with their briefcases and overcoats and blue jeans. The whole day had the off-center, underwater slowness of a dream. No flipping telephone. No secretaries sneaking looks at the clock. No hubbub, no filing dates. No stressed-out aura from all those striving young people running around. I got in early and checked my voice messages and E-mail, thinking I might have heard from Bert, but the only word was from Lena, asking me to call when I arrived.

She came up from the library, wearing a button-down shirt of broad green stripes. She'd gotten the plane tickets and a beachfront hotel booking for Pico.

"What are we going to do there?" she asked.

"Investigate. Meet with a lawyer named Pindling. Find out what we can about an account at the International Bank of Finance."

"Great." She seemed pleased by the prospects, by me.

When she was gone, I took out the file on Toots's case, reviewing some of the records we would be offering to complete the defense, once Woodhull finished mauling Toots on cross-examination. My mind though remained on Bert and his problems, which would soon be getting worse. By now, Gino would have done the arithmetic: he'd seen the note in my datebook; he'd found me in the refs' room. Pigeyes would figure one of last night's refs was involved and would start hunting. I wanted to warn Bert—and finish our conversation about the money.

I tracked down a copy of the morning's *Tribune* in a stall in the john, but the refs' names weren't listed in the box score. After some reflection, I called Media Relations at the U. I figured they might not answer on Saturday, but I got hold of an obliging young woman. Introducing myself as Detective Dimonte, Kindle Unified Police, I awaited a telltale response, something like 'You again?' but she seemed unsuspecting.

"Brierly, Gleason, and Pole." She was reading to me from last night's press handout. Those were the refs' names.

"How about their first names and addresses?"

"Care of the Mid-Ten. Detroit."

"You're not gonna make me send a subpoena?"

She laughed. "You can send what you want. We don't have that information. The conference doesn't even like giving out the last names. There was a lawyer a couple of years ago who wanted to sue one of these guys for smashing somebody's car in the parking lot and he had to get a court order. I mean it. As far as I know, you will need a subpoena. You can call Detroit Monday, but they're incredibly tight with this stuff."

That made sense. No off-color fan mail. No fixes. When I put down the phone, I got out the local phone book. I found an Orlando Gleason, but nothing else close. Bert must have made Orleans's acquaintance out of town. All in all, Pigeyes had more hurdles ahead than I'd figured.

Not long afterwards, Brushy came in, full weekend regalia, blue jeans and running shoes. She looked pretty cute, wearing a big tan hat and carrying her briefcase, big as a saddlebag, and a bundle from the laundry wrapped in bright blue paper. She took just a step or two inside my door.

"That was nice yesterday," she said.

"I'll say."

"You mad? About your rash?"

"Hey," I said amiably. I told her I'd called her doctor.

"How is it?"

"Wanna check?"

"I'll remember you offered." She stood there, small, buttoned up, brimming with a great jolly glimmer. It made me a little sad to think how often Brush had been here before, walking into the office and feeling the thrill of knowing that she had this secret something going, a recollection of the senses in this quarter reserved for the grimly logical and perpetually banal. Everybody else arrived thinking of contract clauses and case names, and she rode up the elevators realizing she was going to share the sort of rosy smile we shared now, ripe with the antic-ipation of pleasure, of things that ought not be spoken of with the door open to the hall.

"I called you last night," I said.

"I was here late. I called you, too, when I got home, but you weren't around."

"Guess who I ran into?"

She actually dropped her laundry and clapped her hands when I mouthed Bert's name.

"He's alive?"

I motioned to close the door.

"Where is he?" she asked. "What's he been up to?"

I reminded her about what she said yesterday, about wanting to stay in the dark.

"Starting tomorrow," she responded.

I told her just a bit—Bert running from bad guys.

"But what did he say about the money?"

"Not clear," I said. "Our negotiations didn't get very far." I explained that we'd been interrupted by Detective Dimonte.

"It sounds like this guy's really after you," she said.

I just made a sound. Boy, was that true.

"So when will you hear again from Bert?"

"I'm sitting by the phone." I touched it, right next to me, the latest in technology, sleek and black, like something from Skylab. "In the meantime, I'm going to Pico Luan tomorrow to nose around."

"Tomorrow? Toots's hearing is on again Tuesday."

"The Committee only gave me two weeks. I'll do a two-day turnaround. Back Monday night. We're ready on Toots, right?" I lifted the brown expandable folder to show her I'd been minding the file. I added, "I'm taking Lena."

"Who's Lena?"

"First-year. From the U."

"The redhead? The cute one?"

"I'd say stylish."

Brushy frowned. "What do you need her for?"

"A prover." A witness—someone who could testify, if need be, in court. "This lawyer I want to see is supposed to be a little slippery."

Brushy wagged a finger and let forth in a self-mocking sing-song, "Don't be forgetting who's your girl now, Malloy."

"Brush, you flatter me."

"Mmm-hmm," she answered. I was not sure whether Brushy was feeling wise to the ways of humans in general or just me, but somehow we'd blown past airy humor; her expression was wizened by mistrust. This mood of few illusions reverberated between us, with its bluesy wave forms, and I felt a momentary commission to get to the point.

"Think you're ready to be a one-man woman, Brush?" It was as close as I could come to mentioning Krzysinski.

"I've always gone one at a time, Mack. It's just now and then the time's been short." She smiled a bit, but I realized intuitively that she meant it. Every one-night stand was a piece of Cinderella inside her head, a part of her always hoping that this slipper was going to fit. People's fantasies, even when they're morbid or trite, are somehow touching; it's the vulnerability, I suppose, the fact that lives, like cardboard cartons, fold so reliably along certain lines.

"You know," I said, "if the gals break my heart again, I don't think anyone'll find the pieces."

"Malloy, give me some credit, okay? I know you. I get it." She looked to the door to be certain it was closed, then walked to the desk and removed her hat before she gave me a smooch. I was still not ready to be soothed.

"How old are you now, Brush?"

"Thirty-eight," she said, then thought twice of it and looked at me fiercely. Jesus, this gal could be tough. She asked what difference that made, as if she didn't know. The riff of the independent person is, I don't need nobody. I used to hear the same thing from certain old coppers. But God never made a soul for whom that was completely true. I sort of felt sorry for Brushy. She didn't really take me as the hottest thing on the market and she couldn't misapprehend my reliability or my nature. She just thought I was the best she could get or, maybe, that she deserved. But we both knew I had certain virtues. I'd do what she told me; I needed her guidance. She was smarter than me. And she thrilled me through and through.

"I was just thinking about you," I said.

"Thinking what?"

"How it is," I answered. "You know. The bright fires of youth burning down. A body gets lonely."

"Very literary."

"The Irish." I touched the inside of my wrist. "Verse is in the blood."

"You have a dislikable side, Mack."

"So I've been told."

"It doesn't give you the right to hold someone in contempt, just because you get their number. You're not such a mystery yourself, you know."

"I see."

"You're a miserable wretch, in case you think anybody else hasn't noticed."

I told her to ease up and got to my feet. I took her firmly by her full shoulders and gripped her to my chest, where she willingly lingered, a foot shorter.

"Lunch?" she asked.

"Recruiters," I said.

She groaned sympathetically at the prospect of committee work.

"Tonight?" I asked.

"It's my parents' anniversary." She brightened. "You could come. Warm Italian family."

"Uh-oh."

"I suppose you're right."

We looked at each other.

"Tuesday," I said. "Toots."

"Toots." From the door, she cast a gloomy eye as I stood by my desk. Maybe there is never really a chance to fully combine after adolescence. Maybe all those tribal types, the Indians and the Hebrews, had it right, marrying everyone off by the age of thirteen. After that it's hit-or-miss, the spirit singing out but forced to surmount the channels, the borders dug deep of what has become recognized, if not cherished, as the self.

"Open or closed?" she asked from the door.

I flicked my hand.

"I'm here," I told her, "either way."

B. Checking My Points

In a bow to democracy and to help with the work, the Committee over the years has created more subcommittees than either House of Congress, each one empowered with dominance over some minor region of law firm life. We have subs on ethical questions, on staff employment, on computer usage, pro bono work, and paper recycling. In this regime, recruiting is regarded as a mixed bag. It wields genuine authority, hiring both summer clerks and the first-year lawyers who join G&G every fall following the bar exams, but the workload is substantial and can never be fully managed in the rush of the week. By long-standing agreement, we meet when we have to for Saturday lunch. At this time of year, when our activities lull, it's only once a month, and after reviewing a final list of summer hirings and calendared interviews for next fall, the five of us—Stephanie Plotzky, Henry Sommers, Madge Dorf, Blake Whitson, me—fell, as we generally do, into gossip.

"So what do you hear?" asked Stephanie. "I saw Martin this morning. He just said, 'Bloodier than ever.' He looked beat and it was nine o'clock." We were two blocks down from the Needle at Max Heimer's, a deli characterized by second-rate food and Third World hygiene. Stephanie had ventured this goody, leaning over the table, her round face, highly made up even on Saturday, close to the container of pickles, whose side was spattered with grime.

"The corporate guys are getting hit," said Henry. "The eighties are over." He was a bankruptcy lawyer himself, on boom times. Madge, a deal person, didn't really agree, and we debated a little among ourselves, as if it made any difference.

The Committee members were over at Club Belvedere today, in one of the elegant conference rooms, licking their pencils and passing out points. Groundhog Day was Thursday. My partners reacted with the same anxieties all the good boys in grade school exhibited on Marking Day, when the nuns sent us home so they could fill in our report cards. I never worried. I knew what was coming—A's and boxes of corrective checkmarks in the sections reserved for deportment.

But I was not as sure where I was headed this year at the firm. I thought my deal with the Committee when I agreed to go looking for Bert was no more pay cuts, but nobody'd actually said that. My four partners on Recruiting were up-and-comers and it was clear that Pagnucci had given each one the treatment—some soothing, some encouragement. They were all going to make more money next year. As for me, I could tell from the sidelong glances that each of them sensed, supposedly privately, that my share was going to be reduced again. It was never ax murder. Just a 5 percent cut every year. Still, I walked back to the building after lunch alone and brooding.

All right, I admit it—these decreases each year hurt my feelings. Money's the big scorecard in this kind of life; there's no winning percentage, no runs batted in. It's always struck me as meaningful how we refer to the percentage of firm income we each are awarded as "points." Your partners tell you each year what they think you are worth. By now I can live without everything the marginal dollar buys, except self-esteem.

I sat in my office. The cold winter sun could be seen through the screen of clouds; its light played on the river, tossing Christmas spangles across the greenish reflections of the big buildings on the banks. I tried to set aside my feelings of deprivation to think about Bert, but I got nowhere with that. How much? I kept thinking. How much were they taking away this year? What an effing load of nerve. I'm running from coppers and they're cutting my pay. I kept this up until I was seething. I was in one of my states, angry and mean, Bess Malloy's boy reeling from what he was missing. I drifted upstairs, not really telling myself where I was going, then looked both ways down the book-lined hall and slipped into Martin's office, figuring he'd have retained a draft of the proposed point scheme somewhere in his drawer where I'd peeked at it three years before. I wasn't worried at that moment about being caught. Let somebody catch me. Fucking let them. I had a few things to say. Eighteen years, for Chrissake. And they're paying Pagnucci on my back.

The most important papers in Martin's office were locked in his credenza behind the thousand-year oak. I'd seen him open the drawer a hundred times before, lifting the rubber belly on his hula dancer clock to reveal the battery and the little gold key. I had the usual drilling sense of isolation when I was alone in the firm and screwing around. The big corner office with its reliquary of goofball objects—the paintings, the sculptures, the weird furniture—was dim and I hesitated to turn on the light. What the hell would I accomplish? I wondered. Would I shit in the drawer, like some badass burglar expressing himself? Could I complain? I might. There were a lot of people around here who lay on the floor and moaned as GH Day approached, or went office to office sniping. It didn't matter, though, really. I was being bad. I felt just like a kid, but I'd felt like that before and there was some peculiar purification in acting on impulse.

Martin's private drawer is a mess. I was shocked to discover that the last time I did this. I would have expected exacting order. Martin is one of those persons, so large and voluble, so much a presence, that it is always disquieting to realize how much of his soul he conceals. I suppose Martin did the filing himself, given the utter sensitivity of the documents, and chaos reigned without a secretary's assistance. There were hanging folders in the drawer but many of the papers had been slopped unstacked on the unfinished slats of the bottom. A lot of the most intimate secrets of the firm were in here. Letters from a shrink saying that one of our first-years would slit his throat if we fired him. (We hadn't.) Financial projections for the end of the year, which looked pretty bad. There was also a file with written evaluations of the performance of each partner. I was tempted to read through the disdainful comments about me, but decided to pass on the chance for more self-laceration. Finally I found a folder marked "Points."

Inside was a photocopy of an early draft, handwritten by Carl Pagnucci, of this year's point distribution plan. I didn't look at it closely, because in the same file I found a memo. It had been folded in four, but the handwritten initialing at the top could not be mistaken. J.A.K.E. John Andrew Kenneth Eiger. Jake loved his initials. They were on everything, his shirt cuff, his beer mugs, his golf bag. Like anything else in his hand, I could imitate the initials so well that I didn't even need a subscript to show I was signing with his authority, but nobody else around here was quite as skillful. I had no doubt this was authentic.

PRIVILEGED AND CONFIDENTIAL

18 November

TO: Robert Kamin, Gage & Griswell
FROM: John A.K. Eiger, General Counsel,
   TransNational Air
RE: First Wave 397 Settlements

I wanted to advise you of a flap concerning the 397 settlement payments which arose while you were trying the Grainger claim. As usual, the plain-tiffs' lawyers are fighting with each other about litigation expenses. It seems that Peter Neucriss engaged a firm in Cambridge, Mass., called Liti-plex for litigation support—apparently they pro-vided crash reconstruction, computer modeling, consulting engineers, expert testimony, analysis of the NTSB proceedings, and records management. Litiplex has a series of invoices outstanding to-taling about $5.6 million. Neucriss says he hired them with the consent of all lead counsel for the

class and says I agreed at the time of the settlement that Litiplex would be paid from the 397 fund.
The class lawyers say there was no such agreement
—not too surprising, since paying Litiplex off
the top, as Neucriss is demanding, will reduce the
class lawyers' fee by about half a million dollars. Both sides are threatening to take up the issue with Judge Bromwich. I am very much afraid that
Bromwich will ask for an accounting, which will
lead to discovery of the fund surplus. Rather than
take that risk, and accepting that I may have made
a commitment to Neucriss, I'll authorize payment
of Litiplex's invoices as a below-the-line charge
against the surplus. Please deliver the following
checks to me.

Attached was a listing of Litiplex invoice numbers and the
amounts supposedly due.

I no longer had to look for what Bert had transmitted to
Glyndora. *'Per the attached, re agreement with Peter Neucriss
. . .'* This, clearly, was it. But I read the memo three or four
more times as I sat there in Martin's empty office, feeling as if
somebody had put a cold hand on my heart. I kept asking myself
the same thing, the voice within speaking in the forlorn tones
of a child. What was I going to do now?

XX. MEMBERS OF THE CLUB

The Club Belvedere is Kindle County's oldest social club, erected in the Gilded Age. Here the true elite of the county, men of commerce and standing, have dined and played squash with each other for more than a century. Not your usual grubby politicians whose power is transient and, worse yet, borrowed, but people with fortunes, the owners of banks and industrial concerns, families whose names you see on old buildings, who will still be prominent here in three generations and whose children are apt to marry one another. These are folks who, generally speaking, like the world as it is, and virtually every achievement in social progress which I can recall has involved a celebrated fracas among the club membership, some of whom have inalterably opposed the admission of first Catholics, then Jews, blacks, women, and even a single Armenian. You would think that a sensible human would find this atmosphere repulsive, but the cachet the Belvedere confers seems to overwhelm almost every scruple, and Martin Gold, for instance, in relaxed conversation spoke of nothing but "the club" for a solid month —how good the food was, how handsome the locker rooms— when he was elected to membership over a decade ago.

The club is an eight-story structure in Revival style that occupies half a block in Center City, not far from the Needle. I dashed over there, Jake's memo in my pocket, and swept in past the doorman. The facility is splendid. The entire first floor is paneled in American walnut, handsomely burnished to a deep tone which seems to embed the glow of low lights and reminds me inevitably of the brown-skinned men who chopped these trees, and their descendants in livery who've kept the wood polished to a sheen like somebody's shoes. An imposing dual staircase of white marble rises at the far end of the lobby, adorned with the club crest and winged cherubs, emblems of the period when Americans felt their surviving republic was destined again to achieve the greatness of Greece.

Naturally, I was not even in the lobby long enough to check my topcoat when here, goddamn it, was Wash. He was carrying, of all things, a golf club, a wood, gripping it like a dead goose by the neck, right below its lustrous persimmon head. I could not imagine what he was doing. It was in the twenties outside and the ground was frozen hard. He was equally surprised to see me, and met my appearance with a member's vaguely scornful air for a known outsider. He was wearing a smashing houndstooth sport jacket, checks of black and autumnal gold, and gleaming tasseled loafers. Squashed down below the neck of his open button-down shirt so that it was partly concealed, as if even Wash recognized that this was a ludicrous affectation, an ascot peeked out, spotted with itsy-bitsy paisleys. I had no idea what I was going to say when he greeted me, but I was saved by instinct.

"Meeting over?" I asked. Wash is far too cowardly to want to discuss with me the Committee's decisions about points, especially mine. That job fell every year to Martin, who, after the formalities of Groundhog Day, would honor me by a visit to my office and clap me on the back, creating the impression that he, at least, maintained firm opinions about my value. Instead, Wash's face weakened at once into a sappy ingratiating expression. Up close you can see a certain studied nature to Wash's amiable mannerisms. Pressed, he has no instincts of his own. He is a collection of everybody else's gestures, the ones he sees as appealing, winning, sure not to offend.

"Not quite," he answered. "Martin and Carl needed a break for the phone. We'll resume at four. Thought I'd take the opportunity to clear my head." Wash hefted the golf club; only the fear that I might actually detain him kept me from saying that I was glad to finally know what it was for. Wash, meanwhile, escaped gladly from my company and headed for the gilded doors of the elevators.

I did not leave the lobby. With my topcoat checked, I took a straight-backed chair in a small paneled alcove near the cloakroom and the telephones. I still didn't know what I was doing here. I had rushed over to confront Martin, but now I was moving as if my weight had tripled, and thinking at the same pace. What would that exercise accomplish? Plan, I told myself, think. Beneath my hand, my knee, to my considerable surprise, had started to tremble.

A few years ago Martin's pal Buck Buchan, who was running First Kindle, got in Dutch in the S&L crunch and Buck made a few calls so that Martin was hired as special counsel to the board. Buck and Martin go back to a time when the mind of man runneth not to the contrary, Korea and the U. when they were both trying to get in the girdles of the same sorority girls. There's a picture someplace of both of them in white socks and bow ties. I was with Martin the morning he had to go tell Buck they were taking his job. It was the end of the line for Buck, the conclusion of an upper-class life of achievement, a daily existence of hopping along the highwire, with the eyes of the world upon him and his body full of the erotic pleasure of power. The tent was coming down for Buck; he would have to tend his wounded soul in the festering dark of scandal and shame. Buck had dropped the ball and Martin was going to tell him, eye to eye, man to man, and remind Buck of what he undoubtedly always knew, that for all the hours he and Martin had spent together matching lively minds and senses of destiny, no one could expect Martin Gold to take a dive, to abandon the noble traditions of his professional life. Martin went off to this meeting with a graven face, shadowed and grieved. Everybody here admired his grit—and so did the board at First Kindle, which has hired Martin since then with increasing frequency. But how good are all those principles when you and your law firm come out on the short end of the stick? The answer—the memo Martin had stashed—was folded in my shirt pocket.

I should have known better of course than to go after Wash. He's a weak person, never any help at all in a crisis. But when push came to shove, I wasn't ready to take on Martin—I lived with my father until I was twenty-seven and never once told him that I knew he was a thief. Nor did I want to confront Pagnucci's icy calculations. That would require more forethought and surer resolve. Instead, I went to an attendant, the kind of good-looking retainer you expect in this sort of place, a guy in a navy blazer and white gloves, retired military probably, and asked if he had any idea where Mr. Thale could have gone with a golf club.

He directed me to the second sub-basement, a cavernous service area that had probably doubled as a fieldhouse decades ago, before a sturdy running track had been put down under a dome on the roof. Now a flooring of green plastic turf had been laid over the concrete and a line of folks stood whacking golf balls. Many of these people were in sweats. Down this low, it was chilly, maybe 65 degrees. The green rug of the tee area extended twenty feet or so to a curtain of netting that was suspended from the ceiling and draped in layers like a veil. Beyond was a region of complete blackness, darker than doom. Somewhere out there must have been some kind of wiring, because mounted from the concrete abutments, directly over each golfer, was what looked like a green electric scoreboard. I watched as the guy nearest me hit and then studied the screen overhead, where a progression of white dots appeared, meant, I eventually realized, to show the predicted flight of the ball. After the last dot lit up, a digital readout popped up, announcing the supposed distance of the shot.

I finally spotted Wash down the line, flailing away. He had a bucket of balls and had laid his fine jacket out neatly behind it. He swung awkwardly. He'd probably been playing his whole life, without ever quite getting the game.

Seeing me approach, Wash's look hardened. I knew at once he thought I'd come to beseech him about my points and he was already drawing himself up to a high-minded stance in which he could remind me, with his usual perfect cordiality with underlings, that I was way out of line. Instead, to disarm him, I took the memo from my pocket and watched him unfold it. He read it standing on the driving mat. His eyes had a sort of hyperthyroid extension from his face anyway and they were quick, with little throbbing veins jumping about. The air around us raced with the steady rhythmic click of balls struck and rising. When Wash finished, he looked utterly uncomprehending.

"It's Jake," I said.

He recoiled somewhat. He checked over his shoulder on the other golfers, then pushed me back toward the steel door I'd come through to enter this area, where the light trailed off and the full subterranean dark began to reach toward you, along with the spooky underground sounds of the building.

"You're making assumptions," Wash said. "Tell me where this came from."

I told him. I didn't know how to explain and I didn't. But even Wash recognized that my bona fides were a side issue. It was obvious from the results that I had good reason to search.

"The memo's a phony, Wash. There's no Litiplex, remember? There are no records at TN. Jake faked this. Maybe Bert's in on it too. There are a million questions. But it's Jake for sure."

Wash scowled again and took a gander over his shoulder. His look was reproving, but he was too well brought up to tell me to keep my voice down.

"I say again you're making assumptions."

"Like hell. You explain this."

The whole notion of a challenge clearly vexed him. I was putting him on the spot. Then I saw Wash's pale, soft face become firm as he fixed on an idea.

"Perhaps it's Neucriss," said Wash. "Some game of his. Maybe he made all this up." Peter, God knows, was capable of anything. But I had realized still sitting in Martin's office why he had contacted Peter. Martin had the memo. He wanted to know what was going on. He wanted to know if the document was real or a fraud, if Neucriss, by some improbable circumstance, could explain. But it wasn't Neucriss jacking us around. It was Jake.

"Sure," I said to Wash, "sure. So we get Jake in Martin's office and tell him there's no Litiplex, and does Jake say, 'Oh my God, Neucriss told me there was'? Hell no. He acts like this whole thing's a shock to him. 'How dare Bert,' he says. 'And by the way, if you don't find him, let's never hear about this again.' This only adds one way. Jake wrote this frigging memo to Bert. Bert gave him the money. And Jake's got it now. He's covering himself, Wash. And Martin's helping him."

"Don't be absurd," he said immediately. He was reacting to the idea of Martin as corrupt. His mouth worked around, as if he could actually absorb the bad taste.

"Absurd? You think about this, Wash. Who was it who said he'd called the bank down in Pico? Who told you that the General Manager, whatever his name is, Smoky, that he indicated between the lines it was Bert's account? Who'd you hear that b.s. from?"

Wash is a good deal shorter than me, and my height seemed at the moment, as it is now and then, an odd advantage, as if I was out of reach of refutation.

"Think about Martin's performance the other day," I said, "dragging Jake in and spilling the beans after you and Carl had decided otherwise. What did you make of that?"

"I was put out," Wash said. "I told Martin so afterwards. But that's hardly the sign of some dark conspiracy, that he felt he had to speak up."

"Come on, Wash. You want to know why Martin whistled Jake in? He *wanted* Jake to know. He wanted it, Wash. He wanted Jake to know that Martin had the goods on him and was keeping his mouth shut."

A certain blankness set in as Wash pondered all of this. He was very slow.

"You're putting this the wrong way. I'm sure Martin found this document somehow and realized, I suppose, that for the time being it was best not coming to light. You're making it sound sinister."

"It is sinister, Wash."

He frowned and torqued away. He took one more look in the direction of the other golfers. I could see that my brusqueness and bad manners had finally stimulated Wash to a sense of offense.

"Look, man," he said, using that term, "man," in an old-fashioned high-born way, "he was following the logical imperatives here. Don't be so quick to scorn. Or condemn. Think this through. This firm cannot go on without Jake. Not in the short run. Tell me, Mack, you're such a clever fellow—tell me. If you run and do something half-cocked, you tell me what your plans are." His aged light eyes, pocketed by all that used flesh, glimmered with rare directness. The plans he was asking me to specify were not an investigative scheme. He meant what plans did I have to make a living without Jake. I actually took an instant to let the little logical steps descend. Nobody was going to reward my virtue if I put a knife in Jake's heart. I knew that. I'd been hugging his hind end for years with that realization. Nothing had changed really. It's just that the cost would be a little bit higher, in terms of my own self-respect.

"So that's it? I'm supposed to say dandy? That's Martin's answer. Let Jake steal. Just so long as he sends business. 'Hey, Jake, you know that I know. So cut the crap with the firm in Columbus. Let's resume the gold rush.' Come on, Wash. This is making me sick."

There was a sudden thunderous rumble above and we both jolted. One of the golfers had bounced a shot off the heating ducts on the ceiling. They were padded in foam but still let forth a tremendous sound on impact. The instant of brief fright seemed to prompt Wash to an effort at candor.

"Look, Mack, I can't read Gold's mind. Obviously he prefers to keep his plan, whatever it is, to himself. But you've known this man for years. Years. Are you telling me you can't trust Martin Gold?" Wash and I, in this basement, snapping in whispers, posed close as lovers, both stood struck by that question. Wash was doing what he always did—what he did the other day when the Committee talked over Jake's proposal that we stay silent if Bert didn't return. Wash was posturing, shooting airballs, taking the easy way out. He knew just what was happening. Not every detail; neither did I. I still found it impossible to calculate how Bert fit in, how Martin had been able to blame him confident that he would not reappear. But Wash nevertheless had the lowdown on this scene: it was grubby and evil. He knew that instinctively because it was exactly what Wash, with no reflection, would have done—swap Jake the money for the survival of the firm. And he was keeping himself from speaking that sooty truth by pretending that Martin might have been up to something better.

"You're a fool, Wash," I said suddenly. In the midst of everything else, the seething emotions, the basement gloom, I walked away feeling great. Pure primitive pleasure. I had needed to say that for years.

I had wrested the memo from Wash without resistance. I folded it into quarters again and jammed it in my pocket as I strode up the gray steel stairs that had led me down. It was all clear now. By the time I was back up in the grand surroundings, amid the wooden walls and the cut-crystal sconces, I felt motivated and strong, mean and myself. I was done being little boy disappointed. I was man among men. When I forged through the revolving doors to the winter street, I was starting to plan.

XXI. THE INVESTIGATION BECOMES AN INTERNATIONAL AFFAIR

A. International Flight

The TN Executive Travelers Lounge, where I waited for Lena Sunday morning, afforded a rare vantage on a world askew. The place looked terrific. The interior designer produced the kind of tasteful space-age effect I'd have strived for in my office if I ever decorated, lots of curved woods and big windows, sleek leather chairs and granite end tables upon which were perched those special telephones operated by credit cards with two or three jacks for your portable modem and fax. The elegant-looking ladies guarding the door examined the entrants, who, every one of them, flashed their membership cards with the same air, Hey, look at me, I'm in the front of the boat, I really made it. Nipponese businessmen flying for thirty hours dozed on the fancy furniture; well-turned-out executives cracked away at their laptops; wealthy couples conferred, one of them always looking anxious with the prospect of flight. A waiter in a white jacket wandered around with a tray to see if anybody wanted a drink, while voices from the Sunday-morning TV news shows emerged from the bar.

Here met is the Flying Class, a group ever expanding, whose

real workday is spent in the sky, whose true office is an aisle seat on a DC-10, folks who have so many million award miles they could fly to Jupiter free. These are the orphans of capital, the men and women who have given up their lives for the corporate version of manifest destiny, who are trying to fling far some company's empire in the name of economies of scale. I had an Uncle Michael who was a traveling salesman, a sad sack with an ugly brown valise, one of those lacquered boxes that seemed welded to his hand. His was regarded as the fate of a misfit. Now it's a badge of status to be away from home four nights a week. But on God's green planet is there anything more depressing than an empty hotel room at ten at night and the thought that work, privilege, economic need not only claim the daylight hours but have, however briefly, entitled you to these awesome lonesome instants in which you're remote from the people and the things, tiny, loved, and familiar, that sustain a life?

Listen to me. What was *I* missing but my easy chair and the TV set and bloviating moments interacting with Lyle? And I'd have Lena's youthful company. My briefcase and travel bag were between my knees. I'd packed light—underwear, a suit to do business, swimming trunks, and a few items I'd need: my passport, my Dictaphone, some TransNational Air stationery from the office, an old letter signed by Jake Eiger, and three copies of TN's annual report. Plus the memo I'd found in Martin's drawer, which was never going to leave my sight. Like Kam, I'd also taken a $2500 cash advance on my new golden credit card, which had been messengered to the office on Friday. I had been up most of the night scheming and I shut my eyes, imagining the wind on Pico, fragrant with sea salt and tanning oil as it rattled the palms.

"Yoo-hoo." The voice was sweetly familiar, but I still jumped a little when I opened my eyes.

"Brushy Bruccia, as I live and die."

"So," she said, seeming perky and young. She looked happy

and pleased with herself. Her bag was slung over her shoulder and she carried her coat. She wore jeans.

"Where you going?" I asked.

"With you."

"Really and truly? What happened to Lena?"

"Emergency assignment. She'll be in the library all night."

I got it then. I told Brushy I didn't need to ask from who.

"That girl has a lean and hungry look."

"She's got a look," I said, "I'll give you that."

Brushy punched me solidly in the arm, but I was too embarrassed to carry on in front of all these men. We walked over to the leather chairs. Neither of us said anything.

"You're supposed to be pleased," she told me eventually.

"How could I not be?" I was feeling impinged upon. I had my plans for Pico, which depended on a traveling companion who was more credulous than Brushy.

"Let's try this again."

She walked away and came around a handsome rosewood divider that sported CRTs listing arriving and departing flights.

"Mack! Guess where I'm going."

"With me, I hope."

"Now you've got it."

I told her she was odd.

"By the way," she said, "what are we doing down there?"

" 'By the way' nothing," I said. "Forget 'we.' Remember our deal? No askee, no tellee. You're not on the team."

A gal with a radio voice announced our flight, while Brush absorbed my rebuff lightly. She hung her head sideways; she fluttered her eyes.

"Oh dear," asked she, "whatever will you do with me?"

B. That Old Dance Step

This, the high season, was not my favorite time in Pico Luan. I had last been here years ago during the summer, when the capital, Ciudad Luan, was almost a ghost town, but in this season the homebound travelers, grownups and kids in their bright clothes, were crowded in the airport like the huddled masses from a steerage vessel. Their tanned faces were as surprising as the sweet breath of heat that greeted us as we descended the TN airliner staircase. Even in the long light, the tropical sun was compelling, so vital that winter at once was only a sad memory.

"God," said Brushy, shaking her hands free in the mild air.

There was a rental car waiting. TN, as usual, had coughed up great accommodations right on the Regent's Beach, a nine-mile stripe of sand, white and uncluttered, that polishes the toes of the Mayan Mountains. Enormous and green, the foothills loom above the coast. In this season, with all the high-flyers and snowbirds down here, the narrow roads were crowded, and I found a back way out of the airport. Brushy opened the windows and took off her hat and let her short dark hair rise in the breeze. We whizzed along past the little lean-to houses with their metal roofs, the hand-lettered signs of occasional stores and stands offering local foods. Huge plants with leaves the size of elephant's ears grew in clumps at the roadside. The eternal Luanders strolled unmolested in the middle of the narrow roads, yielding for the car and then returning, pacing along down the center stripe, frequently barefoot.

The Luanders are pleasant people. They know they have it made, having mastered the white man through his greed. They have been bankers since the Barataria Bay pirates began storing their gold in the caves above Ciudad Luan—C. Luan to the locals—and the Luanders today remain as casually indiscriminate about clientele. International narcotics magnates, tax cheats from many lands, and upper-crust bankers mingle congenially in this land of little restraint, sharing the tiny nation with its polyglot people in whose blood is mingled the DNA of Amerindians, African slaves, and a variety of runaway Europeans—Portuguese, English, Dutch, Spanish, and French. Pico has survived despots, Indian conquerors, and two centuries of Spanish rule, which ended in 1821, when Luan chose to become a British protectorate rather than be subsumed by the sovereignty claims of nearby Guatemala. In 1961, when Pico achieved independence, its parliament adopted the strict bank-secrecy laws of Switzerland and some of the B.W.I. islands.

With the acceleration of the offshore economy and the vast riches of today's pirates in neighboring Latin nations, who trade in powder rather than pieces of eight, Pico has gone through startling development in the last three decades. All the dough that's stashed here goes untaxed, and for that reason is not apt to leave. There's a $100 airport tax, a $10 tariff for every wire transfer, and a flat 10 percent VAT on everything that's bought or sold. Burgers for the family in a restaurant in C. Luan can cost one hundred bucks. But the combination of no income tax and financial privacy means there is steady commerce and plenty of jobs. The Luanders remain remote, cordial, even, as British discipline made them, correct, but confident about the native way of wanting less. Fast-paced and ham-fisted, white people are regarded with whatever good nature as freaks.

Our hotel, at the far end of the beach, three or four miles outside C. Luan, was terrific. We had two little thatch-roofed cabanas side by side, self-contained units, each with a kitchen, a bar, and a bedroom that looked out on the water. Brushy had to reach her secretary at home to rearrange tomorrow's appointments, and I stepped outside on the small terrace of my unit as her voice rose in occasional frustration over the difficulty of getting a U.S. connection.

The sun was heading down now, a great rosy ball burning away in the clear sky. We'd been traveling all day most companionably, doing crosswords on the plane, holding hands, gossiping about our partners and items in the Sunday *Times*. Out on the beach, various mothers, weary at the end of the day, called for their kids with fading humor. Pico, originally the haven either to guys who stepped off planes with wraparound shades and a firm grip on their valise, or a few archaeologists drawn by the enormous shrines the Mayas had built high in the mountains in sight of the ocean, is, after decades of promotion by TN, taking hold as a family vacation spot. By air, it's an hour farther than the islands, but it's less overrun and sports more notable sights. I watched kids scramble around between the legs of their parents, the little ones flirting with the waves and running screaming up the beach. One boy was lugging coconuts, still in their smooth brown husks, so that it looked a little like he was mounting a collection of heads. The sailboats were still out, but the water was losing its color. In the blazing sunlight it was a radiant blue, the result perhaps of copper deposits on the coral floor, a hue you thought existed solely in ads for color film.

"All done." Brush was off the phone. She'd put on a kind of sundress and we walked up to the hotel and had dinner on the veranda, watching the pink fingers take hold of the sky, the water licking down on the beach. With my blessing she had a couple of drinks while I knocked down iced teas. She was looking happy and loose. Halfway through dinner a native band started playing a few rooms away in the bar inside, and the music and laughter came through the open french windows. The rhythm and themes were haunting, that Central American sound, pipes and flutes, sweet melodies like an echo out of the mountains.

"What a place." Brushy looked with yearning at the sea.

"I kind of think this is charming," I said. "Your following me."

"Somebody had to do something," she told me.

I was as ever dishonorable, and pretended to have no idea what she might mean. She peered into her drink.

"I thought a lot about that conversation. In your office yesterday? People are entitled to change, you know." When she raised her eyes, she had that look again, all pluck and daring.

"Naturally."

"And you're right about me. But I don't have to apologize for that. It's a natural thing. The older you get, the more you wonder about things that are—" She faltered.

"What?"

"Enduring."

I flinched. She saw me.

She put a hand to her eyes.

"What am I doing?" she asked. Even with the candle guttering on the table, I could see she had flushed suddenly, maybe the liquor, maybe the heat adding to the effect of the strong emotion. "God, what do I see in you?"

"I'm honest," I told her.

"No, you're not. You're self-deprecating," she said. "There's a difference."

I gave her the point. "You deserve better," I told her.

"You're not kidding."

"I mean it." I was as resolute as I could be. It was not, I swear, easy for me. But I was having one of those lucid moments when I could tell just how it would go. Brushy would always blame me for not being better and herself for not wanting more.

"Don't tell me what's good for me, okay? I hate when you do that, like you're Lazarus, who crawled out of his cave just to do Ann Landers's column for a week."

"Jesus Christ," I said. "Ann Landers?"

"You try to make people dislike you, Mack," she told me. "You lure them in, then drive them away. If that's supposed to be some form of winning Irish melancholy, I want you to know I don't find it charming. It's sick," she said. "It's nuts." She threw her napkin in her plate and looked out to the sea to gather herself.

After some time she asked if it was too late to swim.

"Tide's out. It's shallow for a quarter of a mile. The water is 83 degrees year round." I tried smiling.

She made a sound, then asked if I'd brought a suit. She held out a hand as she stood.

The path to the beach was carved through the high ragged weeds and Bermuda grasses and lit by little fixtures on stanchions at the point of each stair. Sunday night, even in Pico, was quiet. There was action on the beach, but that was closer to C. Luan, where the big hotels were clustered. Down here, where it was mostly condos, there was a deserted, summery air, except for the band that struck up periodically a few hundred yards off in the hotel bar. We swam a little, kissed a bit, and sat there while the water washed around us. Middle years and acting like eighteen. Every time I thought about it, I wanted to groan.

"Swim with me," Brushy directed, and she splashed out a bit to a deeper point. Closer to shore the gathered shells were hard on the feet, but about fifty yards out the sand was soft and she stood lolling against me. The moon had been up for a while but was growing brighter, a blue neon glow spilling down like an apron beneath a few boats moored for the night. The hotel and its little outbuildings and the giraffe-like coconut palms hulked on shore, dark on darker.

"There are fish in these waters," I told her. "Gorgeous things. Stoplight parrot fish, and sergeant majors trimmed in yellow, and whole schools of indigo hamlets with colors more intense than you see in your dreams." The thought of this great beauty, below, unseen, moved me.

She kissed me once, then placed her face on my chest and swayed to the band that had struck up again. The small swells rose and fell about us.

"Wanna dance?" she asked. "I think they're playing our song."

"Oh yeah? What's that?"

"The hokey-pokey."

"No shit."

"Sure," she said, "don't you hear it?"

She left her bikini top on, but she removed the bottom and

then wrestled off my trunks. She held our suits in one hand and with the other grabbed hold of the horn of plenty.

"Salve work?" she asked.

"Miracle drug," I said.

"And how do you do the hokey-pokey?" she asked. "I forget."

"You put your right foot in."

"Right."

"You put your right foot out."

"Good."

"You put your right foot in and you shake it all about."

"Great. What's next?" she asked and kissed me sweetly. "After the foot?" She boosted herself up on my shoulders and with the slow controlled grace of a gymnast parted herself in the dark water and settled upon me so that I was somehow reminded of a flower.

"I don't think this'll work."

"It'll work," said Brushy with all her familiar confidence in matters sexual.

So there we were, Brushy Bruccia and me, hokeying and pokeying, cruising through the tropical waters among the beautiful fish, with the silver of the moon spilled out like glory around us. In and out and shaking it all about.

Mon, it was something else.

T A P E   5

Dictated February 1, 1:00 a.m.

XXII. BANK SECRECY

A. Staying Alone

With a woman beside me, I suppose I should have slept well, but I was away from home and near the heart of darkness and I could not pass through the portal to my troubled dreams. A high-voltage anxiety coursed through me, like some grid from which the tortured lightning seems to leap. I sat on the edge of the bed with my face screwed up in the dark and begged myself not to do what I had a mind to, which was head to the bar, where the band was still tootling, to get one of those five-dollar shots of rye. It is not really an illusion that liquor makes you brave. It does, because it is so much harder to be hurt. I have a catalogue of significant injuries inflicted while I was crocked —second-degree burns from cigarettes and boiling liquids which went awry; twisted ankles; sprained knees; and some walloping insults from an angry wife that were hurled with the force of a cannonball. I survived them all with only a little Mercurochrome or an occasional trip to the emergency room. I had a right to think that was what I'd need.

I got up and, for comfort, like a child who fixes on a blanket or a teddy bear, went back across the veranda to my cabana, and found my Dictaphone. I spent an hour telling my story to myself, my voice hushed but still seeming to travel on the sweet evening wind so that I worried that Brushy might hear.

It was my father I thought about, my father and mother both, actually. I tried to figure how it settled with her, his being a thief. Many of the little treasures he carried off in his pockets were offered to her first. Perhaps I flatter her memory to say that she never seemed at ease. 'We don't need this stuff, Tim.' Encouraging him, I would say, to be a better man. She wore a brooch once that especially pleased him, a large ruby-colored stone in the middle and a lot of antique filigree, but usually she ended up declining anything, which led naturally to many quarrels when he'd had something to drink.

I talked to my mother about what was happening on a single occasion. I was sixteen then and full of opinions.

'He's no worse than everybody else,' she told me.

'They're thieves.'

'Everybody's a bit of a thief, Mack. Everybody's got something they're wantin to steal. It just takes the rest of us watching to make most folks stop.'

She was not so much trying to defend him, I thought, as standing a parent's high ground. Either way, I didn't buy it. I was still at the age when I wanted to be a better man than my father. It was a thirst in me. Unquenchable. One of those many appetites I tried to sate thereafter with the fiery taste of liquor. I never wanted to see a woman regard me with the blighted disappointment he saw from my mother. But, you know, life is long, and I loved my old man too, all those moody Irish songs and his hapless affection for me. He never told me to be better than he was. He knew what life was like.

I fell asleep upright on the sofa, briefcase in my lap. Brushy's searching about woke me. Even groggy, I recognized from the fretful way she inspected me that this was a woman who had awakened before to discover herself disappointed and alone, and I was quick to comfort her, having had some lonely mornings of my own. We had a fine time together, in bed and on the terrace, where we eventually took breakfast squinting and sweating in the unremitting sun. Around 11:00, I stood.

"I'm going to meet that lawyer," I said.

Still in her robe, Brushy asked me to wait for her.

"You stay," I answered. "Get some snorkel gear from the beach attendants. Go look at the fishies. It'll make the trip."

"No, really," she said. "I knew there was work to do."

"Hey. You don't want to know. Remember?"

"I lied."

"Listen." I sat down beside her. "This whole thing's turning mean. Just stand clear."

"Mean in what way?" she asked. Her face became absorbed in lawyerly precision. She wanted to ask more, but I held her off. I kissed her quickly and headed downtown with my briefcase.

B. Foreign Banking

The International Bank of Finance, whose block stamp appears on the back of each of the eighteen checks cut to Litiplex from the 397 escrow account, is a little tiny place, almost a storefront, except for the grand mahogany interiors. Since my days in Financial Crimes, it has been known as reliable. Ownership, as ever, is a mystery, but there are impressive correspondent relationships with some of England's and America's biggest banks, and rumor always had it that it was one of the American royal families, Rockefeller or Kennedy, somebody like that, with an ancient knowledge of the relationship between wealth and corruption, who was really behind it. I don't know.

I said I wanted to open an account, and in the cordial Luan way the manager presently appeared, an angular black man in a blue blazer, Mr. George, an elegant fellow with that peculiar Luan accent, an island lilt fugued with the patois still spoken by the coastal peoples. George's office was small but richly paneled, with wooden columns and bookcases. I told him I wanted to discuss a seven-figure deposit, U.S. funds. George didn't even twitch. For him stuff like this is every day of the week. I hadn't told him my name yet and neither one of us thought I was going to. This is an entire city where nobody's ever heard about I.D. I want to be Joe Blow or Marlon Brando, that's fine. Bank passbooks down here all have your photo pasted inside the cover, no name.

"After deposit, if I want to transfer the funds while I'm Stateside," I asked, "what's the procedure?"

"Telephone," he said. "Fax." Mr. George wore round black glasses and a bit of mustache; he had long fingers which he raised in a steeple as he spoke. For phone transfers, he said, a customer was required to give an account number and a password; prior to the transaction the bank would telephone to confirm. I considered it unlikely that Jake was sitting in his office at the top of the TN Needle taking calls from bankers in Pico Luan. I asked about fax.

"We must have written instructions, including a handwritten signature or other withdrawal designation," he said. Very artful, I thought. Withdrawal designation. For all those who didn't like names.

"And how long before the transfer takes place?"

"We wire to Luan-chartered institutions within two hours. If we receive instructions before noon, we promise good funds in the U.S. by 3:00 p.m. Central Time."

I reviewed all of this thoughtfully and then asked him for whatever I would need to open an account and whether I could do it by mail. George replied with an enigmatic Luanite gesture: white man can do what he likes. He opened a drawer for the papers.

"The account holder should kindly supply two copies of a small photo. One for the passbook, one for our records. And here, in this space, we should have the account holder's handwriting,

whatever designation will be used to authorize withdrawals."
'The account holder,' he said, surmising that I was a stand-in
for somebody too important to be seen in C. Luan. And of course
he never used the words "signature" or "name." It struck me
then that Martin had to have spoken to this guy. His description
was dead on. 'Like trying to grab hold of smoke.'

In the office there was a small window, discreetly shaded by
jalousies, through which you could see the street traffic passing.
There was no screen, since on this side of the mountains there
is nothing as troublesome as a bug. At that moment a bird landed
on the windowsill, a little wrenny-looking thing, no make I recognized. He, she, it hopped around and finally took an instant
to look straight at me. It made me laugh, I must admit, this
birdy scrutiny, the thought that you didn't even have to be a
mammal to wonder what gives with Malloy. George whisked
the back of his hand and told it to shoo.

With the papers, I returned to the street. The sun was high
now, savagely bright and thrilling after the indoor weeks in the
Middle West. Down here I always understood how people could
worship the sun as a god. The business district is only a few
blocks, close-set buildings, three and four stories each, stuccoed
in Caribbean pastels with roofs of Spanish tile. The tourists
roamed among the business folk. Good-looking gals in straw hats
and beach coverups, their legs tanned and fully revealed, strode
among the suits with their briefcases.

I looked around for more banks, the names of which were
unobtrusively displayed on the building sides in English and
Spanish, both of which are official languages. Many of the great
names in world finance are present, with Luan affiliates housed
in pocket-sized spaces like the International Bank's. In this mod-
est fashion a $100 billion economy thrives, Luan-chartered cor-
porations and trusts, funded with fugitive dollars, borrowing and
buying and investing around the world, money without a country, as it were, and happy to stay that way.

I found the office of one of the big banks from Chicago, a

name I knew—Fortune Trust—and told them I wanted to open a personal account. Same drill as across the street, except this time I wasn't just fishing and did it. I put down $1,000 American in bills and they took my picture twice with one of those machines. When the photos dried, they pasted one in my passbook and the other to their signature card. I elected to keep all deposits in dollars—I could choose from a menu of fourteen currencies—and said I wanted no statements, which saved me from the need to provide an address. Interest would be posted whenever I showed up to present my passbook. I checked a box on a form authorizing them to debit the account $20 U.S. any time money was wired.

"And what will be the designation for purposes of identification?" asked the smashing young woman assisting me. By her accent I took her for an Aussie, here to scuba and be free of something, parents or a guy or the throttling force of her own ambitions. The whole place was free, with the gorgeous fish that decorated the warm waters, the sun, the rum, the sense that many of the world's rules were disregarded. I eventually realized she wanted my code word.

"Tim's Boy," I answered. She asked if I cared to write it, and I did that as well. I was now free to transfer money in and out, to check my deposits by phone.

According to my prior calculations, I still needed one more account. For that, I did not even have to leave the building. There was a Swiss bank on the second floor, Züricher Kreditbank, and I listened to the lecture on their procedures, which included access to funds out of either Swiss or Pico facilities and the full benefit of the secrecy laws of both nations. I deposited another thousand. I had two new passbooks now in my briefcase.

Outside, I stopped a guy on the street and asked if he knew of a secretarial service, somewhere I could have a letter faxed. I wandered down toward one of the big beachfront hotels where he directed me. I had my suit jacket off, tucked under my arm with my briefcase. I looked into the windows, as if I was shopping, but I was thinking solely about myself, wondering who I was, what I was going to be. A guy getting ready to cheat on his wife has to feel like this, examining the island curios and the fancy knits, the scuba gear in vivid colors, seeing but not seeing, senses focused mostly on his heart and pondering why this is necessary, what this hunger is that he just has to feed, how he'll feel forever after, with some fraction of him cringing whenever he hears words like "faithful" and "true."

U You, I know what you think: usual Catholic upbringing, the only sin not forgiven is sex. But I'm looking at a bigger picture than that. Okay, it's true, most people's secrets are sexual; that's still the realm where a soul is most often unknown. Just ask Nora. Or Bert. We tell ourselves that nobody's hurt when the wishes become real, it's consenting adults, so who cares, but you can't sell that story to Lyle—or to me. Hurting happens. But we still have our needs. That's the point. Whatever it might be, sex or dope or stealing things, everybody's got some weird not-oughta-be that lights them up when it crosses their brain. Nora, Bert, and, in a few minutes, me—we were all members of a teensy-weensy minority group, having fulfilled our sly, unspeakable yearnings. For most people it goes the other way, hanging on that fulcrum where the greatest despair is not really knowing if misery is larger in the realm of fulfillment or restraint. Me, I'd about had it with that balancing act.

I was down at the Regency on the Beach now, and I walked through the hotel, its lobby of fronds and air like dry ice. I sat on a cane chair to think, but I was frozen up, unable to feel much. I asked the concierge to direct me to the secretarial service, and he introduced me to the attendant of their Executive Center. His name was Raimondo, short, sun-coppered, perfectly groomed. I told him I needed a typewriter and a fax machine and gave him fifty Luan. He took me to an area in back, right next to the hotel offices. Raimondo set me up in a small booth that resembled one of the firm's library carrels; an old IBM reposed there like a roosting bird. He offered to arrange for a

typist, but I declined, and he left me alone after pointing out
two phones and the john around the corner.

I ducked into the head then and studied myself in the mirror
one last time. I was still me, a big graying galumph in a suit
rumpled up like some elephant's knees, with this gone-to-pot
face. I knew I was going to do it.

"Well, well," I said, "Mr. Malloy." Then I looked around to
make sure nobody was lurking in the stalls who could overhear
me.

Back in the carrel, I withdrew a piece of TN stationery from
my case. I typed:

```
TO: International Bank of Finance, Pico Luan
Please immediately wire-transfer the balance of
account number 476642 to Fortune Trust of Chicago,
Pico Luan facility, Final Credit Account Number,
896-908.
```

John A.K. Eiger

In my briefcase I found the letter from Jake I'd brought along.
I didn't remove it, just spread the sides of the case to get a good
look, eyes reminding the hand, then signed Jake's name, the
way I customarily do, a perfect imitation. Examining my work,
I felt an odd flare of pride. I really am world-class. What an eye!
Someday, for amusement, I'd have to take a whack at G. Washington on the dollar, frame a copy for Wash. I smiled at the
thought and then below the signature wrote "J.A.K.E." I was
guessing, of course. As a code, Jake could have used his mother's
maiden name, or whatever was written on his last mistress's
shoulder tattoo, but I'd known him for thirty-five years now and
this didn't feel much like gambling. If he needed a password,
he was hard-wired to come up with only one thing: J.A.K.E.

I gave the letter to Raimondo and watched him feed the paper
through the machine. My heart suddenly bolted.

"The origination line," I said.

He didn't understand. I tried smiling and discovered my mouth dry. On the fax, I explained, there was a line printed on the top to identify the sending machine. Some of the people I was dealing with were under the impression I was Stateside. I wondered if he'd be able to block that line out.

Raimondo went mutton-mouthed and hooded his eyes. This was C. Luan, nobody had names or a sure point of origin. He just shook his head in silent reassurance that no one around here would even consider setting that feature. At the other end, they wouldn't know if the fax had come from around the corner or from west Bombay.

After watching the letter buzz through the machine, I felt like a drink. I wandered out through the garden. I laid my jacket over my lap as I took a seat by the pool. The waitress came by in sort of a safari outfit, pith helmet and khaki shorts, and I ordered a rum punch, no rum. I wondered if I could stand this for the rest of my life, this nation of rock hounds, archaeologists, inland tribes, and sunning exiles.

Around the pool at this time of day there was pretty much nobody, a few scuba widows and a number of the babes who various big buckeroos stash down here and shtup whenever they pay a visit to their secret, hidden dough. These young ladies, each one generally better-looking than the next, naturally attracted my attention, but in a somewhat abstract way. They spend their days working on their tan, oiling down their perfect flesh, reading or plugged into headphones, and then when the heat is too great, they strut to the shower and cool down so that the nipples peak up in the tops of their skimpy little string suits. They excite the few guys around—the towel boys, the old goats like me—and, having made sure that they're still full of magic, lie down again for another couple of hours. I've never been in another place like C. Luan, where the cookies on the side all gather and are laid out together as if on a baking sheet, and it makes you wonder, What do these gals think, twenty-five or twenty-six years old, who are they and where do they come from? How does a person settle for life as a trinket? What do you tell yourself? This is great, this old guy's only here to paw me every other week, I'm living rich and free. Do they all need daddies? Or do they wish they'd had the luck and stuff to get through law school? Do they puzzle about where they'll be when they turn forty-three? Do they hope the guy is going to sack the wife, like he's always saying, that someday soon they'll have babies and a house in New Jersey? Do they figure they're just the same as an athlete, in great shape till the body goes? Or do they think, as I think, that life is neither sensible nor fair, that this, however objectively miserable it may be as an outcome, is the best that luck will allow and they'll enjoy the moment, since there will be time to suffer down the road?

I sat there about half an hour, as long as I could stand it, and then went back to the Executive Center to call the Fortune Trust office where I'd been today.

"Tim's Boy, checking a deposit by wire transfer to account 896–908." I thought the voice on the other end belonged to my girlfriend, the glamorous young Aussie. The image of her, long-haired and lean, deeply tanned with eyes so light they verged on yellow, lingered—but there was a coy absence of recognition and I was simply shifted to hold, that electrical nowhere, as empty as whatever is between the stars. Up until then I'd been in control. A day in the life. But at that point, where I was, hoping and having no real connection, my bloodstream froze over and I was sure I'd lost my mind. I knew this was never going to work. Please, please, *please*, I thought and the only thing I wanted was not to get caught. I realized, with the exactness of clairvoyance, that I'd done all this simply to give myself an instant of pure fright. The man awake at midnight offers solace to his tormentors: Don't bother torturing me, I'll do it myself.

Now I could see it had to unravel. Jake in all likelihood had adopted a different code word, or had long ago transferred the money somewhere else. Maybe I'd miscalculated and the money

was not even Jake's. It was Bert's after all. Or Martin's. In any
case, Mr. George, the General Manager at the International
Bank, was probably out on the street, frantically waving to attract
the police. This was not a casual infraction. They would ransack
the nation. Bank secrecy was a national treasure, the key to an
entire people's way of life. I remembered Lagodis's words with
a painful clarity that felt like somebody was putting a brand to
my heart: Watch where you step, mon.

I had escape plans, naturally. Sitting up late on Saturday night
I'd thought of several and I comforted myself by remembering
them now. I'd say I was investigating, trying to pierce bank
secrecy only to confirm the commission of a crime and restore
the funds to their rightful owner. I'd have Brushy phone the
Embassy and her buddy, Tad the K. He'd think I was a hero
when he heard how I was saving TN's money; he'd call his
Governmental Relations folks and his lobbyists who knew half
the pols in this country; they'd get me out in an hour. And who,
anyway, was going to catch me? There was bank secrecy here,
designed even to protect thieves, and no one knew my name.
I didn't care what anyone said to lure me back on the premises
at any of these banks. That there were problems with the wire.
That the Aussie lass wanted to meet me for a drink. They'd never
see me again. I'd thought it all through. It was a lark, a chance,
a lottery ticket.

But standing here, I knew I was done joshing. The scheming,
the fantasies—I'd had my fun. Now it turned out, I had never
been kidding at all. It no longer seemed that Martin or Wash
or anyone else had driven me to this. Instead, I was back with
Leotis: So much of life is will. I'd made my choice. And I had
no idea where it was leading. It was like some scary sci-fi story
about a skywalking astronaut who gets cut loose and can't be
retrieved and just drifts off forever into endless space. At that
instant, if Raimondo'd walked by, I'd have given him another of
those funny-looking Luanite fifties just to touch his hand.

"We confirm a deposit, Tim's Boy. Five million, six hundred

sixteen thousand, ninety-two dollars, U.S." Just like that. Boom.
She didn't even say hello when she got back on the line. From
where I stood in the phone booth, I looked out a mullioned
window to a stout palm and a bed of flowering shrubs with fronds
like spears. A gal in a bathing suit was scolding her child. The
doorman lugged somebody's case, and a little native bird, maybe
against every improbable chance the one I'd seen in George's
office, hopped down the walk, skittering a few steps, as if it was
hoping no one was catching up from behind. All of this—these
things, these people, this little dumb creature—appeared to me
as if they'd been etched on time, distinct as the facets of a
diamond. My life, whatever it was, was different.

I started to speak, then started again.

"Can I give you a further transfer of funds, confirmed by fax?"

That, she said, was fine. I read from my passbook. To Züricher
Kreditbank, Filiale Pico Luan. I repeated the account number.

"How much?" she asked.

"Five million, U.S." I thought I was safer, leaving something
in this account, enough that Fortune Trust would continue to
feel I was a customer worth protecting from inevitable inquiries.
Not that they would think twice about the whole thing. This
happened all the time down here, money hopscotching across
the planet. Nobody asked why. They already knew. It was being
hidden from someone. Tax collectors, creditors, a weaseling
spouse. But I wanted a second transfer to cut off the trail. Jake
would raise hell at the International Bank. They'd show him
they'd sent the money to Fortune Trust at his instruction. But
secret is secret and Fortune wouldn't be saying where the money
went from there, or whose account it landed in in the first place.

I waited more than an hour to call Züricher Kreditbank to
confirm the second transfer. All was well. My money was safe
in Swiss care. I was ready to go back to Brushy. I wished I could
drink wine with her. I wanted to be in the grasp of her strong
skillful hands. Checking my watch, I reassured myself there was
time to make love again before our plane. She would ask where

I'd been, what I'd done. She'd want to know every secret. But I wouldn't tell. She'd inquire about Pindling; her brain would be full of intrigue. She'd envision a character like Long John Silver, with a macaw on his shoulder and a hook for a hand. Let her imagine. Ask me no questions, I'll tell you no lies. I felt dangerous and elusive. Light-headed, light-fingered, amused. On the way out of the hotel I poked my head in the john again, just a quick little look-see, a peek in the mirror to find out who was there.

XXIII. BAD RESULTS

A. Toots Plays for Us

At two on Tuesday, when Toots's disciplinary hearing was scheduled to resume, only Brushy and I were present for the defense.
The members of the inquiry panel looked on dispassionately but
I surmised from their weary disciplined air that they'd already
heard more than enough. After they recommended disbarment,
we had a right of appeal to the Courts Commission. Still, in less
than a year, Toots's law license would be a relic, one more
memento he could tack to his walls.

The old school housing BAD is the kind of structure whose
starkness you don't notice until you remove the color and ran-
domness of children. We were in a grim old classroom, with
wood floors and walls of that shiny functional tile that resisted
abrasion and ink pens. There was a distinct resonance when
anyone scraped a chair or cleared his throat.

By ten after, I knew there was a serious problem. Across the
long conference table where we were arrayed, Tom Woodhull
questioned us about our absent client. The distinguished governmental functionary, enforcer of rules, man with cool white
skin, no dark spots or bug bites, Tom had never cared much for

me—my drinking, my moods, my occasional assertions that com-
mingling client funds was not a crime on the level of treason. I
had long suspected that he had held on to this file for the sheer
personal pleasure of kicking my ass.

Brushy rooted in her purse and handed me a quarter.

"Better find him."

Jesus Christ, I thought. Another one.

As I was on my way to the door, my client poked his head in.
Toots was heaving for breath and he motioned me into the
hallway.

"Got," he said and repeated it many times. "Got someone for
you to meet."

By the dusty stairway, hanging on to the square steel newel
post was a rotund little fellow in the same condition as Toots,
red as Christmas from exertion, breathing hard and spotted with
sweat. Brushy had followed.

"You won't believe this," Toots said. "Tell them." Toots motioned with the cane and again asked the man to tell us.

Taking a seat on a plain wooden bench in the hall, the man
removed his topcoat. At that point I saw the Roman collar. He
was a little guy, bald but for a white fringe and some fried-up
strands growing straight out of his scalp.

He held out his hand. "Father Michael Shea."

Father Michael was Judge Dan Shea's younger brother, retired from a parish in Cleveland and attached to a friary there.
He had come to town last week to visit relatives—Dan Shea's
son, Brian, as a matter of fact, Father's nephew—and in conversation he had heard that Mr. Nuccio here was still having
trouble over that old business.

"I give Mr. Nuccio a ring at once. I talked many a time to
Daniel about this and he always told me he never knew a t'ing
about any generosity from Mr. Nuccio. The dues over there by
the country club had just completely slipped his mind. I was
skeptical, I am the first to say. Daniel was no angel and he
confessed some terrible things to me, as a priest and as a brother.

But he swore on Bridget's memory that there'd never been any kind of funny business between him and the Colonel. Never." Father Shea absently touched the crucifix that he wore.

My partner and the love of my life, Ms. Bruccia, absorbed this intently. Our fine tropical romance was now past. There was sand in our shoes and sweet feelings between us which we had nurtured at her apartment all night. But we were again in the cold Middle West, in the land where the subdued winter light, dull as pewter, makes some people crazy and where troubles abounded. She had a million concerns. Us. And all the stuff I wouldn't tell her. Groundhog Day approaching at the firm. But Brushy was now a trial lawyer ready for trial. In her own theater all the seats were sold to Toots, even the standing room. Her powers of concentration were phenomenal; great performers of all kinds, athletes, entertainers, share this single-mindedness. And when I assessed her now, I saw nothing subdued. Rather, there was glee, the flame of celebration. She was looking from Toots to Father Shea to me, about to win the case that everyone told her she'd lose, ready to prove to the world at large what every trial lawyer secretly yearns to establish, that she was not merely an advocate or a mouthpiece but a palpable magician.

Toots had finally recovered his breath and, if possible, looked happier than she did. His old stoved-in face danced around the fire.

Hitching my shoulder, I strolled them both down the old school hall. There were still those little half-height metal lockers on either side on which various enterprising youngsters had scraped their initials, hearts, and an obscenity or two, all of these symbols now enlarging in rust.

"Can you believe this?" Brushy asked. "It's phenomenal."

"It certainly is," I answered. "Just phenomenal. Right at the last minute. *After* the last minute. So late nobody could even ask this guy boo."

Brushy looked at me strangely.

"Tell her, Toots," I said.

The old guy stared up at me dumbly. He wiped his mouth with the heel of his hand.

"It must have been a tough decision, Toots, to hire someone who looked more like Barry Fitzgerald or Bing Crosby."

"Mack," said Brushy.

Toots wouldn't even feign injury.

"Forget me. Forget you," I said to him. "*She* could get disbarred for a stunt like this. And *she* has a career."

He displayed the rumpled-up sour face that appeared whenever I corrected him. He'd sunk onto another bench and was staring vacantly down the hall, rattling his cane and doing his best not to look at me. Somewhere a radiator spit a bit. I had not quite shaken the chill of winter since getting off the plane.

Brushy, now that it had come through, had lost color.

"Is he a priest at least?"

"A priest? I'll bet you a bundle this guy's name is Markowitz. He's straight from central casting."

"I believed it," Brushy said. She touched her head with her short hands and bright fingernails and sat down next to Toots whom she fixed with a brief, baleful look. "I *believed* it."

"Sure you did," I said. "So would that dope Woodhull, probably. But somebody would figure it out eventually. Here or on the Court's Commission. If anybody ever asked for this guy's fingerprints, I'd book a seat on the next stagecoach."

The old guy still wasn't saying anything. He'd learned from the best. If you get caught, dummy up. No good ever came from confessing. I thought about his luminous expression when he had Brushy going. It must have been music to him every time he fixed something. The unraveling of society was his secret symphony. He was the hidden conductor, the only guy who knew the real score. In a way you had to hand it to him. This was the *coup de grâce*. Imagine corrupting your own ethics hearing. Now *that* would make a story. After all, they forced him. He'd just wanted a continuance.

Woodhull appeared down the hall, outside the door to the hearing room.

"What's going on?" he demanded. His straight thick hair, dirty blond, had fallen down over one eye. Hitler youth. "What are you up to now, Malloy? Who's that guy?" he asked as he came closer. He meant Father Markowitz, who was still on the bench down the way.

"Who's the guy?" Tom repeated. "Is he a witness?"

Brushy and I looked at each other, neither of us answering.

"You have a new witness? Now?" It didn't take much from me to set Tom off. He'd brought a yellow pad with him and he began worrying it in the air, while he let his temper mount. "Eleventh hour, we're going to get a surprise witness? Who we haven't heard word one about? Now? Who we haven't even had a chance to interview?"

"Talk to him," Brushy said abruptly. I reached for her arm, and that gesture of restraint was all the encouragement Tom needed.

"I will," he said and advanced past the three of us.

I whisked Brushy around a corner and asked, concisely, if she'd lost her mind.

"It's unethical to put him on to testify," she said. "I know that."

" 'Unethical' isn't the word, Brush. You do straight time for that stuff."

"Okay," she said. "But you said Woodhull would believe him."

"So what? You don't think he'll drop the case. Woodhull doesn't know how to change his mind. The testimony's hearsay, and even if it comes in, he'll argue that it's worth nothing, that the judge was just too ashamed to level with his brother. You know the pitch."

"But he'll believe him, right? That's what you said."

"Probably. He's probably having a shitfit right now."

"So he'll be afraid he's going to lose. Suddenly. A case everybody thought he was going to win." She was giving me the reverse of her own logic, which is what I mean about her being quick-witted and devious. "He'll be willing to settle. For something short of disbarment. That's what we want. Am I right?"

I finally saw her point. But there were still problems.

"Brush, think about this. You just introduced the Deputy Administrator of Bar Admissions and Discipline to a supposed witness who your client told you is an impostor."

"My client didn't tell me anything. I didn't take any fingerprints. I'm an advocate. And I made no representations. Or introductions. Tom was free-associating. Am I supposed to protect him from himself?" She stared at me. "*I* believed this guy. If somebody else doesn't, fine. The witness won't testify either way. I mean, Mack," she said quietly, "there's no downside."

Toots was gimping our way. He was having a great time. Father obviously was selling well. There was no point in warning the Colonel about consequences. He'd lived his life jumping chasms, scaling perilous heights. I heard Woodhull's voice rising around the corner.

The deal we cut was unique. Under the state law attorneys could be disbarred for five years. After that they were free to reapply, and the Court's Commission, with a frequency exasperating to BAD, tended to readmit them on the theory that for most of these men and women it was the only profession they knew, like shoemakers who could only make shoes. What we offered on Toots's behalf was something better: Toots would promise never to practice law again. Not much of a concession, since he didn't practice anyway, but he would take his name off the door of his firm, give up his office there, and not receive another penny from firm income. If he ever violated the agreement, he would consent to an order of disbarment. In exchange, the proceedings against him ended. No findings. No censure. No record. His name stayed on the rolls. He would never be publicly disgraced.

Toots, in the grand tradition of clients everywhere, refused to be grateful, becoming reticent as soon as the agreement was announced to the panel.

"How'm I gonna support myself?" he asked out in the hallway after we had put on our topcoats.

We both gave him the fisheye. Toots couldn't spend what was in his mattress if he lived to one hundred.

"Toots, it's what you want," I told him.

"I like the office," he said, and no doubt he did. The secretaries who called him Colonel, the phone calls, the pols coming to visit.

"So take an office down the hall. You've retired. That's all. You're eighty-three, Colonel. It's logical."

"All right." But he was downcast. He looked elderly and glum. His color was bad and his skin seemed ripply like the rind on an orange. It's always sad to see the high brought low.

"Toots," I said, "they have never done this for anybody else. It's a one-of-a-kind. We have to swear to God and the Governor that we'll never leak one word of this deal to anyone. They can't admit they backed off on a disbarment."

"Yeah?" He liked that better, being a category of one. "So what's so special about me?"

"You hired the right lawyers," I told him. That, finally, made him laugh.

B. Final Accounting

Back in the office, Brushy and I went for what is called a victory lap, moseying by the offices of various litigators and casually describing the result. The acclaim was universal, and by the time we reached the desk of our secretary, Lucinda, we were feeling roundly admired, a sensation I experienced with a surprising rush of sentiment, since it had been some time.

Brush and I stood there checking out our message slips and

mail. The firm's fiscal year ended today, and all partners had
received a solemn memo from Martin stating that even with
good collections before midnight, income was likely to be down
10 percent. That meant the distribution of points two days hence
on Groundhog Day was going to be a slaughterhouse for the
lower-level partners like me, since Pagnucci would not allow
the top tier to be stinted. As we'd moved cheerfully between
offices, the air was already growing fraught. Brushy ran off with
her phone messages—one triumph behind her, a world of possible triumphs ahead. I lingered by Lucinda's work station.
There was, as usual, not much doing for me.

"Same guy's been calling," she told me. "Keeps asking when
you'll be back in town." She had described these calls to me this
morning, saying they had started yesterday.

"Any name?"

"Just hangs up."

Brushy and Lena and Carl were the only people who'd known
I was leaving. I hadn't even told Lyle much more than the fact
that I might not be home for a night or two. As near as she could
recall, Lucinda said, it sounded like the same man who'd phoned
the office on Friday morning before Pigeyes nabbed me out on
the street. That fit. Gino or someone from his crew had probably
been keeping an eye on the house, maybe even tailed me to the
airport, and was trying to figure out where I was now. If Gino
was good to his word, he was toting a subpoena for me.

Or, I thought, it could be Bert. If he'd spoken to Lyle first,
he might have figured I was gone. But Lucinda surely would
have recognized the voice. Maybe he had Orleans calling for
him?

Lucinda watched me with her usual brimming expression. A
stout, handsome, dark-skinned woman, Lucinda keeps her own
counsel, but it bruises her heart to work up close to such a living
mess. She is a great pro—my salvation, as loyal to me as to
Brushy, even though everybody in the place understands that
I am the underbill and Brush the big star. Lucinda keeps plug-

ging. A picture of her husband, Lester, and their three kids was at the corner of her desk. They were all posed around the youngest, Reggie, at his high-school graduation.

"Oh my God!" I said then, when it hit me. "Oh my God, Orleans." I actually ran the first few steps before I looked back to tell Lucinda I was on my way to Accounting.

Down there, it was chaos. The place was like a campaign headquarters on election night, with computer terminals clicking and adding machines spilling tape and a lot of people running around full of purpose or desperation. Because of the IRS, everything collected had to be booked today. A number of secretaries and messengers were in line to process the booty of fees finally bludgeoned out of clients. Money—collecting it, counting it, making it—thickened the atmosphere the same way gunpowder and blood embitter the air of battle.

Behind her clear white desk, Glyndora started out of her chair the instant she saw me, her intent manifest to avoid any further intimate *tête-à-têtes*.

"Glyn," I said, blocking her way. "Whatever happened to the photo of your son? Didn't you keep it right here?" The picture had been on her desk for years, and on the credenza in her home, a fine-looking lad in his mortarboard and graduation gown. "Remind me," I told her. "What's his name? Orleans, right? Not Gaines, though. Carries his dad's last name, doesn't he?" I'd remembered now where I'd seen Kam Roberts.

Junoesque, Glyndora confronted me in silence, a beautiful totem, her dark face tight in anger. But it was like a closet where you couldn't quite squeeze the door shut because of everything packed inside. There was an edge of something unwanted, beseeching, that undermined her expression and riled her, no doubt worse than anything which I'd said.

"I don't want to hurt anybody," I said to her quietly, and she allowed me to lead her out to the hall. It seemed a bit of a haven, away from the urgent clamor.

"Have Orleans get a message to Bert," I told her. "I need to see him. Face-to-face. In Kindle. ASAP. All Bert has to do is name the time and place. Tell him I have to sort things out with him. Ask him to call me here tomorrow."

She didn't answer. Man, those were eyes she had, black and infernal, sizing me up, her mind flopping about furiously behind them. It didn't take a lot of imagination to figure out what caused all the legendary squabbling in the hallways between Bert and Glyndora, throwing things and calling names. Stay away from my boy. This wasn't a scene that pleased her, her boss and her lad in the mode of the ancient Greeks. She was probably glad Bert was on the run.

"Glyndora, I know a lot now. About your son. And I've got that memo you bootlegged to Martin, which, you notice, I'm not even asking about. I'm going to try not to hurt anyone. But you've got to get that message to Bert. You're gonna have to trust me."

I might as well have asked her for a pot of gold. She despised the position she was in—the weakling, the wanter, the one to say please. Worst of all, she felt something I knew like the back of my hand, as familiar to me as darkness and light, which Glyndora as an act of will had simply abolished from her existence: she was scared. She gummed her lips into her mouth to control herself, then turned to look down the hall where there was nothing to see.

"Please." I said it. It was the least I could do. She shook her head, the mass of dark hair, not so much in answer as dismay, and, still without speaking a word, went back to counting our money.

C. A Word for the Big Guy

Near five I phoned home, rousing Lyle from a sound sleep. He reported that he'd been getting the same strange calls as Lucinda: 'Mack there, when's he back?' He did not recognize the voice.

"Did you tell him?"

"Fuck no, Dad, I know better than that." His pride and his assumptions, the whole tone of his response, struck me in the desperate total way only Lyle could. It was so clear where he was frozen—the latchkey kid of thirteen whose mommy had warned him about strangers. My boy. Listening to him, I felt for a moment I might simply expire from the pain. It eased a bit as he carried on about the Chevy, which he'd retrieved from the pound with two flats. One hundred eighty-five bucks it cost, plus the ticket, and he wanted the money back. He made the point a number of times.

I've come home again with Brushy tonight. We had takeout Italian, fancy stuff, rigatoni with goat cheese and obscure antipasti, which we consumed between screws. I won't say how I ate my tiramisu. About an hour ago, as we were drowsing, her back to me, saved from drowning in my arms, Brushy said, "If I ask, you'll tell me, right?"

"Ask what?"

"You know. What's going on. With the money. Bert. The whole thing. Right? You know, attorney-client. But you'll tell me."

"I think you don't want to know. I think your life is better without this kind of news."

"And I accept that," she said. "I do. I know you're right. I trust you. But if I decide, if I really have to know, for whatever reason, you'll tell me. Right?"

My eyes were wide in the dark. "Right."

So that's how it is. My warped little dreams, private so long, are now hurling themselves through my life with volcanic force. Perhaps the sheer peril made my lovemaking with Brushy vigorous and prolonged. She sleeps as she's slept the previous nights, in the comforted grip of her own improbable fantasies, immobile almost, but I am desolate and awake in the dark, chasing away goblins and spooks, out here in her living room now, whispering again into my Dictaphone.

So you ponder, U You: What is he up to, this guy, Mack Malloy? Believe me, I ask myself the same thing. The apartment is surrounded by the odd silences of winter—the windows closed tight, the heat whispering, the cold keeping idle souls from the street. Since I actually committed this stunt, robbing TN blind and preparing to blame it on somebody else, my ma's barking accusatory voice seems to be with me wherever I go. She regarded herself as devout, one of the Pope's own Catholics, her life whirling like a pinwheel where the Church was at the very center, but her religious thought seemed to dwell mostly on the devil, who was regularly invoked, particularly whenever she was remonstrating with me.

But it wasn't the devil that made me do it. All in all, I think I'm just sick of my life. It seemed like such a terrific idea. But it was *my* fancy, my folly, my fun-time escapade. There's no sharing. Hell, it turns out, is being stuck forever listening to your own jokes.

So who is this for? Why bother talking? Elaine always had the same hope. 'Mack, you won't die without a priest at your side.' Probably right. I'm a short-odds player. But maybe this is the first act of contrition, part of the process that the Church these days calls reconciliation, where your heart, unburdened, rises to God. What do I know?

So here goes. Big Guy, Big Entity, Big Being, if you're up there listening, I suppose you will think what you like. But please forgive me. I need it tonight. I did what I wanted and now I am sorry as hell. We both know the truth: I have sinned, big-time. Tomorrow I'll have my stuff back. I'll be bitter and ready to stick it to everyone else. I'll be the apostate, agnostic, you won't cross my mind. But like me tonight, accept me one moment before I reject you, as I reject everyone else. If you can forgive infinitely, then forgive this, and have an instant of pity for your ragtag creation, sad Bess Malloy's boy.

TAPE 6

Dictated February 2, 9:00 p.m.

XXIV. YOUR INVESTIGATOR

HIDES OUT

A. Waiting for Bert

Brushy had an early meeting and went rushing off at seven, wrestling into her coat as she grabbed her briefcase, a jelly doughnut stuffed whole into her mouth. I was still in bed and lingered amid my lover's possessions. Brushy's apartment had an overcrowded urban air. She was on the first floor of a brownstone with nifty Victorian touches—raised moldings and patterned plaster, and those little breastlike caps in the ceiling where the gas fixtures had been removed. There were tall pine shutters on the street-side windows that ran floor to ceiling, and many plants, and walls of books, stacks of everything. No real art to speak of—a couple of tasteful posters, but strictly representational stuff, no more adventurous than a bowl of fruit. In the bedroom, where I would have expected maybe a mirror or a trapeze, there was little furnishing, except for a king-size bed and heaps of dirty clothing at the corners of her closet, laundry on one side, dry cleaning on the other. She looked, appropriately, like a person with a busy life.

About eight-forty, as I was getting ready to head out, the phone rang. Better not to answer, I figured. What if it was one of Brushy's pinup legion of male admirers? What if Tad Krzy-sinski was asking if he could slip her the big one at lunch? I let it go to the answering machine and heard Brush emphatically telling me to pick up.

"You better stay where you are," she said.

"You're coming home for an interlude?"

"I just met Detective Dimonte."

"Oh Christ."

"He was looking for you. I told him I was your attorney."

"He have a grand jury subpoena?"

"That's why he was here."

"Did you accept service?"

"Told him I wasn't authorized."

"Clever lady. What else did he want to know?"

"Where you were."

I asked what she'd said, then realized the inevitable response and repeated it with her: "Attorney-client."

"I'll bet he was in a mood," I added.

"You might say. I told him I'd have you get in touch."

"When I'm ready."

"He'll come looking for you, won't he?"

"He is already. He may even follow *you*. And I wouldn't talk too much more on this phone either."

"Could he get a wiretap order that fast?"

"Pigeyes doesn't know from court orders. He's got a guy at the phone company he caught buying cocaine or with his thing in a glory hole who he makes throw switches for him when need be."

"Oo," said Brush.

"Attractive guy, right?"

"Well, actually," said Brushy. "I mean, you'd say masculine."

"Don't do this to me, Brush. Tell me you're only saying that because he might be listening."

She laughed. I took a moment to think.

"Look, I better cut out—just in case he got enterprising. I'm supposed to hear from a certain tall missing partner of ours today. Make sure Lucinda forwards the call to you. Don't get into any extended conversations over this phone. Tell him to give you the information I wanted on 7384. Follow?" She assured me she did. 7384 was G&G's fax line. I looked forward to Gino listening in on that screech, the mating call of two machines. He couldn't tap that.

I gathered my briefcase, still packed with everything from Pico Luan, and walked down about three blocks, where there was another location of Dr. Goodbody's. I knew I'd have to deal with Gino eventually. But only after I talked to Bert and figured out what I could say. I had plans—millions, in fact. Soon I'd have to choose.

I spent the day at the health club, hairy-eyeballing the gals in their leotards and playing with the machines. I've passed time like this before. After all those years in saloons, I just get this yen to be near people I don't know. With a towel around my shoulders, dressed in a pair of gray sweats, I hop on the stepper, punch in a bunch of numbers, and jump off shortly after the thing begins to move. I do some pulls at one of the weight stations. Eventually I find someone to talk to, one of those dumb little chats that a drunkard gets to like, where I can pretend to be someone who's never exactly like me.

Today I stuck pretty much to myself. Every now and then I'd try to think through all the alternate routes up ahead, if this, if that, but it was too much for me. Instead, I found myself oddly preoccupied with my mother, feeling as I did last night, punished and without too much hope. I'd made my big move, so why wasn't I happy? At times I sensed myself on the verge of laments I'd heard from her, all this stuff about life being hard, being bitter, barren choices, none of them good.

I called the office now and then. Brushy had heard nothing from Bert and instead ended up describing the intense local anxieties with Groundhog Day tomorrow and firm income down 12 percent from last year. When I called again at four, Lucinda

answered Brushy's line. Brush was out at a meeting. There was
still no word from Bert, but I had two other messages. Martin
and Toots.

I phoned the old guy first. I knew just what was coming: he'd
thought it out overnight and was going to back off the deal with
BAD, he'd rather get clobbered, he was too old to change. The
thought was excruciating.

"I love the deal," he said first thing.

"You do?"

"I wanted you to know, on account of yesterday I might not
a looked too happy, but I love the deal. *Love* it. I told some
guys, they tell me, you musta hired Houdini for your lawyer.
Nobody's ever heard of nothing like this."

I mumbled something, just once, about how Brushy deserved
credit too.

"You done me right, Mack."

"We tried."

"So listen, so you know: you need, you got. Call Toots."

The Colonel was not the kind of guy who was hot air when
he said he owed a favor. It was, in fact, quite a privilege. Like
having a fairy godmother and three magic wishes. I could have
a leg broken or get certain performers to sing if Lyle ever had
anything like a wedding. This was the part of the practice Brushy
was addicted to, somebody saying thanks for the help, not everyone could have done it. I told Toots at length how great it had
been to represent him and, at the moment, meant it.

"Where are you?" asked Martin when he came to the phone.

"Out and about."

"About where?" There was a new note here, a harsh tensile
quality to his voice. I'd heard Martin talk like this to opponents,
the man raised among tough guys.

"About where I am. What's up?"

"We need to talk."

"Okay."

"In person. I'd like you to come in."

It struck me just like that—Martin was doing me wrong. Pig-eyes was sitting there, with his smug smile, loving it as my mentor delivered the sucker punch. Then, just as quickly, I rejected the thought. After all the sewage under the bridge, I still wanted to believe in the guy. There are no victims.

"What's our general subject?" I asked.

"Your investigation. There's a document you found, appar-ently." The memo. He'd talked to Glyndora. He was going to posture. He was going to be magical Martin, potent and charm-ing. However slyly, he was going to ask me to give it back. I breathed in the phone.

"No can do." Sentiment was one thing, but I wasn't going anywhere near the Needle with Pigeyes and his posse posted nearby.

"Just maintain the status quo, will you?" said Martin. "Will you promise me that?"

Without answering, I put down the phone.

I called in again at five-thirty. Brushy picked up herself.

"He's ready to see you," she said.

"Don't say anything else."

"Okay. But how can I get this message to you?"

I thought a second. "Maybe you should come see me."

"What about being followed?"

"You and I had lunch last week."

"Right."

"And then we went somewhere else."

"Okay." The hotel. She got it.

"Before we went upstairs, you went somewhere on your own. Remember?"

She laughed a little when she caught my drift.

"That's where you'll be? Where I went?"

"Center pew. One hour."

"O-kay," she sang. If I said so.

B. Looking for Love in All the Wrong Places, Part 2

The bar at the Dulcimer House hotel has one of those great after-work scenes where the young gals, the secretaries and bank tellers and female functionaries who are not sure if they're looking for fun or a life, go to be ogled and throw back half-price drinks while various guys, bachelors and married fellas with undisciplined dicks, line up three deep at the bar, hoping for some quick drunken action to think of tomorrow at work. As I stood in the distinguished lobby, with its wedding-cake ceiling ribboned in gold, the emanations from the bar intruded, strange as radio signals from deep space: the booming dance music, the garlicky reek of various warm hors d'oeuvres, the carousing voices hoarse with thwarted emotion and ambient lust.

The restrooms were down a short carpeted corridor off the lobby. I waited outside the Ladies', which Brushy had visited as we were checking in last week. Pigeyes would never work with a female cop and he was too old-line and prudish to even think of following her in. He'd wait at the door like Lassie. I spent about five minutes in the hallway, circumspectly checking out the ingress and egress, then stopped a young lady ready to enter.

"Say, my wife's been in there awhile. Would you let me know if she's okay when you come out?"

She was back in a jiffy.

"There's nobody in there."

"No," I said. She was standing at the door, which was decorated with a buxom silhouette, and I held it with one hand and gradually slid into the vestibule, pushing shyly at the inner door. "Shirley?" I called, averting my face so I did not even peek. I turned a little more front and center, yelled in again, and heard my voice ringing off the pink tiles. The girl hunched her shoulders and went back to party.

As soon as she was gone, I stalked into the john and locked myself in the center stall. Resting my briefcase on the toilet paper dispenser, I stood up on the fixture so that no gal would see my wingtips and start yodeling. I squatted there hoping Brushy would be hasty. At 255, my thighs would burn out quickly.

I found myself eye level with two bolt holes originally meant to hold some coat hook or other apparatus. Unutilized, they could serve from this peculiar vantage as a kind of peephole. A gentleman never would, of course, but who said I was Sir Galahad? About a minute along, a great-looking gal in a black dress with tassels entered the stall next to me and I got, as usual, just what I deserved. She didn't touch her zipper or hike her skirt. Instead, she took a minute to remove her rings, then put the middle three fingers of her right hand as far down her throat as could fit. When they came out, she touched each hand to the metal sides of the stall, bucked her head deliriously a couple of times, and puked her guts out. Varoom. Breakfast, lunch, and dinner. The force of it all drove her down to her knees, and she shook her fine head of black curls a little bit, then cleared her throat with a crackling expulsion. A second later I peeped over the top of the stall and saw her by the sink freshening her breath with an atomizer. She tossed out her curls with her long red nails and shoved her boobs back into her push-up bra with a hand underneath each, then lingered to give herself a sizzling look in the mirror. Wednesday night and ready for fun.

I was still trying to figure out what to make of that one when I heard Brushy say my name. She rattled the door. After I closed us in together, she gave me a big smooch, right there next to the toilet bowl.

"I think this is all very exciting," she whispered. That was Brushy, part of what had led her on the world penis tour or ignited some of her interest in me: raw curiosity, the fact that she wanted to see life's every side, savor every far-flung experience. As I've said, I always find female bravery notable and attractive.

"So where is he?" I asked.

"Wait. Don't you want to hear how I shook the tail?" She loved the lingo, the cops and robbers. Brushy thought she was in a movie where I was going to do something smart and save us all, not run away with the money. She described a circuitous route through various buildings in Center City, a stop at a client's, and entry here through the back door of the bar. She would have eluded Joe Friday.

She was searching through her little black purse when we heard the restroom door open. I jumped back up on the bowl, so that I was basically rubbing my zipper on Brushy's nose. Being Brushy, she found this pretty amusing. I covered my lips with a straight finger, and just to let me know she cared, Brush gave my pecker a pat and took the opportunity to start unzipping my fly. I swatted her hand.

The water ran at the sink. Somebody was doing a makeover. Brushy tugged on the zipper. I scowled and mouthed various vituperations, but she loved the circumstance, me in this bondage of silence and place, and pretty soon she was down to business and getting a response. She had old J.P. out there, touch, kiss, prod, and consume, aided by some quick dancing work of the fingertips, and she might have finished if some gal hadn't pulled into the stall next door. The nearby audience diminished my interest, but the whispers and giggling and squirming around were apparently audible to our neighbor, who seemed to jump up. On her way out she put one eye to the breach between the stall door and the post and said, "Weird."

"You are," I said, when we were alone again. "Weird."

"To be continued," Brushy answered. I was in my rough tweed sport jacket, and when she saw my sour look she dug her fingers in. "Come on, Mack. This is wild. Be wild. Enjoy it."

I just shook my head and asked about Bert. She gave me the

note he had faxed: "Behind 462 Salguro. 10 p.m." Recognizing the address, I laughed.

"It's the Russian Bath."

"Aren't they closed then?"

"I suppose that's the point."

"Will you come see me afterwards?"

"They're gonna sit on your house, Brush. They might."

She was funny and melodramatic. "Is this goodbye forever?"

I don't think she liked the uncompromising square-jawed expression she got in response. She wanted to be lovey-dovey and lighthearted here in the bathroom stall, giddy and teenaged, as if singing a chorus or two of "I Got You, Babe" would conquer all.

"I want to see you," she said. "I want to make sure you're all right."

"I'll call."

She gave me the eye. After all, she'd followed me to Central America. So we made a plan. She wouldn't go home, because Gino might pick her up there. Instead, she'd grab a taxi, have it circle the block twice to see if she was being followed. Maybe in the movies coppers can tail somebody for days unseen, but in real life it takes four cars at least, someone to go in every direction, and if the mark knows you're there, nine times out of ten you get lost or he's flipping you off in the rearview or sending you a round when you follow him into a tavern. If she came away without company, we agreed Brushy would go to a chain hotel three blocks down. Just check in for the night. Leave a key at the desk. And buy me a toothbrush.

I told her to take off first now. I waited in the vestibule between the doors and she rapped once to signal the hallway was clear. Then I gave her a few minutes to get a lead and take any trailing companions with her. Naturally some old biddy with flossed-up beauty-parlor hair came in then and did a triple-take and a haughty who-are-you look, and I had to pirouette around and play like I thought this all-pink enclosure was actually the men's room and then bow my way back out the door.

No Pigeyes in sight, none of his pals. I put on a winter hat and drew up my muffler and went out to see if I could talk a hack into taking a ride at night into the West End. I was thinking about Brushy. She had kissed me goodbye in the bathroom, a long, lingering embrace full of all her spunk and ardor, and issued fateful advice before disappearing: "Don't get another rash."

XXV. THE SECRET LIFE OF
KAM ROBERTS, PART TWO

I got to the West End with more than an hour and a half to spare and I spent the time in a little Latin bar on the corner near the Bath where almost no English was spoken. I sat sipping soda pops, sure every second that I was going to break down and order a drink. I was thinking about Brushy and not enjoying it much, wondering what-all that was coming to, whether I wanted what she did or could give it, and as a result, I was in one of my most attractive moods, refusing to move my elbows and waiting for somebody to try to hoist my no-good Anglo ass.

But the fellas here were pretty good-natured. They were watching one of those taped boxing matches from Mexico City on the bar TV, commenting *en español,* and taking peeks now and then at yours truly, figuring all in all I was too big to mess with. Eventually I got into the mood, joshing with them, throwing around my four or five words of Spanish, and recalling my longtime conclusion that a neighborhood joint like this might be the single best class of places on earth. I was more or less raised at The Black Rose, a terrible thing to admit maybe, considering the rumpot I turned out to be, but in a neighborhood of tenements and tiny homes, people longed for a place where they could expand, lift an elbow without knocking down the crockery.

At the Rose, it was all right if your wife came; there were kids running round the tables and jerking on their mothers' sleeves; there was singing and those jokes. Humans warmed by one another's company. And me, as a kid, I couldn't ever wait to get out of there, to blow the whole scene. I recollected this with chagrin, but suspected for reasons I couldn't explain that I'd end up feeling the same way if you put me back there today.

Ten o'clock even, I headed out and walked down the alley. This was a big-city neighborhood where the cops and the mayor long ago installed those orange sodium lights with their garish candlepower that seemed to turn the world black and white, but the alley was still all kinds of menacing shadows—garbage cans and dumpsters, sinister alcoves and iron-barred doorways, a lot of lurking spots for Mr. S/D, Stranger Danger, to smile and wield his knife. Walking on, I had the usual dry rot in the mouth and watery knees. I heard a grating clank and stopped dead. Someone was out here waiting for me. I reminded myself that was how it was supposed to be, I was meeting somebody.

When I got closer, I saw a figure beckoning. It was the Mexican, Jorge, Mr. Third World Anger, who'd questioned me the day I was down here. He stood in the alley in bathroom slippers and an iridescent blue silk robe. His hands were shoved deep in his pockets and you could see the great puffs of his breath hazing above him in a blade of light angling from the doorway behind. He chucked his face in my direction and said, "Eh."

Bert was inside, out of sight of the door. We seemed to be in a supply area behind the locker room, and he greeted me as eagerly as he had the other night. Meanwhile, Jorge engaged the dead bolt on the door and padded off. Apparently he was going back to sleep. He paused to poke his head down the hall.

"When you leave, lock it. And, men, don't leave nobody see your ass. I don' want no fuckin shit here. I tole you a long time ago, *hombre*, you was fucked up, all fucked up." He said this to Bert, but he pointed at me. "I tole you, too."

Jorge, Bert said, had to get up at four, arrange the stones

which had been in the oven firing all night, and make the place ready for the bathers who'd begin arriving as early as 5:30 a.m. I wondered where Jorge stood with the outfit guys. There were a lot of them that came around here to steam off the stink of corruption and ugly deeds. Jorge, I suspected, kept everyone's secrets. But if a guy with a tommy gun or a coat hanger knocked on the front door now, Jorge'd point out where we were and go back to sleep. It was a tough life.

I told Bert we had to talk.

"How about the Bath?" he asked. "You know, oven's on. It's blow-your-brains-out hot in there. It'll be great. Get all that oil and stuff right up to the skin. How about it?"

I had some thoughts, silly bigoted ones, about sitting around naked with Bert, even wrapped in a bedsheet, and then I began to feel sheepish and stupid, sure that if I said no he'd read that as the motive. So we hung our clothes in the lockers and Bert found the way down, both of us in the ocher-colored bedsheets cinched at our bellies and worn much like skirts. Bert didn't dare burn a light near a window. The shower room outside the bath remained dark, and the bath itself was lit only by a single bulb that left a gloomy light the color of tea. The stones had all been shoveled back into the oven and the room was arid, the great fire roasting the air. Even so, the place still had a vaguely vernal scent. Bert cracked the door a bit on the oven and then sat himself down on the top bench in the stepped wooden room and made exultant noises in the withering heat.

You'd have thought he had no troubles, chatting away about the Super Bowl, until I asked him to tell me on the level how it had been. He looked down then between his knees and didn't answer. Scary times, I suppose. Here was a fella who'd flown wartime missions, who knew what it was like being throttled by fright. But time had passed; the imagination takes over; honest memories fade. The pain of fear had plainly surprised him.

"I been eating fried food. Drinking bad water, man. Can't tell what's gonna get me first. You know?" He smiled. Loopy old

Bert. He thought he was funny. Lead from the tap or a gun barrel was lead either way.

"And where the hell have you been hiding out?" I asked.

He laughed at the question.

"Brother," he said and laughed again. "Here, there, and everywhere. Seeing the sights. Tried to keep moving."

"Well, let's take today, for instance. Where'd you start out?"

"Today? Detroit."

"Doing what?"

He fidgeted in the dense heat while words evaded him.

"Orleans had a game up there last night," he said finally. He was looking the other way as he said it and he didn't say any more. I got the picture: Bert was seeing all the best places, Detroit and La Salle–Peru, chasing Orleans, romancing on game nights in funky motels, places like the U Inn.

"And what about money? What've you been doing to live?"

"I had a credit card in another name."

"Kam Roberts?"

That startled him momentarily. He'd forgotten what I knew.

"Right. I thought it'd be better than using my own, they'd have a harder time tracking me down, but they did anyway."

"I thought Orleans used that card."

"I had one, he had one. We scissored them finally. The cards were about to expire anyway. But we piled up some cash. That's okay. What the hell do I need? A motel with cable, I'm cool. It's just those guys, man. They were right on us. They were checking at stores where Orleans used the card, stuff like that. Scared the hell out of us both. Man." He looked at me. "Those guys were cops, you're saying?"

"They're hot on the trail." I had remained on my feet. I figured if I kept the sheet clutched around me and my butt off the boards, I'd make Brushy happy and come home unblemished. "That's our problem, Bert. The coppers. They know I've been looking for you, so now they're looking for me, especially after that runaround at the House of the Hands on Friday. I haven't slept

at home for four nights. You and I have to scope out what I tell
them, Bert, cause 'I dunno' doesn't really seem to cut it. This
whole thing with Orleans—I'd like to know how it happened,
just so we can figure what kind of dance step I do."

I wasn't facing him then. There was no point in that. Even
so, I could feel him sort of hanging, suspended in space as we
sat here in this hot wooden box.

"I mean, you know," he said behind me.

"Right," I said. We were going forward easy. "You met him
when he came to visit his mom at work. Something like that."

"Right."

So we stumbled around in conversation and Bert told me the
tale of Orleans and him in his own half-ass way. We were there
broiling, not looking at each other, just two voices in the tea-
gloomy light and incredible heat. Bert wasn't much of a storyteller. He did a lot of shit-out-of-luck mumbling. "You know,"
he'd say, "you know." And I did, I guess. I got the point. Orleans
changed Bert's life the way people's lives are ordinarily altered
only by human violence and natural disasters—volcanoes, hur-
ricanes, typhoons. You see the pictures all the time, some poor
son of a bitch in his hip waders, looking with zoned-out disbelief
at the roof of what used to be his house, now angled into the
black waters of the flood. That was Bert after Orleans. I'd only
seen the guy across the distance of a basketball court, so I
couldn't tell you a thing about him, except that he was a fine-
looking young fellow. But as I put the pieces together, my two
bits, he was sort of high-strung and erratic. Apparently he'd
been a high-school football star who tore up his knee and suffered
a lot over that, getting cut out of athletics, then started refereeing
various sports while he was still in college. These days he taught
grade school p.e. as a sub and reffed, but his principal occupation
apparently was fighting with his mother. He had a peculiar job
history, moving in and out of town, always coming back, living
at home half the time. I suppose Glyndora wanted him to be
different and he was engaged in the usual parent-child struggle,

always angry with her and wanting her to accept him, the way we all want with our folks at one level or another.

Somehow, though, they connected. For Bert, it was epochal. Orleans, I took it, was Bert's first actual real-life thing, and Bert was in love with him the way you'd love the genie if you'd found that magic lamp. Orleans to Bert was liberty. Destiny. In the midst of his longing, his attachment, Bert was also wild with gratitude. It's hard to believe that this could really happen in this day and age—people who live on the other side of earth from what they're really feeling—but the old copper in me says it occurs every day. Look at Nora. Look at me. Suddenly you're at an age when your own naughty thoughts exhaust you; no matter how much you try to ignore them, they remain. Whatever ugly stamp they place on your soul is impressed there indelibly. You might as well be whatever it is they say you are. You are anyway.

So they got their rumba going, Bert and Orleans, and Glyndora caught on and went wild. I got the feeling that was okay with Orleans, to be causing that kind of ruction.

Bert was walking back and forth now on the tier above me, roaming on his big feet with the long nails and the calluses from his loafers and athletic shoes. His black hair was heavy with perspiration and his unshaven cheeks looked darker in the heat.

"And how'd this betting thing happen? Whose idea?"

"Oh, you know, man," he said again, for the one hundredth time. "There was never any idea about it. We'd talk games. Players. Stuff like that. You know how it is, you hang with somebody, you kind of figure what they're thinking, I mean maybe he'd say— He'd say. You know, before the Michigan game, he'd say, 'I'm going to call Ayres tight, he's a street player, you got to call him tight.' Or Erickson at Indiana. All elbows."

"And you'd bet it. Right? If Ayres was going to be called tight, you'd bet against Michigan."

"Yeah," he said. He was slowed by shame. "It didn't seem like much. Just a little edge. I didn't really think twice."

"Did Orleans know?"

"To start?"

"Eventually?"

"Man, do you know I bet the games?"

"I do," I said. Orleans, he was saying, knew too. I thought
for a sec about Bert as a gambler. What was it that compelled
him? Did he lust to feel favored by chance, or did he want to
dare punishment? What drew him? The men? Or the sport? The
grace, the fact that it was all winners and losers with no com-
promise? Something. It was part of the game of hide-and-seek
he was playing with himself.

"Did he ask if you bet his games?"

"Not like that. He'd just ask what I was down on. You know,
I'd tell him. He wasn't even sure where he was going until 4:30
the day before." This was slow: "He never said I'm gonna fix
this. It was nothing like that."

"But did you notice that he was taking care of it?"

I dared a look back at Bert, who was standing on the top tier,
his head in the rafters, his black eyes still and stricken.

"You want a real fucking yuk? When I knew what he was
doing—when I saw it, you know, I was happy. I was fucking
pleased. God." Bert suddenly reached forward and hooked one
hand on the beam and leaned out, muscles articulate in his long
arm, wincing, holding on to his sheet with the other hand. What
he'd thought was that Orleans was in love with him. That's why
he liked it. Not the money. Not even bragging rights in this
room. Because it was a token of love. Now he was in pain.

"What a sick stupid thing," he said.

I realized suddenly that I had been looking forward to having
this out with Bert for my own reasons. Here we both were, two
middle-aged men, big-deal successes, sort of at least, and both
of us felons. There may be no honor among thieves, but there
is a kind of community, knowing that you're no weaker than
somebody else. And I guess I'd been thinking that cornering
Bert, making him account for himself, I'd have an answer or two

to throw back at that nagging voice of my ma's. But this was a letdown. Bert's was a crime of passion. Not in the sense that the object of the scam was secondary; maybe it was with me too. But because for Bert and for Orleans there was really no scam at all. It was simply a stepping-stone, a point of access to the place they needed to go, Bert especially, where "wrong" didn't even exist.

"And how did Archie find out?" I asked him.

"Well, Christ, he's taking the bets. All the sudden I'm betting one game heavy three times a week and making a bundle. I didn't want him to get hurt. I'd tell him, Watch out for this one. Everybody down here had money in Archie's book." Bert took an instant to explain Archie's system with Infomode, everybody with a credit card and a funny handle. One guy's Moochie. Hal Diamond got called Slick. Bert was Kam.

"We sit here, we're talking games for hours. And, you know, we keep track of each other. Real close. You know how that is. We're all in each other's pockets."

So pretty soon everybody here knew. They'd kid Bert. 'What's Kam Roberts got today?' Bert realized it was a mistake. Afterwards. At the time he couldn't resist. That was his way: talk and swagger. I'm a fella. Who says we'll ever change?

"Archie had no idea where you were getting the information?"

"I wasn't talking, I don't know what they thought. Some connect to the players, I guess."

I paused to put it together in my head. "And Orleans got the credit card?"

Wrong thing to say. Bert popped. He came down a tier, cat-quick, got right up in my face. My favorite madman.

"Hey, fuck yourself, Mack. It wasn't like that. Christ, it's part-time work. Refereeing. He's a teacher. You know, you have money, you give a friend money. Get real. I had this credit card, money to spend. That's all, man. But it wasn't like that. Don't give me that crap." Orleans wasn't really fixing games. Bert wasn't really sharing the proceeds. It wasn't corruption. Not in their minds. It was love. Which, of course, it was.

Behind me I heard a faucet loosen and water begin to run. He had turned on one of the spigots between the boards and was filling a bucket, getting ready to do that number with the icy aqua over the head.

I realized about then that I'd sat down. I jumped up and did some heavy-legged version of the hootchy-kootchy, swearing, swatting at my big broad Irish bottom as if that was going to do any good. Bert watched, but I didn't explain. I pushed him back to the story.

I said, "So play it out for me. Some dude with brass knuckles starts making an impression on Archie, telling him he's got to give up the fixer, and all he can give them is you. And you find Archie in your refrigerator and go for the world tour, right?"

"Sort of. I knew I was leaving. Martin had pretty much convinced me of that."

Bingo. I watched the sweat gathering among all my gray chest hairs, the rivulets running over the swell of my belly and dampening the sheet bundled there.

"Martin had?" I asked. "Fill in the blank, Bert. Where does Martin fit?"

Bert's reaction was amazing. He hooted.

"What a question!"

"Where he fits? Martin?"

"Hey, the answer's like, 'In Glyndora,' " said Bert and, smirking like an absolute juvenile, circled his index finger and thumb and poked a finger through the form a couple of times. The gesture was so silly but direct that we both laughed out loud. What a life! Here we were, me and Bert of all people, giggling about somebody else's peccadilloes.

"*Mar*-tin?"

"Fuckin A," he answered.

"No way."

"It's ancient history. Years ago. Not now. Orleans was in grade school. But they're still like, what would you say—" Bert shifted a hand. "I mean, when things get heavy for her, that's who she goes to. Not just around the firm, man. You know. Life."

"Martin and Glyndora," I said. I was still marveling. I have made addled party-time chatter with Martin's wife, Nila, for years and know nothing more about her than what meets the eye: elegant looks and cultivated manners. I'd always assumed that Martin was happily wed to his own pretensions. The idea of him with a girlfriend was somehow at odds with his projected image of complete self-sufficiency.

"So what problem did Glyndora come to him with?" I asked. "I still don't understand why he got involved."

Bert didn't answer. By now I knew what that meant. Go gently. We were on that subject.

"She was upset about you getting to know Orleans?"

"Right," said Bert. He took his time. "He was in the middle at first. A mediator, I don't know what you'd say. She was just out of control. You know her. She's pretty nuts on this subject." He glanced up bleakly, a one-eyed peekaboo. In the meantime, with that remark, I got a load of the family dynamic. Orleans had grabbed Mom's attention big-time. Not just 'This is how I am,' but 'I am—with your boss. Your world.' I knew Bert would never recognize these intentions. He was like somebody with a perceptual disorder. His own emotions so dominated him that he had little perspective on anyone else.

"Then Martin found out about this, the betting. Man, it was Mount Saint Helens. He was more ticked than Glyndora. He told me straight up we were in way too deep. You know, he learned all about these guys growing up. He said the best thing was for me just to clear out. Disappear.

"And it started to actually sound okay, you know?" Bert said. "New life. That whole thing. Just drop out of sight. For a while anyway. Get out of the firm. You ever hear of Pigeon Point?"

"No."

"It's in California. North. On the coast. I found this ad. For an artichoke farm. I've been out there now. You know it's foggy. Amazing, man. The fog comes in over the artichokes twice a day. You barely have to water them. Great crops. And it's a phenomenal food." He started on the fucking vitamin count, more information in five seconds than a label on a can, and I let him go on, struck again by that notion. The new life. The new world. God, the mere thought still made my heart sing. Then, unexpectedly, I recalled that I had nearly six million dollars in my name in two foreign bank accounts and was gripped by an urgent question I could just as well have asked myself.

"So why aren't you gone?"

"He won't *leave*." Bert threw his big hands in my direction, the fingers crippled by desperation. "The dumbfuck won't go. I've begged him. I beg him three times a week." He stared at me, unhinged by the thought, and then turned away rather than confront what he could tell I was seeing—that Bert had given up his life to protect Orleans, and Orleans, when push came to shove, lacked the same dedication. Maybe Orleans couldn't honk off his mother sufficiently from two thousand miles away. Maybe, in the end, he didn't really have it for Bert. However it went, Bert's crusade was a one-way thing. I saw something else then, that this romance, Bert and Orleans, wasn't the high-flown love of the poets. There was something bad in it, it was tethered to pain; there was a reason Bert was so long telling himself the truth he did not want to know.

And even so, I envied him for a minute. Had I ever loved anybody like that? My feelings for Brushy seemed flimsy in the intense heat. But what about time? I thought. Maybe with time. Life has these two poles, it seems. You go one way or the other. We're always choosing: passion or despair.

"I've told him about the police," Bert said. "He doesn't believe it."

"They'll be pretty convincing if they catch him."

"Can you talk to them?" he asked finally. "The cops? Are they friends of yours?"

"Hardly," I said, but I sat there smiling. It was terrible really, the joy I took at the notion of skunking Pigeyes. I already had a few ideas.

The heat and the hour were gradually making me faint. I turned on the water and poured a cold bucket for myself, but didn't have the stamina or the courage to dump it over my head. I stood there before Bert, dabbing the water on my face and my chest, while I tried a moment to figure out what all this meant for me. There was a whisper about of the oven and the rocks barely sizzling.

"You don't know a thing about what's been going on at the firm, do you? The money? That whole thing?"

The sweat ran into his eyes and Bert blinked. He had his impenetrable black look: he doesn't understand you and never will.

I asked if the name Litiplex rang any bells.

"Jake?" he asked.

I nodded.

"Didn't Jake send me some memo? And I wrote him a bunch of checks on the 397 account? Yeah," Bert let his long body bob. He was remembering. "Something was very touchy. It was a mix-up with the plaintiffs. Jake was afraid Krzysinski would roast his hind end when he heard Jake had to pay these expenses. Big, big goddamn secret. Jake was very uptight on this thing." Bert reflected. "Something's fucked-up, huh?" he asked.

"You might say."

"Yeah," he said, "you know, now that I'm thinking, maybe a month ago Martin asked me about this. This Litiplex. But he was like, no problem, no big deal."

That would have been when Martin saw the memo and the checks. Glyndora, of course, would have come to him first when she noticed.

"So what's the story?" Bert asked.

I laid it out briefly: No Litiplex. The numbered account in Pico Luan. Bert seemed to regard it as remotely amusing until I got to the part where Martin and Glyndora manipulated appearances to make it look like the money was his.

"*Me?* Those *fuck-ers!* Me? I *don't* believe it." He'd jumped to his feet. I was abruptly reminded of trying cases with Bert, his sudden courtroom rages, objecting to a leading question like it was the landing of foreign troops on our soil. I waited for him to cool off.

"Just answer me straight, Bert. There's no deal between you and Martin for you to take the blame for this? The money?"

"Are you kidding? Fuck no, man."

"Nothing? No wink, no nod?"

"No. NFW. That's scumbag stuff." This was Bert, who had deceived millions of Americans about the outcome of sporting events, who had thought with his dick and made a profit besides, but he was on his high horse. He had the same lunatic look as when he talked about the secret poisons some faceless "they" put in his foods. He got back up on one of the moisture-blackened benches and poured the bucket over his head, and came out of the flood glaring. I had an odd thought at that moment of how much he reminded me of Glyndora.

We went upstairs to dress then, both turned pretty sulky and without much to say. Bert had a bag in his locker with deodorant and whatnot and let me use his stuff.

"Who is it?" he asked me suddenly. "With the money?"

"Doesn't matter."

"Yeah, but—" He shrugged.

I'd spent the last few days delving into the depths of the mind of Martin Gold. It was like walking downward in some endless cave. From the start Martin must have figured that if he hung this on Bert no one would ever contradict him. Not Jake, of course. Not Bert, who was on permanent leave, hiding from hit men among the artichokes. Not clueless old me. Not even the

TN board, which, if informed of the loss, had nothing to gain by making a public fuss that would only attract attention to what was left of the 397 surplus. By blaming Bert, Martin would keep everything tidy.

And I could have gone along with that, Martin's scheme to save the world as I knew it. Unless Pigeyes caught him, Bert wasn't going to surface. Any day now Jake would discover that he'd developed a hole in his pocket down in Pico Luan, but so what? Self-preservation would prevent Jake from making an international scene. He couldn't start hollering, Where's all that money I stole? Trumped and taken, Jake would probably blame Bert too. It could work out for me Martin's way. In a couple months I could retire from the firm, vacationing when need be in Pico Luan.

But when I'd steamed out the shellacked doors of the Club Belvedere on Saturday and sat up all night hatching plans, I was gripped by ornery impulses. I'd developed the fixed intention to smite Martin and the whole smarmy scheme. Since then I'd hoped against hope at moments. I came here wanting Bert to tell me there was a galaxy of good intentions involved, some aspect that was wholesome, or at least excusable, which I hadn't seen. But he couldn't. Because that wasn't the case. And recognizing that, I found myself under the same internal momentum. Maybe I was still a cop on the street, committed to my own kind of rough justice. God knows, I never have played well for the team. But I was going to do it my way. Brushy hung there somehow in the balance, an indeterminate weight. Yet there was no reason, really, I couldn't make that work out. I kept telling myself that.

"Jake," I answered at last. "Jake's got the money." That's where this was going. I was gonna be mean. Even so, the details were daunting.

"Jake! Whoa." Bert brought his long hand to his jaw and rubbed it as if he had taken a blow. He was sitting there on the bench in the dim locker room, holding his socks, the only light borrowed from a single bulb burning in the john.

"Martin's covering for him, protecting the firm."

"Jake," Bert said again.

It struck me with an exactness that had completely eluded me before that if I was going to carry through with this, undermine Martin and pass out just deserts, I'd have to figure some way for Bert to return. Without that, it might come down to finger pointing. Martin and Jake could still call Bert the bad guy somehow. Why else was he running? Mystery Thief on the Loose. To make my version fully convincing, Bert had to be here to tell his story: he got the memo from Jake, gave the checks to Jake, listened when Jake told him it was all hush-hush. I couldn't imagine, though, how that could be engineered. Amid the dank atmosphere of the locker room, we sat in silence. One of the steam pipes eventually emitted a distinct clank.

"Look, Bert, I'm going to try to help you. I want to see you get out of all this, but I really have to put my thinking cap on. Just stay in touch. Make sure you call every day."

The guy saw right through me. Not what was wrong. But something. That I had some stake. And he couldn't have cared less.

"Please," he said quietly. He watched me there, his face buried in shadow but still rimmed by some eager hope.

When we were dressed, he took me to the back door and unlocked the bolt, the grate.

"Where you going?" I asked.

"Oh, you know." His eyes floated away from me. "Orleans is in town."

God, he was lost. Even in the dark you could see him, swarthy and lean, in the grip of his sad hopeless love. He was being tortured and teased. Moth and flame. I thought to myself again, What is this? A character like Bert, you figure his gyroscope's wacky. But the head, the heart—who am I kidding? One man's rationality is another fella's madness. Nothing ever really adds up. Either the premises are faulty or the reasoning sucks. We're all of us pincushions, lanced by feelings, full of wounds and pains. Reason is the lie, the balm we apply, pretending that if we were just smart enough we'd make some sense of what hurts.

I'd already stuck my nose into the cold when I realized one question remained. I barred the door with the arm of my overcoat.

"So who moved the body, Bert? Who took Archie? Did Orleans?"

"Fuck, never," said Bert. "He'd freak." Bert shook his head violently at the thought and repeated that Orleans wasn't up to something like that.

"So who?"

We stood on the threshold, eyeing each other, surrounded by the deep alley darkness and the harsh touch of winter, hovering with the unspoken improbabilities of our futures, everything that was simply unknown.

Thursday, February 2

XXVI. MACK MALLOY'S

FIFTEENTH

CONTINGENCY PLAN

A. Step One

So. It was midnight. I was the only white man for a mile, a guy
in an overcoat with a briefcase and a prominent urge to begin
making plans. I stalked through the tough old neighborhood,
headed in the direction of Center City, an exercise in fifty-year-
old daring, striding from the rescuing glow of one streetlight to
the next. A bus came along presently and I boarded gratefully
and bucketed down the avenues with the winos and the workers
returning from late-night stints. A few blocks from the Needle,
I jumped off. Kindle County at night is not lively. The lights
are on but the streets are empty; it has its own spectral air, like
a deserted building, a place even the ghosts have fled.

I entered the lobby of the Travel Tepee, where Brush and I
had agreed to meet. The big lobby was quiet; even the Muzak
had been turned off for the night. I sat in an ugly easy chair
with a horrible bold print and considered the future. Finally the
lone registration clerk asked from behind the front counter if he
could help me. From his tone, I thought he was pretty sure I
was just a better-dressed derelict whom security would have to
give the heave-ho. I went over to make peace, told him he had

a Ms. Bruccia registered, and picked up my key, then I sat down again, counting out the steps in my plan. I thought of waiting until morning to begin putting this together, but I was feeling edgy, compulsive, call it what you want. I was wide-awake anyway and a little reluctant to be with Brushy, now that I actually knew what I was going to do.

About two blocks down there was an all-night pharmacy, another Brown Wall's, built near the exit ramp of the Interstate, a place with a bus station air, a lot of downtown creeps hanging around near the doors, and a cop car parked right at the curb. I bought two pens—one ballpoint, one felt tip—and some glue and a pair of scissors. I asked at the counter if they had a coin-operated copying machine, but the answer was no, so I walked back to the hotel, waved to the desk clerk, and found a little phone alcove which had a laminate surface I could use for a desk.

I already had the rest of what I needed in my briefcase—the signature form I'd received at International Bank of Finance, the letter of Jake's I'd used as a model to forge his signature to the fax I sent from the Regency, and the copies of TN's annual report that I'd toted down to Pico. The report contains pictures of all the corporate officers, including Jake Eiger, and I'd brought copies along thinking Jake's photo might come in handy if I had to do any of a number of things I was then considering to get at the money, such as phonying up a passbook or some form of U.S. I.D.

The signature form was printed on onionskin with a schmaltzy heading in script: "International Bank of Finance, Pico Luan, N.A." There were only four or five lines of information required, the descriptions written in all of the major Western European tongues. Using the felt tip, I filled in the account number that appeared on the back of the Litiplex checks, 476642. I named the account owner as Litiplex, Ltd., Jake Eiger as president. Then just to remind myself of the look of his hand, I took Jake's old letter from the briefcase and signed his name to the form with the ballpoint, dead on again, so close you'd think it was traced. After that, I cut Jake's grinning puss out of the TN annual report and pasted it down where Mr. George had shown me it would go in the upper-right-hand corner of the form. Finally, in the little block labeled "Designation," meaning code word, I wrote out, perfectly, "J.A.K.E."

Then I went back to the clerk at the counter. He was starting to get used to me. I gave him a weary sigh, dragging my hands down my raddled kisser.

"I have a presentation in the morning and I forgot to copy one thing. Just two pictures of it, one page. You must have a machine in the office." I had a twenty between two of my fingers, but this guy, young, maybe a graduate student, somebody still starting out in his life, wouldn't take it. He was still feeling bad for thinking I was a bum. He brought back the copies of the signature form and we talked about the weather, how quiet the city could be at night.

I returned to the phone booth. I took the original of the signature form and tore it into pieces, throwing them in the opening in the long sand-topped trash canister by my feet. The two photocopies the desk clerk had made me went into my case. Then I called information for D.C. The latest Mrs. Pagnucci, a six-foot blonde, answered the phone. She said nothing to me when I explained who I was. Instead, in a voice I'd heard now and then in my own home, the soul of tedium, she remarked, "One of your partners."

B. Step Two

Brushy was asleep when I let myself into the room. It was about 3:00 a.m. She still slept like a child, in a small fetal ball, and her hand was close enough to her mouth that I wouldn't have been surprised if she suckled a digit or two. Vulnerable, with her sly wits turned off for the night, she looked dear to me, maybe precious is the word, and I felt really bad, my heart twisted around like a cloth being wrung. I threw my clothes down and crept into bed. As my night eyes came on, I could see this was not exactly the bridal suite. The headboard had been nicked in many places, revealing the mealy composition of the underlying particle board, and directly over the bed the old textured wallpaper had peeled from its butt joints and hung down from the plaster like an extruded tongue. I drifted a hand against Brushy's solid flank to comfort myself.

"How's Bert?" She still hadn't moved.

"Okay," I said, "safe at least." I apologized for waking her.

"I was waiting for you." She snapped on the light and covered her eyes like a child with the backs of her hands. While she was blinded, I touched her, just kidding around, pulled the sheet down and nuzzled my cold cheek to her breasts, but she held me there and we heated up fast. Every time we had screwed so far it was different. There was horseplay sometimes, as in the hotel ladies' room, and she also had a lot of daring and skill, a bold way of laying her hands on that cut to the basics, that said this was for pleasure so let's not kid ourselves. Now suddenly, in the cheap hotel room, as beaten down as Center City around us, we were quick and desperate, wanting to overcome every-thing else. Real fire, and afterwards, spooned to her from behind, I could tell she thought that was great. We were quiet, with the empty sounds of the hotel and the street reaching us—sirens at a distance and the shouts of drunks and kids like my son who should have been at home for the night. I asked if she had brought cigarettes, then sat beside her on the bed, trading one back and forth with her in the dark.

"Does he have the money?" she asked.

"Come on, Brush."

"Just that. Does Bert have the money?"

"Brush, aren't we too old for Twenty Questions?"

"Attorney-client," she said. "Does he have it? Yes or no?"

"No."

"Really? Did he ever?"

"He doesn't have the money. Go to sleep." I went to the john, found the toothbrush she'd bought me, and lingered there hoping she'd fall off.

When I snuck in beside her, I slept dreamlessly, a velvet pit. Near seven, I snapped awake with a tiny outcry, quickly muted, the sound of inspiration. I dressed quietly and left Brushy a note that said I'd be back.

I had a walk of about six blocks and I jogged a step or two now and then as I penetrated Center City from its grotty outskirts, getting closed in by the morning hubbub, the trucks double-parked and wreaking havoc with the traffic, the silent army of workers marching the streets. It was pretty cold, less than 15 degrees, and I threw myself down into my coat.

Toots ate breakfast every morning with the same guys, old pols, ward types, and lawyers, at a corner table of a Greek joint called Paddywacks right across from his office. This was a legendary event. Toots greeted half the folks in the restaurant and waved to them all with his cane. In the corner booth Toots and his friends gossiped about dirty business in any number of venues—the courthouse, the council building, the mob. A few years ago the feds had put a microphone in one of the salt shakers, but Toots and his pals had got word somehow. One of them, it was said, complained loudly about the taste of his eggs, then slammed the shaker on the tabletop and blew the listening agent's eardrum out.

Paddywacks was slightly overdecorated—brass fixtures and tufted benches and floors that were mopped once a week. I was beginning to be afraid I'd missed Toots, when he came in about 8:15 on his stick, two paisans on either side. One of them, Sally Polizzo, had been a federal guest up until six months ago. Toots greeted me like a visiting king. I shook hands with each of his companions, then strolled him down to a booth where he took a seat alone. I stayed on my feet.

"Did you mean what you said about a favor?" I asked him. Sitting on the little velveteen bench, the Colonel looked tiny, a little guy shrinking worse with age, but when I asked if he'd meant what he said, he just drew back with a look tough enough to make you believe he'd been a killer. I corrected myself.

"This may be too much. If it is, you say so. You remember we talked about my partner?" I went over it quickly, but I told Toots the truth. How his pals were looking for my guy and his friend and how my guy was hiding. Somebody else was going to end up dead, and for nothing. The bookie had paid the big price, and these other guys were scared straight. Justice of the kind Toots practiced had been served. I asked him to get his friends to lay off Bert and Orleans. Favor for favor.

Toots sat there silent, the rubbery old mouth pursed, his eyes still. He was working it out in his head. If he called that guy and reminded him of this thing, then that guy could get to someone else. It was all geometry to him, and power. He wanted to justify my faith.

"Maybe," he said. "Depends. I think so. I'll let you know this afternoon. This fella got any money?"

"Some," I said, then thought of Pico and added, "yeah, he's got money. Why?"

"This here's a business. Somebody's got a point to make. He gets paid, that's his point. Right?"

"I suppose."

Toots said he'd leave word for me at the office. Then I helped him to his feet so he could totter down to the corner booth and his courtiers. There were already two old guys with rubbery faces waiting to say hi.

C. Watch That Step

"I went to see Toots," I told Brushy when I got back to the room.

"Toots?" Sitting by the window at a little cane table arrayed with a light room-service breakfast she'd ordered—coffee and rolls, half a cantaloupe—she considered me intently. The heavy-lined night curtain had been pulled back, admitting the light and revealing a sheer that nestled about her. She was wearing her overcoat as a robe and she'd made up her face. When I came in, she'd been reading the paper.

"Mack," she said, "I want to know."

I didn't say anything and threw my coat on the bed. I was hungry and she watched me eat, measuring the meaning of my lack of response.

"I called the office," she said, "to say we'd be late. Detective Dimonte's been there already."

I made a sound. No surprise.

"And Lucinda said Martin's looking for you. He's left two messages." She looked at the phone as if to guide me, but I didn't move.

"Look, Mack," she said, "I can handle it. I'm a grown-up. Whatever it is. It's just—"

"I thought you were going to take my advice."

"It's my life too."

I hated this moment. But I'd always known it was coming. One of the problems about settling for Mr. Not-Quite-Good-Enough is a sense of peril about accepting his guidance. With my eyes closed I ruminated, then I grabbed my briefcase and looked into its dark, disordered depths. Balled deposit slips rested in the bottom, along with fragments of papers, and paper clips; stick-on notes adhered to the sides. I pulled out one of the photocopies of the signature form I'd made up last night. I laid it down on the rattan table. Litiplex, Ltd. Jake Eiger, line 1.

"Don't ask how Pindling got it. We don't want to know."

She studied the document with a hand on her forehead as the weight of the tangible evidence bore down on her visibly. I got her cigarettes and we shared one, the odor of the smoke filling up the little room. I cracked the sliding window a bit and the curtains flowed around her like spirits.

"Jake?" she asked.

"That's what it says."

"You've known about this all along, haven't you? That's why you were so peeved with Jake." I think I winced when she said that. Even with alarm bells clanging, she was listening for good news about me.

"I've known a lot," I told her.

"Like what?"

I was just sailing here, no charted course. I didn't have the will to resist her and the lying made me feel childishly eager to cry. In my briefcase I found the memo I'd pulled from Martin's drawer. As she read, she picked a fleck of tobacco off her tongue. Her expression was flat, intense. She was being a lawyer.

"I don't understand," she said. "This isn't from Pindling. This memo."

"Martin."

"Martin!"

I told her the story, some of it anyway, about finding the memo, chugging over to the Club Belvedere. I was moved by her pain. As she often told me, Brushy liked these people. Martin. Wash. Her partners. The firm. These were her colleagues, who admired her abilities, who trusted her years ago with the things that mattered to them, who applauded her many triumphs and had received her assistance with a gratitude that was often intense. She knew she'd survive. She had clients, a growing reputation. That was not her worry. The point was commitment, allegiance, shared enterprise. She was devastated.

"They were setting up Bert? Right? To take the blame for Jake. Isn't that how this looks?"

"That's how it looks."

"God," she said, and raked a hand through her hair. I opened the sliding door for an instant to crush out my cigarette on the small cement balcony, and the cold briefly forced its way into the room. The sun was out but seemed to offer no heat, as if it were just posed in the clear sky for decoration. Brushy asked me how Bert fit in and I told her his story and why I'd gone to see Toots. Her mind, though, remained on the Committee.

"Oh, it's so stupid. Stu-pid," she said. "Is this all of them?"

"Couldn't say. Martin obviously. Pagnucci doesn't seem to be in it. Wash—well, I told you what his attitude was."

"Martin," she said again. The Great Oz. She'd taken a seat on the bed, clutching her coat. I'd be willing to bet she wasn't wearing a stitch underneath—not that either of us would be pursuing that prospect in our present mood.

"What are you going to do with all of this, Mack?"

I shrugged. I'd lit another cigarette.

"I'll probably do the right thing."

She watched me, assessing, wondering what that might mean. Then she shook herself in a lonesome spasm of disbelief.

"Something," she said. "I mean Jake. Why? It doesn't make sense. He makes money. His father is rich. Why do this?"

I leaned over the bed. I peered in her eyes.

"Because that's how he is." The sheer viciousness gripped me and she looked on as if it were some kind of spectacle. She didn't care that I was saying I told you so. And she wasn't afraid. She held me at a distance, marveling.

"You're going to blackmail him, aren't you?"

It was the weirdest fucking thing. I felt like I'd been kicked. My mouth hung open and my heart felt hard as a fist and filled with intense physical pain. The humiliation ran like an acid to my eyes.

"Kidding," she said.

"Bullshit."

I walked around the bed and picked up my coat.

"Mack." She reached for me. "I don't care what you do."

"You don't mean that. Don't even ask me to believe it. I know who you are and so do you." Looking into my case, I realized I'd left the papers on the table. I waved them at her as I picked them up. I was hating myself for having said anything.

"Attorney-client," I remarked to remind her she was ears only, that I was the only one with options, the right to act. Then I went down the shabby hallway to the elevator. I punched at the button, calling the car, and leaned against the wall, hollowed out and hopeless, certain that I would never understand the first thing about myself.

XXVII. PLAN EXECUTION

A. Up to His Neck in Sand

"This is distressing," said Carl. Those were the first words from him in a number of minutes. He had read the memo, then looked over the photocopy of the International Bank signature form. When he asked me about Pindling, I used the same words as Lagodis.

"A real snake charmer," I said. "You call him, he won't even know my name. I had to pay him in cash." I'd show the charge on my golden credit card if I ever needed to prove that.

We were at the airport in the TN Executive Lounge, in a tiny conference room just big enough for a small table of black granite surrounded by four chairs. There was a telephone between us, as well as an insulated thermos of coffee which neither of us had touched.

Last night I had told Carl it was urgent. He didn't seem especially surprised to hear from me. It fit both his view of what he did and himself to receive emergency phone calls after midnight. It probably happened a lot, some young genius noticing a snafu in an offering circular three hours before they were going into the market. There was the usual deliberative pause when

I asked Pagnucci to catch an earlier plane, leave himself time before Groundhog night. I promised to meet him at the gate. It was almost one now.

Carl looked at the papers a second and then a third time. His mind was moving at a phenomenal pace, trying to absorb everything, but I could tell from his deliberation that he was having trouble figuring it all out, especially the next move. He compared Jake's handwriting, first on the signature card, then on the old letter I'd given him as an example, and minutely shook his head.

"And what is it you propose?" he asked me at last.

"We'll call one of the nice ladies outside in the service center to make copies of all this. The originals I hold."

"Yes?" He watched me alertly.

"You phone Krzysinski right now. Tell him you have to see him at once. Highest priority. Then you take these documents to him. Say you're proceeding on behalf of G&G. You express appropriate emotions. Horror. Regret. Disclosure of course is the only avenue."

"And I do so without advising Martin or Wash?"

"Right."

Pagnucci was sallow, his eyes small and intent. He nibbled a bit at his little mustache.

"Are they in league?"

I didn't follow.

"Wash, Martin, Eiger," he said. "Are they in this together?"

I shook off the question. "That's beside the point. I've been around G&G a long time. A lot of people have been good to me."

That was not the sort of feeling I'd expect him to share. One thing about Pagnucci I was banking on was that he was as tough as he made out, the kind of guy who, if he was up to his neck in quicksand, would have the brass to tell you to walk on. I knew cops like that, guys who felt they could prove something essential by refusing—ever—to yield to sentiment. They believed what they believed, absolutely. He sat there quite erect in his perfect blue suit.

"Yes, but let's play this out," said Pagnucci, unconsciously patting the bald spot behind his head. "My partners told me that this memo couldn't be found."

"It turned up. It was a surprise."

"And what about that meeting the other day, where you outlined Eiger's proposal to keep all of this mum? What's to be said about that?"

"Tell Tad. It's part of the evidence. Jake wanted the whole matter forgotten. But we continued to investigate and now you're here on behalf of the Committee, the firm, to bring everything out. Look, no one's ever accused you of saying too much, Carl. You can handle it. But it's your obligation to go forward." Talking to Pagnucci about his obligations felt as vain and mindless as saying, Have a nice day. In the stuttering movements of his dark eyes, you could see him calculating, his mind on the roam.

"But who had the memo?" he asked. "Wash?"

I didn't answer. Pagnucci may have had questions, but he'd like what he saw. Carl Pagnucci—man of grit and integrity. Forthcoming with the truth, even when it was devastating to his firm. Pagnucci had already been making contingency plans with Brushy, and this would fit. He understood how his candor was likely to be recalled and rewarded by Tad in the future, now that TN would be floating free as a client. Moving on, he would take some of TN's work with him, even as G&G sank. There was an irresistible cocktail here for somebody like Carl, looped already on the ethers of self-importance.

"And you wouldn't advise sharing this with Martin or Wash before we act?" The fact that his caution exceeded his greed startled me a bit.

"Afterwards you can tell them what you've done, what you've said. They can only follow. If you tell them in advance, they'll try to derail you. They have to. You know that."

Carl continued his silent reflection. The thing that bothered him most, I suspected, was that he was depending on me.

"Carl," I said, "there's no choice. We have a duty to the client. Someone from the Committee has to go to Krzysinski, someone who speaks on behalf of the firm."

He considered me soberly. We both knew I was manipulating him shamelessly. But I'd given him what he needed—a good excuse. It had all the right appearances. Highly principled. Above criticism. And very good for Pagnucci. He could salute the flag and steal the client. Beyond that, it did not matter much what I was up to.

I pulled the phone close and dialed TN. It took some time to get to Krzysinski, but he said he had a few minutes for Carl before two.

B. Some People Want Me and Some People Don't

I waited until three to leave the airport, then took a cab home. Right about now, big powwows were going on at TN: Carl and Tad and TN's head of security, Mike Mathigoris. They were figuring what to do with Jake—question him, crucify him, or just throw his ass out. In another hour or so, they'd be calling the FBI.

When I got home, I stood on the low concrete stoop before my front door and the vines. The rare sunshine had continued, but the air remained cold, with an astringent wind. I looked around for the surveillance vehicles and waved. I raised my hands the way Nixon used to, fingers in V's, and pivoted about for a full minute. Nobody appeared. Inside, I changed into my tuxedo for Groundhog Night and drove downtown. Lyle had even cleaned up the car.

I walked the entire block outside the TN Needle three times, looking for the tail and waiting for them to pick me up, but there was still nobody there. Finally I headed up. Lucinda handed me three messages. All from Martin. He wanted to see me at once. In my office, I went to the phone.

"Financial Crimes," I told the operator at the Hall.

Pigeyes picked up himself. I was relieved to hear his voice. I thought he might have called off his forces because he'd grabbed Bert, but his voice was full of bovine indifference for the paperbound life in Financials.

"You drop your investigation? I thought you were looking for me?"

"Who the hell is this?" he asked, and then, figuring it out, added, "You think you're all I got to worry about?"

"I'm at the office. I'm ready to tell you whatever you want to know."

He was thinking. Something, God knows what, had him buffaloed.

"Ten minutes," he told me. "And don't go running again to the fuckin dark side of the moon."

I found a cigarette in my drawer. Lucinda stuck her head in. Toots was on hold.

"All done," he told me. "All square. Your fellas are in the clear. Had to remind one or two guys a some things."

"Toots, you're a miracle worker."

Over the phone, the old guy basked in the praise. You could hear it.

"Only one thing," he said, "is the money. We gotta talk about that. I think, you know," said Toots, "I think it's gotta be 275."

The number was a blow. I hadn't been thinking of bankrolling Bert like that, but I began to reason it through. Bert was useful to me, essential really. Besides, I was happy to prove to myself that I wasn't quite the lowdown bum Brushy had implied.

Toots was explaining. "This here was big stuff, that's what I'm hearing. So it's gotta be that, you know, 275." This was not so much a negotiation as Toots setting a price. And it came to me—maybe something I was supposed to know from the start —that the Colonel would be getting his share. This was Toots's skill, his profession, fixing things up, making big problems go way. We didn't defend him for free either.

I explained how I wanted to do it. I needed an account number at a local bank. Sometime in the next seven days a wire transfer would hit there from Fortune Trust, Pico Luan.

"What are the ground rules?" I asked. "Is my guy in danger until the money arrives?"

"I got your word, they get my word. It's all done, this here. Never happened. But tell your partner: there can't be no next time."

Next door Brushy was on the phone. She mugged up and made kissy-face when she saw me, sweeping a hand in admiration of my gallant look in my tux. I tried to smile. She put her caller on hold.

"Can I say I'm sorry?" she asked.

"Sure." I closed my eyes. What was I supposed to be angry about anyway? That she suspected me of bad intentions toward Jake? "Anything from Bert?"

He had phoned an hour ago, she said, and promised to call back soon.

"What about Toots?" she asked. "Did he work it out? Really?" I got a great smile. I was some kind of fella. The door was open to the hall, so she just took my hand. We did an instant of that stuff, gazing fondly. We'd found a sick little cycle, swords and wounds and soft rapprochement. I saw her eyes shift to the threshold. Lucinda was there. The policemen had arrived. And Mr. Gold wanted me upstairs in ten minutes.

"He sounds angry," she added.

"Tell him I'm with the police." I turned to Brushy, who had finished her call. "That'll get his attention," I said.

C. I Try to Satisfy Pigeyes

"Okay, Gino, let's see if I've followed the bouncing ball. After talking to Mrs. Archie, Missing Persons made a trip to the Bath, where somebody with a weak bladder snitched out this little game-fixing thing, and Missing did what they always do, lateraled to someone else, Financial Crimes in this case, telling you what a great investigation you had, and by the way, should you run into an actuary or a corpse, assuming you can tell the difference, give Missing a call. Am I guessing good so far?"

He didn't say a thing. We made an odd little group—me, Brushy, Pigeyes and Dewey, scattered around Brushy's high-tech office, each of us visibly wary. Brushy was behind her glass desk, which was sided by the potted jungle plants. I was the only one standing, walking around, waving my hands, having a great time. I was in full dashing formal array, tuxedo and cummerbund and a boiled shirt I'd owned for twenty years and never replaced; it sported silly button-on frills that reminded me of the comb on a cockatoo. Gino'd looked up and down at my getup when he walked in and asked for a T-bone, medium well.

"So that's why you're looking for these guys, Kam Roberts especially, and Archie and Bert along the way, and you're pretty sure you have a hot one and you get half the Force helping out cause here's what you see: A, a bunch of characters from the Russian Bath say they were winning money with Bert, who was getting information from someone he called Kam Roberts. B, Bert has got a credit card in the name of said Kam Roberts. C, we have sightings here and there of said Said. And D, the bookie, Archie, is among the disappeared. But there are a few questions: One, who the screw is Kam Roberts? Two, how does a partner in a big law firm fix basketball games? Three, why is he playing hide-and-seek all over North America? And four, by the way, where's Archie? Am I on the right track?"

Pigeyes gave me something, a shrug, a tip of the hand. He

still wasn't talking. You never explain what you're investigating, not until you tell them the charges when they're under arrest. Still in their overcoats, Pigeyes and Dewey were seated side by side on Brushy's chrome-trimmed sofa. I could tell Gino was uneasy because I was having such a good time.

"Okay, so let's explain some of this. Hypothetically, of course, since if one is a big-goddamn-deal lawyer he has to watch out for BAD and his shingle, which is why you're hearing from me. But let's get one thing straight to start: Nobody was fixing games. Nobody here and nobody anybody here is friends with."

That got a rise. "No?" Pigeyes asked. Skeptical, you might say.

"No. Here's how it ran. Archie is a tout, but he's an actuary to start. Clever with computers. Does his number runs. Let's say there are some gentlemen, we'll call them Valpolicella and Bardolino, V&B, who just always seem to get certain Mid-Ten games right. Let's say Archie notices. The nature of the world is that Archie is supposed to keep such thoughts to himself. V&B are making suckers out of the suckers, and Archie's getting a break on his street tax.

"But let's imagine Archie's got a buddy—a real good-type close intimate friend." I hit Pigeyes's peepers to make sure he got it. "Archie clues him on this info. The friend, a certain hotshot partner in a certain big law firm, starts betting what V&B do, winning big. So far so good?"

Pigeyes somewhere had acquired a photo of Bert and he withdrew it now from the many layers of his coats.

"Good-lookin here? We sayin he's that way?"

"How you talk, Gino. Let's not get too personal, okay? Just remember, you're the one who told me about Archie. Pecker tracks in the porthole, didn't you say?"

He and Dewey liked that one. Brushy covered her eyes.

"Anyway, Bert, which is what I'll call this lawyer hypothetically, he tries to be discreet, but these guys at the Russian Bath are always in each other's pockets and heads, they've got to know everyone's action. One thing leads to another. And pretty soon everybody there realizes that Bert, or Kam Roberts as he's called when he's putting down money, is hitting big on certain games. Now he's not about to explain why. Everybody sweating there is in Archie's book. It's bad business to favor one customer. And the reasons for doing so are highly personal. So Archie and Bert start this little thing like it's Kam Roberts who's got inside stuff. But it isn't. It's Archie all along.

"Sooner than Archie hoped, V&B hear about what's going down at the Russian Bath and they know sure as shooting the info ain't from any Kam flippin Roberts. It's their proprietary confidential trade-secret business-time information and Archie's peddled it, denting their odds, and they let it be known that Archie is about to literally have his private parts fed to some mutt. Archie scoots and V&B start hunting, which brings them pretty quickly to Bert's door. They give Bert the choice— twenty-four hours to dig up Archie or he's the one who's dog food. So Bert scrams too. Until one of his intrepid partners who knows a guy who knows a guy who knows another guy arranges what we might call an amnesty. High-priced. Could be, hypothetically, that Bert is repaying his profits at interest rates that exceed the ceiling on usury."

Brush, when I glanced her way, was sunk back in her desk chair regarding me with an uneasy eye. It troubled her, I suspect, to see me lying with such élan.

"And?" Pigeyes asked me.

"And what?"

"And where's this crumb Archie? Today?"

"I'd look in the sanitary canal. Watch what comes out of the treatment plant. That's the way I hear it. V&B found him. He's got something around his neck besides his tie. And if your people on the street are half as good as they used to be, Gino, you've heard the same thing."

Whacking a guy, making him dead, is not something anybody owns up to, but word spreads. It has to. It's the way those guys keep everybody in line.

Lucinda knocked. "Mr. Gold," she said.

"Tell him five minutes."

"He wants to talk to you right now."

"Five minutes," I repeated.

Lucinda stepped to the phone and pressed a button. She held out the extension. It's been this poor woman's lot for years to protect me from myself.

"We are not amused," Martin said when I put the handset to my ear.

"I'm busy."

"So I hear. What, pray tell, are you and the nice policemen discussing?"

"Detective Dimonte had some questions about Bert." I smiled at Gino when I mentioned his name.

"We're not talking high finance?"

"Bert," I said.

"Did Bert do something else that was naughty?"

"Never kid a kidder, Martin. I'll be up in one minute. We're just about done." I put the phone down without allowing further comment.

Gino was waiting. "So this Kam Roberts thing was strictly an act?" he asked.

"Exactly."

"Except there's a Kam Roberts." Pigeyes sneered.

"No. There's a certain young man who's used Bert's bank card a few times. That doesn't make him Kam Roberts."

"No? Who is he?"

"Friend of Bert's."

"Another one? Good-lookin's real frisky, isn't he? He's two-timing the other guy?"

"Hey, Gino, call it what you like. But remember, I used to

ride with you. I've seen you stop off with three different gals on the same *shift*."

He was flattered, of course, by the memory. He stole a glance toward Brushy, hoping she was impressed. Someday I'd have to tell Pigeyes about *Nueve*.

"Anyway, there's this young man," I said. "Bert's piling up a lot of credit on the card, so he's got plenty to share. Now it could be, hypothetically, this young man, he's got a connection to the U. Maybe he's the one who let a certain middle-aged lawyer into the refs' room the other night so Bert and the middle-aged lawyer could confer outside the watchful eye of the law in the hopes of straightening some of this out."

"That so?" Gino asked.

"Could be," I said and rested on a chair arm to see how it had gone down. Better, it seemed, than I might have thought. I was trying like hell for Bert's sake and my own, vamping like crazy, and when it came to Gino, there was no end to my daring. But I still thought I'd gone over the top. The whole thing was too much, too curious, way too lame. I didn't know what I'd do if, for instance, they wanted to quiz the young man from the U. And there wouldn't be any smart answers if Gino ever started matching the games the guys at the Bath called Kam's Specials with the ones officiated by Friday night's referees.

But the great thing with people is that you never know. After two weeks of riding my fanny, chasing me everywhere, and spooking my dreams, Gino seemed to have run out of gas. Not that he believed me particularly. He knew better than that. But he was clearly afraid the prosecutor's office would toss him out on his keester because he was nowhere near beyond a reasonable doubt. Bogus or not, I'd touched all the bases; it was a comprehensive defense. And my history with Gino was enough to make a conscientious deputy P.A. think twice anyway. Pigeyes didn't come to these conclusions peaceably. When he looked at me, his eyes were stilled by a hatred entirely void of goodwill, like black being the absence of color, but I could see he knew I had him beat.

He turned to Dewey, who shrugged. Go figure. They both got to their feet.

"Great to see you again, Gino."

"Yeah, really," he offered.

Lucinda peeked in, beckoning, and I followed her out, departing with a cheerful wave as Brushy started with Gino and Dewey toward the door. Lucinda had a note: "Bert's on the phone." I picked up in my office.

"Listen," I said. "I've settled your problems. Those guys won't be looking for you anymore."

The line gathered static. I could hear from the gray roar behind him that Bert was on a pay phone somewhere near a highway.

"Humor, right?" he asked.

"Don't ask me how. You're done. D, o, n, e. I've got it squared with the coppers too. What you oughta do is get down here. You'll probably need to answer some questions about Jake." Mathigoris from TN security would want to go over the whole thing many times. The memo, the checks. Jake telling Bert to keep it strictly hush-hush.

"And what about—"

"I covered both of you. Go rent a tux and get over here. It's GH Night."

"God," he said softly. I could tell that in the instant of relief the terror suddenly had hold of him. He'd been flying combat again. Now he was on the ground, torn up by what he'd been through, the great concussions of noise and the light that had rattled the plane and trailed him through the sky. "God," he said again. "Mack, man, what can I say?"

"Just come back," I repeated.

This was getting exciting, everything falling in place. My phone rang again.

"I'm waiting," Martin told me.

XXVIII. H O W   M A R T I N

S O L V E D   T H E   C R I M E

Martin was dressing. He had on his tuxedo pants, striped in satin along the seam, and his wing-collared tuxedo shirt, into which he was nimbly inserting the studs, little diamond jobs that glimmered in the pearly light of the late-winter afternoon. In an hour or so my partners, all similarly dressed, would stroll down the avenue to the Club Belvedere, share a drink or two and some canapeś, and then over dinner get a report on financial results and the size of their share. It promised to be an excruciating evening in every regard.

Martin did not speak at first. Standing, he worked over the shirt for some time. Every now and then he stopped to examine a small blue note card on his desk, reading it to himself. It was, I suspected, his GH Night speech. Rah-rah from the managing partner. Picking up his pen, he made a few corrections. I said nothing either. The large corner office, fully lit from the long windows, was quiet enough that you could hear the whirring of the gyroscope device that powered one of his clocks. I was tempted to play with some of his toys, the shaman stick or the coffee-table games, but I took a seat instead in a wooden side-chair painted up in Southwestern shades. I'd brought along my briefcase.

"I've been too fucking good to you," Martin said at last. He didn't talk dirty and this was meant to be shocking. He wanted me to know he was pissed, that our partnership agreement didn't include a search warrant for his drawer. He continued fooling with the shirt.

"How much trouble is Bert in?" he asked in a moment.

"Now that I've had a little chat with the police, probably none."

He glanced my way briefly to be sure I was serious.

"How'd you arrange that? This policeman an old friend?"

"You could say."

"Very impressive." He nodded. I was sorry, frankly, he hadn't been there to see it. In a law firm it took all types, and I was one of the best bullshitters in town. It was like having a guy in the bullpen who could get away with throwing spitballs. Witnessing that performance would have rewarded Martin's faith in me, all the time he'd spent telling our partners I might come back yet.

"I've been doing a lot of impressive stuff," I said. "I was in Pico Luan over the weekend."

Martin's eyes stayed with me for the first time. Standing there, his figure was framed by the black iron circle of the enormous arc lamp that cut the space over the desk.

"Are we forestalling one another with humor?"

"No, I'm demonstrating my investigatory powers," I told him. "I'm telling you politely to cut the crap."

I took one of the dupes of the International Bank signature form from my briefcase and threw it on the desktop, where Martin studied it at length. Finally, he sat down in his tall leather chair.

"What are you going to do?"

"I'm done doing. Mr. Krzysinski has been informed."

The last stud, which Martin still had within his thick fingers, caught his attention somehow. He considered it briefly, then let it fly at the windows. I heard it bounce but couldn't see where it went.

"Carl's up there with that document and the memo you were hiding, and Tad and he and everyone else are trying to figure out why Jake Eiger would do something like this."

Momentarily Martin covered his whole face with his broad hand, blackly pelted on its back. From the hall I could hear through the closed door the phones, the voices of the workday.

"Well, that's not going to take very long, is it?" Martin asked finally. "The motive is hardly elusive. Jake's planning for his future. He knows that Tad doesn't like him and that sooner or later, when Tad's alliances on the board are firm, Krzysinski is going to be opening the bays and dropping Jake without a parachute, golden or otherwise. So Jake provided one for himself. That's the explanation, isn't it?"

"Seems right," I said.

Martin looked at me through one eye as he canted back in his chair.

"What else is Carl saying?"

"I covered your butt, if that's what you're asking. Which is more than you deserve. You were fucking around with me, Martin."

He made some move to deny it and I challenged him.

"I can give you a hundred examples. I don't have to ask who Glyndora called for advice on how to get me out of her apartment last week, do I?"

"No." He laughed suddenly, and I did as well. I was being a good sport, but a mood of disclosure was also beginning to lighten the air. I suppose it made a great story, the way I went running down the stairs like a little elf, trying not to stumble on my you-know-what.

"Didn't want anybody messing with your girl, huh?"

Martin rolled his jaw. He looked again through one eye. I wasn't sure how he'd take this assault on his secrets, whether it would make him frantic or if he would get up and try to throw me out of the room. But I guess he knew himself well enough, because he seemed to accept this with a faint resignation.

"Don't let me stop you," I said. "You were about to explain."

"My personal life? That's before the flood." It wasn't quite a rebuff. He was looking out the broad windows toward his city and its life, and his tone suggested worlds, universes of emotion suppressed. God, I thought, to have been a fly on the wall for that romance, to have observed these two characters surmounting the many barriers to get into each other's pants. Glyndora must have stuck out all her prominent parts and dared him to touch them—a way to put him in his place. I'd seen that routine: You think you're tough? I'm tough. I'm the best-looking woman in four city blocks. I'd wear you out. I'd get you up four times a night, I'd screw you dry and tell you I needed more, I'd be so much you'd want to unhitch it and put it in my trophy case. You didn't have wet dreams as a puppy 10 percent as good as me. And you won't dare touch it. Cause I ain't gonna have it.

She probably laid it on thick. And he accepted the World Championship Challenge of treating her kindly. Glyndora'd stomp and sulk and he must have signaled in a hundred ways that he thought she was valuable and would never change his mind. He must have worn her down until she had to succumb to the fantasy that everything she rejected before it refused her might, instead, fold her in its embrace. And Martin visited that shadow zone where not much matters, where pretense and power, every one of his bets which was always on the future, had to surrender to the pure sensation of the present. I'll bet until ten minutes before they were screwing it was no more than daily titillation for each one of them, a dirty movie that was always shuttered in their minds.

"But what happened?" I said. "You know. With you and her. Can I ask?"

"It didn't work out," he said. His hand skirted the air. "We were kidding ourselves." The remark hung there, with all its potent sadness—the American predicament. Martin had these kids, this wife—and there was the Club Belvedere, clients who'd snigger that he'd taken up with a colored girl. But the result probably suited Glyndora. It would have been a lot to ask of her, to be herself in his world.

"I am very fond of Glyndora," he said then, impaled on whatever the remark conjured and concealed. He looked at me. "Do you believe in reincarnation?"

"No," I said.

"No," he said. "Neither do I." He was quiet then. Martin Gold, the most successful lawyer I knew, wanted to be somebody else too. It was touching, though. Loyalty always is.

We were silent some time. Eventually Martin started talking about what had happened in a depleted, reflective tone. He had not been fooling with me, he said. Not intentionally. I gave him far too much credit. Circumstances had mounted. Combined. His honesty as he spoke was beguiling. You so rarely got Martin to talk straight from the heart.

"Glyndora came to me with the memo and the checks as soon as they'd cleared. Early December, I think. Around then. It looked odd to both of us, of course, business checks negotiated offshore, but I didn't feel any great concern until I started doing the research—talking to Bert, Neucriss, the banker down there in Pico. No Litiplex registered anywhere. No records upstairs. I was shocked when I saw where it pointed. I never perceived this in Jake. He'd lie to the Pope for the sake of his vanity, but I was stunned to learn he was a thief. And it was gruesome, of course, imagining the consequences."

Martin, like any man with an empire, was accustomed to problems—big ones, situations that could bring him and everyone who depended upon him to doom. Like TN walking out as a client, or Pagnucci making a move. He got used to it, accustomed. He learned to walk the highwire, sailing along with gumption and a parasol. This thing with Eiger was a problem too. He left Glyndora on alert for more checks and took some time to ponder the common good.

"At which point," he said, "Glyndora's life began coming apart."

"Bert and Orleans?"

He emitted a sound, the old wrestler's grunt, a little eruption of surprise, self-consciously controlled, when he was snatched for the takedown. He peered, his squat face immobile, engraved by shadow in the dwindling light.

"You know, Malloy, if you'd done half as good a job around here in the last few years as you did looking into this, you would have made my life a great deal easier."

"I'll take that as a compliment."

"Please," Martin answered.

"What's he like?" I asked. "This son of hers?"

"Orleans? Complicated fellow."

"He's her heartbreak, I take it."

Martin made various ruminative gestures. It seemed he had tried to be good to Orleans as a boy.

"Very bright individual. Mother's son, that way. Very capable. But not steady. Temperamentally. Nothing you could do about that. She thought she was going to prohibit him from being the way he clearly was. And he wasn't willing to be prohibited."

"She found Bert an upsetting development?"

"Not Bert as Bert. It's a situation she's never wanted to confront squarely." He made a sad face.

"Yeah," I offered. I got it. But I felt for Bert. In all likelihood, he'd been largely beside the point with Orleans from the start.

"Did you warn Bert?"

"No one here has accepted my warnings. No one." He remained momentarily forlorn, even as his agitation visibly mounted. "Jesus, what a mess. What a mess! This one may have been the single stupidest thing—" Martin waved. "This ludicrous, insane novelty with these basketball games— And worse, both of them, neither had given a moment's thought, not a bare instant, to the costs of this behavior— Imprisonment, bodily harm, my God, the prospects, and the two of them are *surprised* by this, shocked, absolutely, positively disbelieving, like tiny children, the two most immature grown men I have ever known, neither with the remotest—" Martin stopped himself; he was losing the thread.

"You were explaining how you decided to cover for Jake."

"This is part of it," he said. "I told you. It's happenstance. Circumstances conspire. This is part. This is what led Glyndora to it."

"Blaming Bert? You're saying that's Glyndora's idea? For what? To get even with him?"

He waited. He smiled.

"What kind of mother do you imagine Glyndora is, Mack?"

You could take your choice of adjectives. Intense. Protective. She'd have sheltered Orleans through the ravages of war, scavenged food, or sold her body. For all I knew, that's what she was doing with me that night. But I still wasn't following. Martin saved his partners, his professional life, by covering Jake. I didn't see much gain to the chief clerk in Accounting.

"Look, Mack, Bert's decision to drop out of sight was well-intentioned as far as it went. He thought he was being heroic. But it was hardly a solution for Orleans. Not as far as Glyndora was concerned. She wasn't going to have him running for the rest of his life. She wanted him safe to stay here, and he wasn't."

I still didn't get it.

"You're the one who asked the question, Mack. Last week. 'Where did Bert go?' Where do *we* say Bert went? This is a lawyer. With sixty-seven partners. And clients. Never mind his family. There's not much. His friends, so-called, were all implicated in the same thing and surely willing to keep their peace. But what the hell do we say around here? How do we keep somebody from notifying the police who, in investigating Bert's absence, will promptly discover that whole basketball mess? The only way to insulate Orleans—to completely protect him—was if there was another credible explanation for why Bert disappeared—even if that explanation was understood only by a few people who'd make excuses to everyone else."

I rolled my head around, this way and that. I sort of liked it. Until I saw the next part.

"That's why you needed some hapless stumblebum to go look for him." Someone, I realized, who wasn't supposed to really catch Bert or even figure out what he'd actually been up to— just state convincingly that he was gone. That was what Glyndora had meant in the one sincere moment we'd had. Absorbing my observation about their estimate of me, Martin, I noted, made no effort to differ.

"And that's why you hid the body," I said. It came to me, just like that. "Once I started looking for Bert."

"We *what*?" Martin's entire weight was suddenly planted on one hand fiercely gripping the arm of his chair. This aspect of alarm, of incomprehension, could have been posed, I realized. But Martin didn't look like he was fooling. Instead, I recalculated: Orleans and Bert, already shamed and scolded, yelled at, told they were irresponsible fools, hadn't confessed the worst. Martin and Glyndora thought Bert was running only from threats. Archie's disappearance, when it hit the papers, must have terrified them.

"Figure of speech," I said. "The memo. You hid the memo."

"Oh," said Martin. He relaxed. "Right. We hid the body." He made a brief effort to smile. For an instant, I wondered again about who'd moved the body. The only thing certain was that Archie couldn't have walked.

In the meantime, Martin had resumed his explanation, telling me how they had come to blame Bert for stealing the Litiplex money. The first few times Glyndora and he had discussed it, he said, the whole plan, it was in the vein of magnificent fantasy, a perfect future where all problems came to an end. He worked it out with her dozens of times, calculated how the dominoes would fall, saw at once how advantageous it would be to the firm not to have to sacrifice Jake. It was fun to discuss, lots of laughs, like a couple saying they'll rob a bank to pay the mortgage. Eventually he recognized that she was urging him to pursue what he'd regarded as jest.

"I told her this was lunacy. Worse than that, impermissible. A fraud. But you see. Really." He sat up. He faced me squarely. "It's me. It's mine. It's my precious values. My law. My rules. Take that out of the equation— My right," he said, "my wrong. My precious abstractions." He halted in the midst of the litany he must have heard from her for years and lingered like some bug in the breeze, manifestly pained. Watching him, my heart spurted with sudden hope that Brushy and I might resolve what divided us the same way, until I recollected, as quickly, that we were both supposed to believe in the same thing.

"Here are these people," he said. "Glyndora and Orleans. My partners. Jake. Bert. Even you, Mack. Even you. This is an institution. It's the product of lives. Hundreds of lives. All right. I sound like Wash. Forgive the sanctimony. But do I lay that all on the altar? I've made worse compromises."

Both hands were thrown wide. He had a touch of priestly majesty. He thought he was revealed.

I said, "It doesn't hurt you either, Martin. We all know who gets the biggest share." I was enjoying this—being the man of greater rectitude, even if we both knew it was situational and I knew it was an act. Fact is, I've enjoyed my acts, every one of them—copper, hard guy, smartass, lawyer. I can be a good anything, if it's only part time.

Martin had absorbed my remark with a lingering, rueful grin.

"Not me," he said. He backhanded the little note card he'd had on his desk so it spiraled through space; I picked it up off the rug. Martin's handwriting is atrocious—slashes and squiggles indiscernible to me, even after all these years. But certain words were clear enough. "Resigning." "Mayor." "Riverside Commission." "Long-held passion." In tonight's speech to the partnership assembled, Martin Gold was going to quit.

"Think the public sector can handle me?" he asked.

"You've got to be kidding." I couldn't believe it. The circus without Barnum.

He muled around. Stubborn. Set. It was time, he said. The deal was done. Martin Gold, head of the Riverside Commission. Starting April 1. He talked about thirty years in private practice, giving things back, but I understood the imperatives. If he took a dive for Jake, if he didn't march stalwartly to Krzysinski's office and let his law firm pass into the great beyond, then Martin would punish himself instead. His people might survive, but he wouldn't get to the promised land. It was an old idea, and its mixture of shrewd practicality and highfalutin principles was quintessentially Gold. Lawyerly, you'd say. But still nuts.

"You should have been born a Catholic," I told him. "You really missed your chance. There are all these obscure fast days and penitential rites. We've been working for centuries on strategies for self-denial." He thought I was funny of course. He always did. He laughed out loud.

All these years I've figured that if I somehow eluded Martin's defenses and peered into his core it would be a vision of glory: I'd see a lionheart, beating at mach speed and enlarged by passion. Instead, what was within was some little gremlin that made him believe that his greatest nobility came from cutting himself off from what he liked best. Glyndora. Or the law firm. He was cheap with himself, with his own pleasure. It was crushing to recognize: he was more productive than me, but no happier. I didn't want his life either.

He was still disagreeing.

"As of today"— And he nodded toward me—"I'm not giving up much. Not once the dust settles upstairs. Whether Tad instructs his new General Counsel to cut us off or just cut us back, this place won't hold together. A fellow like Carl—" Martin stopped himself; he never spoke ill of his partners. "Not everyone will settle for less. In the end, frankly, there will be those who paint me as an opportunist. First man to the lifeboat."

There was, of course, a subtle accusatory element to these observations. Martin had removed a limb or two for the team. I'd destroyed it. The Catholic boy, ever guilty as charged, still reared up to defend himself. It was comic, of course. I'd stolen nearly six million bucks and wasn't beset by thoughts of giving it back. But in that goofy way we have of thinking we are what we're seen to be, I cared about Martin's impressions.

"Am I supposed to apologize?" I asked. "It's an ugly deal, Martin, the one you were trying to cut with Jake—five and a half mil of the client's money so he continues throwing slops to G&G."

Martin went still—just the way he had when I mentioned the body. He gave his head a distinct shake.

"Is *that* what you think?" He smiled suddenly. Luminously. He used the chair arms to boost himself. What I'd said actually pleased him. I knew why too. I'd made some error that allowed him to resume his familiar supremacy.

"Oh, I see," he said, "I see. I was bartering with Jake. TN's business for the money. Is that it? That's it?" It was a contest now, a stalking. I just kept my mouth shut as he kept moving in. "I plead guilty, Mack. I was trying to preserve the firm. I was even trying to save Jake from himself. And God knows I was hoping to shelter Orleans. I trimmed some corners off my conscience in the process—I admit that too. Maybe more than corners. But do you honestly think the object of this was that —that crass?"

I didn't answer.

"I can't imagine how you viewed this. Why would I confront Jake with Wash and you last week? Why not just whisper in his ear that I knew he was a thief and demand he send all business now and hereafter?"

He was safer, of course, not confronting Jake openly, but I knew he would ridicule that suggestion.

"Don't you see?" he asked. "Look at this, for God's sake, from Jake's perspective. We tell him the money's missing, we believe Bert's got it, we can't locate any records related to the disbursement to Litiplex. But we also say we're looking high and low for Bert, and when we find him, we'll beg him to give the money back and come home. We even tell Jake we want his blessing for that arrangement. You were sitting right here. You heard that. Now how does Jake know that you're not going to find Bert? How can he be sure?"

This was like law school. The Grand Inquisitor. I swallowed and admitted he couldn't.

"He can't," said Martin, "that's right. He can't. He can't be certain. And when Bert is found, when he returns from whatever exotic detour he's taken, Jake knows where Bert is going to be pointing. Straight at Jake. There's no safety for Jake in the fact we blame Bert. He *knows* it's a misimpression.

"But now let's consider an alternative. You're out searching up Bert, trying to get him the message that all is well if he just gives back the money, and lo and behold, lo and behold, Jake Eiger, Glyndora, someone is able to report that mysteriously, wonderfully, a wire transfer has come in from Pico Luan. God bless Bert. God bless us. Case closed. As promised, not another word will be spoken on the subject. My God, Mack! Could you really have missed this? Don't you understand that the point was to offer Jake a discreet way, a last opportunity to give the goddamned bloody money *back*?"

It settled in then, like the mystical presence of some nearby angel. Martin, of course, was speaking the truth. It had all the delicate signs of his typical engineering. Nothing so direct as a confrontation with Jake. That would have been shabby and extortionate—and risky as well, if Jake ever told tales. This way the world could go on, with all its false faces. Oddly, it would be exactly as the Committee had told me from the start. Except for the identity of the thief, the plan was precisely the same: Get the money back, sweep it under the rug, kiss and make up.

"He could have run," I said to Martin.

"He could have. But he hasn't run yet. Jake obviously wants to hold on to this life. He just craves some security to which he's not entitled. I was letting him know it was time to make a more realistic choice."

"And what happens when he doesn't give the money back? You're not telling me you were actually thinking of turning him in?"

He looked at me like I was nuts.

"What other choice is there? That was the one limit I set with Glyndora to start." He could see I was astonished. "Look, Mack, if I was determined to say nothing, no matter what Jake did, I would have burned that memo, not kept it in a drawer."

"But you *didn't* say anything."

"Why should I? You're the one who brought us Jake's message last week: Be patient, Bert's not to blame, it's not what it appears, future accountings will show that there's been a mistake. That was clearly the prelude. Jake was planning to get the money back."

A strange qualm passed between us then, some recognition of the differing planes where we'd stood which was transmitted in a stark look. Martin got to his feet.

"My *God*," he said. It was just coming home to him, not the dimension of our misunderstanding—he'd seen that before—but rather, its consequences. He'd assumed I'd sent Carl to Krzysinski out of disdain for the grubby arrangement Martin was orchestrating—protecting Jake and the firm, breaching our duty to TN to fully inform them of what we knew about the General Counsel. Martin saw only now that I'd been propelled by imagining malefactions far grander. He spotted his stud on the floor and pitched it at the windows again—full force, so the jewel flew off in a kind of musical ricochet. He pointed at me. He called me names.

"You goddamned dumb bastard! You wouldn't even talk to me on the phone."

He stood there huffing and puffing. And how did I feel? Pretty strange. Confused. In a peculiar way, I was actually relieved. When I recovered some sense of myself, I realized I was smiling. I'd misjudged Martin and his complexities. You wouldn't call his conduct saintly, but he'd done better than I thought—and, God knows, a hell of a lot better than me.

There was a knock on the door. Brushy. She had put on her formal, a sleeveless black floor-length job with sequins. She wore long white gloves. A rhinestone tiara was perched in her hair like a sparkling bird. Her eyes went to the desk where the copy of the form from the International Bank still lay and she tolled that, as usual, at the speed of a Univac. I whistled at her and she diverted herself for a fraction of a second to smile.

"Is Wash here yet?" she asked. "He just called and asked me to come down. He sounded upset."

Wash arrived presently. In the condition she'd discerned.

"I'm just off the phone with Krzysinski. All hell's broken loose up there." He was in his tux, with a jazzy red bow tie, but his face was pale and he had broken a sweat. "Tad asked for everyone TN works with—'my dependables' was how he put it." Wash closed his eyes. "He wants all of us upstairs. You. Me. Brushy. Mack. Bert as well. What do we say about that? About Bert?"

Martin waved his hand to pass off the question; Wash, as usual, was missing the point. Martin asked what precisely Tad wanted and Wash at first seemed unable to bring himself to answer. The old age descending on him, where he would be bewildered and addled, seemed at hand. He stood there with his mouth vaguely moving and his eyes never quite fixed. He answered at last.

"Tad said he wants to figure out what to do about Jake."

<u>XXIX. A N D   T H I S   T I M E</u>

<u>I T ' S   T H E   T R U T H</u>

A. Office of the Chair

In Tad Krzysinski's huge office we found the disjointed air of a
large, unhappy family. Tad's assistant, Ilene, met us and said
that Pagnucci had stepped out to put on the tuxedo his secretary
had brought up. Mike Mathigoris, the head of security, was also
elsewhere for the moment, while Tad's four o'clock meeting was
going on in his adjoining conference room. Only Tad and Jake
remained here, paying no attention to each other. Krzysinski
was taking a phone call and Jake was abjectly hulked on the edge
of his chair, staring without much comprehension at the many
portraits of Krzysinski's children that were the principal decoration on the far wall, between the three doors that led to Jake's
office, the office of TN's CFO, and the conference room. You
could tell from the empty way that Jake first looked at us, the
wan smile, that he couldn't explain what was wrong with this
picture, why Brush in her floor-length gown and the three men
in tuxes appeared out of place. Martin's bow tie was still hanging
loose through his collar, and his shirt was held closed over his
stomach principally by his cummerbund, since he'd never managed to insert the last stud.

"I wanted you to hear this." Krzysinski had gotten up to shake each of our hands, the usual crushing grip. In college, I'd heard, Tad's nickname had been "Atom" and that about said it all— size, structure, the barely contained power. Tad, of course, had a vast corner office. The parquet was covered by an enormous Oriental rug—fifty grand at least—and his view ran all the way to the airport on a clear day. When the weather was good, Tad liked to stand at the long windows and watch TN's planes rise, giving you the flight numbers and the names of the pilots.

Now, once he'd greeted us, he jiggled a commanding finger at Jake, instructing him to proceed. Jake recounted the story somewhat methodically, drained of emotion. You could tell that he'd repeated it about six times already and it was beginning to get routine. He was, as usual, perfectly groomed, hair stiffly parted, his gray herringbone suit buttoned at the waist to add to the impression of his ordered form. But his face was out of focus. Jake, for once in his life, was under the crush of sensible pain and it threatened his sanity. I felt only a twinge of regret. Asked to speak, I might well have said, "Goody."

In November, Jake said, as we were thinking about making the final disbursements on 397, Peter Neucriss and Jake had a talk. Actually, Peter took Jake out for the evening, a characteristic manipulation, wooing the enemy. Royal treatment. Dinner at Batik. Many drinks. Hockey game. Afterwards, as Jake and Peter were having a nightcap down at Sergio's, Peter got to what he had been leading up to all night. He had a business proposition for Jake. For TN, really. Neucriss had three different settlements on 397. Huge cases, naturally. A mother and child one of them. The total was nearly thirty million. Peter was working on the usual third. He had almost ten million in fees coming.

"He told me this long farfetched tale, how a fortune was owed to this litigation support group, Litiplex. He said their work had benefitted all the plaintiffs, but the class lawyers were acting as if they'd never heard of them and Peter was in a spot because he was the one who'd retained the company and made some cozy deal with them, these Litiplex people, something a little unsavory. You know Neucriss when he gets like this. You'd expect him to leave a spot on the wall. At any rate, he felt it was his obligation to pay Litiplex even though I—me supposedly—I'd said at one point it would come off the settlement fund. I objected. A number of times. I mean, I'd had a few drinks, but I knew I'd never said anything like that.

"I couldn't imagine what was going on, until suddenly he made this proposal: If we'd pay Litiplex offshore—$5.6 million was the number he'd come up with—set up an offshore account in their name, disposition subject to Peter's later direction, then Neucriss would let us reduce our remaining payment to Peter's clients to $22.4 million. That way, TN would be two million dollars ahead. He assured me his clients would net the same amounts. You know how it goes—we pay him, he deducts his share and remits to the clients. He'd just cook his books so it looked like he was working on a 10 percent contingency instead of a third. Why should I care? It's two million to us. That's the bottom line."

"I'm not following," said Wash. "What does Peter get out of it?"

"It's a tax dodge." It was Brushy who spoke. As usual, she didn't need a book of instructions. "There's no Litiplex. Not really. It's a sham for Neucriss, who gets his fee offshore and never pays income taxes on it, not this year, and not on whatever it earns in the future. That's why he was willing to take two million less. He'd save two or three times that in the long run."

Jake was nodding eagerly as she ran it down. Eagerly. Even Jake had understood this much.

"Neucriss denies all of this, by the way, the entire conversation." It was Pagnucci, in the doorway. Carl was dressed in a double-breasted dinner jacket, blue sharkskin no less, smoking a cigarette and looking somewhat haggard. Considering the assembly, he said dryly that he'd already listened to this story several times.

"Mathigoris and I were just on the phone with Mr. Neucriss," Carl said. "He states, most emphatically, that the only time he's heard of Litiplex was when Mack and Martin spoke with him recently."

"Naturally," said Jake, "naturally he denies it. I told you he would. He's engaging in tax evasion. I don't expect him to put up a billboard. But I'm telling you, that was the deal. I set up the account with that understanding. When he presented me with signed releases on our cases, I'd give him the balance of the settlements and a letter of direction entitling whoever he designated to the account. Don't you see? I wasn't stealing anything. This for the company. For TN."

He looked at Krzysinski, but Tad's attention was on Ilene, the assistant, who stood at the door signaling obscurely. Tad stepped into his conference room to attend to whatever fire was burning there.

"And what were you thinking the IRS would say about the company and you, Jake?" Brushy asked this. Wash in the meantime was peeking up hopefully. He didn't understand everything, but Jake's last lines had buoyed him. He could see it coming. Undeserved salvation. Story of his life.

"Me? We haven't lied to them. We haven't filed any false documents. I haven't even seen Peter's return. God knows, I've got suspicions, but who can fathom the mind of Peter Neucriss? If the Service ever asked, I'd tell them the absolute truth. And I'm certainly not hiding any income. We *want* to declare it. It'll be on every return and financial statement. That's the point. Let's not pretend. We all know the story. Tad has been *very* concerned about the level of legal expenses. And quite pleased with the way 397 has turned out. This is two million, straight to the bottom line. We need that. All of us. The company and everyone here."

"I still don't think you'd get a good-conduct medal from the Service," said Martin to Jake.

"Or the SEC," said Pagnucci.

"Or Tad," Brushy said.

"Admittedly," said Jake, "admittedly. True on all counts. Krzysinski hates it. *Hates* it. Look at him. It's not his style." Glancing darkly at the conference room door, Jake lowered his voice. "But he'd *love* the result. So would the board. Friends, really. A tree falls in the forest. Is there sound if nobody hears? If I'm discreet, what does anyone know? Neucriss won't say a word. The IRS has no reason to audit an escrow account. We're showing a *surplus*, for crying out loud. That's why I told no one. I sent the memo to Bert, explaining that it was very sensitive. I left no records here. And I made my own hell by doing it that way. I'm the first to admit it. The very first. There was not a thing I could say when all of you began looking into the matter, except what I told Mack last week: If we just wait, it's going to turn out all right. When the disbursements were made, there would be *no* money missing. There'd be two million more than expected. Who would complain? Don't you see? I'm not a thief." He looked around the room at each of us. He was being achingly sincere, wounded and vulnerable, that Jake-thing I'd probably last seen when he talked to me about the bar exam.

Krzysinski had returned for the latter stages of this performance, but he did not allow it to hinder him as he walked back to his desk. He addressed Jake without rancor. Tad was just himself—completely in charge. His job was deciding things. He was better at that than most people, the way certain guys can jump a foot over the rim. He roamed an empyrean landscape where he figured out what would happen with the perfect instantaneous reflex of a machine. He asked Jake where he wanted to go while we spoke.

"Home," said Jake, and Tad nodded. That was a good idea, he said. Go home. Stay by the phone in case there were more questions. Jake departed, clearly at a loss for the right gesture of farewell. He reverted to his friendly little wave, a politician's touch that he'd absorbed from his father. It was, in the circumstances, sadly wrong. His departure, disappearance, seemed fateful and left a silent, troubled wake.

"So what do you think?" Tad asked after a moment. "I wanted your opinions. You've all known him much longer than me." He swiveled about in his big chair. This might well have been Tad's ultimate test—would G&G's lawyers shoot straight when the target was Jake? Maybe, in order to decide about us, he was matching our estimate against one he'd derived already. But I thought he was merely making smart use of the available resources.

"I believe him," Wash said instantly. He had summoned himself to sound stalwart. He brought all that upper-crust nobility back into his face.

Krzysinski pursed up his mouth. "Mathigoris thinks it's a cover story. Carefully planned. Carl shares that opinion."

Carl nodded. As usual he wasn't saying much. But his ego would suffer no blows and he preferred the sinister to admitting he had failed in divining the situation. Now and then he had looked darkly at me, suspecting, I imagine, that I'd set him up. But I'd hung in there, meeting his eye meaningfully, and now he was not backing down.

Martin, when Tad addressed him, wasn't there, lost instead at mystical depths within himself. He'd still not fit the last stud into his shirt and he was tossing it up and down in one hand, in a mindless way, the jewel glinting as it turned in the air. He caught me eyeing him and gave me a wry look.

Tad asked the question again to gain his attention. What did he think?

"Oh," Martin said. "Do I think it would tickle Neucriss to see your General Counsel doing tricks for him like a streetwalker? Naturally. Neucriss's favorite pastime is proving that all human nature is as base as his. On the other hand, do I think Jake is capable of this deception on his own?" Martin smiled fleetingly

at me, with his usual deep appreciation of irony. "Quite," he
said. "Quite. Frankly, Tad, I don't know what the hell is going
on."

Martin stood up in his half-secured formal wear and hoisted
his striped trousers; he threw his stud in the air one more time.
He was enormously cheerful. You wouldn't quite say he didn't
give a damn. But you could tell he felt free of this life. Martin
was on the road to being somebody else. He smiled again when
he looked at Krzysinski.

"To me it sounds typically Jake." That was Brushy. "I hate to
say it, but we all know Jake's consuming interests are corporate
politics and what makes him look good. Frankly, Tad, I'm not
even sure he realized he was breaking the law. I believe him."

I wasn't certain I'd ever seen Brush in the same room with
Krzysinski and I watched them for signs. But all that showed
was Tad's native intensity. His searching look lingered with her
even after she'd spoken.

"I think I do too," Tad stated finally. "You see," he said to
Wash, picking up on some dispute from the boardroom, "this
is what I never liked. Always the easy way out. Well, he's gone
today. That's given. Given. And I have to advise the board. But
I need to know what to recommend. Everyone will prefer to
avoid the scandal. I'd hate to turn him over to the authorities if
I didn't have to. I guess you go on your gut. I just wish I had
some experience. What's your view, Mack? You're the one who's
done this for a living. What do you say? Does Jake look to you
like a crook?"

We were back to where we had been last week. I had their
attention. Everyone's. The fly ball once more was coming my
way. I knew I could save Jake. I could tell one of my wonderful
wild-ass stories. There were already six of them in my head.
Say, for example, that Jake must have forgotten that long ago
he had vaguely mentioned some shady deal with Neucriss which
I'd told him to avoid. That would do it. Give me five minutes
with a fax machine to rip off messages to Pico Luan to the

Züricher Kreditbank and Fortune Trust and I could even re-
plenish Litiplex's secret account. I could do it all.

But I wasn't going that way. It's happened to all of us, especially as kids. The screen goes dark; the music fades and the
speakers hiss; the sudden lights sting the eyes. How can it be
over, the heart cries, when the film's still running inside me?

It turned out that it no longer mattered what had actually
happened. I was set on my way—another direction. I felt that.
Somewhere new. Somewhere else. Me and Martin. I'd made
the decision. Brave new world. No turning around. If I wasn't
headed for a better life, at least I was going toward something
unexpressed in the life I presently had.

Looking back, I suppose it's sort of funny that we'd all been
so willing to believe Jake was a thief. That slippery side of him
must be out there for everybody to see—which was why we
were still hanging in doubt. Isn't that life? Seeing it, hearing
it—how much is there we don't really understand? Caught in
our own foxholes, we never see the battlefield scene. I had
wanted to believe they were no better than me. All of them.
But we think what we do for a reason. Call me a fool or the
victim of my own expectations. The one guy I wasn't wrong
about was me.

"I believe him," I said. And I did. Not because Jake was too
honest to steal. God knows, he wasn't. It was the story he'd told.
About Neucriss. It wouldn't come to Jake in one thousand years.
Not in REM sleep. Tad had it right. Jake always took the easy
way out. If Jake was going to need phony cover, he'd find some
fall guy, some flunky. Somebody like me.

"I believe him," I said again, then added, "assuming there's
no problem getting the money back."

"No, no," said Krzysinski. "He and Mathigoris ran off an hour
ago to send a fax to the bank. Mathigoris has been standing by
the machine waiting for a confirmation. Wait, here he is now."

There he was, Mike Mathigoris, security chief, nice-looking,
right-in-the-middle kind of guy, former vice-commander of the

State Police, out after twenty and in a great job here, fending
off future skyjackings, ticket frauds, travel agents with commission schemes. I'd worked with him a lot before Jake let my well
run dry. He handed the papers he was carrying to Tad without
any ceremony. Tad read them and started to fume.

"Son of a bitch," he said. "Son of a bitch."

Brushy, in her vaguely familiar manner with Krzysinski, stood
to read over his shoulder. Soon the documents were passing
among the rest of us. The first page was a fax cover sheet from
the International Bank of Finance N.A., Pico Luan, with the
following message at its foot:

```
Account closed, January 30, per attached letter of
direction.
Best wishes,
Salem George
```

The letter I'd faxed over on Monday from the Regency was
attached. When I looked at the signature, I admit I smiled.
Handwriting analysts can't work with a copy. And I'd fool them
anyway. Brushy, it turned out, was watching me, something
solid, maybe even fatal, in her eye. She mouthed: "Why are
you having such a good time?"

"It's ironic," I said aloud and turned away.

Pagnucci was reading now, looking quite smug. He made little
pontifical sounds but might just as well have said, Told you so.

"What in the hell is Jake up to?" asked Tad. He had said this
already a couple of times and nobody had replied.

"He's running," I answered. "He put together this story about
Neucriss to buy himself time. Now he's headed for the hills.
And the money."

"Oh Christ," said Krzysinski. "And I let him out of here. Oh
Christ! Let's go. Let's get the police." Krzysinski was waving at
Mathigoris.

Wash had turned to wood right in front of me. He was dead as a stump.

"Who do we call?" Tad asked.

"Mack has friends on the police force," Martin volunteered at once from across the room. "He just had one in the office before."

"Wrong guy," I said immediately. "Not for this case."

"Who's that?" Mike asked me.

"A dick named Dimonte."

"Gino?" asked Mike. "Tough cop. He's working Financials now. He'd be fine."

In desperation I looked to Brushy, but she'd turned away.

"Don't you think the Bureau would be better with an international case?" I asked Mathigoris. He was indifferent. "This guy's idea of investigative technique is to scare you to death," I told Tad.

"That sounds like just what Jake deserves. Call him. Go," Tad said to me. "Quickly, please. Jake can't get away. We'll move from bad to worse."

Because the conference room was in use, I ended up in a little phone closet off the TN reception area, where there was a colonial print of a woman in a Dutch collar, a poor cousin of Rembrandt. This was a kind of in-house phone booth, designed for visitors, a place they could take a call from their office in privacy. There was a small bowl of potpourri that sweetened the tight air. I considered the alternatives. I had none. 'I couldn't get through' is not a credible excuse on a call to the police. 'I called him' wouldn't work, because when he didn't show up, somebody would just call him again.

"Gino," I said. I tried to be upbeat and bright. "When you hear this one, you're gonna love me."

"In another life," he answered at once.

I told him the story. If he ran quick, he could get Jake at home. I gave him the address. Jake of course would be sitting there. Like some beaten hound. Right by the phone, as he promised. Maybe he'd called a lawyer. Or his dad. But he'd be there. I'd have paid some money to see the look on his face when Pigeyes grabbed him. God, I thought. God, I hated Jake.

"You won't need another collar before you retire," I told Pigeyes.

"I just want you to know," Gino said when I finished, "I didn't buy one word of that."

I had no idea what to say.

"Not one fucking word. I don't want you going home and laughing in your beer tonight, or whatever you drink now. Postum. I knew that whole routine was a crock. About these three guys all doing the bunny hop." He was talking about what I'd said when he'd come to the office, the tale I told about Bert and Archie and the could-be-Kam from the U. This was *mano a mano*, him to me. He wanted me to know I hadn't gotten the best of him after all.

"It's all wrong," Pigeyes told me.

"How?"

"Archie ain't bent, for one thing."

"You're the one who told me, Pigeyes. About Archie. Rocket up his ass? Remember?"

"No. You told me. I said, What if. I said, Give, and you said, Has this guy got an elastic asshole? and I said, What if. This mutt Archie, I know the story of his life and his mother's life. He's straight. He don't got nothing but dingleberries back there, same as you and me. So it's a crock. That whole routine. Just so you know."

Just so I knew. The other one, his young bootlicker, Dewey, he was taken in. Not Gino.

"I'm not following."

"What else is new?"

"Are we done here or what?" I asked.

"Are we done, you and me done, is that what we're asking?"

"I mean Bert."

"Fuck 'em."

Nothing but fuzz on my screen. I did not understand. Which was just what he wanted.

"So what is this? Favor done, favor owed?" I thought maybe with the big collar on Jake, he was calling the score even.

He laughed, he roared. There was a phenomenal clanking wallop in my ear when he banged the phone on something hard.

"You done me enough favors. When you're miserable in hell, suffering your sins and thinking it can't get no worse, you look behind you and I'll be there. Payback time with me and you ain't gonna end, Malloy. Just so you know. I'm telling you, you're dirty somewhere. I said that from the git-go and I still say so. You're covering your ass, same as you were doing with Good-lookin. So stay tuned. Same time. Same fuckin station." He slammed the phone again and this time it went dead. Maybe he'd hung up. Maybe he'd broken it.

But he'd done what he wanted. I sat in that tight little space and broke a sweat. This time I was really scared.

B. Closing the Circle

In the elevator, on the way down, Martin announced his resignation. I suppose he was forewarning Wash and Pagnucci. He seemed to regard his statement as dramatic, but it fell flat. This group had already been through too much, and as Martin had acknowledged before, there was not much left now to resign from. Brushy, a good kid to the last, started to talk to him anyway about changing his mind.

When the elevator doors parted, back on 37, Bert was standing there. He was dressed in supposed formal wear—a leather coat as a dinner jacket and four days' growth. He looked like a rock star. I guess Orleans was picking his clothes. He remained in the elevator doorway confronting us all in an auspicious posture, sneaking a glance to see who was inside. A lot had gone on since we'd last seen him here, and there was an instant so still it could have been suspended animation.

Martin, in particular, seemed undone by the sight of Bert, finally bereft of all his survivor's aplomb, that intense belief in his own powers which ordinarily sustains him. He stared a bit, then shook his head. Finally, he took note of the last diamond stud, still in his fingers. He seemed to weigh it. I think he had some impulse to throw it again, but in the end he simply paused to insert it in his shirt.

"Well," he said presently, "some of us have an appointment at the Club Belvedere." It was time to worry about the future. For the person of importance, the moment never waits. Martin was going to read the firm its epitaph. He was good at that kind of thing. When we'd buried Leotis Griswell last year, Martin had made the eulogy, the usual funeral folderol, stuff he did not fully believe about how Leotis was a lawyer's lawyer who knew that the law in the end is not a business but is about values, about the kinds of judgments that were not meant to be bought and sold. The law, as Leotis saw it, said Martin, is a reflection of our common will, meant to regulate society and commerce, and not vice versa. God knows what Martin would tell the partners tonight. Maybe just goodbye.

Wash, Carl, Brushy all followed him, going off to get their coats. I tarried with Bert but gave Brushy a palsy little wink as she departed. She responded with a blistering look over her bare shoulder, the motive for which eluded me entirely. Here we go again. Fuck did I do? She said, coolly, that she had a call to make and would wait in her office to walk over with me.

Standing with Bert, I could tell he was shook up to be back. He was near the windows behind the receptionist's desk, facing the glass where his reflection loomed, vague and incomplete, like an image on water. He looked bleak.

"I wish I'd done it," he said to me, out of nowhere.

"Done what?"

"Stolen the money."

I recoiled a bit and gripped his arm to quiet him. But I could see his problem. He had a future again suddenly. His high times and adventures were over. He'd been out there on the edge, mad with love, crazy from danger. Now, if he liked, he could go right down to his office and answer interrogatories. He had lived for a while with all those neat shows playing in his head. Gangsters and athletes—his honey and him doing weird stuff in the moonlit artichoke fields, being covered and chilled by fog in the perfect still nights. Never mind that it was mad. It was his. Poor him. Poor us. Dragged to sea in our little boats by the tide of these irresistible private scenes and crashing come daylight on the rocks. But who can turn back?

"Somebody beat you to it," I told him. He laughed at that. Eventually, he asked if I was coming to the Belvedere, but I sent him along on his own.

XXX. T H E   E N D   A N D

W H O ' S   H A P P Y ?

A. Brushy Isn't

I went home. A man in a tuxedo boarding a plane would grab
too much attention. And although I distrusted the sentiment, I
wanted a word with my boy. It was time for the get-tough speech:
Hey, I know you think your life is grim. But so is everyone
else's. We're all grinning in spite of the pain. Some do better
than others. And most do better than I have. I hope in time you
grow up to join that majority.

For Lyle, this talk figured to be largely beside the point, but
I could feel I'd made a final effort. Upstairs at home, I found
him asleep, knocked cold by some intoxicant.

"Hey, Lyle." I touched his shoulder, sharp-boned and bitten
by ugly acne marks. I shook him some time before he seemed
to come to.

"Dad?" He couldn't see straight.

"Yes, son," I said quietly, "it's me."

He froze there on his back, trying to focus something, his
eyes or his mind or his spirit. He gave up quickly.

"Shit," he said distinctly and rolled back so that his face went
down into the pillow with the lost despairing weight of a felled

tree. I understood Lyle's problems. As he saw it, his parents owed him apologies. His old man was a souse. His mother pretended all his young life to be something she only later told him she wasn't. Having found no adults to admire, he'd decided not to become a grown-up at all. In strict privacy, I couldn't even quarrel with his logic. But what's the further agenda? Granted, all of it, guilty as accused, but you tell me how to repay the debts of history. I touched the tangles of his long dirty hair but quickly thought better of that and went off to pack.

I had been at it about twenty minutes when the front door chimes jingled. I was feeling cautious and glanced down through the bedroom window that overlooked the stoop. Brushy was there in her sequins, no coat, stomping one patent-leather pump on the concrete and casting occasional foggy breaths behind her as she looked to the taxi which waited in the street. Once I hadn't shown in her office, she must have checked at the Belvedere, then called a hasty search party of one.

I opened the various locks and bolts I've mounted on the front door to shield me from the Bogey Man and his captain in arms, Mr. S/D. We stood with the glass of the storm door between us. Brushy's long white gloves were wrapped about her, and the flesh of her upper arms, where the daily workouts had never quite slackened the softness, was mottled and goose-bumped from the cold.

"We need to talk," she said.

"Attorney-client, right?" I'm afraid I was smirking.

She turned to wave off the taxi, then snatched the door open in her own decided way and, as she stepped up on the threshold, smacked my face. She struck me open-palmed, but she's a strong little person and very nearly put me on my seat. We stood in the doorway in the midst of a nasty silence, with the rugged breath of winter flowing around us and invading the household.

"I just predicted to our partners that all the money was going to be returned by tomorrow at 5:00 p.m.," Brushy said.

"Did anyone ever tell you that you're too smart for your own fucking good, Brushy?"

"Lots of people," she answered, "but they've only been men."

Brushy smiled then, but the look in her quick eyes would have fit well on Hercules. She was not taking any crap. Not that she'd never forgive me. But she wouldn't back off. Those were her terms. I rolled my jaw to make sure I was all right, and she stepped in beside me.

"You've misjudged your man," I said.

"No, I haven't." When I didn't respond she approached me. She put her sly little hands on my hips, then slipped her chilly fingertips into the expandable waistband of the tuxedo pants I was still wearing. She shook her wind-draggled hair out of her face so she could see me squarely. "I don't think so. My man is attractively nuts. Impulsive. A practical joker. But he's in touch. Really. In the end."

"Wrong guy," I said. I touched my cheek one more time. "What's going to happen to you when the money doesn't come back? Huh?"

She kept watching me with the same intent light, but I could see her beginning to melt down inside. Her bravery was fading.

"Answer me," I said.

"I'm in big trouble. Everybody will ask what I knew. And when."

I put my arms around her. "Brushy, how could you have been such a chump?"

"Don't talk to me like that," she said. She laid her head on the silly frills of my shirt. "It makes me sad when you pretend you're mean."

I was going to tell her again she had the wrong guy, but went instead to the front closet and groped in the gummy pocket of Lyle's leather police jacket where he hid his cigarettes. I brought the pack back for us both. I asked her what she had in mind.

"What about the truth?" she asked. "Isn't that an alternative? Telling the truth?"

"Sure, I'll just give Gino a jingle: 'Pardon me, Pigeyes, you got the wrong guy behind bars. I'd like to swap places with Jake.' Gino's already hoping for that."

"But doesn't somebody have to file a complaint? I mean, what if it's all right with TN? I can explain this to Tad. Mack, I *know* Tad. Give me twenty minutes with him. He'll *love* you for scaring Jake this way. He'll think it was just what Jake deserved, having someone turn the tables on him for a while."

"Twenty minutes, huh?"

Her face fell. "Go to hell," she said. She sat on Nora's old rose-printed sofa and scrutinized the spotted meal-colored rug, caught between anger and some scandalized sense of her life.

"What's your deal with this guy?"

"Not what you think."

"So what is it? Pals? Sodality meetings?"

She went through a retinue of reluctant gestures—evasive looks, nervous fretting with her cigarette—always committed to protecting her secrets. Finally, she sighed.

"Tad's asked me to be the new General Counsel at TN. I've been thinking about it for months."

"You replace Jake?"

"Right. He wants somebody whose independence he trusts. And who'll spread TN's business around a lot more over time."

Tad of course had not arrived at the top by accident. He knew corporate politics, too, and this move was slick. Wash and his coterie on the TN board wouldn't have stood in his way if Jake's replacement came from G&G.

"Martin doesn't think the firm can survive without a big share of TN's work," I told her.

"Neither do I. Not in the long run. That's why I was reluctant."

Jake was gone now, though. Tad would make the change anyway. Brushy's course was clear. I saw the future.

"And what happens to Mack under the Brushy plan for the world, with Emilia as General Counsel of TN and G&G a wreck at sea?"

"You're a lawyer. A good one. You'll find work. Or"—she smiled somewhat, the shy-sly routine—"you can be kept." She got up and put her arms around me again.

I still had my cigarette in my mouth and I drew back with the smoke in my eyes.

"Wrong guy," I told her. I broke away and headed upstairs. She followed to the bedroom eventually. She considered my canvas, the Vermeer mounted on the easel, before turning to watch me pack.

"Where are you going?"

"To the train. Which will take me to the plane. Which will take me far away."

"Mack."

"Look, Brushy, I told you. My pig-eyed former colleague, Detective Dimonte, already smells bullshit in the air. He said so when I called him."

"You can handle him. You've handled him for weeks now. Years."

"Not now. He's flat-out said he thinks I'm dirty. He's thick-witted but he's like a cow. He always ends up in the right place." I went to the easel. I thumbed through my sketchbook and threw it in the bag.

"Why, Mack?"

"Because I'd rather live rich and free than in the penitentiary."

"No, I mean, why? The whole thing. How could you do this? How could you think you wouldn't get caught?"

"You think everybody's as smart as you are? The only reason *you* figured it out is because screw-loose here ran his mouth. You really believe you'd have seen it if I hadn't told you from the jump about how much I'd love to steal the money myself or how much I hate Jake?"

"But don't you feel bad?"

"At moments. But you know, once it's done, it's done."

"Look." She started again. She put her hands together. She lifted her pert rough-skinned face. She tried to sound even and rational, to look persuasive. "You wanted to make a point. You wanted to get Jake, all of us, you wanted to hit us where we live. And you did it. You felt ignored, undervalued, wounded. Deservingly. And—"

"Oh, stop."

"—you want to get caught."

"Spare me the psychoanalysis. What I wanted was to do it. There's such a thing as infantile pleasure, Dr. Freud. And I got mine. And now I'm doing the adult and responsible thing and saving my ass. Just like you're going to do very shortly when they ask you to account for five and half million dollars which you said would be repatriated tomorrow." I pointed at her. "Remember the privilege," I said. "Attorney-client."

"I don't understand," she said and bounced herself off the bed in sheer frustration. "You have to hate everyone. You do, don't you? Everyone. All of us."

"Don't manipulate."

"Come on. Don't you see how angry you are? My God. You're Samson pulling down the temple."

"Please don't tell me about my own moods!" I'm sure for a moment I looked violent. "Why would I be angry, Brush? Because I had such great choices? Should I have whored around like Martin to cover Jake's hind end? Just so Jake could ignore me while Pagnucci pushed me toward an ice floe, after I've surrendered my adult years to this place? I mean, how does Pagnucci put it when he bothers to justify himself? 'The marketplace speaking'? I forget the part of the theory, Brushy, which explains why the people the market fucks over are supposed to let the tea party continue for everyone else. So I showed some initiative, entrepreneurship, self-reliance. I helped myself. Those are free market concepts too."

She didn't say anything for a while. I took off my pants and my shirt and hopped around in my underwear, putting on clean slacks and a pullover. I wore my athletic shoes. Ready to run.

"What about your son?"

"What about him? He'll fend for himself. Or live off his mother. It's high time, frankly, for either one."

"You're twisted."

"Sick," I said.

"Hostile."

"Granted."

"Cruel," she said. "You made *love* to me."

"And meant it." I looked at her. "Each time. Not something every fella could say to you."

"Oh." She closed her eyes and suffered. She wrapped her long white gloves around herself. "Romance," she said.

"Look, Brush, I've seen ahead of the curve from the start. I told you this was a bad idea. I think you're a great human being. Honest Injun. I'd share your bed and your company for the foreseeable future. But Pigeyes is now on the scene. So that leaves only one alternative: You have a passport, you're welcome to come. As I've always said, there's enough for two. The more the merrier. Wanna start a new life? My impression is that you're pretty attached to the one you have here."

I held out both hands. She just looked at me. The idea, I could tell, had never crossed her mind.

"No sweat," I told her. "You're doing the right thing. Take it from your old buddy Mack. Cause I'll tell you the real problem, what I keep coming back to: Honey, you ain't gonna respect me in the morning, not when you think this whole thing through."

She eventually said, "I could visit."

"Sure. Tell Mr. K. He'll love hearing that from his new General Counsel: I'm going to visit that crackpot who destroyed my law firm and looted your company. Face it, Brush, your life is here. But hey, prove me wrong. I think you've got ties. And" —I closed the case—"I've got to go."

I grabbed her by the shoulders and kissed her quickly, hubby speeding off to work. She sat on the bed and put her head in her hands. I knew she was too tough to cry, but I said something anyway.

"Let's not be mushy, Brushy." I whined it. I made it rhyme. I winked at her from the doorway and told her goodbye. I saw Lyle down the hall, dressed only in the jeans in which he'd fallen asleep, groping to make something of the voices. Maybe he'd been roused to check out his dream that it was Mom and Dad, home again and happy, one of those dream things that never really happened. I stood on the threshold considering them both, enduring one of those moments. Up to now I'd been beset by great emotional constipation. Pour me a couple of drinks and I could bawl my eyes out, but in the present I'd felt smug and stuck on myself. Only with the actual instant of departure at hand was the pain beginning to mount.

"God, Mack," said Brushy, "please, *please* don't do this. Think about what you're doing to yourself. I'll help you. You know I will. You know how hard I've tried. I mean, at least, Mack, think about me."

Oh, what about her? She imagined, no doubt, I was running from her. And I'd succored myself with disarming comparisons to the devotion of others—Bert to Orleans, Martin to Glyndora. But who was I kidding? My heart was suddenly sore and afflicted, full of a hurt that seemed to double its weight.

"Brush, there's no choice."

"You keep saying that."

"Because it's the truth. This is life, Brushy, not heaven. I'm out of alternatives."

"You're only saying that. You're doing what you want."

"Fine," I said, though I knew in a way she was right. Standing with her now, I was abruptly some kind of suffering blob, ectoplasm without boundaries in which the only point of form was a hurting heart. But even in that condition there was a sense of direction. It wasn't hope, I saw now, that drove me. Perhaps I was at one of those passes again, doing what I most fear, because otherwise I'm paralyzed, worse off than some slave in chains. But the compulsion was strong. I was like that figure of myth, flying with his wings of wax toward the sun.

"Mack, you talk about my life? What am I going to say? How am I going to explain why I let you run, why I didn't just call the police?"

"You'll think of something. Look." I took one step back into the room. "Here. Go to your pal Krzysinski. Right now. Today. Tell him the *whole* thing. Everything. Tell him how you couldn't stand by and let me ax Jake. Tell him how noble you are. And smart. You were going to sucker-punch me. Get me to give the money back. *Then* turn me over to the police."

She was sitting on the bed, holding on to herself, contracted with pain, and she recoiled a bit. The words seemed to strike her with the reverberating force of an arrow. I thought at first she was again overwhelmed by shuddering wonder at my facility when it came time to lie. Then, at once, I saw something else.

I held absolutely still.

"Or did I just get it right?" I asked her softly. "Was I finally reading your mind?"

"Oh, Mack." She closed her eyes.

"Grab me and love me and let them haul me away? The Brushy-first plan?"

"You're lost," she said. "Do you even know the truth? When you're seeing it? When you're telling it?"

She thought she had me with that one, but you could nail most folks like that from time to time. I refused to back off anyway. Brushy, as I well knew, was a four-wall player. She had all the angles in her head, and I'd found something, some notion, some line of reflection she couldn't keep herself from seeing, any more than I could help being myself at that moment, full of a liberating spite, an anger so generalized but intense I didn't really know what was making me mad—her or me or some unnameable it.

"Was that the idea?" I put on my coat. I picked up my bag. "Well, you haven't been listening." I said it again and I suspected by now she believed it.

"You've got the wrong guy."

B. Pigeyes Isn't

The little light-rail system that ties Center City and the airport
was one of those genius planning notions for which Martin Gold
occasionally takes some credit. He was counsel to the Plan Commission and our bond folks worked out the financing. The thing
doesn't always run on time, but in rush hour it beats the traffic,
which you can see stalled on either side as the train rambles
down the divider strip. The LR, as it is known around town,
terminates in an underground station, a big cantilevered space
with the rising ceiling of a cathedral and various-colored block-
glass windows lit from the rear to simulate daylight.

I arrived there lugging my case and still yelling at Brush in
my head, purging my guilt and explaining again how she ought
to be blaming herself, there are no victims. I was a few steps
from the train when I saw Pigeyes at the end of the platform.
I'd had a few intense and unsettling visions of Gino nabbing
Jake, booking him, printing him, putting him in the police station
cell where the gangbangers would grab Jake's Rolex right off
him without even saying thanks, and I briefly hoped I was seeing
things. But it was Gino. He was leaning on a pillar in his scruffy
sport coat and cowboy boots, picking his teeth with a fingernail
and eyeballing the passengers as they alighted from the cars. No
doubt about who he was looking for, but I didn't have too many
places to go. He'd caught sight of me already and the return trip
to the city wouldn't begin for another five minutes. So I kept
walking. It was daytime, but I was dead in my dreams, headed
for that mean dangerous stranger. He had me now and my blood
was suddenly pumping at 30 degrees.

As he watched me approach, Gino's little black eyes were still
and the rest of his big face harsh with purpose. He was ready
to chase me, maybe to shoot. I took a quick peek for Dewey
but it looked like Pigeyes was flying solo tonight.

"What a delightful coincidence," I told him.

"Yeah," he said, "what. Your girlfriend gimme a call. Said I ought to track you down." Pigeyes faked a smile without showing his teeth. "I think she likes me."

"That so?"

"Yeah." He was not near my height. But he got good and close. His face was in mine, all his heavy breath and body odors. He was chewing gum. I was taking in a lot at that moment. I'd been soft about Brushy. I thought she believed all that stuff, attorney and client, my secret to keep and hers not to tell. She could give me one hundred reasons the privilege didn't apply; I could probably give you fifty of them on my own. But I hadn't thought she'd sell me out. She was always tougher and quicker than I figured.

"What'd she say?" I asked.

"Nothing much. I told you. We talked about you."

"How good I am in bed?"

"I don't recall that being mentioned." Pigeyes smiled the same way. "Where you off to?"

"Miami."

"For?"

"Business."

"Oh yeah? Okay I look in your little case there?"

"I don't think so." He had one hand on it and I tightened my hold.

"I think maybe there's a bankbook in there. I think you got a connecting plane for Pico-whatever. I think maybe you're about to take flight."

He took a step closer, which didn't seem physically possible.

"Careful, Pigeyes. You may catch something."

"You," he said. He opened his mouth and tried to belch. He was standing on my toes now, so that if I moved I'd fall over. If I pushed him, God knows what he'd do. "I knew I'd catch a piece of you. Guy asked me to do this thing, this whole caper, and I said to myself, Maybe you'll meet up with your old pal Mack."

I believed that. Pigeyes was always looking for me, and I was always watching for him. Immovable object. Irresistible force. In that moment that is worse than dying, the flaming terror that wrests me from sleep, Pigeyes will always be there. How do we explain that? I turned this over in my mind, that same old thought, that there are not accidents, there are no victims. And then, God only knows why, I had one last revelation. I was okay now. I knew it at once.

"I think," said Pigeyes, noting the intensity of my expression, "you just wet your socks. I think when you walk, your shoes'll go squish."

"I don't think so."

"I do."

"No, I've got this too well figured."

"That's what you thought."

"That's what I know. You always talked too much, Gino. Especially to me. Couldn't live with me thinking I'd skunked you one more time, could you? You couldn't resist straightening me out when I called to tell you about Jake this afternoon."

His belt buckle was still under my belly, his nose was one inch from mine. But a certain caution had set in. Once badly bitten, Pigeyes was an unusual creature in the depth of his respect for me.

"All of these things I should have seen," I said, "I couldn't explain. Why you never arrested me. Or served me. You must have thought I was deaf, dumb, and blind. You say you knew I was spreading manure this afternoon with that myth about Archie and Bert, but you left Bert alone even so. Why? Why didn't I see it? You'd been called off. Whoever hired you in the first place unhired you. The capo, or whoever. What are they holding your marker for, Pigeyes? Gambling? Dope? G-Nose take one sniff too many? Or are you doing it for one of the old buds from the neighborhood? You're the guy, though, right? You're the one who was supposed to get Archie to give up his connect. You're the one who was going to make the connect grateful for staying alive so he could throw basketball games for some ungrateful types. It's you."

I had his attention now.

"How could I not catch on? I should have known as soon as you said you were following Kam with the credit card. Christ, where the hell do *you* come by that card? I know where I found mine. And the envelope was open. There were footprints on the mail. You were in there before me, Gino. At Bert's. And that wasn't the first time.

"The first time, Pigeyes, was when you guys put Archie in the icebox. You were gonna scare Bert into telling what you wanted to know. Big-time lawyer? I don't care whose windpipe is severed. Bert couldn't call the police, because he can't answer their questions. He's not gonna throw away the money, the shingle, by admitting to the coppers how he's been fixing national sporting events. He'd be meat when he saw that body. He'd be yours. Bert would cry on the telephone. Beg for his life. He'd tell you just where to find this Kam fucking Roberts who Archie kept mentioning. Bert would even have to take care of dumping Archie himself. It never figured he'd run—not when all he had to give you was a name. But he wasn't there when you called."

Pigeyes's dark eyes were caving in. He was not as smart as me. He'd always known that.

"So that was trip number two to Bert's, right? Looking to find where he'd gone. That's when you picked up the credit card. And decided you better lujack Missing Persons' case. That way you'd be the only cops looking for Archie. You got Missing to send the case to Financial—those guys are always happy to lose one—then you went sniffing around the Bath to see if you could get a hot lead on Kam.

"And if guys didn't do dumb things, Gino, they'd never get caught. Why didn't you get the body out of Bert's when you had the chance? What was the problem? Upstairs neighbor at home that week? Not enough help? But when you nabbed me with the bank card down at U Inn you knew where I'd been. And what I'd seen. I mean, Gino, who's the guy who taught me to look first thing in the refrigerator? But dim-bulb Malloy, he gives you the perfect excuse to go back in. With a warrant, no less. That's why the body disappeared then, right? Before I could tip Homicide. That's why we had our scene in the surveillance van. So you and Dewey could get me on paper in front of a prover, saying I never saw anything of interest in Bert's apartment. I mean, Christ, was I dumb or what? Why would *you* wanna make me say that? And that's why you didn't want to run me in on any of the chickenshit that you could have. It wasn't worth it. I'd be out in an hour, so why take the chance that I'd have second thoughts and start free-associating to some stray Homicide dick about this body I'd seen?"

Somewhere along there he had gotten off my toes. If we had been having this discussion out on a dark road, he'd have shot me. But we were standing in the subway stop underneath the airport, and various passengers burdened with heavy cases and garment bags were coming and going on the platform, glancing back to get a load of what looked like it might turn into a fistfight. Pigeyes was not a happy dude.

"Tell me you didn't start out to murder poor Archie, Pigeyes. Tell me you just got carried away when Archie wasn't coming up with Kam's real name. Tell me you felt sorry." I pulled away the briefcase from where he had continued resting his hand.

"What do they pay for a job like that? Fifty? Seventy-five? You getting ready for retirement, is that it? I'll make that in interest in a couple of weeks." For emphasis, I tapped him right over the heart, grazing my fingertips on the same dirty knit shirt he'd been wearing for days. We both knew I had him.

"So turn me in," I said. "Think I can swing a deal for immunity if I give them a hit man who walks around with a star?" He didn't answer. He'd been to Toots's school. "The guy I hung with," I said, "my old partner, he wasn't that bad. He cut some corners, he did some things. But he didn't torture people for money. Or dope." I picked up my suitcase and nodded to him.

With that, I had a serendipitous recognition. If you gave Pig-eyes truth serum he'd explain to you how this was partly my fault. Years ago I'd taken his good name. And cheated to do it. The neighbors, his ma, the people in church—they now knew what he was. He couldn't pretend. He looked to them suddenly the way he looked to himself. I put it to him out loud, here in the public way.

"You're a bad guy," I said.

You know how he responded: *Fan-gul! Fan-gul!* "I gotta take that from you?"

"Have it your way, Gino. We're both bad guys." I didn't mean it. I wasn't as low as him, not in my mind. We were two different types, two different traditions. Pigeyes was like Pagnucci—really tough, really mean, capable of courage and cruelty. One of those men for whom it's always wartime, where you do what you have to. I was the second in a line of thieves—deceivers. But we'd both touched bottom, Gino and I, and I saw then that was the point of all the bad dreams: I am him and he is me, and in the dark feelings of night there is no discernible difference between wishing and fear.

So that's where I left him, on the train platform. I looked back once, just to make sure he was absorbing the full effect of letting me go. I made my plane to Miami, and now the connection to C. Luan. I'm sitting here, in first class, telling the end of my story to Mr. Dictaphone, whispering so that my voice is lost below the engine's great hum.

When I get off, these tapes, every one of them, are going to Martin. I'll send them Federal Excess. I will be wildly pie-eyed by then. At the moment, on the fold-down table in front of me, four little soldiers, hot off the attendant's drink cart, are dancing with the vibration of the plane, the sweet amber liquid bobbing in the throat of each bottle so that I can almost feel it in mine. I will be drunk, I promise, for the rest of my life. I'll travel; I'll sun. I'll engage in prolonged dissipation. I'll think about how ecstatic I was sure this gig would make me and how, in that frame of mind, I couldn't tell the right guys from the wrong ones, the merely plain from the plain ugly.

Now that I'm done, I'm thinking that telling this whole thing was for me. Not for Martin, Wash, or Carl. Or U You. Or Elaine up above. Maybe it's me I meant to entertain. A higher, better me, such as Plato described, a kinder, gentler Mack, capable of greater reflection and deeper understanding. Maybe I wanted to make another of those failing efforts to figure out myself or my life. Or to tell it all in a way that is less ambiguous or boring, remembering it with my wit sharper and my motives more defined. I know what happened—as much as memory serves. But there are always blank spots. How I got from there to here. Why I did whatever at a particular moment. I'm a guy who's spent so many mornings wondering just what happened the night before. The past recedes so quickly. It's just a few instants under the spotlight. A couple of frames of film. Maybe I recount it all because I know this is the only new life I will get, that the telling is the only place where I can really reinvent myself. And here, I am the man who controls not just the words but with them the events they record. The higher, better Mack, sovereign over history and time, a fellow more earnest, honest, more fully known than the mysterious guy who has always recovered from one disaster just in time to rush on to another, that incomprehensible being who blinks at me in the reflections on windowpanes and mirrors, who treated most of the settled items in his life with scorn.

Nonetheless, I've had the final word. Taking blame where it is due and otherwise assessing it. I don't make the mistake of confusing that with an excuse. I have regrets, I admit, but who doesn't? Still, I had it wrong. Completely.

There are only victims.

ACKNOWLEDGMENTS

A number of friends allowed me to prevail on
them with an early draft of this book. To all
of them—Barry Berk, Colleen Berk, David
Bookhout, Richard Marcus, Vivian Marcus,
Art Morganstein, Howard Rigsby, Teri Talan
—and to the sustaining lights, Annette Turow
and the world's greatest literary agent, Gail B.
Hochman, special thanks.